THE VALLEY NEARBY

KANG SOK-KYONG

THE VALLEY NEARBY

Translated by Choi Kyong-do

HEINEMANN
Portsmouth, NH

Heinemann
A division of Reed Elsevier Inc.
361 Hanover Street
Portsmouth, NH 03801–3912

Offices and agents throughout the world

The publication of this book was partly made possible by the generous support of the Korean Culture and Arts Foundation.

Library of Congress Cataloging-in-Publication Data

Kang, Sŏk-kyŏng, 1951—
    [Kakkaun koltchagi. English]
    The valley nearby / Kang Sok-kyong ; translated by Choi Kyong-do.
        p.   cm.
    ISBN 0-435-08146-2 (alk. paper)
    I. Title.
    PL992.38.S615K3513   1997
    895.7′34—dc21   97-5087
                                                                                          CIP

Editor: William Varner
Cover design: Jenny Jensen Greenleaf
Cover illustration: Louise Goldenberg
Manufacturing: Louise Richardson

Printed in the United States of America on acid-free paper

01 00 99 98 97   DA   1 2 3 4 5

Contents

1

The Root Drifting in the Sky

It looked as if it had snowed overnight; the stone front step lay buried deep in snow. The whole village was shining silver-white in the sun, the mountains beyond were a white ridgeline beneath the cutting wintry sky. As is usual in the winter, it felt deserted in this village and, because of the snow at the beginning of the year, not a single soul was visible. Tan-bee, who usually got up late in the morning, awoke from the sun shining through the window, made a path through the snow, and fed the geese.

Indeed, color has such a sophisticated effect; any color modifier awakens a sleeping imagination and brings it to feverish life. The "crimson" lie, as it is called, leaves us dazzled, while the whorish "yellow" house tempts us to break taboos.

In reality, color is close to our instinct; hence, the colorlessness of the robes of a priest or a Buddhist monk is closer to an essence rather than to an instinct. Consequently, no colors are stronger and more magnificent than black and white, which are commonly used for a ritual outfit. Black implies absolute obedience, while white is the manifestation of light. And so, another aspect of the world presents itself when the snow covers all the earth. At that time both grown-ups and children become purified and exhilarated with the appearance of the new world, feeling tempted to go out to find someone, or even, like Hee-jo, to wander in the mountains with a bottle of liquor in his pocket.

In the snow, Yun-hee too was awakened from a slumber as cozy as death. She remembered that in *Dr. Zhivago,* which she had read twice, the crimson serviceberry blossoming in the snow was associated with blood, and that this description had made her wish for death and further slumber.

At first, such an association visited her with a certain sorrow. When Yun-hee had been at rest in her parents' home in Seoul after giving birth to Sae-bul, her second child, the drunken Hee-jo had brought her a pink carnation blossom, then had fallen asleep as if unconscious. The following morning he secretly returned home to Choha-ri in the heavy snow, without even waking Yun-hee. She watched him walking aimlessly into the dim light of dawn—his body looking like a dried root—until his appearance from behind became almost a dot. At the time Yun-hee had thought she would never have peace while living with such an indifferent husband.

As she turned, heavy-hearted, toward the mountains where her house was, Yun-hee saw the fields at the base of the mountains expanding their bosom of pure white. It was truly an enormous seduction, she remembered, since she felt instantly like escaping from life as from a scuffle—from the life that had overshadowed her with an indefinable torment. She wished she could have lain in the bosom of pure white and slept as cozy as death. If so, she could have shed a tear of joy. But thinking that at home a newborn baby might be anxiously seeking her mother, Yun-hee rubbed her blood-shot eyes with a handful of snow and headed home.

Clang, clang . . .

Once in a while the wind-bell rang, even though there was no wind, but with this sound Yun-hee was awakened from her reveries. As she swept the snow toward the corner of the front yard and opened the pen, the geese were moving about in the yard contentedly. In the winter the color of their feet and beaks turned deeper, and their red, webbed feet pressed upon the white snow like starfish. When Tan-bee, with her boots on, took the grand-father goose into her arms from behind, the goose stood motionless.

"Do you like this kind of snow, Gu-chul?" said Tan-bee, talking to the goose. In a moment she told Yun-hee, "Mom, I like the look of our house best around this time."

"It's absurd to stress the word 'best' as you can simply say it's 'good'," said Yun-hee, rebuking her daughter's obscure expression. Then she saw Hee-jo coming out of his studio. At the sight of her father, Tan-bee spoke, raising her voice a little.

"You see, the word 'good' is used too often, so I think it should be changed into 'really good.' Nevertheless, this morning is really good because nothing went wrong in spite of all the snow last night. Can you imagine how frightened I was last night when I was walking toward the house with Mom? I almost thought our house was on fire. When I saw it from far away, our house looked as bright as if it were blazing."

"The area around the house was lit up all over by the light reflecting on the snow, so Tan-bee's face turned purple with fear." Yun-hee was about to explain the situation on behalf of her child, but Hee-jo laughed grimly.

"What on earth made you have such a strange idea at the beginning of the year?" he countered. "You believed an evil spirit would be driven away by fire, didn't you? If the house looked so bright, it might have looked like a feast."

"I said it first out of surprise. For a moment the house looked like it was burning," Tan-bee replied.

"Since you once made a poster against fires, you just had fire on your mind, I suppose," Hee-jo explained.

With a vivid memory of her surprise, Tan-bee drew in her shoulders. But Hee-jo left without further joking as Yun-hee stood still, staring at him with confused eyes. While Yun-hee and Tan-bee had been returning to Choha-ri the day before from Yun-hee's parents' home, where she had left Sae-bul, the snow had come down so heavily that it covered their feet. Emerging from a shrub-lined path into the fields, they saw a brightly lit, solitary, tile-roofed house in the distance that looked as if it were soaring up from the ground. In their fantasy, the house seemed engulfed by a low flame, illuminating even the sky, and so Yun-hee and her daughter shouted simultaneously. At this time, however, Yun-hee's legs trembled momentarily as she recalled the face of Hee-jo laughing like someone bereft of his senses. Just as the flames fluttered like a banner, the face of Hee-jo appeared to overlap Yun-hee's and both seemed to be laughing in one contorted face.

Three years before, when Hee-jo had been leaping about as wildly as a horse, threatening to set fire to their house and pouring oil upon it, Yun-hee herself should have gone mad. Perhaps it pricked Hee-jo's subconscious like a thorn that Yun-hee had started building their house with assistance from her mother, not thinking about her husband's mood. About the time he started work in their newly built house, Hee-jo had drunk for several days, not saying anything. When Yun-hee took the liquor away from him, he had leaped up wildly, shouting, "This house is going to grab the nape of my neck," and proceeded to set fire to the house. Ultimately, Yun-hee, splashing water on the pillar of fire, had had to get out of the house in her bare feet, holding hands with her wailing children, after having roughly folded the blazing quilts and throwing them out into the yard.

It was the day before an athletic meeting at the children's school. As it was the first such meeting since school had started, Yun-hee had bought new running shoes for the children, and it happened that Sae-bul, even in the midst of such commotion, had gotten out of the house holding his running shoes tightly. Like refugees, Yun-hee and her two children were temporarily lodged at an inn in town—not getting a wink of sleep—and the new shoes Sae-bul had put on in the window of the inn rose distinctly before her view. At the sight of the children's running shoes, something like a stone had weighed on Yun-hee's mind, a tremendous anger raging within her. "What's the use of art?" she had lamented. "How could art help us when you constantly torment the whole family? I haven't the slighest idea why you're dragging us down to your dungeon! We wouldn't understand how chaotic your mind is, nor do we dare to know."

Now the words that had stuck in Yun-hee's mind like a dagger since that day woke her again, but Hee-jo stole out the door. The geese were walking in the snow in search of something to eat, while Tan-bee blew on her frozen hands to thaw them and started to make a snowman. Still, the wind-bell was ringing peacefully in the surprisingly mild January wind. Finding herself getting on her own nerves since morning, Yun-hee set off toward the living room. As she exchanged the briquet in the stove for a new one and went out to the front yard, Yun-hee saw a man walking toward her house across the bridge over the brook. A stranger was making a path through the empty fields, the distance unwinding like a string as he approached, his feet sinking into the snow.

"Hello, Mr. Hong."

As the stranger stooped to pass through the iron front gate to the house, Yun-hee shouted, startled. "Hello, Mr. Keichi!"

He was a potter from Japan who had visited Korea the previous

4

autumn as an exchange professor, taking lodgings at Choha-ri while working with Hee-jo. Hee-jo seemed to have heard his voice in the studio and came out in a moment to see the visitor. With a rucksack on his back, Keichi held a liquor bottle and a wrapped box in his hands.

"Happy New Year!" the visitor said cheerfully.

"I wish you many blessings," replied Hee-jo, who, after exchanging brief greetings, practically pushed him into the house.

"So, how did you get back to Korea without even letting us know?"

"Well, I've been so anxious to come again. All of a sudden, I wanted to see you, Mr. Hong."

"Anyway, you're most welcome here. In truth, the snow makes me feel like having a drink. You seem to have brought liquor all the way from Japan by intuition."

As Keichi presented the bottle of liquor, Hee-jo handed it to Yun-hee and asked her to set a table for drinking. Yun-hee just stood there smiling—as delighted to see the visitor as Hee-jo. Keichi did not forget to greet her, either, saying, "I've been looking forward to seeing you too, Mrs. Hong."

"Oh, thank you. You're welcome any time."

Yun-hee replied in the little Japanese she had learned from him during his previous visit, and then she went promptly into the kitchen. Luckily, since New Year's Day was approaching, there were many things for him to eat. First, she warmed up some grilled food and the liquor, then put some soft bean curd on the table. When Keichi had stayed with them before, it was his habit to eat soft bean curd for breakfast and, since her family came to enjoy it all the time, she had bought some bean curd the day before at the market.

"I bought this bean curd because I expected you might come, Mr. Keichi," explained Yun-hee. "I bought some groceries on the way back from my parents' home yesterday."

"Thank you so much. I prepared a gift for you, Mrs. Hong. It's an electric thermos, so you can have hot water whenever you want."

Smiling brightly, Keichi gave Yun-hee the box he had brought with him. As she thanked him and unwrapped the box, she saw a large electric thermos with a flower pattern. In fact, the electric thermos she had been using was so ineffective that the water inside became cool within a day. It seemed Keichi's Japanese sensitivity had led him to notice it and Hee-jo, recognizing his own insensitivity, laughed uneasily.

"I'm certainly not a good husband, because I'm completely ignorant of what is needed in this household."

"You've only got to concern yourself with making pots, Mr. Hong. It's enough just to show people what you've made, then enjoy yourself with the liquor you like."

"He's careful in drinking as long as he enjoys it with you," interposed Yun-hee. "But this is not to say he drinks carefully all the time. I'd object to his drinking if he goes to such an extreme as to destroy his health. Naturally, his health is more important than the pots he makes."

While Yun-hee spoke like a medical nurse with Hee-jo on her mind, Tan-bee had set a bowl of hot shellfish stew on a tray and carried it into the room before her mother knew it. Tan-bee, an older child who often helped Yun-hee, brought another spoon and glass for her mother, who was in such a hurry that she had put only two sets of spoons on the table. Finding such thoughtfulness in Tan-bee, Yun-hee looked at her gratefully. Keichi praised the child's attitude and filled the glasses, Yun-hee's first, and they drank a toast.

"I hope both of you will make fine works of art again this year and live long," remarked Yun-hee.

"Even though I'm Mr. Hong's senior by a generation, there is still a lot I must learn from him."

Upon the words of Keichi, Hee-jo responded. "Oh, no. You're just being modest."

Although Hee-jo paid no attention to what Keichi had said, Yun-hee noticed a shadow of resignation crossing the visitor's face. Keichi, who was a professor at Kyoto University in Japan, was over fifty. On his first visit to Korea several years before, he had bowed politely to Hee-jo, treating him as a teacher. Actually, Keichi was so gracious a person that his artistic work took on a graceful appearance. He had seemed to be attracted by the way Hee-jo used his brush on the *punch'ong* ware, which appeared somewhat crude but unrestrained, and had spent nearly three months just brushing the *punch'ong* ware with Hee-jo. But whenever he found an unintended brushmark on the ware, he grew discouraged and made additional strokes. He was so careful in handling the potter's wheel that not even a spot of clay fell on his white working clothes. To Yun-hee's eyes, such an attitude seemed a uniquely Japanese delicacy, and a limitation as well.

Lifting his glass, Keichi said smilingly, "I'm really glad to see you both again."

He was back in Korea only a month and a half after having returned to Japan the previous November, but his visit this time was not boisterous at all. Rather, it brought a feeling as if a ray of sunshine were coming down to make the leisurely winter air warm and soft. Keichi was so discreet in everything that on his previous visit to Yun-hee's family, he would go for a walk alone to avoid disturbing Tan-bee's homework—but he enjoyed drinking so much that he often sat drinking with Hee-jo all day long. Yun-hee, who knew her husband's drinking habits, had inevitably felt strained when Hee-jo drank day and night. However, with Keichi around, she sometimes joined them.

One day they got on the subject of Korean politics. Hee-jo said the opposition New Democratic Party had outrun the ruling Republican Party by one and one-tenth percent in the parliamentary election the previous winter. He went on to criticize the so-called Revitalizing Reform advocated by President Park Jung-hee because it had its roots in the imperialistic education that had prevailed during Japan's colonization of Korea. "Incidentally," Hee-jo mentioned, "this year marks the sixtieth anniversary of the March 1st Independence Movement from Japan." Remembering this historic event, Keichi bowed silently toward Tan-bee who was sitting with them, her hands pressed together.

"In remembering the history of Japan's invasion of Korea," Keichi began, "people of my generation in Japan feel a need to atone. Long ago your ancestors came to my country and left a splendid culture there. It's clearly visible in my hometown of Nara, for instance. In truth, we Japanese respected Korean culture and were willing to accept it before the Meiji era opened. It's since the Meiji era, I believe, that Japan began to distort its history in order to establish a strong nationalism."

Despite this brief explanation for the child, Keichi's expression was sincere. He went on to say that during the Hideyoshi invasion of Choson, many Korean potters had been forcibly taken to Japan, and it was they, he explained, who had started making white porcelain and *punch'ong* ware in Japan. He added that *punch'ong* ware similar to what Tan-bee's father was making originated in Choson and was later transplanted to Japan. It was for this reason that Keichi came to Korea—to learn to make *punch'ong* in its mother country. Then he ended his remark by explaining carefully to the child, "Tan-bee, you should be proud that your father is such a great potter that he transforms the spirit of Choson *punch'ong* ware into modern form."

Hearing this, Yun-hee told Tan-bee, "You must know Mr. Keichi's father was also a famous potter. In truth, he was considered a human cultural asset in Japan."

When Yun-hee, while scrutinizing Tan-bee's face, which had been lost in thought, told her daughter of Keichi's family history, the child began to show delight. Giving Keichi a nod of friendship, Yun-hee said, "You belong to the pro-Korean group, Mr. Keichi."

Keichi left them after three days. The day before leaving he sat on the stepping stone and merely watched the geese moving about in the yard for a while. Feeling that the appearance of his small body from behind looked lonely, Yun-hee asked him, "Do you already miss your home?"

But Keichi shook his head, making room for Yun-hee beside him. "I feel as comfortable here as in my home," he answered. "I wish I could live in a place like this, since this country—though indigent and barren—has a certain depth that my country lacks. It's like the stream of spirit, so I find Mr. Hong's works resemble his environment."

"Well, I feel his works have changed since moving to the countryside," Yun-hee said of Hee-jo. "It looks like the jar he's making is imbued with the line of the clouds and with the wind. However, his disposition hasn't changed in the least. Since you left, he broke his knee in a traffic accident. Luckily, it was a slight injury, so he was discharged from the hospital within two weeks. Still, he remains the same in spite of his work."

Yun-hee smiled vainly, looking in the direction of the stream where the snow still lay. Her soliloquy continued in spite of herself, since she felt this foreigner always inclined to make the people he encountered comfortable.

After a pause Keichi resumed: "To be engaged in art, I feel, is ultimately to fight against the invisible enemy that lies within oneself. The enemy called self-limitation, I mean. Although I can see the things I strive to attain just ahead, the path that leads there is out of my reach. My helplessness in such a moment is like a state of death."

In spite of his placid expression, his tone was grave, as he seemed to be suffering himself. Though Yun-hee was not able to gain access to what he was trying to attain, she nevertheless could feel it. A solitary struggle Yun-hee called it. And so, it made a person who watched it from outside feel lonely as well.

One of the geese moving about in the front yard flapped its wings and then began to rub its body with its beak. Originally domesticated from the wild goose, which has nearly become extinct, the goose made an elegant sight when it spread its wings. At the sight, Keichi uttered with some amazement, "Even the goose gives the house a sober atmosphere!"

"During the first days we lived in this house," Yun-hee explained, "we kept dogs because we felt a little lonely with the big lot. At the time, I had an amusing childhood memory of being bitten by a goose while I was visiting a family grave. So, on account of my memory, we ended up raising the geese, and the goose over there belongs to the third generation. If you come to stay again in Korea, Mr. Keichi, I'll hatch a goose egg this spring and give you a young goose."

"I would appreciate it. And I promise to be back next spring. Even if I cannot take an animal to Japan, I'll at least take an egg with me secretly."

While talking with Keichi, Yun-hee could make herself roughly understood by using a mixture of English and Chinese. When she wrote the Chinese character meaning egg into the palm of her hand, Keichi responded by writing the same character. After that

Yun-hee said, "I really hope you'll come again, Mr. Keichi. Then I'll make some *water-kimchi* for you."

The previous autumn when Keichi had come to stay with them, Yun-hee had made *water-kimchi* for him because he didn't like spicy food, and he had enjoyed it, saying it had an incomparable taste. In truth, he loved hot Korean food, like bean paste stew, not to mention *kimchi*. On his very first visit, Keichi tended to eat his meals from his own bowl, like the Japanese do, but soon rejected such a custom in order to express his intimacy with Yun-hee's family.

The day Keichi left them, Yun-hee presented him with a case for spoons wrapped in *hanji*. Remembering that Keichi's wife enjoyed doing embroidery, Yun-hee chose a case she had bought at the exhibition of a traditional Korean embroiderer she once knew. "This spoon case was made by a Korean embroiderer," she said. "Though it's a humble gift, I preserved it till now for you to give to your wife. Please accept this as my New Year's present to you."

As Keichi reached for the spoon case, his eyes began to glisten with tears. In a moment the tears flowed from his eyes so much that Yun-hee couldn't look him in the face, and in the end Keichi had to cover his face with a handkerchief. When he had left Korea about a month and a half before, he had cried so. It seemed that while staying nearly three months with Hee-jo, who was completely simple and innocent, this foreigner had discovered something different from what he found with his fellow Japanese. Now Hee-jo, who was going to accompany Keichi to town, touched him on the shoulder like an older brother and set out first onto the snow-covered path. Trying not to show his tear-reddened eyes, Keichi followed Hee-jo silently. Then Yun-hee called after the utterly tender-minded foreigner, "Don't forget to come back in the spring, Mr. Keichi."

᠅

The frozen stream made another snow-covered path, yet the wintry air with little wind seemed bearable. Sitting on the wooden floor where the sun was pouring down, and looking out the window, Yun-hee found the stillness of the snow-covered fields a place of exile. More than the season when visitors would frequent her house, Yun-hee liked the winter season, which gave her a sense of isolation—of being cut off completely from the outside world. How is it that she came to like this season, she asked herself. There seemed to be something in winter like a virtue of moderation in which she could submerge herself, shaking off any external sound. Yun-hee believed she would find a certain truth in the winter by taking away the shell of vanity and gaining access to the essence of things. Since moving to the village, Yun-hee had occasionally strained her ears to observe such a winter silently. But she had gotten caught up instead in the life she led—like snow melting into the ground.

The deep winter, when Hee-jo was usually off work, was a time of rest, and after Keichi had left, Hee-jo did not go out at all, spending his time reading books. One day as she was cleaning her living room, Yun-hee happened to discover on a stationery chest a work by Dostoevski that she had not seen before. Despite its thick binding, the book looked worn and faded with age. Because Yun-hee liked Dostoevski's works, she opened the book and found four short stories as well as the novel *The Possessed*. Finding that someone had circled the title of "Farmer Marei" with a brown pencil, she turned to that story. Her curiosity was aroused because she had not read it before. Since the story was only four pages long, the length of a regular *conte*, Yun-hee began to read it on the spot.

The story opened with a scene in which the writer recalls his experience in prison when he was twenty-nine. It was the second day of Easter week, so the prisoners, who were not forced to labor, were spending the holy day drinking and playing a card game, or in bawdy talk. There were even several prisoners who had been beaten almost to death by their fellow prisoners, lying like corpses upon boards. Disillusioned with the insanity of these prisoners, the writer was losing himself in thought, his eyes closed, lying on his cot. Suddenly he remembered an incident that had happened when he was nine years old.

Hearing someone shout that a wolf was dashing toward him while he was playing in a grove, the nine-year-old boy rushed to a farmer who was tilling the land nearby. The gray-haired farmer of about fifty was strong and very tall. He was Marei, a tenant farmer

11

who had been working for the boy's father. The boy held on to the arms of the farmer, his whole body trembling, while the farmer tried to relieve the child's fear by saying over and over that there was no such thing as a wolf around. "Calm down," the farmer said, "I'll watch you from behind. While I stand here and watch you, the wolf wouldn't take you away from me, my dear. Look, Christ is with you, so don't be afraid. Go on." Crossing himself the way the boy's mother did, the farmer stopped his work, his mare next to him, watching the boy until he had disappeared into the hills.

The smile of the humble farmer as if coming from a mother, the sign of the cross he made for the boy, and the words he said, nodding, "You must be frightened, my dear"—all of these entered deeply into the boy's mind, as did the serenity of the farmer who, his fingers stained with the soil, slowly but tenderly put his hands upon the boy's still trembling lips. . . . The boy wondered later how such pure and humane feelings could exist in the heart of a humble farmer. Thus, vividly recalling his encounter with the farmer in the big, empty field, Dostoevski was able to regard the miserable prisoners with totally different eyes, and expressed the momentary vision as a miracle.

Forgetting to clean the room, Yun-hee read the story, feeling drawn into its charm, and remained sitting for a while. On her back she felt the warm sunshine streaming down like the touch of Marei's hands. Tapping the thick cover of the book with her nails as she idly turned over the pages, Yun-hee noticed on the lower left page the Chinese character *Wha,* meaning brilliance, printed in full size. While staring at the character, Yun-hee was suddenly reminded of the writing of Han Min-wha.

Han Min-wha was a weaver artist who three years before had moved to Eunti, a village not far from Choha-ri. Yun-hee was not aware they were living in the same area until a woman painter had introduced them to each other the year before. Han Min-wha was said to go to Seoul once a week for a lecture, but the way she led her life as a half-recluse in the countryside and engaged in her work was similar to Hee-jo. Moreover, their ages being about the same, the two people, upon meeting each other, were delighted like old friends. Afterward Han Min-wha had visited Yun-hee three or four times and once, by invitation, Yun-hee and Hee-jo went to Han Min-wha's home. But Yun-hee and Han Min-wha had not seen each other since the previous summer.

If the work of Dostoevski belonged to Han Min-wha, Yun-hee wondered, did Hee-jo borrow it from her directly? In a moment Yun-hee realized she had never seen the book in Hee-jo's studio before. No doubt he had borrowed it recently. It occurred to Yun-hee that the last time Hee-jo had gone out was when he accompanied Keichi to town. If so, had her husband visited Han Min-wha and borrowed the book that day? Yun-hee pondered. Eunti is a village on the same stream, around the corner of the mountains at the end of Choha-ri, and the snow must have lain deeper in that village. How could Hee-jo manage to walk through the snow-covered path at the beginning of the year just to borrow a book? If he had kept seeing Han Min-wha, why hadn't he let Yun-hee know?

A chain of thoughts starting in her mind, Yun-hee suddenly recalled something. Talking of Han Min-wha to his wife, Hee-jo had once said, "I am very impressed because her appearance is so like yours." Because of an air of coldness around Han Min-wha, Yun-hee had not at the time accepted the comparison, merely suspecting that her image aroused in him a familiar feeling. Perhaps because of the rumor that Han Min-wha had parted with her husband shortly after her marriage and lived by herself ever since, Yun-hee had been interested in her from the first time she had met her. It must have been the instinct of a woman who had a husband, she thought. But nevertheless Yun-hee wondered why she was overcome with suspicion merely by seeing a book. Feeling reproachful toward herself, she replaced the book.

Because Hee-jo had worked for several days on a sketch of a bowl, Yun-hee suspected something was afoot. Then she received a telegram from the Hanwoori Company about their intended visit to Hee-jo. About a month before, they had written to express their intention of visiting Hee-jo, who had met with them a couple of times around the end of the previous year. It seemed to Yun-hee that they were suggesting production of the *punch'ong* ware. Yun-hee considered their offer reluctantly, but Hee-jo had been concerned with distributing the traditional dinnerware for the general public, and seemed to have made up his mind to do it.

It was nearly two o'clock when people from the company arrived. A successful businessman, President Chang had made his way in the world by introducing traditional Korean folktales into the field of children's books, which had been dominated by foreign fairy tales. In addition to publishing books, he had started selling brass ware as a business activity to boost the traditional Korean image. President Chang, whose broad, neat forehead attracted Yun-hee's attention, stepped inside the house with another man, who seemed to be one of his senior staff members.

Rubbing his frozen hands, President Chang began. "Well, I really didn't know you lived in this secluded countryside. You're living in total seclusion without even a telephone." Then he continued: "As the snow is deep, the road leading to this house is too rough to drive, so we parked the car at the restaurant at the entrance to the village. The road is quite rough, and I suggest you have the road leading to this house paved, just in case you buy a car in the future."

"Despite that," returned Hee-jo, "people frequent this area when the days get warmer. Just imagine how things would turn out if we paved the road."

As Hee-jo replied flatly to the visitors, Yun-hee broke in with a smile: "Actually, some people are suggesting that I start a restaurant here. I'm willing to do that if we're unable to support ourselves by selling pots."

People living in the big cities are liable to look upon convenience as the most important value, Yun-hee realized again, but few of them know that living surrounded by nature is a blessing not to be replaced by any convenience. Greeted by Yun-hee's children, President Chang stepped onto the wooden floor and gave Tan-bee what the other man had brought in.

"These are the cassette tapes my company makes for learning English," President Chang said to Tan-bee. "Since they are for beginners, you'll be able to use them in middle school. People are getting more interested in early education recently. I also brought a collection of paintings by Yi Jung-sup. Take this, too."

Looking at the book of paintings, Yun-hee said in wonder, "Oh, you're even publishing a collection of paintings!" Although Hee-jo had always said the bull painting by Yi Jung-sup did not resemble a native Korean bull, and had given it little attention, Yun-hee had thought it worthwhile to write about the artist, since he was somewhat mystical.

Asked to set a wine table for the visitors, Yun-hee made a dried-pollack stew and brought it into the living room. After exchanging greetings with the chief of the company's business department, Yun-hee sat and listened to Hee-jo's words.

"The exhibition of dinnerware that I gave last year was probably the first of its kind," began Hee-jo. "At the time I had some purposes of my own for the exhibition, I must say, but as the price for the works had been decided I found it something of a fraud. As you remember, each set of cups and teapot cost more than ten thousand *won,* and the price of two sets of rice and soup bowls exceeded the price of a bag of rice. But because I made them all by myself, there was no choice but to increase the cost of the product then. Anyhow, this is why I judged we ought to set up a production team, so that we could lower the price. And while I was thinking about it, President Chang here consulted me, and I put off making a work of art for the time being, intending to be involved in producing the dinnerware. But the problem is, if you put the price four times higher than the price I set, it will only appeal to a limited range of people, as proved by my exhibition. With such prices, I believe, there is hardly any reason to try to distribute our ware for the general public."

After Hee-jo had made his point, the man who accompanied President Chang interposed to express his view.

"Well, I'd like to say that the idea our president and Mr. Hong hold is a little premature. As a potter you might have your mission, Mr. Hong, but our president also started this kind of business with a certain foresight. I was told he was shocked when his mother threw away her *bandaji* in the sixties and replaced it with a lacquer table, which was in fashion then. From then on, he determined to devote himself to things related to our native culture. As you may know, Mr. Hong, the brass ware made by our company—which are now on sale—have received a favorable response in the market, even though their price is by no means cheap. But I daresay customers tend to buy products mainly because of their nostalgia for antique things, or from their taste, or even out of a bit of vanity. In any case, it's not for the price alone. What's more, the dinnerware we're planning to make is not made irresponsibly in a pottery mill but in the workshop of a distinguished potter like you. So it's quite natural that it be somewhat expensive."

Judging from what the man had said, there seemed to be something obviously farsighted about President Chang. Yun-hee too remembered the time when the lacquer table was in fashion in every household, and it seemed to her such a table was more gaudy than the chest of drawers inlaid with mother-of-pearl that, because it appealed to the taste of the nouveau-riche, had been in fashion before. Apart from their different views on prices, Hee-jo once again expressed the necessity of distributing the dinnerware.

"If you thought it necessary to preserve our native things by looking at the lacquer table, President Chang, I'm sure you'll have a certain feeling when you look at wares these days. Whether in a restautant or in a supermarket, most of the wares we find lately are *Japanized*. You may remember that this year marks the 60th anniversary of the March 1st Independence Movement. To my knowledge, we're now in the third stage of the pottery war with Japan. The first stage, I think, took place when the Japanese carried off many Choson potters into their country during the Hideyoshi invasion, and the second was when Japan forcibly annexed Korea in 1910. As you know, Japan prohibited the use of native Korean bowls as part of its colonial policy, since those bowls were believed to awaken a national spirit in the mind of Korean people each day. Afterward the neat-looking Japanese wares began to invade the country everywhere, and naturally our native kilns gradually disappeared. In other words, while people sought the cheap, exotic Japanese wares, the native ones went into decline. But the accusation that Korean potters are to blame for not handing down their skill is groundless, because they were forbidden to do so by Japan's colonial policy. When we look back upon the entire period of the Koryo and Yi Dynasties, we come to know that pots continued to be made, although under Japan's rule we were unable to keep that tradition. What's serious, however, is that we're now abandoning our heritage by our own will! Though I admit culture is a thing that progresses by mixing with other environments, we're now forgetting what we must do."

"Absolutely true," agreed President Chang instantly. "In fact, that's why a businessman like me keeps arguing for the preservation of our tradition. In addition to my liking your work, Mr. Hong, I find a mutual bond between us, so I think it's really a great occasion to start doing business together. The instant I saw your work in the exhibition last year, I told myself I had finally found what I wanted. Then the only thing to settle is how to set the price, but in this respect I'd like you to trust us, since it'll be decided in relation to other items we're dealing with, as well as our experience in sales."

Following the words of President Chang, the chief of the business department spoke again.

"Once the dinnerware is in production, we'll guarantee to sell at least two hundred sets a month, including tea sets. Of course you won't be dissatisfied with what we offer you, Mr. Hong, because we'll certainly compensate you fully for your work. As you know, white porcelain is widely used for dinnerware, but as far as I know there is no *punch'ong* ware offered for that purpose. So if you trust us in distributing them, we'll make every effort to do so."

"As for the white porcelain," resumed Hee-jo, "it looks artful and showy in comparison with the *punch'ong,* but in contrast to the white porcelain, the *punch'ong* ware is stubborn and healthy. So wherever it is on display, the *punch'ong* ware is always in harmony with its surroundings. I hope our native ware like the *punch'ong* would be put on the dining tables of every household."

After Hee-jo had reiterated the importance of mass distribution of the dinnerware, President Chang got up to leave, asking Hee-jo to consider both his intentions and the actualities. It seemed to Yun-hee that the price was already decided; with the consent of Hee-jo, they were on the verge of putting their plan into action. But, to Yun-hee's relief, Hee-jo finally revealed to the visitors his skepticism about making the dinnerware, and put off his decision for the time being.

After President Chang had left, Hee-jo lost himself in thought, sitting in front of the wine table. Yun-hee, pretending not to notice, watched Tan-bee open the box of cassette tapes. Inside there were three large, hardcover binders, which were a little bigger than college notebooks. Opening the first binder, Yun-hee found twelve English cassette tapes arranged in it, so she assumed the rest of the binders contained similar tapes. Tan-bee seemed to have the same idea but, opening another binder, she muttered to herself, "God, what's all this?"

Looking into it, Yun-hee discovered thick sheets with drawings in strong colors, a little like cartoons, below which were brief English conversations. The drawings were a supplement to the English cassette tapes, and the four sets of drawings, which were intended to illustrate a sentence in each of the English pattern drills, were actually all alike. The remaining binder was nothing more than an instruction manual.

After scrutinizing the instruction manual, which was filled with meaningless drawings, Tan-bee laughed in disappointment. "Look, it's just packaging. I thought all of these binders contained cassette tapes."

"Right. A big waste, isn't it?" responded Yun-hee, pleased that the child had not been seduced by the fanciful drawings. In truth, she too felt deceived. And the price was unreasonably high for only twelve cassette tapes. Putting aside the collection of paintings by Yi Jung-sup she was about to look at, Yun-hee went over to talk with Hee-jo.

Glancing at Yun-hee, Hee-jo spoke first: "If I understand correctly, I'm supposed to be paid twice what it costs to produce the dinnerware. And that's what President Choi estimated earlier. It's a reasonable offer, since they set the actual selling price at almost four times the cost of production. But although I understand that they must make some profit for their workers, I'm still not at all convinced they need to raise the price nearly four times. And I had a good feeling about them, since there was little about them that was commercial."

President Choi, owner of the Dawool Gallery, was the person who had taken charge of Hee-jo's exhibition of dinnerware the previous year. He had developed his discriminating taste in his father's antique shop, and now he was running an antiques shop as well as the gallery. As a connoisseur and an art dealer, he had taken responsibility for Hee-jo's first exhibition and kept in contact with Hee-jo ever since—willing to give brotherly advice to him in everything.

Finding Hee-jo's mind wavering, Yun-hee calmly suggested, "I'll grant you that President Chang has exceptional foresight, but still he is no more than a businessman, you know. Although he's proud of engaging in the cultural business by emphasizing the cause of tradition or something, I don't think we have to regard him as a philanthropist."

"Damn it! Who in the world doesn't need money?" Hee-jo spat suddenly. "If the price they suggested was reasonable, I'd be willing to go into business with them. Then I could indulge in works of art without having to worry about making a living. I wouldn't even have to sell the pots I want to keep."

"If, as they assured us, you would be selling two hundred sets a month, you could earn almost ten million *won*. That's remarkable, isn't it?" Yun-hee said half-jokingly.

"It wouldn't be that easy," Hee-jo answered skeptically, not seeming to grasp the irony.

Yun-hee became serious, "I don't approve of what you're going to do. In the end, I believe you would end up being a puppet for the people who want to make their profit in the name of tradition. Of course, you could make a lot of money, but what would you do with it? Have you worked hard all this time just to make money? We've almost paid off our mortgage; do you intend to burn down this house and build a magnificent mansion instead? If you're going to succumb to the lure of money, all we've been striving to sustain till now will collapse in a moment. The torment I've had living with you cannot be repaid with money."

Hee-jo's eyes bulged, but he evaded her glance after a moment. He was again lost in thought, since he had not drunk so much as to lose his senses. Yun-hee remembered how, less than a year after their marriage, her husband had to sell his watch to pay off a debt, and they had lived an aimless life for some years, occasionally even unable to fill the rice chest. Before moving to the countryside where they lived now, Hee-jo had had to give lessons to students in his workshop, but all the money he had earned there was spent on alcohol. They had been forced to borrow money, and he had paid it off only after his exhibition. Anyhow, that's the way they had lived in those days. Yun-hee herself was as used to such a life as she was to her own flesh. Wasn't it possible that now Hee-jo, feeling his burden as the head of a household, was ready to take the money, which was by no means a small amount? In truth, there was something in the way he acted that showed him to be childlike. As Yun-hee saw, deep in Hee-jo's mind was wriggling a guilty conscience, because, while he regarded the making of the pots as the most valuable thing in his life, he had never made enough money to support his family.

It all had started from his arrogance, Yun-hee felt. Many potters subsidized their income by teaching in a college, but Hee-jo was simply indifferent to everything except his pots. Then, one day, when a truck loaded with clay stopped before the gate of the house, or when he saw some sign his mother-in-law had come to his house to fill the rice chest, he began drinking without a word. In Yun-hee's eyes, it was a kind of declaration of war for him, and such arrogance was the very energy of Hee-jo himself, as well as a thing that might lead him to a dungeon.

In the winter, when there was no work to do in the fields, there were hardly any villagers around. One morning Jae-chull's mother came to Yun-hee to borrow money, which she promised to pay back when her younger sister, who was working in an industrial complex, returned home for the lunar New Year. Around the end of the previous year, Jae-chull's uncle had deceived a painter friend of Hee-jo's by coaxing him to buy a building site that was, in fact, classified as forest land. As such, he was the very person who had got Yun-hee in trouble, since she had introduced the painter to him, and now his younger brother's wife was asking her for money. Though it was not a large amount, Yun-hee had never gotten back money she had loaned to the villagers. In the previous autumn Young-sun's mother had borrowed ten thousand *won* from her, and only repaid it with sesame oil. The way the villagers would pay off a debt had something to teach her because, unlike people in the big cities, they didn't adhere to the ownership of any particular things. So Yun-hee asked the woman first when the lunar New Year was. "It's five days from now," the woman replied. "I'm already hard up to stay alive—even though I feel as if I did a harvest just a few days ago. . . ."

Then, all of a sudden, Yun-hee realized the lunar New Year was only a few days away. Looking up at the calendar, she discovered that the next day was Sae-bul's birthday. But for Jae-chull's mother, Sae-bul's birthday would have passed unnoticed, she felt. Inwardly blaming herself for her indifference to her children, Yun-hee lent the money readily, as if admitting her disadvantage as an outsider from the city. "In return for the money, just plow the farmland in spring," she said.

Finding that Hee-jo happened to be going to Seoul, Yun-hee asked him to buy a birthday gift for Sae-bul, and she herself set off for the market to buy ingredients for the birthday meal. For the birthday dishes Yun-hee intended to make seaweed soup and fried bits of fish, and after making sweet rice and the sweet rice drink Sae-bul liked, she could use them for the upcoming lunar New Year as well.

As she watched Sae-bul poke around the kitchen idly, smelling the foods she was making, Yun-hee recalled the old times. In childhood she would recognize the approach of the New Year by the smell of the glutinous rice jelly boiling. With the sweet rice drink being made and slices of oil-and-honey pastry spread out in the middle of the room, many kinds of food kept accumulating right up to the night before. In those days, even golden apples in the chaff or some similar gift would make children giddy, and what remained the most vivid in Yun-hee's memory was a patch of cloth for a quilt sent to her home by a linen shop her family frequented. The quilt top was made with all kinds of splendid colors by tightly putting together triangular and square pieces of silk fabric. In short, it was a ground for nurturing her dream as well as its ultimate realization.

In the old days feasts had been times when she could enjoy herself instinctively, but now that they were a mere occasion for the children, Yun-hee had lost the spirit of the old days. On the first lunar New Year after marrying into her husband's family,

Yun-hee remembered, she had been so perplexed to find such a chilly air. The dried rice cake soup without even dried seaweed, a bowl of leftover *kimchi,* and a dish of boiled pork . . .

What lingered in her mind for so long was the memory of her mother-in-law, who, with the breakfast table before her son and his wife on New Year's morning, was sitting like a stone Buddha deep in the room. While Yun-hee had been in bed after giving birth to Tan-bee, her mother-in-law had cooked herself a wheat-flake soup. A thoroughly incompetent woman, she didn't even know how to sterilize a baby's milk bottle by steam and would scorch the milk in it every time she tried. As a matter of fact, there was nothing in her except a childlike instinct for self-protection.

After marrying into a farmhouse, that woman had had no interest in working in the fields. Once, induced by her neighbor, she had indulged in the worship of the Jesus religion but, after being taken forcibly back home by her father-in-law by the scruff of her neck, she had lived in seclusion, cutting herself off entirely from the outside world. Until her death, the woman had never again gone out of the house, even to a relative's or a neighbor's home. Nevertheless, Hee-jo had treated his mother as if worshipping a goddess, becoming infuriated unless Yun-hee served even a simple piece of steamed potato to her first. He would buy a dozen pairs of socks for the aged mother who, oddly enough, changed her socks several times a day.

Yun-hee had encountered countless hardships since marrying into the Hongs, one of which was Hee-jo's morbid protection of his mother. In Yun-hee's eyes, the old woman was neither a devoted mother to her children nor a person of respectable disposition. Above all, there was nothing sagacious about her. Although Yun-hee admitted that loving one's family is instinctive, Hee-jo's blind attachment to his mother was quite exceptional. Was it compassion for a person who was totally incompetent, or the ardent protection of a weak human being? Perhaps her husband had identified himself with his mother; if he were to exclude the pottery and arrogance from his life, Hee-jo would come close to becoming like his mother.

Because there were many things to be taken care of, Yun-hee

was not able to have dinner until seven, and then she could take a rest as Tan-bee helped her with the dishes. In the meantime Sae-bul, who had finished his art homework, showed Yun-hee a sketchbook containing a portrait of his father. Sae-bul's drawing of his father's head and shoulders was natural as he captured the figure at an angle from the front, and the figure looked more vivid on the left. Yun-hee found there was little to find fault with in the drawing, let alone such a trivial part as an eyebrow. In particular, the brow was so vividly drawn that she felt as if Sae-bul had made the drawing with a living model before him. The drawing was scrupulous from the composition to the sketch, so Yun-hee found it hard to believe the child had made it without help. Leaning comfortably against the wall, Yun-hee recalled a picture Sae-bul had made the previous year: showing his mother a picture in which only the head and front legs of a dog were captured in a corner of the paper, Sae-bul had said the dog was walking into the picture.

"You deserve to be called an artist, Sae-bul," Yun-hee said admiringly.

Seeing the approving expression on his mother's face, Sae-bul replied assuredly, "I wouldn't become a painter, though."

"Why? You don't like it?"

"Mmm, I have no wish to become a painter."

Yun-hee looked hard at the child to fathom his mind. Though barely eleven years old, Sae-bul must have been disillusioned with the way his father led his life, so, deep in his heart, he might harbor some animosity toward the life of an artist. As his eyes met Yun-hee's, Sae-bul made an abrupt remark: "I'd rather be a zoologist like Seton, Mom." Hearing it, Tan-bee broke in, "You're going to draw a baby bear like Seton did, aren't you?"

Judging from Tan-bee's words, it seemed that each child already knew what the other was going to be. Yun-hee knew Sae-bul had a deep interest in dogs and geese, to the point of reading Seton's *Wild Animals I Have Known* almost seven times, but she never imagined he had been dreaming of becoming a zoologist. That's not bad, she thought. Although people would compare a ferocious human to an animal, it's more than unfair to the animal, since mere observation of animals proves they're the pure prototype of human beings. Though presumably the highest of all creatures, the human being must be degenerating in proportion with the progress of civilization.

So, in a praising tone Yun-hee told him, "Really? I never knew you wanted to be a zoologist, Sae-bul, and Father might be surprised to learn your plans. He went to Seoul today to buy your birthday gift. I guess he might have a lot of trouble choosing it."

As he usually did when he went out, Hee-jo returned late—about midnight. He never failed to smell of wine, but this time he brought a new bicycle into the yard with him. The instant Yun-hee saw the smart-looking bicycle gleaming silver in the darkness, a smile came to her lips. Actually, she had not in the least expected her husband to buy a bicycle as a birthday gift, even though she had left him to decide for himself. Trying not to betray her delight, Yun-hee said, stepping onto the wooden floor, "My! How did you bring such a heavy thing into the house? If you bought it in town, why didn't you ask them to bring it here tomorrow morning? At any rate, Sae-bul may have a nice dream tonight."

When Yun-hee brought a bowl of warmed sweet rice drink to Hee-jo, he was already in bed, having turned off the light. One side of the sliding door was open, the dusky front yard shaded by a tree was visible through the westfacing window, and the wind chime rang as a cool, gentle breeze shook the dry boughs. Lying in bed, Yun-hee felt a fatigue as if her backbone were collapsing, which she forgot while working. Thirsty, Hee-jo swallowed the bowl of sweet rice drink in one gulp and began: "I told the Hanwoori Company today I've given up the idea of making dinnerware. There's no sense in such an expensive price as they proposed."

"Great! You made a wise decision. You know there's no need to be in such a hurry now."

Yun-hee felt assured she was right in urging him to turn down the offer from the Hanwoori Company. Cracking his knuckles one by one, Hee-jo then said he had met his close friend Park Young-soo, who was an oriental painter.

"He told me he'd tried *hanji* at home some time ago. As an oriental painter, I think he was very interested in materials for his paintings. He told me he watched the entire process of papermaking, after inviting two professional *hanji* makers and preparing all the necessary equipment. It seems he was much impressed because, in spite of making a variety of *hanji* depending on the size and thickness, he found it less expensive than when he bought it in the market. At any rate, businessmen are all alike."

"Sure. You'll have another chance to make dinnerware later on," replied Yun-hee. "I believe you can even run the business yourself if someone will finance your project. Then you could lower the price."

"Maybe." Regretting his lost opportunity, Hee-jo accepted this new idea readily. He was convinced it was his mission to distribute dinnerware, and Yun-hee wanted to support him. As Yun-hee was lying in bed, a white object past Hee-jo's head caught her eye and, looking at it carefully, she saw it was a drawing by Sae-bul.

"Have you seen Sae-bul's drawing?" asked Yun-hee.

"Yes—he draws very well."

"But he told me he has no intention of being a painter," Yun-hee continued as Hee-jo kept silent. "Instead, he wants to be a zoologist."

"Really? It's a relief, though, he's not dreaming of becoming the President."

Pleased that Hee-jo was feeling proud of his son, Yun-hee turned on her side. "By the way, Sae-bul will be very surprised to find a new bicycle. What caused you to buy such a thing?"

"I came across Ms. Han at the South Gate Market," replied Hee-jo unconcernedly. "As a matter of fact, I met many people today."

"You mean Ms. Han of Eunti village?" inquired Yun-hee.

"Of course. It seems she went to Seoul to buy some thread. I saw a woman whose head was bowed low walking toward me in the street, merely watching the ground. I almost didn't recognize her, but when she happened to look up I realized it was Ms. Han. I told her I needed to buy a birthday gift, and she suggested a bicycle, saying the road to Eunti village from our house is good for a bicycle."

"That's true. The road has a scenic view since it parallels the stream." Yun-hee imagined the stream flowing grandly toward Eunti village across the fields in Choha-ri, the ripples becoming a wave. In the roaring wave she saw the little house where Han

Min-wha lived, aloof in a grove near the stream. Her face, transparent and arousing a feeling of trepidation, lingered in Yun-hee's mind for a moment and then disappeared. Yun-hee nearly said, "Haven't you met her once before?" but stopped herself, because she didn't want to question him so blatantly and betray her suspicion. Instead, she lay flat on her back, her face toward the ceiling.

"I haven't seen her for a long while," Yun-hee said calmly. "Why didn't you invite her to come to see us?"

"Well, she seemed to be involved in her work this winter and confined herself to her house," answered Hee-jo.

"I wonder if she feels at all lonely—although she always felt lonely even when she was married."

"She's strong, I think."

"But being strong isn't the same thing as not being lonely, you know. I suppose being strong might help her get over her loneliness, but she would still feel it."

Looking through the darkness, Yun-hee suddenly thought of the times when she had been pregnant before moving to Choha-ri. When she was pregnant with Tan-bee and then Sae-bul, Yun-hee, even in her difficulties, had felt encouraged to think she would become a mother soon. Awed by the thought of the being that would come into the world, she was more emotionally stable than at any other time. However, when she found out she was pregnant with her third child, Yun-hee had experienced a confused feeling she couldn't put into words. She felt like a dull female who conceived children irresponsibly, and hated the idea of motherhood. Selfish and lonely, she felt with her whole soul that her entire existence was threatened.

"Did I tell you I had an abortion before moving to Choha-ri?" Yun-hee asked abruptly.

"You did?" At the sudden remark from Yun-hee, Hee-jo looked startled and turned his head toward her. "Why didn't you tell me then?"

"I had no intention of having another child. And you seemed to agree with me."

Looking into her uncertain and wavering eyes, Hee-jo took her into his arms. Was it an apology? Yun-hee thought to herself.

Breathless, she felt a cold wind surging through her even though Hee-jo's breath was hot against her. Something in her was ready to revolt.

❧

With the weather not as cold, Yun-hee expected Hee-jo to start work but, even at the onset of the spring after the lunar New Year, he simply wandered through the mountains. He drank in the air of early spring; as the days started to become warm in February, he wandered over mountain after mountain. Every year at this time he would come home with muddy sneakers, his eyes seething like water flowing beneath the ice.

Seeing Hee-jo in spiritual communion with the spring before anyone else made Yun-hee feel lonely, but she kept busy by replacing the briquets in his studio, indirectly urging him to take up his work again. She made it a practice not to go to the studio once Hee-jo got to work; it was better to leave him alone as much as possible, since he was usually on edge.

Hadn't it happened when Hee-jo was drying wares off the potter's wheel? One day Hee-jo had confined himself to the studio, working far into the night; while taking rice out of a chest at the entrance to the studio, Yun-hee had peeked in where he was working. Hee-jo was sitting before the potter's wheel, grinding a half-dried jar, surrounded by a blue flame, and she'd jumped as if she'd seen a ghost. At the sound of someone approaching, Hee-jo had glanced at her, ready to attack her with the iron tool in his hand. It had happened so unexpectedly, Yun-hee had been stunned; the look in his eye was not Hee-jo's. He wasn't just mad, he had seemed possessed, his bulging eyes warning Yun-hee not to approach the world where he lived. The air of evil stirred even her innocent soul.

One day, entering Hee-jo's studio to check the briquet, Yun-hee discovered it had already been replaced. On his chair was an ashtray filled with cigarette butts, and his sketchbook was open on the shelf. Finding signs of Hee-jo's presence there a moment before, Yun-hee suspected he was now ready to take up his work. Relieved, she sat on the chair and noticed the writing in the sketchbook:

27

What am I supposed to express in my wares? The purest thing in the world, or something comfortable and unforced— that is, nothingness.

The pots are being made out of the state that conforms to clay and yields to firing, out of the state that does not assert my own will.

A certain shape is not made intentionally, it is simply made. And its being made means something exists beyond my sight.

The whiteness the Chinese character So *implies is to accept all colors thoroughly, while the character* Pak *is compared to the stump of a tree that has endured a long hardship. This state of simpleness and humbleness I always have in mind, but aren't these things also being made beyond my sight?*

Paging through the rest of the sketchbook, Yun-hee saw some fragmentary thoughts written in several places, mixed with sketches. In particular, the writing scribbled in pen on the last page expressed his impatience at not being able to grasp some image that he had sought but that had slipped away from him like fog. Now it's time for him to start work, Yun-hee said to herself, like a stern mother urging her child to do something. Looking at a page in the front of the sketchbook while putting it back, she found another fragmentary thought she had not noticed a moment before.

A disappearing point on the surface of the water disappears into the water. Is it possible to give an expression to the gravity in the water? All the objects in the sky disappear into the air. A state of the fourth dimension.

Yun-hee had no idea what this meant. Reading it again, she still didn't: what was the state of the fourth dimension? Hee-jo would jot down idealistic thoughts as they came to mind, but Yun-hee was unable to comprehend them at all. Yun-hee didn't believe anything unless it took a tangible form; how was it possible to accept the world of the fourth dimension? Naturally, Yun-hee

28

could not figure out why Hee-jo made pots as if he were making war. In addition to what he imposed on her, her children burned her memory like a scar.

Each time Yun-hee had experienced hardship, her mother would tell her it was, after all, a fate Yun-hee herself had induced. An old-fashioned woman, her mother had never spoken to her husband informally, so Yun-hee could not accept what she said—not only as a mother, but as an independent human being. Deep in her heart, Yun-hee was taking revenge for the indescribable torment she had suffered.

Her revenge was to goad Hee-jo into creating a work of art as great as her inner torment. But this was not to be defined as either sadistic or a compensational mentality. Instead, she compared Hee-jo to the heights through which she must pass to the world beyond. A well-made pot would therefore soften her heart toward Hee-jo, compell her to surrender to the world he lived in.

It was not until the next morning that Yun-hee learned someone had died in the village chief's house. Stepping into her house, his face pale with shock, Yi Sung-ju informed her that Hong-taek, one of the chief's sons, had committed suicide the previous night by swallowing agricultural chemicals. Some years younger than Hee-jo, Hong-taek had been the head of a household with three children. "Let me have a cup of grain tea first," Yi Sung-ju said to Yun-hee. "Anyway, the site of his house is ill fated, I suppose, so he ended up paying the price."

A young leader in the so-called common folk literature, Yi Sung-ju, whose name was often mentioned in the papers, was a poet of the participation group. He had involved himself in the work of awakening young people to the ideological matters of the day by conducting a masque dance for college students and a theatre group in his hometown. While preparing to launch a randomly published literary magazine, *The Literature of Liberation*, to stir up a dissident movement, he had been looking for a house close to Seoul and happened to find it at Choha-ri the previous autumn. The house he rebuilt to live in was one that Hong-taek, driven by debt, had sold to him.

Sitting down, Yi Sung-ju said immediately, raising his voice: "You know what? There could be no worse doomsday than this, since the whole country is being driven to greed. All this regime has done so far, I think, is emphasize being rich—witness those money-hunting ladies who speculate on real estate in the remotest countryside. On the other hand, people in the rural area are deserting their homeland, which has been the base of life. What's worse, they're even taking their own lives in spiritual starvation, gambling all their fortunes away. Can you imagine? In this age when people, no matter who they are, covet easy money, how empty is the ideal of the farmers! In fact, overcome with the smell of agricultural chemicals, they have little choice but to till a small piece of farmland. Besides, the purity of labor that has supported community life has dissolved into the reality of an industrial zone. I mean it's sacrificed for a policy that only encourages production as the supreme end—with no principle of distribution. Within the past twenty years, the life of the people and their surroundings have been devastated in the name of modernization. You've lived nearly four years in this village, Mr. Hong, so you can easily see how antagonistic people here are toward people from the city."

Following Yi Sung-ju's vehement criticism of the realities of the day, Hee-jo began slowly. "Well, I heard the gross national product per person has gone from nine hundred and forty dollars to twelve hundred and forty dollars. Despite that, life in the city is filled with fiendish avarice, while people in the countryside are frustrated and full of despair, hating each other. I think there's more to be lost than gained in this situation. So what we really need is the idea 'small is beautiful.'"

As she set the wine table, Yun-hee told them what she herself had gone through before. Because one of her relatives was a house builder, she had let him take charge of building the house when she moved to Choha-ri, but he ended up in a great deal of trouble with some people in the village. At the beginning of the work he had hired people from the village but, finding them lazy, he brought some workers from Seoul.

"That seemed to have provoked them," Yun-hee went on. "One day three people in the village came over to us. And they complained that such wretched people as themselves, with no one else to rely on, had no chance of changing their course of life, even though they began working early in the morning. They asserted that people from Seoul could lead a better life and own their homes without difficulty. Coming around us in that way, they bullied us with no special reason, and eventually we had to make a fence with a gate in it. Even so, they harrassed us, coming through the hills behind the house, and accused us of rejecting the ways of the countryside by making a fence around the house, just as people in Seoul did. Moreover, they started a fight with our workers, so that within five days all the workers we'd brought left. I was so horrified that I even thought of giving up building the house then. If it were not for the pots, we would have given in to them completely."

Listening to what Yun-hee said, Yi Sung-ju remarked: "So you've already paid in full a penalty you didn't deserve. In the eyes of villagers here, people like us seem no better than the whites who forcibly robbed Indians of their land. When I first moved here, people in the village stole into the house at night and spoiled my water pipes. I learned some time later that when a magazine reporter who had come here in a car was about to go back, they dug a hole so that the car couldn't be moved. Then I told them I was a poet who, like themselves, owned nothing and that I had once engaged in the campaign for the farmer, only to realize I could not communicate with them at all. I had intended to give lessons to the young, brilliant ones if I found them here, and have them work with me, but I find it hopeless in this place."

"Isn't that another aspect of the common folk you are with?" Hee-jo, who had remained silent, spat out petulantly and emptied his glass. As it was the first time he had shown such contempt, Yi Sung-ju looked bewildered. Of a different temperament from Yi Sung-ju, who aspired to be a social revolutionary, Hee-jo had a sense of antipathy toward the poet, who used the expression the "common folk" in every sentence each time he visited.

In an effort to ease the tension, Yun-hee spoke of the dead Hong-taek to Yi Sung-ju: "Well, I feel sorry for the young widow. Why don't you go to the mourners' house and express your condolences? It might be a good idea to suggest they burn an offering to console the soul of the dead. After all, he is the former owner of your house." And Yun-hee got up, saying she was going to the mourners' house to express her condolences.

31

2

The Stream Thawed

In big cities, each day is vividly marked with an abundance of news and information, but at Choha-ri, time merely dissolves into nature itself. This winter had been so warm that people did not mind the cutting wintry wind blowing in the fields.

Because of the unusually warm weather, winter birds such as white-naped cranes and swans were said to have left for northern Siberia two months earlier than other years, and Yun-hee too had spent the whole winter without once having to fix the water pipe. She would make a fire in the brass stove only for the enjoyment of roasting nuts, but with the coming of March she cleaned the ashes out of the stove and put it back in the attic.

It was in the evening just after supper one day that Sae-bul, opening the sliding door in the wooden floor to go out to the toilet, called out, "Mom, look here!" Stopping her kitchen work, Yun-hee looked toward the wooden floor since Sae-bul shouted again, beckoning, "Look at these frogs, Mom."

Tan-bee quickly looked out, too. Responding to the excited sound of the children, Yun-hee left the kitchen, removing her rubber gloves. A swarm of frogs, small and large, had gathered from somewhere, completely covering the front step. There seemed to be more than twenty frogs, some younger ones filling Sae-bul's sneakers and a few of them jumping at the glass window in vain. All living things are sure to come again! Staring at the backs of the frogs glittering in the reflected light, Yun-hee uttered a low exclamation of wonder. Tomorrow would be the day of the lunar calendar, which marks the coming of early spring. All of a sudden, spring was coming all over the earth.

It is so wondrous, Yun-hee thought. The days are like unwinding a ball of thread: today is the continuation of yesterday and tomorrow just the extension of today. Yet, at the sound of the word "spring," yesterday and today feel completely different. To Yun-hee, the word "spring" called to mind such nostalgic things as warm sunshine, broken bits of glass, a flowering stalk, a command for physical exercises in the playground of elementary school. For a runaway girl, Yun-hee imagined, the spring might evoke an aspiration for things like a train and high-heeled shoes. Thus the expectation of the return of living things makes such splendid images possible.

The stream beginning to thaw, and Yun-hee tried to push the broken pieces of ice away when she set her foot in the water. Though the weather was still chilly, she could use the pump in the yard and hang out the clothes. Also, the start of the new school session made Yun-hee busier than ever: in addition to preparing lunch for her children early in the morning, she regularly had to help Sae-bul finish his homework as well.

Although everything was moving faster than in the winter, Hee-jo was still roaming over the mountains, showing no intention of getting back to his work. Replacing the briquet in the studio regularly, listening to music, or even looking into some books or sketchbooks, he did not so much as touch a bit of clay. Before, he would have felt agitated if he were off work for such a long time, so what he was doing now bewildered Yun-hee deeply.

One day, returning from Seoul, Hee-jo brought a pair of wooden fish with him and showed them to Yun-hee, saying they were given to him by President Choi of Dawool Gallery. It was an antique work, which was made by carefully carving a piece of wood no bigger than her hand into the shape of fish and painting eyes and scales on both sides. It looked not the least bit crude, nor was it so polished as to evoke a feeling of smartness. Though ordinary looking, there was no appearance of anything superfluous in it. The marks of the knife shaping a scale, carefully cut by hand, shone with a trace of the flow of time, and as such, the whole shape felt comfortable in her hands. Drawn to the wooden fish, Yun-hee said, "Oh, he gave you a really remarkable thing."

"Indeed. President Choi said that he felt like giving it to me for sure when he obtained it some days ago. He knew I would like such things," Hee-jo replied, contented. Still, he kept looking at the fish, his eyes filled with a look of wonder, and though he said no more, a smile curved his lips repeatedly. As Yun-hee knew, it was the expression when he was most delighted.

While observing Hee-jo, Yun-hee recalled the time when they had visited a museum together before their marriage. After looking at all the exhibits such as celadons, white porcelains and *punch'ong* wares, the reticent Hee-jo had become particularly giddy in front of the *punch'ong* wares. Looking hard at a *punch'ong* vessel with a bird pattern, he sought Yun-hee's opinion whether it looked amusing or not. Then he muttered that in comparison with a celadon vase with a willow pattern, which he had seen a moment before, there was no mark of artificiality in the *punch'ong* vessel. At the time, though, Yun-hee was more drawn to the exquisite, elegant patterns of peonies or willows on the celadon wares than to the patterns in the *punch'ong* wares that Hee-jo had pointed at. However, she was at a loss as Hee-jo chuckled in a muffled way at seeing the pattern of the wooden fish. On the surface of the *punch'ong* flask, which was carved with flowers and fish, was a fish smiling like Hee-jo himself.

That night Hee-jo went to bed with the wooden fish at his bedside, and the next day he made a point of carrying it in his pocket. He seemed to continue to enjoy looking at it even by himself, because he couldn't resist smiling when he came out of his studio. To Yun-hee, it was so silly to enjoy himself by merely looking at an antique thing, not engaged in the work he should be doing.

One day, Park Young-soo, an oriental painter, visited Yun-hee after a long while, accompanied by another man. He introduced the man accompanying him as Yi Jung-dal, saying he was a new writer who had received the ten-million *won* prize in a letter-writing contest sponsored by a national newspaper the previous year. Then the man whom Park Young-soo had introduced bowed his head and said, "I'm Yi Jung-dal."

"I enjoyed reading your novel *The Long Journey*," Yun-hee greeted him.

"You already finished it?" Yi Jung-dal made a delighted look as Yun-hee mentioned the title of his novel.

Unlike its musty-sounding title, the novel was set in a town near a military camp, which had been upset by the announcement of the withdrawal of American Forces from Korea, planned by U.S.

President Jimmy Carter. And its title, *The Long Journey,* referred to the fate of a group of comfort girls near the camp, who symbolized the adverse history of the country as well as its economic subordination.

"Even though I'm not familiar with the world of the novel," Yun-hee began, "it was so vivid and sustained such a thrill that I could not help reading it all the way through. But after reading it, one thing has lingered in my mind."

Yun-hee then expressed candidly what she had felt about the novel. The hero of the novel, a pimp at a bar, resolved to escape the town he lived in with a woman he intended to rescue. As a comfort girl, she led a miserable life—being brutally beaten by an American soldier and driven deep into debt. But on the day the man was about to leave, the woman refused to accompany him: though she had been totally exploited, she had already given in to the life of evil pleasure she had led. In the end the man did likewise because he too was accustomed to the life he had led. He had no choice but to accept the miserable conditions that made him unable to lead an independent life, and found he had the same fate as the woman. To Yun-hee, then, the hero seemed to have a self-proclaimed mission as a redeemer of the woman, which disgusted her.

At the reference to the man's mission as a redeemer, Yi Jung-dal asked, "Is this what you thought?" but Park Young-soo expressed his sympathy with Yun-hee: "There's something penetrating in your remark. It seems the writer would be presumptuous to regard his protagonist as a redeemer. No wonder that in the eyes of a woman, *The Long Journey* is considered just as you thought."

"Well, I like everything depicted as being equal," asserted Yun-hee. "Since I find that is hardly possible in the real world, I hope that at least in literature everyone will be given equal value. But I believe Hong Myong-hee's novel, *Im Guck-jung,* is a good example of this, since all the characters are depicted as being dignified in their own way—whether they are bandits or belong to the upper-class *yangban.* Besides, how vigorous the women in that novel are! They are by no means stereotypes who at best appeal to the compassion of men. For instance, the women in the novel would not simply give in to the men who attempt to take them. While pretending to comply with the demands of men wishing to have intercourse, these women threaten them all at once with a dagger in their face asking a lifelong commitment. Actually, the way these women behave there is hardly anything sorrowful like what we often find among the repressed class. In this sense, they're totally different from the traditional type of Korean women we've heard of so far. I mean, of course, those traditional women who would, for better or for worse, be faithful to their husband throughout life—just as Chun-hyang does in *The Tale of Chunhyang*—and sacrifice themselves entirely for the success of their children. In any event, Hong Myong-hee's novel helped me realize how the attitude of our traditional women goes against the instinct for life. While reading the novel, I even thought that I might have a misguided concept of what life should be like for women, and then I assumed that because all the characters in the novel come from the low class, both men and women are portrayed as being equal. But it did not prove so. Even a writer of our time, I daresay, would not have portrayed them the way that novel did. Perhaps Hong Myong-hee himself was the one who stressed the equality of human beings, since he genuinely loved life. And I'm really yearning for such a writer now."

As soon as Yun-hee's long praise of Hong Myong-hee's novel was over, Yi Jung-dal looked stunned. But Park Young-soo slapped his knee with one hand, saying, "Well, I didn't know our dear lady in Choha-ri was a true feminist!"

"I believe in the principle of equality and nothing else," replied Yun-hee. "As you know, I'm such an old-fashioned woman as not to know what feminism is about. Sometimes, when I'm depressed, I feel like expressing myself through writing, but I have no such talent."

"No one is meant to be a writer by birth, you know. Only in the course of life some people incidentally become novelists or poets, just as I happened to be a painter."

As Park Young-soo mocked himself, Yi Jung-dal said to Yun-hee. "Why don't you begin writing anything you like? You might as well get into the habit of writing a diary first. Because of their habit of writing, I heard people in the West often become successful writers, even though they don't specialize in writing. For instance, the biography of Marcel Proust was written by his maidservant, and indeed it's well written. Who knows, Mrs. Hong? You may end up with a good biography of your husband."

"Oh, there's no point in writing the biography of my husband. I feel like writing my own biography instead."

"That makes no difference," replied Yi Jung-dal.

Since, as an avid reader of books, she couldn't resist the opportunity to talk about her views, Yun-hee prolonged her remark: "Any petit bourgeois who hasn't done remarkable things in her life deserves to write her own biography, I suppose. I don't believe only artists or writers can claim an inner world for themselves. Ordinary people—even fools—can have their own view of life."

In the meantime Hee-jo had poured tea twice for the people in the room. Giving little attention to what they said, he continued to stare at the wooden fish. Glancing at him, Yun-hee stopped talking. But Hee-jo put the wooden fish before Park Young-soo as if he had been waiting for such a chance.

"Look at this work," he began. "An obscure woodworker must have created this piece with no purpose in mind. Indeed, it looks incomparably natural because there is nothing superfluous here. It also gives a comfortable feeling, since, though plain looking, there is nothing to find fault with in this. I doubt if any craftsman would be able to create this kind of work if he attempted it on purpose."

"As a matter of fact," Park Young-soo broke in, "our ancestors had truly incredible craftsmanship. Who could make this kind of thing in our times? In the old days, I'm told, a craftsman would make a full-dress costume for people ordering it, without even having to measure them. He merely exercised his feeling and ended up making a costume that fit them exactly. And so, in receiving an order for clothes, all the craftsman asked was when the customer had passed the civil service exam. Interestingly enough, he would make the front part a little longer for people who passed the exam in their youth, because such people were likely to lean backward, feeling superior to others. On the other hand, for people who passed the exam later in life, the craftsman would make the back part of their costume a little longer since they tend to lean their body forward due to the hardships in preparing for the exam. How wise it was! Indeed, people in the old days would make a garment, however humble, through the exercise of their feelings only."

"That's quite interesting," marveled Hee-jo. "In fact, the way they made a garment seemed at first glance cruder, yet its result was more natural. Although everything seems so polished these days, it turns out so shallow and artificial. I've always aspired to create something plain and simple, but I feel there is something artificial from modern life in me. Despite the fact that the state of simplicity is closer to our instinct, we're destined to stick to more polished forms in proportion to what we see around us in the course of life. True, there's no denying polish is the instinct of the modern spirit. Nevertheless, we must get rid of it."

While exchanging words with Park Young-soo, Hee-jo picked up the wooden fish again and continued: "I should have done this kind of wooden work myself, because all things made out of wood are really to my taste. If I were born again, I would become a woodworker."

At Hee-jo's words Yun-hee interrupted at once. "Are you trying to say you can make enough pots to satisfy your taste in one lifetime? Stop looking at the wooden fish and give it to Mr. Park."

With this remark Yun-hee picked up one of the wooden fish and put it before Park Young-soo, who, given it all of a sudden, merely blinked uncomprehendingly. Like one who had been ambushed, Hee-jo remained silent, smoking. Once again Yun-hee urged Park Young-soo to take it, because she knew he had been collecting antique things. As she urged so earnestly, Hee-jo gave him the other fish with resignation. "One is not enough, take this one with you," he said.

In the yard the goose was squawking out of boredom. Following the visitors to the front gate and returning, Yun-hee saw Hee-jo washing teacups with the water left in the teapot. His mouth closed, he was apparently expecting an apology from Yun-hee for what she had done a moment before. Wiping the *ondol* floor with a damp cloth, however, Yun-hee said unconcernedly, "Rather than being moved by others' work, you must create your own work to move others."

All that day Hee-jo kept frowning, but early the next morning he entered his studio. Looking into the studio from the yard through the open door, Yun-hee saw him scooping out clay. Since frozen clay would break to pieces, it was necessary to crumble it with a shovel and then sprinkle it with water to get the air out. As far as she knew, all this would take several days. Now that he was about to begin his work, loitering no more, Yun-hee felt relieved as if a heavy load had been taken off from her shoulders. Just as the stream thawed and the frog awakened from its winter sleep, so Hee-jo must go on with his work, breathing life into the inanimate clay.

Opening a sack of grain to feed the geese, Yun-hee took the thread from the seam, thinking that the strong thread could be used to cut the clay loose from the potter's wheel. Then she put the thread and the empty sack into the tool box by the entrance to the studio, intending to use the empty sack as fuel for the kiln. The habit she had gotten into of making use of whatever she found had something to do with the progress of Hee-jo's work.

One morning, along with a big envelope with the name of a professor from Hee-jo's alma mater written on it, came a letter from the Korean Consulate in Osaka, which had sponsored Hee-jo's exhibition there two years before. When Yun-hee brought in the packet and the letter to Hee-jo, he was spading, his bare feet and forearm all covered with clay. Asked to open the mail, Yun-hee tore them open to find that one was a pamphlet for an exhibition and the other, sent by the Consulate, was typewritten, so she read aloud:

I had intended to send a telegram to you immediately after I was informed of the news about Mr. Keichi yesterday. But because I was afraid you might be shocked, I send this brief note instead. Mr. Keichi committed suicide by hanging himself in his studio . . .

Yun-hee couldn't read it anymore and closed her eyes. "What in the world is this about?" she mumbled to herself. And Hee-jo, groaning, snatched the letter from her hands. According to the brief letter, there seemed to have been no external causes for Keichi's suicide and, judging by what people around him said, his natural diffidence may have caused him to be obsessed with his sense of self-limitation as an artist. The letter concluded with mention of praying for the repose of the soul of the dead and the signature of the consul himself. It appeared the consul had sent minute information about Keichi to Hee-jo, because he had introduced them to each other, telling Hee-jo the Japanese artist wished to work with him while in Korea.

Having read the letter over and over, Hee-jo went out somewhere. And sitting alone vacantly, Yun-hee heard the sound of water boiling peacefully in the studio as the sun was going down. She couldn't make herself believe such shocking news, either. Distinctly into her mind came the sight of Keichi, who would use a brush over and over on the *pun'chong* wares and who, sitting on the front step, would look forlornly at the snow-covered fields. Hadn't he already been anticipating his death then? Yun-hee asked herself. Even if he hadn't considered suicide, he might have been close to the state of death. Perhaps it was no more than a death of consciousness, Yun-hee suspected, because she too had felt more than once a sense of despair, as if abandoned in dark mountains. However, even in the midst of the state of death, humans are awakened like weeds to their instinctive aspiration for life, she sensed. Yun-hee remembered having read that after Gandhi once considered suicide in his youth and quickly changed his mind, he had never paid attention to anyone who was thinking of suicide. Isn't it true, then, that people learn almost instinctively not to confront directly a life as hazardous as an ice ridge?

At the news of Keichi's death, Yun-hee felt a sense of pity and a feeling of awe at the same time, and mourned him silently. To the artist, art is the imperative goal of life, but how could it be possible that Keichi had to hang himself at an age when he could make a compromise with himself? Yun-hee wondered. Keichi was said to be obsessed with his sense of self-limitation as an artist, but wasn't it enough just to live with the title of professor at a prestigious university, which would allow him a sense of worldly success?

Since receiving the news of Keichi's death, Hee-jo hadn't said a word, confining himself to the studio all afternoon. When Yun-hee went to call him for dinner, he was gone. In spite of his agony, however, he had begun to tread clay, because Yun-hee saw a heap of clay piled like a small hill, covered with vinyl. It looked as if he did not plan to go far, judging that he had changed to his normal outfit from his working clothes.

When Hee-jo returned just before ten at night, he had a bunch of chrysanthemums in his hand as well as a liquor bottle clinking in the pocket of his parka. He must have drunk wine alone in town and bought a bottle of *soju*. His face weary, he lay flat on the bare floor the instant he entered the room, and murmured: "What a fool! You could have lived life, enjoying it to the full."

Tears were running down his cheeks and, holding his breath, Hee-jo closed his eyes. Obviously, the death of Keichi, who had lived with Hee-jo three months like his own flesh, saddened and shocked him. Unlike Hee-jo, who would struggle with himself like a fiend, Keichi kept all his pain in his heart, and sank into the depths of despair. His struggle was more intense than Hee-jo's because he had sought all his life to perfect his art.

The next day, in the corner of the studio was set a small table, upon which lay the bottle of *soju* as well as the bunch of white chrysanthemums. At sundown, Hee-jo went out somewhere with a flower in his hand and returned late at night, dragging his feet and smelling of liquor like he had always done before. But the flower was no longer in his hand. It had been Hee-jo's habit to take a flower with him whenever meeting someone he loved. Perhaps, in search of the spirit of Keichi, he might have let the flower drift away on the stream as an expression of his mourning for him.

For nearly four days after that Hee-jo did nothing but roam about like a ghost, and Yun-hee was anxious for him to return to his work. Then one day Wan-kyu appeared like a wind. A graduate student majoring in pottery, he had often visited Choha-ri, intending to be a student of Hee-jo ever since he saw Hee-jo's exhibition two years before. As Yun-hee learned later, he was the brother of a student Yun-hee had met as a teacher. In the summer the year before, taking lodgings at Choha-ri, he had helped Hee-jo for a month. At first, Hee-jo had asked him to pull weeds in the yard for a whole week, and so he did it without a word. Then, one day, he was overcome by the work, unable to continue it any more, and lay deadly still on the bamboo bed.

Yun-hee was a bit amused to recall it. Wan-kyu, for his part,

41

expressed his intention: "I've got to get to work. It's spring, you know." Then Yun-hee was relieved to think Hee-jo might be moved to work by the presence of his student. When she led Wan-kyu into the room, Hee-jo was standing before the sliding door to the wooden floor.

Upon entering the room, Wan-kyu took out a bottle of western liquor, saying his father had asked him to give it to Hee-jo. However, Yun-hee was perplexed to see it, since Hee-jo had not eaten even a spoonful of rice in the mornings lately, and though she prepared a hangover-relieving soup for him he would merely drink liquor at his meals. As Hee-jo quickly opened the bottle that Wan-kyu had brought and filled his glass, Yun-hee couldn't stop him. She was angry to think that even in the morning he tried to gulp down the strong western liquor, which with even a little sip would burn his throat.

In the meantime Wan-kyu offered an envelope to Yun-hee, who brought in a cup of ice with her mouth closed firmly. "I guess you love to see traditional dances, Mrs. Hong," he said. "There happens to be a performance of Buddhist dance by Chang Ji-yeon tonight at the *Sarangbang* theatre, so why don't you two go and see it together? I'll take care of the house for you."

"Where did you get the tickets?" At this unexpected suggestion, Yun-hee softened her expression.

"One of my friends works as a designer at the *Sarangbang* theatre. Since I remember you once went to see a performance by one of our Korean human cultural assets, I supposed you'd like to see a traditional performance of something else, too."

"I remember when I was a child we would go to see the oral theatre group."

After expressing her gratitude to Wan-kyu, Yun-hee said there was actually something to be done in Seoul, but her husband, she added, wouldn't care to watch any of the dance performances.

But as Wan-kyu kept urging her to take the tickets, Hee-jo glanced at them, murmuring, "Isn't it where the exhibition by Dean Yoo is being held?"

Dean Yoo was a professor at Hee-jo's alma mater who had sent a flower basket on the occasion of his exhibition; naturally, Wan-kyu, a younger student at Hee-jo's school, knew him. So Wan-kyu urged again: "Come to think of it, this is opening day. Just drop in at the exhibition and enjoy the performance. It's better to take Mrs. Hong with you on this spring day after so long."

"Hah! Do you suggest I go as far as Seoul for such a playful exhibition?" Hee-jo replied unenthusiastically. But in a moment he smiled, showing his teeth like a fiendish child. "Shall I go there just to have a drink?"

Because Wan-kyu had given them an unexpected chance to see the performance, Yun-hee had an opportunity to go on an outing with Hee-jo. As it was Saturday, Sae-bul got home from school earlier than usual and willingly accepted his mother's outing. Hee-jo, who had drunk more than half a bottle of liquor, set out with a chrysanthemum stuck in the upper pocket of his suit. With his worn-out suit and a loose necktie that was out of fashion, Hee-jo gave the impression of an ascetic of the nineteenth century. So shabby was his only suit, which he wore each time he went out, that Yun-hee had asked him several times to get a new suit, but Hee-jo paid no attention to her words. Eventually Yun-hee's mother had sent a gift certificate to him for a new suit, but Hee-jo ended up giving it to a destitute student he was teaching. Because of such peculiar behavior, Yun-hee had never even bought a necktie for her husband, yet the old necktie he had on now—not fashionably wide, but as slim as a string—suited him well.

Glancing at Hee-jo, who was somewhat elated with liquor, Yun-hee turned her head to the sky. Though she still felt a slight chill around her neck, an air of spring was hanging in the clear sky. In the morning Tan-bee had left the house, saying, "Spring comes with a bird's song." In truth, a bird was flying across the sky and all the plants were wriggling out of the newly-thawed ground. Along with them, the wild pickpurse flowers coming out here and there came into Yun-hee's view as she walked.

In the first spring she had spent at Choha-ri, Yun-hee had gathered wild vegetables, which looked miraculous to her then, and filled the dinner table with them, so no meal was without vegetables. At the time, though, no one in the family complained—all enjoying the meals. Perhaps it was because all the dishes she made were coming directly from the earth that the dinner table would look alive with the smell of vegetables, fresh from the soil. That spring her children had barely eaten when they visited their grand-mother in Seoul. Although no one could truly equal their grand-mother in cooking skills, there was something inanimate about a meal eaten in the city.

Whether plants grow or worms wriggle, Yun-hee felt, the land where living things are moving about is good to live in. The fields in front of her house were now lying fallow because they had been used for nearly six years in cultivating ginseng. The resting fields, nevertheless, looked abundant, as if dreaming of another fertility. Before moving to Choha-ri, Hee-jo often visited this place to make pottery, since he did not have his own kiln then, and he discovered this village by coming for a drink after work at the peppery-stew restaurant.

The then owner of the restaurant was a widow living with her two children. People working at the nearby kilns had called her a "Philippine Widow," because, with her swarthy face, she had somewhat of an exotic air around her. Being attracted to the house and walking down along the stream, Hee-jo was taken by the magnificent natural landscape of the ginseng fields, with an area ten thousand or more *p'yong* that lay stretched out before him. That night, rolling excitedly about in the bed, Hee-jo said twice he saw a vision of *The Dream Journey to the Peach Blossom Spring*. Hearing about it from Hee-jo, Yun-hee went straight to the village the next day, and with the smell of ginseng that greeted her, she grasped a handful of soil and made up her mind to move in.

Choha-ri is situated somewhere between the cities of Sungnam and Kwangju. The nearby city of Kwangju had been a center for white porcelains during the nearly five hundred years of the Yi Dynasty, as well as the site of the central government kiln, which had regularly produced court vessels. Naturally, near the village were scattered many kilns where white porcelains were made. Considering the history of this area, with many kilns thriving, it seemed not merely a coincidence that Hee-jo had chosen this place for his home, Yun-hee thought.

Sometimes Yun-hee wondered about Mr. Yi, a villager, who would borrow money from her and bring some pieces of ginseng instead. Most of the fields near her house belonged to a clan, so it seemed like a blessing that Yun-hee's family could move in despite having no family connection and still take this place as their home, enjoying the view overlooking a long stretch of fields in front of the house, with low hills surrounding the house like an embroidered folding screen.

When Yun-hee arrived at the exhibition from her parents' home, which she had visited alone, Hee-jo was already quite drunk. At the entrance to the gallery she came upon Yi Jung-dal, the novelist, who told her he was to meet Park Young-soo there. Because Yoo had a position as the dean of college, the building where his exhibition was being held bustled like the opening of a business, with flowerpots all lined up at the entrance. Going down along the narrow steps, bumping shoulders with others, Yun-hee found Hee-jo, who was drinking wine and standing face-to-face with Park Young-soo and another man. Approaching, she greeted them with her eyes, then walked around the gallery alone.

The works in the exhibition were mostly abstract paintings. Each canvas was painted with diagonal lines as if swept by a broom, on a deep white background that was scratched over and over, to which some paint had been added. And some of the canvases were painted with repeated spiral lines. Some works expressed a state of disinterest by emphasizing the unpurposefulness of the creative act, whereas other works caused Yun-hee to promptly call to mind an oriental spirit, which was rather familiar to her. But while staring at the paintings, which all seemed similar to her, Yun-hee thought they simply looked like a pose. Though not a specialist in painting, she did consider the abstract paintings in the exhibition a meaningless play with an idea.

When she returned to Hee-jo after looking in earnest around the exhibition, he challenged her with a smirk. "Damn! There are really so many artists who, like myself, are good at a fraud. All they've been doing these past ten years is the manipulation of a broom and nothing else."

At this moment Yi Jung-dal, who was not interested in the paintings, pointed at the white chrysanthemum stuck in the pocket of Hee-jo's suit. "Look, I heard Marcel Proust carried a camellia blossom with him all the time, but I didn't expect the same chrysanthemum in a place like this. I didn't know you were a true stylist, Mr. Hong."

Not pleased with the word "stylist," Yun-hee defended Hee-jo: "One of his close potter friends died recently. It was a shocking incident because he committed suicide."

Then Park Young-soo responded, "Is that so?" but Yi Jung-dal cocked his head, looking skeptical. "Well, I understand some artists attempt suicide in the face of the recognition of their limitation as an artist. But I'm sure there might be other reasons we're not aware of. For instance, the sculptor Kwon Jin-kyu was believed to have committed suicide on account of his frustration with art. In truth, he was sexually impotent, I heard."

"You sound like one who never considered suicide, Mr. Yi." Displeased with the reference to impotence, Hee-jo made a sarcastic remark to Yi Jung-dal, who, in turn, showed little attention to Hee-jo's words.

"Never! Why should I be concerned with things like suicide, with so many things to be done?"

Upon the words of Yi Jung-dal, Hee-jo replied brusquely. "Really? I've always thought what makes humans different from animals is that only humans are able to give meanings to suicide. Then I must conclude there's something wrong with both of us."

As Hee-jo retorted looking down at the floor, Park Young-soo gave his opinion: "Like Hemingway or Marilyn Monroe, some people die at the peak of their careers. Though Monroe enjoyed the highest popularity during her life, I easily imagine she was afraid of losing her popularity. Can you understand the fear she had?"

"You mean the peak of one's career should be considered the highest kind of success in a realistic sense. But can we possibly imagine complete success in art?" countered Hee-jo at once.

When Hee-jo was about to return to the table for more wine, a middle-aged gentleman with curly hair, silver-framed glasses, and a small body, walked toward him. Though it was the very first time she had seen him, Yun-hee was instantly able to recognize him as Mr. Shim Jung-kwan, who had designed the famous *Sarangbang* building. Proclaimed as a leader by those who gathered around that building in search of something liberal, he had designed the college Yun-hee's youngest brother was attending. As Yun-hee remembered, that gray-brick college building looked oddly like a prison accommodating well-trained prisoners. Besides, the labyrinth-like *Sarangbang* building was inconvenient to use, even if it did arouse an aesthetic curiosity in people.

Approaching, Mr. Shim said, "Hey, Hee-jo! What's up? Living as a hermit? What made you come to a secular place like this?"

"Just for the wine, what else? Who could drink up all this wine except me?"

"Ha, ha! By the way, we're expecting your exhibition this year. I imagine your *punch'ong* wares would be good enough to relieve the troubled minds of city dwellers. Your works, I suppose, might be imbued with the robustness of the potter from Choha-ri and suffused with the sound of the wild wind. Am I right?"

"Um, I'm beginning to realize everyone has, in his own way, something to show," Hee-jo murmured. Then, suddenly raising his eyebrows, he said. "I know there is an erratic artist who, by means of sex, attempts to offer repose to the fatigued city folks. The buildings you designed, Master, are no better than a space for sex. I admit those darkish labyrinth and small windows are seductive and polished, but they are at best an invitation to sex since they aroused in me a sexual groan. Of course I myself am addicted to sex, but it's not everything in life, because there is something more important than that man and woman embrace each other. I mean there is something eternal!"

As Hee-jo finished his words, the face of the architect was momentarily out of shape, the wrinkles in his broad brow deepened. Just then, Yun-hee asked for rescue by her glance at Park Young-soo, who instantly snatched away Hee-jo's glass from his hand, grinning.

"This prudish fellow," said Park Young-soo, "never takes wine without making an acrimonious remark. With his tongue, he's giving no mercy even to the architect of the day. Please be merciful to him, Mr. Shim. You must know that nothing offers him a better chance to speak sharply to a master like you than this occasion. Once sober, he'll completely forget what he said now."

"Indeed, I feel awakened to hear such a peculiar comment on my work."

The architect, worthy of a master who had many people in his command, promptly changed his complexion, not minding Hee-jo's words anymore. As he left, Yun-hee asked Park Young-soo to let Hee-jo go with her to the dance performance. Then Park Young-soo suggested, "Let's greet our respectful dean."

When Yun-hee got out of the building by practically pushing Hee-jo out, though he kept coming around to find something to argue about, a girl sitting at the entrance offered a guest book. Hee-jo, staggering, held up the writing brush and scrawled a whole sheet in mockery of the painters whose style did not seem to change at all for so long.

Not all the plays by Shakespeare are good!

—Hong Hee-jo

At this time Park Young-soo, who followed Hee-jo immediately, patted him on the back. "As you still have a mind to make a sarcastic remark, I think you can have more wine. I'll buy another drink for you. Let's go."

"Please don't insist on your idea. It's the first outing for us in a long while," Yun-hee argued against Park Young-soo. But even before she had finished her words, Hee-jo tried to stop her by waving his hand. Though she had suspected Hee-jo wouldn't part with his friends to see the performance, Yun-hee was much annoyed that Park Young-soo insisted on taking the drunken Hee-jo with him to have more wine.

"Just do whatever you wish. I'd be better off opening a tavern myself to serve all of you." With this sarcastic remark she departed, giving a stiff nod to them.

With the front gate open, Yun-hee had waited anxiously for Hee-jo all through the night, but he did not return. On Sundays when the children were at home, there was virtually no time for her to relax in the room, but today she occupied herself with the housework, sweeping the front yard with a broom and cleaning up the goose droppings scattered around. As she moved from the house to the front gate sweeping, Yun-hee saw a mother goose sitting beneath the wall of the studio to lay eggs. Standing before her were the father and grandfather geese to protect her. Once, looking at such a scene, Yun-hee told Hee-jo that ganders were even better than humans.

Meanwhile Sae-bul showed his sister two of the goose eggs, the first this spring, nearly twice as big as chicken eggs. Because goose eggs were so hard to hatch, Yun-hee had heard, people in the old days would let their servants put Chinese ink around the eggs to soften the hard shell, so that a hen could brood on them; nevertheless, the rate of hatching was less than half. Knowing that the goose feather had been the most popular pen in the West, Yun-hee remembered a portrait of a famous musician sitting before an open book of music, holding a goose-feather pen. But with the development of civilization the use of geese would gradually disappear, she suspected.

Wasn't it because the geese seemed somewhat aloof from civilization that Keichi was captivated by them? Sitting on the front step, Yun-hee recalled Keichi who had written the Chinese character *Ran* upon her palm. It occurred to her that such a suicide should be the last thing she would witness in this age.

In the afternoon after lunch, Sae-bul, who had been doing homework since morning, made haste to take his bicycle outside. On Sundays he would roam about the nearby path, using the bicycle by turns with Tan-bee. Now he told his mother he was going toward Eunti village.

"Ah, I myself have something to do at that village. Let's go together," Yun-hee replied as if she had been waiting for his suggestion, and Sae-bul asked her why she was going there.

"Do you remember the woman who works with textiles? I mean your father's friend."

"Yes—the woman who looks like a cartoon."

"What do you mean?"

Sae-bul explained to the curious Yun-hee: "She's living like one caged in a castle, bewitched by a magician."

Then Yun-hee smiled. It seemed the sight of Han Min-wha, who spent most of her time before the loom weaving, must have given the child such an impression. And Sae-bul might be remembering one of Andersen's fairy tales with a princess weaving clothes from nettles in order to release her brothers who were turned into swans by witchcraft.

Having put into a bottle the fresh-made *kimchi* she had taken this morning out of the jar, Yun-hee left the house carrying a young sea bream that she had brought from her parents' home, feeling as spirited as if she were going on a visit to her relatives. A meal of rice mixed with a seasoning of sesame oil—together with fresh-made *kimchi*—was known to be representative of her cooking skills, the impeccable taste of which only she knew the secret. But the fresh-made *kimchi*, which had been preserved deep in the ground, had not yet attained its full taste.

Sae-bul pedaled slowly to keep pace with his mother, who was trying not to miss any scene that came into her view. A swarm of frogs filled the rice paddies, which still retained the roots of rice plants since the harvest the previous autumn. Between the ridges, the sun came down on the moving frogs, and as the surface of the water was trembling, the sunshine that reflected upon it shivered. The frogs, croaking pathetically at night like baby ghosts whose spirits did not seem to be risen yet, were just getting out of their winter hibernation, and began to stretch their legs spiritedly in the sunshine to confirm their life.

"Look, it's spring everywhere. Where are you going now?"

At the sound of the cracked voice behind, Yun-hee turned to find the old woman in the Pear Tree House. Accustomed to seeing her only in the field, Yun-hee felt somewhat strange to see the old woman who seemed to be on an outing in old *chogori* with long sleeves.

"Hi, where are you going with such a heavy bundle?" Yun-hee greeted her as she was taking the bundle from the old woman's head. Turning, Sae-bul bowed to her and was about to put the bundle on his bicycle, but the old woman held back and walked side by side with Yun-hee.

"My youngest daughter told me some days ago she needs old bean paste," replied the old woman, "so I'm going to Seoul with some old bean paste and soybean malt. Since it's my first visit in a long while, I had to make soybean paste fresh for her."

"Are you still taking pains to make soybean paste for your daughter? True, my mother did everything for me at the beginning of my marriage. But although I managed to learn how to make soybean paste later on, I discovered I could never equal her skill."

"Well, regardless of the skill, the air in the city is so bad the bean paste does not get its full taste. Whenever I go to Seoul, I can barely take a walk in the street because the air constantly makes my eyes sore. Though it's difficult to resist my daughter's request, I can hardly stay there more than two nights. It's horrible."

"In fact, it's the same with me since I moved here. I rarely go to Seoul, but once I get there I try to return instantly after finishing my business. I wonder how I'd ever live in a place like Seoul."

"You aren't like the younger ones these days, Sae-bul's Mom, since you'd never pass an old woman like me without bowing."

"I have a mother to serve, too. She is as old as you."

Yun-hee showed her modesty. In truth, while living in the countryside, she had made it a custom to offer a word of greeting, however short, whenever she met old people in the village. Despite the fact that people living on the outskirts of big cities had been much affected by the modernization drive, the old people of her mother's generation were still preserving the same simple and honest minds as those in the old farmhouse.

It was when Yun-hee first moved to Choha-ri that a strange old woman she thought insane had broken into her house to get some water from the pump. After drinking water as if thirsty—her face all stained with the soil—the old woman turned around to see Yun-hee and said, "You don't mind my taking water here, do you?" Although Yun-hee had assumed that the old woman would have a dreadful look on her face, her expression turned out as nonchalant as an innocent child. Finding that the face preserved unhampered humanity, Yun-hee momentarily thought her an angel descended to earth—as in a story from long ago. From then on, Yun-hee occasionally saw the old woman from the Pear Tree House who was working ceaselessly in close touch with the earth, neither complaining nor criticizing anyone. In truth, she felt something akin to piety toward this soul who lived in harmony with the earth.

In the meantime Sae-bul, who had made his way alone ahead of Yun-hee, stopped his bicycle at a hillside and waited for his mother, looking over the stream. And the old woman went across the bridge to take a bus. With Yun-hee hastening her pace, Sae-bul pedaled again, emerging out of the pine grove. He said, "Mom, will you ride on the back of my bicycle?"

As Yun-hee asked if he was anxious for her to keep pace with him, the child shook his head. "Not at all. I want to let you know the feeling of riding a bicycle. It might feel good since we're moving straightway along the stream."

"Then I'd rather walk. I can ride on the bicycle later on." Yun-hee smiled secretly, perceiving Sae-bul was much excited with the bicycle.

Soon a village emerged around a bend in the stream, and while walking along the meadow up to a yellow mud path that looked like the tail of a snake, Yun-hee saw a solitary shanty. Since she had been to this place once before, Yun-hee, looking at the meadow and the solitary shanty before her, had no difficulty in finding Han Min-wha's house. The garden back of the house planted with potatoes the previous spring had already been tilled. Stepping into the front yard, Yun-hee called out, "Hello, are you in?"

While washing dishes by the pump, Han Min-wha just stared at Yun-hee, not instantly recognizing her visitor. In a moment she said, "Oh, my! What makes you come to this place?"

"I simply followed a child who went bicycling in this direction. Besides, it's a fine day."

"Hello," Sae-bul greeted Han Min-wha, pulling his bicycle into the front yard and stopping it.

"I heard from my husband you helped him select the bicycle for Sae-bul," Yun-hee said. "I'd have bought it sooner for him if I had known how delighted he would be with the bicycle."

"It's a relief he likes it, though."

With a smile on her lips, Han Min-wha got up before finishing the dish washing. As Yun-hee urged her to finish her work, Han Min-wha said to Sae-bul, "Will you pump the water?" and hurriedly washed the dishes. To wash the dishes, she mixed straw with some grit piled at the corner of the yard and then rubbed the dishes with it, instead of using a detergent.

So Yun-hee asked with curiosity, "Do you always wash the dishes in such a way?"

"Yes. I've never used detergent for washing them. If we threw away the water after using the detergent, we would end up drinking it. I've only to wash off the dregs of fatty food with wheat flour and boil the dishes once. In fact, people in the old days washed dishes without detergent, you know. While living in the countryside, I'm getting to know how to live in harmony with nature."

"Actually I feel dizzy whenever I see the farmers using agricultural chemicals in the fields," replied Yun-hee. "It's been many years, I heard, since foreigners living in Seoul stopped drinking tap water, being afraid of its pollution. Moreover, even people in the countryside cannot feel assured of the water they're taking, on account of the agricultural chemicals."

"Good Lord! When I went to the drug store a few days ago to buy something for disinfecting the toilet, they gave me hydrochloric acid. I intended to get rid of that chemical after using it once, but I gave up since I was afraid the earth might suffer for it. Then I ended up keeping it in the barn. As I live closely with the earth, I'm getting to realize the earth is indeed the root of all living things. I believe what people are doing with farming these days really goes against the earth."

Because they had something in common to talk about, their first meeting in a long while was far from being awkward. Going into the house with the basket of dishes in her hands, Han Min-wha led Yun-hee and Sae-bul to the room. The loom at the upper end of the room attracted Yun-hee's eyes. In a corner were lined up a carved wooden bowl containing small pieces of artwork and a bamboo basket full of thread. On a shelf at one end of the wall were a variety of colorful skeins of thread, heaped up in disorder, and on the opposite wall two pieces of weaving were hanging side by side, one in a blue tone and the other in red-brown. On her first visit to this place, Yun-hee had felt the room had the peculiar air of a woman living alone—not affected by the burdens of everyday life at all—but now the room appeared like a toilsome workplace. Bringing sweet wheat cakes to Sae-bul, Han Min-wha prepared to make tea by opening a straw container. Inside were a set of gorgeous-looking *punch'ong* teapots in a brownish hue. It was a set made by Hee-jo himself.

A *punch'ong* jar filled with pear blossoms was set on the chest, which was the only furniture in the room. That jar, with blue speckles like a halo on the upper part of it, was not intended for sale, even at Hee-jo's exhibition. As such, Yun-hee had cherished the jar steadily, with its single line like a flower branch. When Han Min-wha had visited Yun-hee's house for the first time, Hee-jo suggested they exchange works with each other, and she chose the jar without hesitation. But Yun-hee had no urge to yield it to anyone, and Hee-jo also said it was not made for others. When Han Min-wha replied shortly she wouldn't take any other thing but the jar, Yun-hee thought she was quite a determined woman.

Sae-bul, who had been looking around the room, pointed at the paintings hung side by side on the wall and asked if they were paintings of mountains.

"Oh, do they strike you as mountains?" Han Min-wha asked the child.

"One of them looks like mountains at twilight, and the other is like a night scene."

In fact, the paintings Sae-bul had mentioned were abstract art, but they gave him such an impression. Though the composition of each painting was somewhat different, in one of them blue and black mountains seemed hidden here and there, making the whole canvas look like a valley at night.

"Since I'm living surrounded by mountains," explained Han Min-wha, "I tend to paint mountains in spite of myself. I'm told that in the West many paintings are figure paintings, so there are few painters who depict mountains, because the mountains do not overwhelm people as they do here. You know, I'm always amazed by the ridgelines of the deep mountains in our country. As the spring comes, I feel tempted to do something else rather than painting. So in the dyed work I try these days, mountain images appear continuously."

Then Han Min-wha took dyed silk cloths out of the chest and spread three pieces on the floor, each being about twice as large as a palm. They were works of art in which the mountains and the moon were painted against a black background, and the mountains made of two different colors looked like rainbows. The colors of red, blue, green, and purple, in harmony with the black background, were as distinct as a fluorescent light, thereby making each work look like a mountain village dreaming in the darkness.

"You see, these are dyed paintings," explained Han Min-wha, "so they look very colorful and give a different feeling in comparison with my weaving."

Yun-hee stared at the silk cloths, recalling the ridgeline and moon which had appeared in Hee-jo's pots. At the sight of them, Sae-bul broke in, "It looks sad."

"What makes you think so?"

As Han Min-wha was looking into Sae-bul's eyes, the child blinked, lost in thought. Suspecting that the primary color used might arouse such an impression in him, Yun-hee expressed her opinion. "They say what children feel is usually accurate."

"Perhaps. But deep in my heart there might be something suffused with sadness. Whatever it is, a work of art is meant to be a reflection of one's mind. Though looking much the same, the mountain scene I painted when I was on edge has something pointed like this."

Han Min-wha then pointed at the painting of mountains on the left side of the wall. Scrutinizing it for a moment, Yun-hee discovered that the mountains in this painting were quite pointed, like triangles, while the mountains on the other two canvases had softer ridgelines.

After pouring boiling water into the teapot to warm it, Han Min-wha asked Sae-bul, "Will you try tea or just a cup of cocoa?"

"He has been drinking tea since he was three years old," Yun-hee explained.

"So? Maybe it's because your father is a potter. You're ten years old now, aren't you?"

"No! I'm eleven," retorted Sae-bul suddenly, angry and blushing.

His raised eyebrows indicated he was genuinely upset, and Yun-hee was at a loss to comprehend it. But it was Han Min-wha herself who grasped the feeling of the child. "Oh, I'm sorry I didn't know your age exactly. You seemed so hurt because I miscalculated your age by one year. Well, he has a very strong self-respect, Mrs. Hong, just like his father."

"You understand him very well," responded Yun-hee, feeling uneasy. Judging from the Dostoevsky book or the teapot, her husband and Han Min-wha must have maintained a close relationship with each other. Reflecting that Han Min-wha may already have heard about Keichi, Yun-hee told her of him.

"What? He committed suicide?"

At the sudden news Han Min-wha raised her eyebrows. Being at a loss for a moment, she fixed her eyes on the floor and then took two cigarettes out of the case she happened to have. Putting them on the table in the shape of a cross, she picked a small, white flower from the jar and placed it next to the cross. With the pure, small altar setting completely, Han Min-wha dropped her eyes for a moment. Then she said, raising her head: "Certainly Mr. Hong must have been shocked. I'm afraid he cannot concentrate on his work because of the confusion. Why don't you suggest he take a trip for a change?"

ళ

Hee-jo did not return that night, and actually it was not unusual for him to stay out. When Tan-bee had once awakened in the night, sobbing, to tell her mother she had had a dream in which she could not see her father anymore, Yun-hee had implored Hee-jo to have a convincing reason that his children could accept for his staying out or else come home, however late. Since her entreaty had been made in the name of the children, Hee-jo had seldom stayed out since then, but nonetheless he occasionally troubled the sleep of other family members by arriving home in a taxi from Seoul the instant the curfew was lifted.

On Monday morning, Yun-hee went to the peppery-stew restaurant in town with her children to telephone to Seoul. In a half-asleep voice, Wan-kyu answered her call, but Yun-hee couldn't help explaining the situation to him, asking him to find out the whereabouts of her husband, because he hadn't returned since following Park Young-soo at the exhibition the previous Saturday. If her husband was still in Seoul, she continued, Wan-kyu should accompany him to her house by telling him something had come up at home that he must take care of. Yun-hee felt she could confide in Wan-kyu, since he was, after all, Hee-jo's student. Besides, she didn't feel like asking even a friend of Hee-jo about the whereabouts of her husband by a telephone call in the early morning.

It was past noon when Wan-kyu returned, and upon entering the house he inquired, "Is Mr. Hong still not home?" He then conveyed what Park Young-soo had told him: both he and Hee-jo had dropped into a Buddhist temple in Seoul the day before to meet a monk who specialized in painting temples, and after drinking all night they went their own way the following morning. "He told me then that Mr. Hong might go to see his children at school," Wan-kyu added.

"To the school?" Yun-hee felt suspicious at the words, recalling that about two years before Hee-jo had made an abrupt visit to the school and brought his children home. True, Yun-hee too occasionally had an urge to see her children at school, but it goes without saying that no children would greet their father if he arrived drunk to see them at school. As Yun-hee made haste in search of Hee-jo, Wan-kyu stopped her by waving his hands: "If Mr. Hong is drunk, I must carry him here on my back. You couldn't do that, right?"

As the spirit of midday was waning, Wan-kyu, who had left the house with a joke, returned with a grave face. Because Yun-hee had been impatiently waiting for him, afraid that misfortune might have befallen Hee-jo, her heart sank suddenly as she saw Wan-kyu walking home alone. Hee-jo, according to Wan-kyu, had lost his senses while roaming about the children's school. While Wan-kyu was walking around the school fence looking for Hee-jo, a woman passing by informed him a man was lying nearby, and when he rushed to the place a few children were standing around the corner of the street, whispering. Finding Hee-jo, who had fainted on the ground like a disabled man, Wan-kyu had taken him to a nearby hospital.

"It seemed he'd lost his senses because of severe pain," Wan-kyu explained. "As soon as I brought him to the hospital, he emptied his stomach suffused with blood. It was diagnosed as subgastric mucosal bleeding, so he was given an injection of Ringer's solution—not just one, but two—in order to counteract the poison. At any rate, he needs to be in the hospital for about two weeks for treatment. But I think we might as well decide how long he should be there as his condition develops."

Yun-hee, unable to listen anymore, closed her eyes. In the meantime Wan-kyu took out a cigarette and brought it to his lips. "The moment I saw Mr. Hong lying down in the street, I felt he might end his life if he continued to live this way. As odd as this may sound, he must not destroy himself, since life is never as long as he might think."

"Although I've been living with him over ten years, I still have no idea why he did such a ruinous thing to himself," sighed Yun-hee.

When Yun-hee went to the hospital, Hee-jo was lying beneath the dim fluorescent light of the hospital room, with an intravenous bottle of Ringer's solution connected to each arm. Stepping into the room, Yun-hee could figure out what Wan-kyu had told her. She had not been so alarmed in the past, even when Hee-jo had been hospitalized from a traffic accident. At that time he was practically dragged to the house, unable to keep himself steady, but he began to drink the next day, making Yun-hee wonder how he still maintained the spirit to do so.

Before moving to the countryside, Hee-jo could not endure his life in Seoul, where he was constantly overcome with drink and pestered by people around him, so once in a while he escaped the city without telling anybody. At times like that he would telephone Yun-hee at midnight from cities as far away as Taejon or Mokpo, with a bottle of wine in his hand, and murmur he would die. After Yun-hee had spent several nights worrying deeply about him, Hee-jo would return home holding in his hand a blossom he had torn to pieces, like a scar on his heart. Just five years before, when a close poet friend was arrested for criticizing the dictatorial government, Hee-jo had disappeared for nearly a week, haunting Yun-hee with nightmarish thoughts. The day before his poet friend was arraigned after the arrest, Hee-jo got together with other friends for a drink and happened to leave earlier than usual to do something with his painter friends, who had scheduled a group exhibition the next day. As a result, the whole group except Hee-jo had the ordeal of being taken to the police station for investigation.

With the tubes of Ringer's solution stuck in his arms and lying on the white sheets with both of his hands stretched down his sides, Hee-jo looked like a sacrificial offering. To Yun-hee's eyes, it was a portrait of a defeated man who lived in a small corner of the world with little to rely on, risking all his dreams on his pottery and ruining himself because he was unable to adapt to his times. The sun that slanted into the room through the west-facing window was setting, but Hee-jo didn't open his eyes even once. The deserted village below, in which many houses were clustered together, changed color with the evening glow, while a ray of sunshine crossed the back of Hee-jo's hands.

Yun-hee touched his distinctly curved knuckles, feeling that it had been a long while since she held his hands. To hold hands, she believed, would give a deeper sense of intimacy than any other act of love. She remembered a friend who had argued for the supremacy of the kiss, saying that sex without a kiss was like a kitchen table without salt. For her part, however, Yun-hee could have a deeper communion with Hee-jo by holding his hands than when she was in sexual intercourse. Obviously, holding hands let her confirm a sense of union, as with a comrade, or feel humanity, since it helped confirm something greater than mere physical desire. A prostitute would surrender her body to anyone who seeks it, Yun-hee reflected, but nevertheless she would be as prudent in holding hands as if she were selecting a gem.

Holding Hee-jo's hands for the first time in a long while, Yun-hee felt his knuckles looked thicker and rougher than before. His hands seemed more suitable for labor, not for love, because they looked like the hands of a farmer who labored too much in the fields. At the same time, they reminded Yun-hee of her mother's gaunt hands, which would stroke the silk cloth of the children's clothes in the New Year, making a crisp sound. Most of all, hands at work would arouse in Yun-hee something akin to an image of her old home.

As the index finger of Hee-jo's right hand came into her view, Yun-hee felt relieved, since the long fingernail of the finger, which Tan-bee had called a demoniac fingernail, looked the same as before. Hee-jo had grown this fingernail long so that he could use it in drawing a fine line on the *punch'ong* wares. While the commercial potters habitually made the pattern by using both of their thumbs, Hee-jo used to do it with the long fingernails of his thumb and index finger.

It was only since he had seen an exhibition of some finger paintings by painters of the Yi Dynasty that Hee-jo began to draw using his fingers. At the time he wondered why those painters used their hands in drawing, rather than using a brush, and Yun-hee suggested the finger paintings at the exhibit had a bold and some-what dynamic touch. It was still vivid in her mind that she had laughed at herself when Hee-jo, feeling content with her comment, had gone so far as to compliment her excessively, saying she deserved to be the wife of a painter who would make a drawing with his fingers.

After studying Hee-jo's hands, Yun-hee felt reassured he would be getting back to work soon. While she, with a relieved spirit, kept looking at the Ringer's solution dripping like rain drops, Wan-kyu turned up and said he would take care of Hee-jo for the night. Although Yun-hee dissuaded him from staying with Hee-jo, whose condition now was not so serious as to require surgery, Wan-kyu urged her to return promptly, reminding her of her children. "You have to get them ready for school in the morning. While staying with Mr. Hong, I myself have to think about why he nearly drinks himself to death."

At the news that her father had been taken to the hospital, Tan-bee, awake far into the previous night, made a vase by putting colored paper on an empty can. Incidentally, a magpie cawed when she set out for school in the morning with some money to buy a flower. Looking up at the sky, she told herself that someone might visit, though her father was away from home.

While Yun-hee, having finished her housework, was waiting for Wan-kyu to return, Monk Hyeo, to her surprise, came to her house. He was a Buddhist monk at the Sunwoon Temple where Hee-jo used to visit for meditation each winter when he was off work. After taking charge of a secluded temple near Tamyang the previous year, Hyeo frequently dropped by Choha-ri whenever he had occasions to come up to Seoul. Since this visit was his very first this year, Yun-hee nearly jumped down to the yard to greet him, without even putting her shoes on.

"Please come in. I thought you might have been in meditation for a long while, since I haven't seen you at all recently." Yun-hee greeted him heartily, putting her hands together, and Hyeo did likewise, bending his tall frame to bow.

"As I now take charge of all the affairs of the temple, I have many things to do outside." Hyeo explained.

"Where are you coming from, Monk?"

"I went to the main temple in Seoul last night to do something about business and now I'm on the way to Tamyang."

Stepping onto the wooden floor, Hyeo looked for Hee-jo first, and so Yun-hee couldn't help but tell him the exact situation. "Everything that happened to him has something to do with wine," she added. "He kept drinking wine for a whole week—not even eating a spoonful of rice. No wonder he was taken to the hospital."

"That's because he depends upon wine for his existence," Hyeo replied calmly. "People have an inclination to depend on something, so the weaker they are the more they depend on whatever they find. They depend on their husband, children, money, or even fame. I know that these days even religious people depend on worldly things."

"But if we turn to people, we could at least expect human affection," sighed Yun-hee.

"It's because Mr. Hong is strong that he has been able to sustain such patience. In the course of living we encounter countless crises, as if standing on the edge of a cliff. The important thing is that when we feel driven as to the edge of a cliff, we must abandon ourselves in order to come up with something. However, because of an uncertain dread about what the bottom might be like, ordinary people strive to cling to something. And it's the same with a monk like me. Mr. Hong seems to be strenuously driving himself as if to the bottom of a cliff. Though in the process he falls back on the support of wine, it's never easy to abandon himself in such a way."

"As a monk, do you also have moments of feeling driven to the bottom of a cliff?"

As Yun-hee asked in earnest, Hyeo laughed slightly. "A monk is human, after all. We are no better than worldly people in the way of feeling lonely and uncertain. I am always conscious of a moment when the entrance of the mountains begins to surge in silence after sundown. Actually, one of the monks in my temple makes it a habit to wash his feet in the basin exactly at that moment, watching the sun waning through the rice paper of the window. As you know, a monk is destined to wander about the world, but it's because we're truly lonely. All we have to attempt, then, is to get over such thoughts through a process of spiritual discipline."

"I understand you have the goal of attaining Buddhahood, though," remarked Yun-hee.

"To be honest, I haven't even thought about it myself. They say that to attain Buddhahood deprives us of the right to be born again. So, instead of accomplishing such a goal, I wish I could be born again in the afterlife as the son of a rich family, so that I might study to the best of my ability."

The words of Hyeo were always so candid that Yun-hee felt drawn to such a human side as he possessed. He was said to have worked well through middle school, being always at the top of his class, but he had gone into a temple to become a monk because of his family's meager condition. In spite of his towering stature, however, Hyeo was so weak as to have nosebleeds while in meditation, and so he would recite just a Buddhist invocation until his voice cracked. Three years before, when she had gone to see Hee-jo at the Sunwoon Temple, Yun-hee had heard Hyeo's invocation and found that it gave her the impression of cool air like dawn. Attracted to the tone of his invocation, Yun-hee had recorded it, thinking that anyone who listened to it would feel as refreshed as if washed by chilling water.

It was already eleven, and remembering that Hyeo was in the habit of skipping breakfast, Yun-hee got up to prepare lunch for him. "Oh, you must be hungry, Monk. When I was returning from the hospital yesterday, I dropped in at the market and bought a salmon. I'll serve it for lunch if you like."

Hyeo didn't decline, saying, "I'll take with pleasure whatever you make if you put it on the table."

While broiling the salmon, Yun-hee washed the vegetables she had gathered the previous day and seasoned them without garlic. The meal table was set very simply, with only the broiled salmon, but Hyeo emptied each dish to the last particle. Bringing the table outside, he said a word of gratitude with a look of satiety. His unpretentious way in which there was no disguise could be compared to the very atmosphere of the *punch'ong* ware, so Yun-hee momentarily wondered if Hee-jo would be able to have peace by him.

"As soon as my husband gets out of the hospital," she said, "I wish he would go down to Tamyang for a rest. If you take care of him for even a few days, he'll get better soon."

"In fact, I've worried about him since I had a dream in which Mr. Hong at Choha-ri kept walking forlornly in the rain. So be sure to tell him to come down to my temple. Though there will be little I can do for him, he might feel settled with spiritual discipline in the temple. Instead of seeing him here, I'd rather leave now, because I might feel uneasy to meet him ill in bed."

As Hyeo was about to leave, Yun-hee took out a large teapot from the stationery chest. Hee-jo had made it last autumn with Hyeo in mind, and was content with its modest and clean look. Yun-hee explained to Hyeo, "As he made it especially for you, Monk, it evokes your image."

"Leave it where it is. If I visit again, I'll have tea using the teapot I entrust to you."

He laughed heartily, and as Yun-hee was preparing to wrap it he dissuaded her by waving his hands. Hee-jo had at first intended to make a formal teapot, but decided instead to make a humble one, thinking it might go against the disposition of Hyeo, who didn't like possessions of any kind. Despite that, Hyeo considered even that small teapot a burden to him.

When Yun-hee went to the hospital, Hee-jo's endoscopic test had already been done, and his symptoms were confirmed as sub-gastric mucosal bleeding. Because of the severe stomachache in the morning, Yun-hee heard he had been given a pain-relieving injection, but as the pain still continued after about twenty minutes, he was given a sleeping pill. He was now lying in bed as if unconscious, with the tube of Ringer's solution in his arm.

Tan-bee, who came straight to the hospital from school, filled the vase she had made at home with an armful of freesia. Not being content, though the scent of freesia wafted about in the room, she placed a separate bunch of flowers upon her father's head. Since she had already seen her father hospitalized in a traffic accident less than four months before, Tan-bee did not cry this time as she did before. When Hee-jo awoke, opening his eyes dimly at hearing someone talk, the child brought her face close to him and said in an accusing tone, "Father, what on earth did you have that much wine for?"

After four days in the hospital, Hee-jo began to show signs of recovery. The bottles of Ringer's solution being reduced to one a day, he started taking gruel and milk. He lay vacantly in bed all day long and the next day wrote down some fragmentary thoughts in the sketchbook that Tan-bee had left behind. Yun-hee found a short entry:

People often say they "have no time," but does time really exist as they think?

On the next sheet was a sketch of a big porcelain dish, upon which were drawn some patterns representing mountain ridgelines and nature. Along with a sketch was written another passage:

Several suns and several moons. They're circling the whole universe. Do they leave any mark behind them or not? It seems that at one moment they do and at another they don't. Do they have the same shape or not? How about humans? They're all alike.

Although Hee-jo, like an alcoholic, was overcome with the effects of wine, his spirit still seemed as alive as before. Yun-hee had so far been conscious of the passage of time, feeling anxious that Hee-jo was off work, but she too wondered if time really existed. When she looked out the window, closing the sketchbook, Hee-jo opened his eyes and looked for water. After breathlessly taking a gulp of the barley tea Yun-hee had poured into a cup, he began to talk for the first time since he had been in the hospital.

"How did Wan-kyu find me before I was taken to the hospital?" he asked.

"I telephoned him in Seoul on Monday morning to ask him to go in search of you. Because I had no mind to make such a call to any of your friends."

"It would have been better if you had sent Wan-kyu home last night. I called out in the morning since I felt as if my head would explode, so Wan-kyu awoke to find a nurse."

"Should I have to stand all this trouble myself?" Yun-hee responded to Hee-jo momentarily in anger. "Should I have to feel disturbed to the innermost place in my heart by just watching you destroy yourself? I have no more mind to see all this. But for Wan-kyu, I would have called anyone else."

Though Yun-hee spat out in anger, it was what she had been trying to say. After a pause she made a low moan, looking at the blank wall. "Now that you're in the hospital, don't mind anything else and just take a rest. The doctor said you need to be in the hospital for nearly two weeks."

"Damn it! What's the use of being in the hospital that long? I'll get out of the hospital tomorrow. I just feel like a disabled man since I am always drowsy from the pills I'm taking."

"But you're liable to be a disabled man if you continue to lead your life in such a way," Yun-hee said without revealing emotion, and then told him of Monk Hyeo's visit. "He said he had dropped in, anxious to see you, because he had had a dream in which you were walking forlornly in the rain. He asked me to tell you that when you're out of the hospital you ought to come down to his temple and stay for a few days."

3

The Land of Survival

There came a season when the mountains, which had been silent all winter long without revealing their color, turned light green, unfolding another dream of life. Each day the young leaves of the mountain plants emerged from their buds, and the good earth, opening its wide bosom, welcomed the seeds to the open ground. The undistracted air of the early spring, which gave a feeling as of turning up one's collar, was so exhilarating that Yun-hee stopped hanging out the laundry and inhaled deeply.

Stepping onto the wooden floor, Yun-hee heard the sound of the front gate opening and saw a woman entering with a bundle on her head. Seeing this stranger, the two geese that were drinking water at the water pail started running to her, craning their necks.

"Ouch! What wild and crazy animals," shouted the woman in surprise with the accent of Kyongsang-do Province.

"Because it's mating season for them, they grow wild," replied Yun-hee.

Stepping down into the yard, she led the threatening geese into the back yard. Since the geese started to lay eggs in the spring, there were about four eggs accumulated in the nest. Following Yun-hee onto the wooden floor, the woman put down her bundle and said, looking toward the open field through the window, "The scenery is so beautiful! Auntie, how about buying some hemp cloth made in Andong?"

Though it was not the thing Yun-hee needed in this season and, moreover, she couldn't afford to buy it, she nevertheless inquired about its price, recalling how her mother would prepare the hemp cloth even before the summer arrived.

"Oh, it costs about fifteen hundred *won* a foot," answered the woman instantly. "You see, if you use it as a quilt cover, I'm sure you can spend the whole summer without minding the heat."

"It appears this can be used only as a quilt or something. If I use it for a quilt cover, I think its structure would loosen."

"Looks like you've used hemp cloth before. Of course you can use it as a quilt," the peddler coaxed Yun-hee again.

"Before I got married, I saw a heap of hemp cloth and some other quilt covers in the *bandaji* in my parents' home. They were completely packed so as not even to allow a single bit of space. Long ago, we used starched cotton cloth."

"So? Your mother must have been frugal in everything," the peddler said with elation.

"As a matter of fact, she's such a person as would make a quilt cover out of silk cloth dyed in the winter and use the remaining raw silk for a tablecloth. While providing her children with a different set of clothes each season, she always wore mended clothes."

"Indeed. In fact, that's the way parents raise their children although they are themselves in shabby clothes."

As Yun-hee was chatting face-to-face with the peddler, her mother, Madame Shin, came unexpectedly through the sliding door to the wooden floor. Because Yun-hee had not inquired about her recently, even on the telephone, and she had dropped in at her parents' home no less than a week earlier, she had not anticipated this sudden visit of her mother.

"What has brought you here? We're just now talking about you, Mother," Yun-hee said in surprise.

"Speak of the devil, they say," replied Madame Shin. Putting down her market bag, she glanced at the unpacked bundle, asking, "What's this hemp cloth for?"

"It's from Andong, this woman said. It reminded me of you, Mother."

"Then, did you bring this stuff yourself all the way from Andong to sell? Well, you've really come a long way here." Turning to the material, Madame Shin asked about the price and ordered the woman to prepare two seven-yard pieces of the cloth. Then she instantly took out money to pay the peddler before Yun-hee could dissuade her.

Upon receiving the money, the peddler rubbed it against her head. "Thank you so much. A good start for the day! Certainly so."

After the peddler had left, delighted, Madame Shin asked Yun-hee immediately if something had come up in the house. With the absence of Hee-jo, she seemed to figure something had happened in the family, and as Yun-hee told the truth, Madame Shin responded by saying she had felt tempted to come here for no reason. In a moment she said, "I'm fed up with whatever he's doing."

No sooner had Madame Shin sat down than she went out to the jar stand in the yard. The soy sauce made the previous year was still there, but since it is believed the taste of soy sauce turns bad with the turn of the year, Yun-hee had made it all again with the onset of spring. Opening the lid of the jar now, she discovered that the soy sauce inside had diminished a little in the meantime. So she murmured: "Because I had used little salt last year, a white foam had appeared in the jar. But I suppose I put in enough salt this year. . . ."

Yun-hee believed she had managed to do the household work to the point of not being reproached by her mother, who often visited her to see if her daughter was doing rightly with the housework. Meanwhile Madame Shin opened the jar containing the old soy sauce, the first Yun-hee had made after she had moved to Choha-ri. Since it was made nearly four years before, the jar was almost empty, and at the bottom was deposited some hardened salt as white as ice.

"In the pickling season this year," Madame Shin told her daughter, "you can preserve cabbages with this hardened salt. Then you'll get *kimchi* tastier than before."

"Really? I was about to throw it away." Yun-hee murmured.

"For the woman who manages the household, there's nothing to throw away. Even the rice that turns sticky in the summer will have a better taste when you put it into the bean paste."

To Yun-hee's eyes, her mother was meant to be a born housewife: whenever finding a fully ripe squash in the market she couldn't resist buying it to make basic side dishes for the family, and she would also make vinegar out of oranges bought cheaply in the market. Besides, with the change of the season, she would prepare all kinds of fruit wine, and have groundnuts spread deep inside the *ondol* floor, to the point that they could look shiny, for preparing them as a side dish. Under the influence of such a perfectionist mother, who had considered womanhood a kind of mission, Yun-hee often wondered if she had been striving to be an ideal woman in spite of herself. While working for her daughter, Madame Shin did not even straighten up until after she looked into the jar of pepper paste.

"I brought some ground soybean malt with me," Madame Shin said, "and you could make pepper paste using ground barley this year. As I suspected you might not have barley at home, I asked someone in the rice store to bring some barley here along with a bag of rice."

"Why, how did you suppose I don't have barley at home?" Yun-hee responded shortly. But that's the way Madame Shin had supported her daughter, so as not to wound her pride. At times Yun-hee had felt a coldness toward her mother, who was so formal as not to open the drawers of the chest without reason when she visited her daughter. Still, Yun-hee could not but marvel at the sagacity with which her mother led her life.

When Yun-hee stepped out to the yard, Madame Shin pointed to a hilly spot directly facing the front gate. "What's that hut over there? I saw it on my way here."

On the hill, where nothing more than a thatch-roofed house had been standing, was something similar to a small tent, covered with vinyl. It did not seem to be a substitute for a house. In truth, Yun-hee had paid little attention to it, since she did not notice it until just the previous day.

The vinyl-covered tent, however, expanded into two the next day, and the following day grew into four. Madame Shin, staying at Yun-hee's house while Hee-jo was in the hospital, continued to watch them, and finally told her daughter to ask about what was going on there. Going toward the hill across the brook, Yun-hee happened to meet a villager passing by and asked him about the tent.

"They're building a henhouse over there for raising chickens, I heard."

"Who started this?" inquired Yun-hee.

"The land belongs to the old man in the Electric Pole House. Probably he is letting Chung-man's father use the lot."

Yun-hee knew the old man and Chung-man's father very well. When she first moved to Choha-ri, the people in the village had cooperated to make a gravel road leading to her home, but these two men demanded that she pay for the work done. Although the work for the road was done for the whole village, they attempted to impose a burden on Yun-hee's family as though they had been forced to work for her sake. They were, as she found later, notorious in the whole village for their greedy acts.

When Yun-hee returned and told her mother of what she had heard from the villager, Madame Shin hardened her expression. "If they build a henhouse over there," she said, "you could hardly live in this place, since the excrement of chickens would contaminate the stream, and flies would swarm all over the house. What's worse, no one would come to your house, because the odors would linger. Naturally, the price of the land in this area would drop sharply."

Yun-hee, who had known nothing about it, was startled to hear her mother's warning. To make her daughter aware of the seriousness of the matter, Madame Shin continued: "Of course the excrement of chickens could be used as a fertilizer. But if used excessively, it becomes poisonous enough to kill the plants it is used on. Because of this, it's forbidden to build a henhouse in a residential area, I believe."

"This region, however, is part of a residential area. Therefore, it's illegal to build a henhouse," Yun-hee responded anxiously.

"Check with the people in the village first. If people had complete dependence on the law, they wouldn't have to worry about anything."

Upon hearing this, Yun-hee immediately started out to consult Chung-ki's grandmother, who lived nearby. Her house being situated right across from the henhouse, and being a senior person in the village, she was the suitable one to talk to about this matter. Fortunately, the old woman was sitting on the wooden floor in the sun, as if she had been awaiting Yun-hee.

"Now that my mother happens to be staying with me, I learned how badly we'll be affected by living close to a henhouse," Yun-hee said. "I know it's illegal to build a henhouse in a residential area, so how is it that the people in the village did nothing but look on? No doubt all of us will be badly affected."

"I heard Kwang-ho had acted as a broker in this affair since he was in touch with the old man in the Electric Pole House. Because he is such a bastard that even his parents would give up, there might be no one to stop him. Huh!"

With this remark the old woman clicked her tongue. Then Yun-hee urged the old woman: "Please ask Chung-ki's father about this because we must stop them from doing this. If only we could make all the villagers aware of this, I suppose they might be moved to cope with what will happen."

On the way from consulting Chung-ki's grandmother, Yun-hee came upon Mr. Yi, who was Jae-chull's uncle. Because he was the one who had coaxed one of Hee-jo's friends to buy a piece of land the previous year, they had since then had no associations with each other. Fortunately, Hee-jo's friend was later able to resell the land. Finding it hard to treat him as a foe while living in the same village, Yun-hee greeted him by bowing a little. The only high school graduate in the whole village, he, now in his thirties, was one of the few people in the village whom Yun-hee managed to communicate with.

"Where have you been?" asked Jae-chull's uncle.

"To Chung-ki's house. By the way, would you stop by at my house right now, because I've got something to ask you about?"

Jae-chull's uncle readily accepted her request, and walking side by side with Yun-hee, he exchanged words with her. People in the village for the most part had already known about the building of a henhouse, it seemed. In return for acting as a broker, Jae-chull's uncle informed Yun-hee, Kwang-ho was expecting to receive the manure of the chickens for use as fertilizer.

"Then the people in the village have kept silent intentionally all this time, even expecting what will happen," said Yun-hee in surprise.

"All of the people involved in this are notorious for their behavior in the village. For fear of retaliation from these villains, I think, people won't dare defy them. Besides, since most of the land in this area belongs to a clan, people are closely related to each other, and make concessions among themselves. Naturally, they're quite indifferent to this matter."

"Because the henhouse they're building is so close to the village," replied Yun-hee, "the cow flies will swarm all over the stream that flows by the village. In the end we'll have no better water to drink than the water contaminated by the chicken manure. So we should not just stand by and watch. If they raise chickens over there, we've nothing to do but leave this place."

Yun-hee candidly revealed what was on her mind, and asked advice from Jae-chull's uncle. Stepping inside the house, he gave his suggestion: "Even though we can distribute a written petition throughout the village, we shouldn't take such measures until the last moment. For the present, I think it's better for you to meet our town chief. He might give you some suggestions, because this area is under his control."

As it had been a week since Hee-jo had entered the hospital, Yun-hee was impatient, because the money made from the exhibition the previous autumn was nearly spent. Not only feeling burdened by the hospital charges, but also by a morbid dislike for spending time not doing anything, Hee-jo had insisted on leaving the hospital at any moment. In fact, Madame Shin had given her daughter half a million *won* for the hospital charge on behalf of Hee-jo. Although the money had been intended for her daughter from the beginning, Yun-hee did not dare give a pledge to return it, since the money was to be spent entirely on her husband's care.

Having helped her daughter make pepper paste and put rice paper on the door, Madame Shin left as soon as Hee-jo returned from the hospital. Because they had been not on good terms with each other, Hee-jo greeted his mother-in-law only outwardly. Displeased, Madame Shin replied with an irrelevant remark. "Hmm! It's good weather."

Less than three years after her marriage, when Yun-hee, weary of married life, had suggested divorce to her mother, Madame Shin sternly warned her that she would never be allowed to see her mother if she mentioned divorce again. In reality, a divorce was simply unthinkable to someone like Yun-hee's mother, who was affected by the dictates of feudal society. Yet she did not approve of the disposition of her son-in-law, who appeared to be destroying himself. Hee-jo, for his part, had an instinctive dislike of the perfectionist attitude and coldness of his mother-in-law. Once he had ridiculed her, saying she looked like a Queen Mother, the moment he saw her photo in a traditional costume for commemorating a silver wedding anniversary.

The meeting with the town chief took place even before Hee-jo was discharged from the hospital. However, after giving a vague pledge he would reveal the truth, the chief did not carry out his promise. Now that she needed to bring this matter to an end as early as possible, Yun-hee sought again the town office in the morning three days later. But she found something dubious in the manner of the town chief: while not giving his answer readily from the beginning, he, as before, tried to leave his place for no reason and finally avoided confronting her. Yun-hee just then remembered her mother's remark that it was because they might have someone to rely on that those people plotting the henhouse did not hesitate to start raising chickens illegally in the residential area.

When she was about to leave, Yun-hee encountered an officer she was familiar with. The officer, who had his wife's home in Choha-ri, knew that Yun-hee's visit was related to the henhouse. Feeling pity for Yun-hee, who left the office with no result, he spoke first. "You're going home now?"

"Yes. I've no idea why the chief keeps putting off giving his answer to me. I know some rumor is going on that this office secretly approved the henhouse. Isn't it true?"

"Well, that's beyond my knowledge . . ." replied the officer, smiling half agreeingly, and then gave his suggestion. "In this matter of administration, the county chief is in a more influential position, so you might well meet him first."

Hee-jo did not learn of what was going on until after Yun-hee met the county chief. Of course she couldn't venture to tell Hee-jo of the henhouse matter, since, lacking energy even to work with clay, and devoid of any will, he would go out alone to spend a good part of the day by the stream.

The county chief was a friend of the director of the general hospital in town, and both of them had visited Yun-hee's house about two years before. Recognizing Yun-hee, the chief listened attentively to her explanation of the henhouse matter. After hearing it, he asked, "How would you deal with this if poor people did such things just for their means of living?"

"If raising chickens is a means of livelihood for them," returned Yun-hee resolutely, "the land is to us the place for survival as well. And if the whole village will be damaged for the interest of only those three people, don't you think something is going wrong, regardless of the law itself?"

"In fact, while I was working as a county chief at Susan-kun before, I went through a similar case related to poultry raising. At the time I ordered the illegal henhouse to be cleared away, but one of the people involved in it finally committed suicide, leaving behind a letter addressed to me." He added that the incident had been reported in the newspaper, and had got him into trouble.

Because of the influence of that incident, the county chief seemed reluctant to accept Yun-hee's request. After a pause Yun-hee suggested to him what Jae-chull's uncle had mentioned: "If so, I'll start something I can manage myself. If I get sufficient support from the villagers by distributing a written petition, I'm going to submit it to your office. I expect you'll handle the rest of the matter according to the will of the villagers."

As Yun-hee was determined in her stance, the county chief gave a pledge that he would be giving special attention to this matter. Actually there was little time for her because they seemed to be about to start raising chickens, so she went straight to Jae-chull's uncle, intending to ask him about how to start the written petition. In addition to informing her about it, Jae-chull's uncle suggested she get approval from at least ten people in the village, adding that it might be more effective to get approval starting with the people who owned the most farmland.

His advice proved to be realistic. First, Yun-hee went to see her neighborhood head to ask for his help. Although most of the farmland in the area belonged to a clan and was used mostly as property for burning an offering to ancestors, the head, who possessed a good house and a farm of his own, did not hesitate to put his seal on the petition. Angry, he said the henhouse should not legally be built in a residential area, asserting that it was an ignominious act that the old man in the Electric Pole House let others use the tenanted land. He then informed Yun-hee of several other families who might give approval to the petition, saying he would take care of the rest of the matter because of the obvious conspiracy involved.

It was a season when the air was shimmering. In the spring sunshine, the old woman from the Pear Tree House was tilling the land before her house. Barely able to feed herself by tenant farming, she seemed to be willing to lend Yun-hee a helping hand. As Yun-hee approached and greeted her, the old woman nodded her head with a hoe in her hand. Her brown skin tanned in the sun and her deeply wrinkled hand made her look like an old tree that had gone through all sorts of hardships living in this world.

"You look healthy since you're always working in the field," Yun-hee said to the old woman.

"Well, I can barely stand still, and I must lend a hand to whatever it is. What's the use of sparing the flesh, only to have it extinguished at death?"

Then she straightened herself, looking at the sheet of paper in Yun-hee's hand. Following the old woman into the house, Yun-hee explained how she had been occupied with the henhouse matter, telling her the reason for having to call on each person with a written petition. After patiently hearing the details from Yun-hee, the old woman brought her seal without a word.

"In fact, my son had entreated me not to be involved with this," she explained to Yun-hee. "He was afraid I might be engaging in a troublesome matter, I suppose. But since it's a thing to be corrected, I must help you. You're working so earnestly, Sae-bul's Mom."

"Oh, thank you for helping me."

"Young people these days are far better than old ones. In our time people would not exercise their will and simply endured everything."

With a faint smile, the old woman put her seal on the petition. And when Yun-hee gave her a ball-point pen, asking her to write down her name on the sheet, she declined, saying, "I cannot read any letter at all."

By the next day Yun-hee was able to get approval from twelve people in the village. Though she had had difficulties persuading people, one by one, to give their consent to the petition, they were generally on her side, because what she was doing was believed to be against a conspiracy. There was even someone who made a sarcastic remark that getting consent from them should be done, not by a woman like Yun-hee, but by her husband, but most of them took sides with her.

Later, the neighborhood head who came to see Yun-hee was satisfied with the petition. Giving a pledge to take care of the remaining procedures, he told her to be cautious about those three people involved with the henhouse. Hee-jo, who had entered his studio in the morning to sprinkle water on the clay, asked Yun-hee what was going on, because he saw the neighborhood head coming to the house. And Yun-hee judged it necessary for Hee-jo to be informed of everything, since it would be decided pretty soon whether those people would have to stop building the henhouse, or whether people on her side would get into deeper hardship.

Hearing from Yun-hee about developments concerning the henhouse before his knowledge of it, Hee-jo was startled. Yun-hee, who felt rather relieved to have the petition done, said: "Living with you, I became an all-round being. I used to be so timid that I wouldn't even go to school for my children. But while you're ignorant of all this, I went so far as to visit the county office to meet the chief."

"You mean the one who once called at our house?" asked Hee-jo.

"Right. Since he's the person you're familiar with, you should have gone to see him yourself. Of course, you wouldn't go to such a place . . ." Yun-hee said to him in a half-accusing tone.

"I wish I could concentrate on my work with a new determination, but my head is still in a complete void. I wonder if I would feel awakened with another drink." Making this irrelevant remark, Hee-jo got up abruptly to leave.

Although her mother helped her with housework, Yun-hee had not been able to spare time even to assist her children with their homework since Hee-jo had entered the hospital. Sae-bul, who found in the morning he had missed one of his assignments, hurriedly finished the written homework, and got home from school with a frown after four in the afternoon. As Yun-hee asked him if he'd had a fight with his friend, Sae-bul was silent, shaking his head.

"My homeroom teacher," he said after a while, "slapped me three times on the palm in the classroom. She reproached me for scribbling. But there are quite a few students in the class whose handwriting is even worse than mine. I was chosen to be slapped, though, because I'm a class monitor."

"Really? But a class monitor is supposed to assume responsibility, even for something that goes wrong," Yun-hee soothed her child. "Unless you set a good example for other students, you should be blamed. It's natural."

"No! It's not so," Sae-bul replied quickly. "I was slapped because she hates me, you must know it. Before, I even got slapped as many as five times on my palm just because other students made noise in the classroom."

"Why do you think your teacher hates you, then?" asked Yun-hee calmly.

Sae-bul, who had become a fourth-grader this year, had a new woman homeroom teacher. Since it was all Yun-hee knew about, she reasoned with the child composedly about why the teacher had slapped him.

"I don't know, either," retorted Sae-bul. "That makes me more angry."

"I suppose there must be some reason for that. Because your teacher is a grown-up, you're too young to understand her."

Sae-bul did not respond any more, but he did not appear to accept his mother's explanation. Wasn't he, Yun-hee wondered, hated by the teacher because of his stubborn character? Something that had happened long before came suddenly to her mind. It was when the child had been five months old that his father had yielded to him completely. Looking at a kettle steaming on the electric heater, the child of five months kept trying to crawl toward it, wanting to put his hand above the steam. Twice taking the child back to where he was, Hee-jo threatened him with glaring eyes not to approach the steaming kettle—as if at the point of slapping the child with his hand.

In spite of the threat, however, the child kept stretching out his hand to touch the steam, so Hee-jo pulled down the child's trousers and tapped him on the buttocks. Even so, the child still attempted to stretch his hand toward the kettle and Hee-jo, annoyed, spanked him on the buttocks to the point of making a sound. Since the child had got slapped several times on his buttocks for refusing to comply with his father's demand, there appeared the clearly visible mark of a hand. Though he did not cry when his buttocks were slapped, the child had cried out all through the night, being ill. Yun-hee had been so astonished with Sae-bul even then, finding it difficult to break him of his stubborness, though he was only an infant.

The next morning Sae-bul grumbled, putting on his shoes, saying, "Should I have to go to school today to see that awful teacher?" and then looking up at the sky as if pitying himself.

Hearing it, Yun-hee felt like rapping him on the head, but she soothed him instead. "Don't lead your life in such a way. If you have someone you like, you must also expect to encounter someone you *don't* like. There are a good number of people in the world you must confront, regardless of your will, and to be a grown-up you must get over this."

"I wish I could be in the fifth grade sooner."

Discontented, Sae-bul left the house and, looking at the child for a while, Yun-hee quietly took a deep breath. To live in the world, she said to herself, wouldn't be as easy as you might think, and while living in the world, you learn that everything does not turn out as you wish.

To Yun-hee, Hee-jo seemed lacking in energy, but preparing to take up his work again, he had worked with clay for two days in a row. Holding a rope suspended from the ceiling in one hand, and expressionlessly treading clay with his bare feet, he appeared like a slave in ancient Egypt in a movie, and his foot marks left the lump of clay in the shape of a blossom. It was a relief, though, that he could recover his spirit while working. As if to soothe a child, Yun-hee put a glass of fruit wine she had made secretly the previous year on the dinner table. Although the doctor had warned he would be liable to have chronic gastritis if he took wine again, Hee-jo wouldn't keep it in his mind.

Hee-jo had worked with clay all day, slipped out somewhere at dusk, and returned after having a drink. Now that he resumed his work and took wine with his meal, Hee-jo, even in his exhaustion, got so spirited he played the *changgi* game with Sae-bul. Playing a game with his father after such a long while, Sae-bul became excited, his face flushed. Quickly finishing her homework, Tan-bee joined them, too, sitting by Sae-bul.

When Sae-bul was going to the toilet after finishing the game, he called out in surprise that someone had intruded into the house. Looking out through the sliding door to the wooden floor, Yun-hee noticed Chung-man's father stepping up onto the stone front step and standing firm before the foundation stone like a devil post. It was surprising that he should come to her house at night. Yun-hee held back because he was the very person who had started the henhouse problem.

Upon encountering Yun-hee, the intruder shouted in his cracked voice. "Auntie, why are you so impeding our work, eh? You're disturbing us with a damned petition while we try to raise chickens just to feed ourselves."

"Because it's illegal," Yun-hee retorted. "And I don't believe the whole village should be damaged for the interest of only three people. Certainly, you knew all this yourself."

"What? How do you suppose such worthless country men as us know anything about the law, eh? It's an affront to us that a woman like you interfered in this affair."

Chung-man's father was openly informal in his speech with Yun-hee. In a moment Hee-jo, who had listened to all this from inside, emerged out to the wooden floor and told him: "Look, if you have something to say, make it in broad daylight. Don't make such a commotion at night, because my children are in bed now."

"You get to sleep, eh? I can't get to sleep. Well, a worthless brat like you whose stomach is full is only concerned with whether your land value will drop or not. But wretched country men like us are worried only whether we'll manage to feed ourselves. 'Hunger makes anyone a criminal!' You know this phrase?"

His face flushed, Chung-man's father must have taken wine somewhere before he arrived. In a moment Yun-hee told him composedly, "If I'd done something unreasonable, the petition would be ineffective. But since it's properly done with consent from the villagers, all we have to do is wait for the decision from the county office. It's late at night, so please go away."

"Damn you! Why are you trying to destroy us by wandering

into this remote countryside, eh? People like you should be sticking in Seoul, stretching your legs and relaxing. Hmph! I shall watch if things turn out as you wish."

It was only the beginning of the intimidation that Chung-man's father had sought to create at Yun-hee's house that night. Three days later, the town chief called upon her, saying he had dropped in on his way to the village. He immediately blamed Yun-hee for having gone so far as to talk with the county chief about the henhouse, rather than waiting further.

"How could I possibly wait for such a busy person as you to handle this matter? Anyhow, a person in a hurry must settle things, like the old saying goes." Yun-hee retorted sharply and left without even telling him Hee-jo was home.

Apparently the town chief had been bribed to permit the henhouse, Yun-hee judged, and so he seemed to be in trouble now that the petition had already been handed in to the county office. Then he set off toward the hilly spot where the henhouse was temporarily set up—presumably to discuss the situation with Chung-man's father. The tents for raising chickens that had been expanding one by one each day, as if with a mystic power, lay shabbily under the sun, but Yun-hee did not lower her guard hastily.

Late that afternoon Park Young-soo came suddenly to her home. Normally an affable man, he greeted Yun-hee roughly this time. And immediately after entering the room, he asked for Hee-jo's opinion, since he was about to buy a reasonably priced house near Namhansansung.

"With a land lot of four hundred *p'yong* or more," Park Young-soo explained, "the house has a little garden and is very spacious. Although the house is in poor condition, it won't make any difference to me because I'm going to have it repaired. While living in Seoul, I'm overcome with materialism, I must say. I urgently need to move to the countryside since I'm growing to feel limited in my brush painting. To be honest, I've always marveled at you, Hee-jo, because you moved so boldly to the countryside. At the same time, I must admit that our friend, Jung-dal, is also an extraordinary fellow because he does not yet even own his house—proclaiming himself a devotee of letters. Because by nature I don't like to feel bound to something else, I've so far accomplished nothing but engaging myself in teaching about painting. But now I realize there has been little purpose in the cumbersome work I did for petty cash."

Park Young-soo seemed to make up his mind after serious thought. He was the man who had twice been awarded a big prize in the National Art Exhibition, in recognition of his bold coloring and skillful manipulation of the canvas. And with the thriving of apartment communities in the Kangnam area in Seoul, he had become a popular painter, with the increasing demand for oriental painting considered to be in good harmony with mother-of-pearl chests. In proportion to his increased income, Park Young-soo had enjoyed material well-being to such an extent as to buy antique works by old masters such as Chusa or Kyumje, but while continuing to produce paintings on order, he seemed to have a deep conflict within himself.

Hee-jo, who had been always afraid that Park Young-soo's painting would degenerate into a technique without spiritual depth, was delighted to hear of his friend's decision, and soon set the drinking table himself.

"It's by no means easy to live in the countryside, cut off from the city," said Hee-jo. "But it's still worthwhile to try, because living in the countryside will ultimately stimulate your work. When I first moved to this area, I believed that being surrounded by the mountains and the stream would affect me in a way that more of the mountains might appear in my work. Actually, we're more dominated by what we see than we're aware of. There is, after all, nothing in particular to be conscious of, because what we're conscious of does not enable us to go beyond it. For this reason, I'd say we're more affected by what we're *not* conscious of."

With this remark Hee-jo turned to his own experience when he had gone to Japan six years before to study pottery. Finding Hee-jo's works at the exhibition of modern Korean pottery held in Kyushu, a descendant of a Korean potter in Japan had expressed his willingness to support Hee-jo, who came from his motherland. At the time, too, before leaving to study in Japan for three years, when Hee-jo called on a senior potter in Korea who had been encouraging his art, the old master had given his advice.

"As he was engaged in traditional pottery," continued Hee-jo, "the first thing he told me was that three years was too long. He added that what I should learn was not the Japanese art, but how to manage the kiln, or their attitude toward pottery. As I realized later, the old master's advice was quite right. Within a year after I had gone over to Japan, I had sent some works to Korea for the Korean Pottery Exhibition. Upon looking at them, he sent me a letter saying that even if there were no harm in the artistic sensibility I had acquired in Japan, I had been too quickly affected by the foreign art. In about one year since then, I came to know what the old master had meant, as I realized that artistic quality is destined to be a result of its own environment. During the time I was in Japan, I attempted some pots together with German and American potters. I then discovered that a work made by a German potter was unimpressive, since his work was deeply dominated by Japanese art. At any rate, that's why I shortened my stay and returned to Korea within a year."

"The environment," observed Park Young-soo, "has a very subtle effect on people, and any nationality or culture will naturally be affected by it. I'd say painting is no exception in this regard. A friend of mine, who has engaged himself with abstract painting, once lived in a black community in the United States while studying there. And I felt that somewhere in his canvas lay hidden a touch of the black people, because it had a rough, audacious air with something to express. If I had expressed that image in my cloth, it might be more suitable for a black woman to wrap around her body."

As soon as Park Young-soo's statements were over, Hee-jo resumed: "People are often worried that living in the countryside might deprive them of a sense of reality. But, in truth, it's not so. Since I moved to this place, I've discovered more than at any time how badly traditional human value has been destroyed by the force of a modernization drive."

With their conversation in full swing, Hee-jo and Park Young-soo seemed not to mind that the sun had already set, even forgetting to turn on the light until the room became dark. When Yun-hee was about to turn on the light after bringing something into the room for dinner, she heard someone calling outside: "Hong Hee-jo, out!"

Hearing it, all three people in the room were stunned and stopped talking. But this time a sudden burst of shouting reached their ears.

"You damned Hong Hee-jo, come out!"

As Yun-hee looked out the window, Hee-jo was already stepping onto the wooden floor. In the darkening front yard was standing the old man from the Electric Pole House.

"Sir, why are you coming to my house at this hour?" asked Hee-jo politely.

"You damned one! Just mind your own business—whatever happens. Because it was so hard to raise children despite toilsome work in the field, I let some people use my land. But you're now impeding us with that petition, eh?"

"Because there was something wrong with what you were trying to do," Hee-jo said reservedly.

"If it was wrong, why did you let your wife make all this fuss—not doing it yourself? Aren't you ever ashamed to do that cowardly thing, as a man with balls?"

"No matter how old you may be, sir, you're going too far to accuse us," interposed Yun-hee. "The whole thing was done without my husband's knowledge because I carried it out all by myself."

"What? You're still insisting you did the right thing, eh? All you pretty women ought to just stay in the kitchen! How dare you interfere with men's work?"

"You men are always doing magnificent work," Yun-hee nearly told him but swallowed her words, thinking it would doubtlessly make the matter worse.

Finding it unwise to wrestle with the intruder, Hee-jo went inside, but the old man continued to curse alone, pointing his finger at Hee-jo. It seemed those three people had planned in advance to trouble Yun-hee's family, and so two days later Kwang-ho came again to her house and made a commotion.

As it was Sunday, people continued to visit her house. With the *ume* blossoms beginning to come out, people seemed more frequently to enjoy the spirit of the spring. One of Yun-hee's friends and her husband, both of them patrons of pottery, visited Yun-hee's house and happened to join Madame Ji, who was running the Ji Gallery in Seoul. After they had left, four people from the pottery mill in town came in a group to seek Hee-jo's suggestions concerning pottery.

Around the time these people from town had left, Yi Sung-ju and two other people visited, and by that time the sun was slanting through the west-facing window. One of the people who accompanied Yi Sung-ju, was a woman in white clothes, and her figure beneath a paulownia tree drew Yun-hee's attention. Her glossy hair, dropping down over her shoulders, was attractive, and the big, deep eyes, which seemed mystic, aroused the image of a martyr. As Yun-hee was going to lead her visitors into the room, Yi Sung-ju insisted on sitting on the bamboo bed in front of the window.

"Why should we confine ourselves to a musty room on this glorious spring day?" he asserted. "It would be splendid to have a drink amid the apricot blossoms here."

"How could you talk about the blossoms with such a beautiful blossom at your side?" At Yun-hee's joke, the woman laughed silently.

Then Yi Sung-ju introduced each person he had brought with him. "These are all my favorite ones. This is Yun Ki-sup, an oriental painter, and there is Kim Ji-woon, who is working for the Saebyuck Company."

"Isn't that the company where *Simone Weil: A Life* was published?" Yun-hee inquired.

"Oh, did you read that biography?" Ji-woon was delighted to hear it, her eyebrows raised.

"Our Big Sister always turns to books, even while she's working," Yi Sung-ju interposed. "I suppose it's because she feels empty that she keeps some paperbacks even in the toilet."

"You're right. I turn to books because I feel empty," Yun-hee admitted. "From the beginning I liked biographies, so I've read biographies of such famous women as Isadora Duncan and Edith Piaf. Because I'm interested in the lives of other women, I wondered how those people had led their lives."

Had she been happy, Yun-hee thought, she wouldn't have had such an interest in the lives of other women. And so, whenever she was wearied with the realities surrounding her, Yun-hee would arrange her thoughts by reading books, as if associating with her friends.

"Aren't those biographies of women called a 'flirt series'?" Ki-sup said, joking.

"Ha, ha! That must be an official judgment of those books, since they're referred to that way in the newspapers," Yi Sung-ju replied with a grin, following Ki-sup's words.

While looking at the empty sky, Ji-woon turned her glance toward Yi Sung-ju and said, "I'm so frustrated to hear such an expression even from a poet. I'd say it's another form of violence."

"As a whole," Yun-hee remarked, "Korean men won't admit women have their portion of life, too. They're convinced of the patriarchal viewpoint derived from the feudal society, and consequently don't consider women in human terms. It's absurd that anyone would attempt to write dissident poetry with such a prejudice against women."

"Ah, I'm petrified whenever I get to this house," said Yi Sung-ju jokingly, shaking his head.

Feeling curiosity about the young painter who was sitting earnestly with his glasses on, Hee-jo asked Yi Sung-ju about him. And Yi Sung-ju spoke excitedly about the painter.

"Ah, he is your school junior, Mr. Hong. I was so impressed with the paintings in his first exhibition last autumn. You see, I'm all against those literati paintings or the paintings of mountain landscapes, which seem to me anachronistic. But in the paintings of Ki-sup, I often discover a tangible side of life. For instance, a woman carrying a child on her back while waiting on the wharf for the return of her husband, a scene of a bed in which a young prostitute is lying as still as in death, and a dish of cold fried egg on a dining table—all these took possession of me. They are not mere lifeless paintings in which a whole facet of living is simplified to an abstract form. Rather, they contain the geniality of the life of the estranged common folk. I think Ki-sup is following the tradition of folk painting in the simple sketches he makes as well as in creating contrasting effects with color. I believe, Mr. Hong, you'll like his paintings once you see them."

"Well, I'm very anxious to see them."

As Hee-jo showed his interest, Ki-sup asked him, raising his glasses: "If all art is regarded as the development of the spirit of each age, as well as the outcome of social activity, what would you say about pottery? I'm wondering if you could express the concrete spirit of our time through the pottery you're engaged in. In other words, do you think it's possible to apply the spirit of folk art to pottery?"

"Hmm, you're talking about the common folk like other people did," replied Hee-jo. With his eyebrows raised, he turned to the art of *punch'ong* he'd devoted himself to.

"Unlike the Koryo celadons or Choson white porcelains," began Hee-jo, "*punch'ong* originated only in Korea. I remember its birth dates back to when Mongolia invaded Koryo in the early and middle twelfth century. At this time, the country had had to move its capital temporarily to Kangwha Island because of the war. Naturally, it was difficult to obtain precious materials, or to build the facilities that were necessary for making pottery. In addition to this, there was the growing distrust and revolt of the common folk against the central government. As you imagine, this is why the standardization of Koryo celadons ceased. Unlike the celadons, however, *punch'ong* was from the beginning not so discriminative in the use of clay. In making the *punch'ong* wares, all the clay around us can be used as material. And this means that the more selective you are in the choice of clay, the more limited you are in the use of material! In fact, I've willingly taken up *punch'ong* as my lifelong mission because I am drawn to the idea of being released from any limit, which is the art of *punch'ong* itself. So, from the choice of clay to its color and the way of firing, *punch'ong* is not the least bit fastidious. Indeed, it's very much attached to where its material originates. As you may realize, the *punch'ong* form is stubborn and simple, unlike that of the delicate celadons, and so it's not bound to the pursuit of precision and perfection. What's more, its pattern is different from the monotonous air we find in the celadons, since it need not be confined to the imitation of nature. For instance, the pattern of fish appearing in the celadons is anything but alive, but the same pattern in *punch'ong* looks cheerful. After all, in the very nature of *punch'ong* is contained the spirit of common folk you're thinking of."

As Hee-jo finished his defense of the art of *punch'ong*, Ki-sup replied. "I see, that's how *punch'ong* was born. I understand the Koryo celadons and the Choson porcelains were made separately either in government or in private kilns, but the *punch'ong* wares were made in the same kiln whether they were intended for the upper class or the lower class."

"I must say," Hee-jo went on, "that a form of art is best understood as one in which all the practical, spiritual elements of a society are symbolized in a certain aspect. Therefore, getting a picture of our time does not necessarily mean that we must put the spirit of the workers or the common folk into the art. In the *punch'ong* wares, I would express the spirit of the common folk by emphasizing their spontaneous beauty and simplicity. At the same time, I try to stress the diversity of creative work by means of the artistic sensibility of our time. But if people are obsessed only with the ideology of the common folk, they will never surpass the limit of that ideology, I believe. Because the creative act will not come out of a rigid mind, the flexible mind becomes a prerequisite for the creative process."

As Hee-jo explained to Ki-sup what he believed art was meant to be, Yi Sung-ju, who had listened without a word, contradicted him at once.

"Well, well! You're oversensitive to the term 'common folk,' Mr. Hong. When we're saying the common folk, it implies the life of the people embodied in the development of history. Like political or economic activities, I think culture or art exists only for the enhancement of human life. In this sense, the nature of culture or art considers everyday aspects of our life in the perspective of our neighbors or society, so that it can have a critical view of the unjust phenomena of our time. As you may know, the primary reason we try to establish the common folk culture is to turn a life that is shrunken and materialistic under the current regime's slogan of Development First into the basic force of life. By doing so, we strive to attain a more concrete vision of our time."

"If so," responded Hee-jo, "I wouldn't object to a movement that aimed to enlarge the creation of the common folk culture into the central issue of our time to develop it further. But as I observe, all this is carried out only among a few intellectuals. In spite of all the definitions of the common folk culture, it's hard to tell what the substance of the common folk is, which, I believe, should be a central concern of this ideology. What I feel animosity about is not the concept of the common folk itself. Rather, it's the attitude of those intellectuals involved in the common folk movement who are trying to be educative and patriotic. To me, they're simply ignoring the reality of the common folk."

In the circle of painters, people often discussed the subject of the common folk. And because Yi Sung-ju had devoted himself to the cause of the common folk movement and became so enthusiastic about that subject, their talk now seemed unlikely to be finished soon. Three bottles of *makkoli* Yi Sung-ju had brought were already emptied, and they also drank all the fruit wine in the house. The window was suffused with an evening glow as the sun went slowly down. Sitting by Yi Sung-ju, Ji-woon listened calmly, then began to hug her body with both arms, shivering. Though it was spring, the temperature in the countryside would drop sharply at sundown.

When Yun-hee got up to bring a sweater for her, Yi Sung-ju turned to Ji-woon and said, "You look cold. Take my coat."

"I think I can bear it," she replied softly.

But Yi Sung-ju had already taken off his coat and put it over Ji-woon's shoulders. The way they exchanged words seemed so natural that they looked like a brother and sister, or long-term lovers. At first Yun-hee conceived them to be merely friends, and it took a moment to realize they were involved in a close relationship with each other. Out of her instinctive curiosity, she asked Yi Sung-ju how they came to Choha-ri today.

"Well, my collection of poetry will be published soon by the Saebyuck Company, and Ki-sup is in charge of designing the cover. Since we needed some pictures for the book, we went together to the Paldang Reservoir to take pictures, and finally arrived here to have more to drink."

"Then, will you give me a copy when the book comes out?" Yun-hee urged.

"Who else can I give the book to except you, Big Sister?"

With this remark Yi Sung-ju turned to Ji-woon, saying, "Won't the book be published in ten days or so?"

"It'll be coming out along with *The Decline of the American Indians.*"

As Ji-woon replied, Yi Sung-ju put down his glass and said to Yun-hee: "That is a book to be published by my company and you must read it, too. As soon as it'll be published, I'll send you a copy of it. It's a book you would like, because it gives a vivid description of how cruelly American soldiers slaughtered Indians to occupy their land."

"Please don't forget to bring it. You often forget what you promise," Yun-hee reproached Yi Sung-ju.

"I'll send you a copy without fail."

At Yun-hee's request, Ji-woon herself made a promise. So Yun-hee thanked her, showing a sign of intimacy. "Will you come to my house again? I'll be treating you with wine as a celebration of the publication of the book."

Upon the words of Yun-hee, Ji-woon brightened up. "Do you really mean it?"

"Of course," answered Yun-hee heartily.

It was when Yi Sung-ju and his company were about to leave that Kwang-ho and Chung-man's father, smelling of liquor, stepped into the house. With the shirt of his working clothes opened wide, the small-statured Kwang-ho was walking toward the bamboo bed while Chung-man's father was standing firmly in the yard, his feet spread. Yi Sung-ju and his friends were sitting halfway, uncomprehending, and Yun-hee was at a loss because the guests were still in the house.

"What's all this for again?" Hee-jo presented himself before the intruder, being informal in his speech since Kwang-ho was not yet thirty.

Then, all of a sudden, Kwang-ho spat on the ground. "You cursed Hong Hee-jo! If you consider yourself an artist or someone, just mind your own business, eh, instead of trying to destroy people like us who are poor and helpless. Why are you determined to destroy us? Does it satisfy you to see our Big Brother completely ruined, eh?"

"You damned one!" cursed Chung-man's father, too. "What have we done to make you think of us as foes? You're determined to destroy the prospects of our life while never giving us even a tiny piece of pottery to smash out! You didn't show the slightest consideration for our means of life through chicken raising, eh? Just ask anyone else in the street which is more important. Is it your pottery or our effort to feed ourselves that counts?"

Kwang-ho and Chung-man's father made absurd accusations, pouring their curses upon Hee-jo. These two people, Yun-hee judged, must have been drinking purposefully somewhere before they came to her house to make a fuss by this sudden breaking in. From behind, then, came the remark, "Who are these scoundrels?"

Finding that it was from Yi Sung-ju, Yun-hee stepped forward. "Please don't make trouble anymore. There's nothing wrong with what we've done. We distributed the petition around the village, not because we had some powerful men behind us, but because the people in the village willingly gave their consent to it. Since it's a thing of the past, don't make trouble. What rudeness you're showing in front of my guests here!"

"What? You completely destroyed our meager means of life and still pretend not to care at all about what you've done, eh. You're wise enough to coax the villagers to harm us. But with your stomach full you get together to stuff food in your mouths. Shall I try to act like you, eh?" Talking gibberish, Chung-man's father walked toward the bamboo bed and impudently sat next to Ji-woon.

Then Yi Sung-ju sprang to his feet to stop the man. "What are you trying to do to these decent people, Brother? If you're dissatisfied with what happened, you must first of all bring the people who approved the petition together and reason with them. It's absurd to afflict someone who is not in a position to initiate all this."

"Where is this man from?"

As Chung-man's father asked, Kwang-ho answered, recognizing Yi Sung-ju. "Hmph! He must be a poet or someone living in the village beyond. He bought Hong-taek's house at a cheap price when the poor man was driven to debt long ago."

"What the devil is the use of a poet? All you're doing is simply playing with a woman, so don't interfere with somebody else," Chung-man's father began to roar.

Hearing him, Yi Sung-ju became angry and was about to seize him by the collar, but Hee-jo stopped him in time. Telling Yi

Sung-ju that he could never make himself understood by the intruders, Hee-jo took him away from Chung-man's father, and even Ki-sup persuaded the man to go back.

Far from stopping his attack, however, Kwang-ho once again sprang at Hee-jo. "You damned Hong Hee-jo! However hard you try to prevent us from raising chickens, we'll bring the excrement of chickens from somewhere and fill the stream with them. I'm sure to fill your throat with the stench of the chicken manure. Remember!"

As the intruders left, Hee-jo turned to Yi Sung-ju and said: "You've seen all this yourself today. As you've always said, the common folk have self-righteousness as their own force, since it is the very means to accomplish their goal of freedom and equality. But it's not always so. You must realize that those people, who have given up being human, obsessed with the interest at hand, are another aspect of the common folk."

"Damn it! It's the distorted side of the common folk," Yi Sung-ju replied with a bitter face.

The revenge of the people who had plotted the henhouse continued for many days after that. They would suddenly intrude into Yun-hee's house to speak their curses one after another, and even the old woman from the Electric Pole House came and cried wildly, calling Hee-jo a cursed one. What they did was almost comic and, having been afflicted, Yun-hee felt herself brainwashed and asked herself if she really had done something wrong. Worried above all about her children, Yun-hee asked them to always stay together when returning from school. About the time the children returned, then, she would wander about the yard, looking across the fields.

Hee-jo, too, was completely on edge and would get angry about trivial things. He was vexed at Yun-hee whenever she began kitchen work, so she had nothing to do but leave the dinner table, smelling of the side dishes on the floor. Once Sae-bul entered the studio intending to do his art homework with clay, but was driven out. Feeling pity for the child crying, Yun-hee soothed him, saying he should not disturb his father. But Sae-bul responded in a sullen voice. "I was sitting by Father doing my homework. When I got bored with the music from the radio, I told him I'd like to listen to Mozart. That's all!"

That evening Kwang-ho began to shout again toward the house from the direction of the stream. As he called out Hee-jo's name, trying in vain to intimidate him, Hee-jo lost his patience and ran after him with a shovel in his hand. His eyes glowing with anger, Hee-jo looked as if ready to commit mayhem, so Yun-hee shouted at Kwang-ho to run away immediately. Taken aback by Hee-jo's threat, Kwang-ho kept trying to irritate him even while he was running away.

Since Hee-jo had been in an angry mood, Yun-hee served dinner a little later than usual. For the children, who liked fish, she put a piece of broiled mackerel on each tray. But staring at the meal table, Hee-jo put down his spoon and spat out petulantly: "Look at all these side dishes we eat! Don't you know we eat to live, not live to eat?"

On the meal table were a broiled fish, some salad, boiled burdock, and sliced radish *kimchi,* together with meat soup. As a matter of fact, Yun-hee always prepared three or four side dishes for each meal, but this time she added only a little leftover tofu stew. When she looked up at him without a word, Hee-jo made a remark as if to appease her. "I believe we eat to live. We even drink wine to lead a better life; otherwise we might feel bored."

After finishing the kitchen work, Yun-hee prepared coffee for the first time in a long while and brought it to her children. She made two more cups of coffee to have a talk with Hee-jo in the living room. Over the coffee, she told him: "Listen, I think we should not remain troubled like this. Why don't you meet the county chief yourself?"

"Do you think it's necessary for me to meet him?" countered Hee-jo unconcernedly.

"Because they continue to afflict us in spite of our asking them to tear down the henhouse. So you'd better entreat the county chief to support us. Since he has a good disposition, I think he'll certainly give his advice once you consult him."

Instead of responding to Yun-hee's request on the spot, Hee-jo remained silent. Even without her mentioning it, Hee-jo in his own way should have found some measures to settle the henhouse matter. Although her request was burdensome to him, Yun-hee continued to urge him: "The first thing you have to do in your visit is express our gratitude for his concern for the petition. After explaining the matter at hand, be sure to tell him we'd like to invite him to our house for lunch."

To Hee-jo who was merely looking at the wall, Yun-hee made one more suggestion that would not be displeasing to him: "Once you get the whole thing done, you can take a trip to Tamyang for several days. You can go there alone and enjoy sketching, or you can even bring someone you love with you without having to tell me."

"Don't be silly!" He put on an expression that suggested that her words were totally ludicrous. Not revealing her faint suspicion, however, Yun-hee smiled nonchalantly. She could still remain emotionally cool, having not yet confirmed a relationship deeper than friendship between her husband and Han Min-wha.

The next day Hee-jo went to the county office. Returning, he said right off, "I told the chief what you said." As Yun-hee sat down to hear some details about the visit, Hee-jo changed his clothes and entered his studio immediately. Was it that he had not been given a pledge in the office? Or was it that he was angry since he returned with no accomplishment, in spite of his unwilling visit to the office? While speculating to herself, Yun-hee didn't attempt to speak to him all night, but the next morning she saw a van marked Criminal Investigation Unit stopping in front of her house, making a big noise. A policeman emerged from the van and stepped into the house, asking, "Is Mr. Hong in?" As if expecting a guest, Hee-jo had already changed into his other suit and led the visitor into the living room. Feeling curious, Yun-hee entered the room with a tray of apples and Hee-jo let the two exchange a greeting.

Then he explained the situation to Yun-hee: "Because of the problem we had, Chief Huh from the police station has come in person. He happened to be in the county office yesterday when I was there to meet the county chief. He was told about all that had happened in this village."

"Well, I've already patrolled the village twice and even gone to the henhouse before I arrived here. Since the people in the village have seen the police car, they may not dare to come around. However vicious they may be, those scoundrels must have been frightened, because they know they did something wrong."

Judging from what the police chief had said, Yun-hee could figure out how things would be turning out. In truth, Chief Huh reassured her there would be nothing more to worry out, having much confidence in his appearing on the spot. Nevertheless, Yun-hee, who was appalled at the outrageous acts of those three people, revealed her anxiety. Taking a bite of apple, Chief Huh spoke confidently: "Don't you know that in childhood we'd often be frightened with no reason to see a policeman? Since we stopped the patrol car in front of your house, people might believe you have a very powerful man behind you."

What the police chief had said turned out to be not a mere exaggeration. Reluctant to express her gratitude to the man from the police station, Yun-hee decided to present a *punch'ong* pencil case to him, then put the whole thing out of her mind. But the next morning the old woman from the Electric Pole House came to see her with a frightened face.

"Listen, dear. My old man found it unbearable to leave the land useless, so he made Chung-man's father lease it. Moreover, he was unable to predict the land would be used for raising chickens. He didn't know it was illegal, either. Only our ignorance was to blame! So don't accuse us anymore. All this happened only because we were unaware of the whole thing. I'm imploring you not to remember my reproach to you, too. At any rate, we'll have the land leased back. Then, nothing will happen to us, right? You're sure we wouldn't get put in jail or something?"

When the old woman came upon Hee-jo, who just stepped into the yard, she looked pathetic, grabbing his hands. The spirit she had shown no less than six days before when she called out wildly to Hee-jo, "Don't you even have parents to respect?" was nowhere to be seen, and now with a lowly gesture she asked for his mercy. Hee-jo was at a loss so he couldn't find a word to tell her. Then Yun-hee spoke to the old woman on his behalf.

"You don't have to make such an apology to us. I think your old man was simply coaxed by Chung-man's father to let his land

94

be used for other purposes. Because you admitted your mistake, we won't ask any more from you. Actually we have nothing against your old man, who did not harm us. Also, we don't have any harmful intention to you, since we have no other desire but to live peacefully."

"Thanks, thanks. Your generosity is known to all of us. Certainly so. Now I'm convinced you're not going to harm others with no reason. I feel relieved and will go back to tell my old man of your intentions."

With nothing more to say, the old woman hurriedly set off. Looking at her, Hee-jo spat out with a bitter smile. "Why don't you continue to be imposing, eh? We all belong to the powerless and wicked common folk and have no better interest than to turn to the powerful, obsessed with self-interest. So we're not brave enough to stand up to the power that threatens us."

That evening the light didn't come on at the studio until sundown. Preparing the dinner table, Yun-hee asked Sae-bul to check on his father, because he hadn't even dropped by the living room once after lunch. Coming back immediately, Sae-bul said that he was not in the studio, and so Yun-hee herself went there. The studio was all cleaned up, with not a single scrap of clay on the floor, and the familiar working clothes hanging on the wall. Though the sun had gone down, the air inside was still warm with heat from the kiln chamber, and Yun-hee noticed the moisture condensed on the potter's wheel. Finding signs that Hee-jo had very recently used the potter's wheel, on which was a ball of clay, she wondered where he had gone in the meantime.

Five of the large jars, which had been put in the kiln chamber before lunchtime, were now on the floor. Since these jars had a longer neck than the ordinary ones and were generally bigger than those Yun-hee was familiar with, they easily attracted her attention. On the wall facing the potter's wheel was a sketch of a jar with a similar shape. She noticed a passage on it:

A shape appearing all of a sudden. It gives a feeling of familiarity and its commanding attitude arouses an air of singleness. . . . A tension that arises from the design clearly distinguishing the neck from the shoulder that connects the neck to the body.

Even in the midst of his inner turmoil, Hee-jo seemed to have begun a new work, Yun-hee suspected. Living with a man devoted to his art, Yun-hee would tacitly enjoy a kind of sheer pleasure. Actually it was because of this that her bitterness toward Hee-jo melted away temporarily whenever she found a work that took possession of her.

Then Yun-hee remembered an incident five or six years before she had moved to Choha-ri. With Hee-jo's exhibition two weeks away and the whole family strained, Yun-hee's mother-in-law had come to inform her of an accident that had happened to her brother-in-law. While escorting his fiancee home, Yun-hee's brother-in-law had encountered a street hoodlum who hit him over his bladder, springing at him for no reason. As if talking about someone else, Yun-hee's mother-in-law had said briefly how her son was hospitalized, and remained sitting vacantly like a stone Buddha. Since Yun-hee's brother-in-law was jobless, even after thirty, he couldn't afford to pay the hospital bills, so the burden fell on Hee-jo as if by agreement.

Finding the money at hand barely enough to cover living expense for her family, Yun-hee had had no other choice in a difficult situation but to seek the support of her own parents. When Yun-hee had arrived home late at night from Seoul, her husband had asked about her absence, since she had left without telling anybody. Hee-jo, who had already drunk so much that his face was flushed with liquor, had pressed her hard, because she had neglected his mother for the day. Yun-hee, too, had burst into anger and shouted: "You're not the only one acting like a filial child. I went to my parents' home to borrow money. Of course, you're sure to pay it back pretty soon." Usually Yun-hee would not speak of money to Hee-jo because he seemed to consider it a burden in his mind. But no sooner had she finished her words than Hee-jo had thrown a liquor bottle from the stationery chest at her. Feeling as if her bones had been smashed, Yun-hee fell to the floor, hitting her forehead against the broken pieces of a pot scattered around. Her face had got bloody all over, the flesh on her forehead torn so the bone inside was exposed.

While in the hospital for about two weeks for treatment, Yun-hee had received a catalogue of his exhibition from Hee-jo, on the front cover of which was shown a cylinder-shaped vase. The *punch'ong* vase, which had an inlaid triangle pattern like a reflection in a mirror, had seemed like the visualized form of a Zen poem. Lying in bed looking at the printed material, Yun-hee had told herself, "You deserve my expectation, though."

It was not quite nine when Hee-jo returned. In the usual outfit he wore at home, he didn't seem to go far, and though not drinking wine, he didn't eat dinner, either. After entering the studio to see if the clay had dried, he told Yun-hee in bed that he would go on a journey to sketch. "Tomorrow I'll make some slip for the ware and leave the day after. I think they won't make any more trouble about the henhouse. I feel something is waiting to be grasped by my mind, and I expect it'll be made concrete after a trip."

Three days before, when Yun-hee had suggested a trip to him for a change, Hee-jo had not responded at all, so she wondered why he had made up his mind that suddenly. Even though Yun-hee felt unburdened because the thing that had troubled her was over, she nevertheless looked at Hee-jo with envy.

Ever since the police chief had visited, neither Chung-man's father nor Kwang-ho had come around her house. The house was ghostly still now that Hee-jo had gone on his journey. In the meantime Yun-hee brought the goose eggs out to the hatchery, supposing that with nearly twenty eggs accumulated so far, the geese wouldn't lay anymore.

As soon as the day became warm, Yun-hee sowed lettuce and radish seeds in the field that she had tilled with Jae-chull's mother. Because Yun-hee didn't plant anything on one of the ridges, intending to buy potatoes at the market and plant them, the old woman from the Pear Tree House brought her some potatoes left in the house. Looking at the old woman, Yun-hee stopped working to greet her, and expressed her gratitude that she helped her circulate the petition around the village. But the old woman said, shaking her head, "Not at all, you did all this yourself. And I found you very tenacious. Since I settled in Satgol when I married at sixteen, I've never seen any outsiders live in this place for more than three years."

The part of the village called Satgol belonged to a clan, and only people with the family name of Yi had lived there for nearly two hundred years. There were only two families with other family names in the village, but one of them had deserted their house. Later, someone from Seoul had intended to repair it and live there, but gave up that idea, being appalled at the exclusive atmosphere of the village. Even Yun-hee's family couldn't have lived in the village if they had regarded their place as something like a villa. Although they lived surrounded by nature, it was not a thing to be enjoyed at leisure. As for the natives engaged in farming, the land was for Yun-hee's family not only a place for survival, but the root and master of life.

"We're not like the whites who intruded to rob Indians of their land by force," Yun-hee murmured to herself. As she looked across the empty fields, the old woman from the Pear Tree House spoke of her family event.

"Tomorrow is the birthday of my oldest son. Though there's little to treat you, come over to my house and have a spoonful of rice. . . ."

4

A Human Affection

It had been cloudy since morning, and then the spring rain began to fall. It was a timely rain. Yun-hee had transplanted the red pepper seedlings the previous day, but the rain was not heavy enough to get down into the roots, merely wetting the surface of the ground. Not carrying an umbrella, Sae-bul stepped out into the yard with his school bag on his shoulders and called out, "It's a timely rain—a timely rain!"

Following her younger brother from behind, Tan-bee, whose name means 'timely rain,' glared at him for calling out her name repeatedly.

"Look, we've got a timely rain. I didn't call your name, Sister, but am only referring to the rain," Sae-bul said lightly.

"Don't mind it. I'm not irritated at all."

Tan-bee countered rather reservedly and, feeling something miraculous about the rain, tried to touch it by stretching out her hand. "I wish I were ill today. Then I could spend my time lying in the white bed in the school nurse's room, instead of studying."

"Classes will be finished pretty soon today. You see, this is Saturday," Sae-bul replied.

Yun-hee was amused at what the children were doing, and then turned away after urging them to hurry. As a child Yun-hee disliked the rain extremely, because on such days the earthworms swarmed on the ground. Also, on rainy days she could not play the jump rope game on the school ground since some perverse boys would kick the water in puddles at the girls and get their clothes dirty. It had only been since she had grown up that Yun-hee could appreciate the rain, as she began to know the bitterness inherent in life. But Tan-bee had no reason to be sensitive to the mood that rain had brought. Some days before the child said to Yun-hee, "I wish I could become rain after death, Mom" and went on to say: "The rain has brought a strange feeling to my mind ever since I saw an insane woman walking up and down the school yard in the rain, doing a ritual."

Yun-hee saw the goose sitting in the yard like a picture; she seemed to appreciate the rain. Having rubbed her body with her beak to spread the oil, the mother goose went in search of something to eat. Finding a time of her own for the first time in a long while, Yun-hee entered the living room after kitchen work. She picked up a book she had intended to read since a few days before, but then a crimson azalea blossom came into her view through the window. The azalea blossoms in the shadowy corner of the house were so thick and colorful that under the gray sky the crimson almost gave a feeling of cruelty. Hee-jo once mentioned that its color was so provocative as to induce him to fondle himself. In truth, if she were to express tears in color, Yun-hee would choose the red of the azalea blossom. Colorful yet faint, turbid yet transparent, its color aroused in her an odd feeling.

It was quiet with the house empty, and with no wind even the wind-bell did not ring. Once in a while a cuckoo sang, adding to the mood of spring. With Hee-jo, whom she would attend to, on his journey, Yun-hee was able to relish the utmost sense of satisfaction. It was because she herself needed time to rest that Yun-hee had suggested that Hee-jo go on a journey for a change.

Hee-jo used to say eating meals is not everything in life; to Yun-hee, however, being a housewife was not the sole purpose of her life. Just as she breathed out after breathing in, so she needed a moment to be alone, away from her own family. As Monk Hyeo put it, Yun-hee might have been secretly dependent upon her family like most people, but in proportion to the degree of her dependence she also felt tempted to be away from them.

Fear of Flying. Looking at the cover of the book in her hand, Yun-hee opened to the first page. It was said to be a novel by an American woman about women's liberation, and Yun-hee remembered having read in the newspaper that even in Korea five companies competed to publish it. "The Most Candid and Revealing Self-confession of Female Sexuality and Consciousness." "A Refutation of All Established Ethics." Commercial phrases like this had attracted Yun-hee's attention from the beginning, and while she was planning to buy the book, her friend Young-ae sent it to her with a short comment: "I'm curious to know how you—a good and wise wife—will accept this kind of novel. I really hope you won't stop reading it in the middle."

Rereading her friend's comment, Yun-hee smiled slightly. While in college, her friend Young-ae had enjoyed a courtship known in all corners of the campus. Even after marriage, she had been brave in everything to the point of suggesting a divorce to her husband after she had gone through a passionate love affair with someone. Her husband, who worked at the public prosecutor's office, was such a model of what every person ought to be that he didn't accept her request for divorce. And after some time she announced her resignation with the remark, "I chose the death of my individuality." Though Yun-hee couldn't see her friend very often since moving to the countryside, suddenly, after nearly four months, Young-ae sent her a copy of *Fear of Flying*.

The novel began on an airplane bound for Vienna in which a group of psychiatrists were passengers. Unlike the figures in conventional novels, the heroine in the story was characterized as a lively woman, naturally endowed with both intellect and sensuality. Sitting by her husband, the woman contemplated some other desires presumably suffocated by her marriage, in spite of the advantages her marriage had brought—that is, to have the best mate called a husband in a hostile world. Finding such emotions as solitude, self-realization, and sex suffocated by her marriage, the woman, now yearning for them, created a fantasy scenario called the "Zipless Fuck."

The scenario gave a bold description of a sexual encounter: In the shabby passenger compartment of a European train, a soldier, sitting between a widow in black and a fat woman, went so far as to push his hand deep between the thighs of the widow and committed an obscene act. The story of the zipper being opened like a rose petal until two people finally became one, suggested something more than a mere love affair to the writer, who had dreamed of escaping her monstrous selfhood; it suggested something like a Platonic ideal. Though brief, the scenario was as revealing as a pornographic film. But it was not until after Yun-hee had read the writer's comment on the final page of the first chapter that she was able to capture the meaning of the novel in a new perspective. That comment read: "The Zipless Fuck is absolutely pure. It is free of ulterior motives. There is no power game. The man is not 'taking' and the woman is not 'giving.' . . . No one is trying to prove anything or get anything out of anyone."

Feeling as if she had been struck on the back of her head, Yun-hee stopped reading after the first chapter. She recalled what she had undergone with Hee-jo before she married. While they had been working together as teachers at a girls' school in a provincial city, Hee-jo had come into the teachers' room one spring day to exchange a day of duty with Yun-hee, and he had put a yellow tulip on her desk. Yun-hee remembered that the yellow tulip, with its air of the spring afternoon, had embarrassed rather than pleased her.

It was nearly a month later that she had accepted his request for a date, after careful consideration. After that, Hee-jo would bring a flower each time he met Yun-hee. It was not the least bit awkward for the young art teacher, with his knife-edged face and long hair drooping over his forehead, and so it attracted Yun-hee's attention.

The third time they met, they had walked aimlessly along the stream and, finding a paulownia in blossom at dusk, sat on the bank. A light spring rain fell ceaselessly that day, and by the bank a *moodang* was striking a gong. They were told that, a few days earlier, a neighborhood child had been swept away by the current after a heavy rain and had died. The *moodang* performed her *gut* to appease the soul of the child, throwing some food on the bank. And Hee-jo and Yun-hee sat beneath the paulownia tree, staring at the ritual until dark.

The sound of the gong ceased. As the *moodang* and the child's family disappeared along the bank beyond, Hee-jo had kept Yun-hee from getting up and brought his face toward hers. With his face pressed against hers, Yun-hee had become breathless, startled, but even in the darkness she could see the tears on his face. In spite of her stubborn struggle, all energy had drained from Yun-hee as she was overcome by the tears of the man who embraced her. When the crude pain visited, however, she had thought with maiden fear and shame that there was no choice left to her but to marry him or to be abandoned.

Unless Yun-hee had confessed how she had surrendered her body, her parents would not have consented to the marriage she chose. Her father had said flatly that there was no need for a woman to know about the social world when Yun-hee once revealed her intention of getting a job after school. As a matter of fact, he had gone so far as to ask any man who telephoned Yun-hee's sisters what they were asking his daughters for.

Yun-hee's mother would call her husband "Master" in the presence of other people. Of all the brothers and sisters who had grown up under such authoritarian parents, Yun-hee was the most unconventional in her attitude. Despite that, she was still utterly polite when talking to Hee-jo, simply calling him "This Man" in front of others. Perhaps her daughter Tan-bee, when she grows up, will call her husband by his name as if talking to a close friend. As for sex, Yun-hee thought, it's not a thing obtained by a man nor is it given by a woman, so it might move toward something more reciprocal.

In sending the novel to Yun-hee, Young-ae had written that she was the same as ever. As Yun-hee looked at the writing on the cover of *Fear of Flying*, thinking of her friend, who looked like a cactus blossom without fail, the grandfather goose rapped on the window with its beak. The goose was trying to be friendly with its owner, who looked lonely, and opening the window, Yun-hee stroked its head. The goose would never flatter people or beg for something to eat, even though hungry, but simply expressed its desire by sounds. It seemed pleased with Yun-hee's stroking, letting her stroke its whole body. Seeing this, Yun-hee thought that both humans and animals tend to rely on each other, exchanging affection. Taking the goose back to its family, Yun-hee looked forlornly at the rain wetting the surface of the ground. Then, suddenly, Han Min-wha came into her mind.

Because it was Saturday, her children came home earlier than usual, so Yun-hee asked them to stay home and set off toward Eunti village. In the fields the grown barley was making a fresh wave, and along the corner of the path the yellow cabbage was in full bloom. With the spirit of the earth beginning to expand everywhere, the season made people weary, but it also gave them a moment to enjoy the colorful changes in the fields.

In spite of the rain, Han Min-wha was making a fire in a fuel pit in an open shed, with dried twigs stretched over it. While letting the air into the pit, she lit the fire, and so smoke scattered in the damp air. When Yun-hee approached her from behind, Han Min-wha smiled quietly with no air of being surprised.

"Hi! What are you doing in the rain?" asked Yun-hee.

"Well, it's been cloudy since morning. So I was a little worried as I intended to have some thread dyed today. Fortunately, though, the rain isn't very heavy."

Finding the twigs ablaze, Han Min-wha took more firewood and pine cones out of the bag and put them into the fuel pit. The dry wood sparkled in the pit. Closing the lid of the kettle, Han Min-wha led Yun-hee into the room.

"I just started my work. Will you wait a little while in the living room? Because I've got to filter some ground charcoal and put it in water."

"Sure," replied Yun-hee, "I won't disturb you and I'd rather watch. Anyhow it'll do me good to learn how to dye something."

"I feel sorry that I'm ignoring you, a guest. . . ."

"It's me who should feel sorry, because I came unannounced."

"Not at all," said Han Min-wha, wagging her hands. Then she went toward the table in the kitchen. In one corner of the kitchen was a drying rack on which there was a thread of gray skein, and a small iron mortar was on the table. Han Min-wha took a bowl with her and, spreading out a piece of gauze, took a black powder out of the mortar with a spoon and poured it onto the gauze. Yun-hee asked if she was using charcoal powder for dyeing, but Han Min-wha answered that she used burnt azalea root for it. "I can make gray dyestuff with azalea root. Yesterday I used a Chinese ink for a dyestuff. So I'm curious how it'll turn out, because the results are not all the same."

Han Min-wha filtered the powder through the gauze and, having put the bowl from the charcoal powder and the salt bottle into the sink, she begged Yun-hee to bring it to the barn. With a white skein of thread held between bamboo sticks, she followed Yun-hee immediately and stirred the kettle with her hand. The way she stirred suggested that the water was lukewarm. Putting the skein of thread into the kettle, she stirred for a while and then took it out again to bring it into a sink. Only then did she dissolve the charcoal powder in the kettle, put the washed skein of thread into it, and finally hold the bamboo stick across the kettle. While dyeing the thread evenly by pulling it with her rubber-gloved hand, Han Min-wha smiled to herself as if something had come into her mind.

"As a child," she said, "I saw a man at the neighborhood laundry start a fire in the street in order to dye some thread. While looking at the tangled winding thread, I felt it must have been used by someone else before it was brought to the laundry. I was so interested in the work that I continued to watch it each time he dyed something. Who could have imagined I would grow up to dye thread myself?"

"Right. It's only human never to know what will happen tomorrow," Yun-hee replied.

"But, as I come to think of it, there have been some elements in me that would destine me to be what I am now. Since I grew up among many brothers and sisters, I always found it unbearable to live in a small house. Actually I was so amazed when I saw the Secret Garden for the first time that I was determined to live in such a spacious place in the future. While in college I had a strange desire to marry a Chinese man, because I was told that young men in Taiwan would not start to seek their bride until they had a spacious house of their own. Since I kept talking about a large, spacious house from childhood, I ended up living by myself in a big place like this, I suppose. Living in a house surrounded by hills, I take the open fields as my yard. What more spacious place could you find than this house?"

Finishing her words, Han Min-wha stirred the skein of thread. Every five minutes she took it out to put salt into the kettle, and then repeated the process. Some firewood had been added to the blazing fire, so Yun-hee's face was suffused with the fire as she was sitting before the fuel pit. Staring at the blaze, Yun-hee asked

105

quietly, "Apart from enjoying the spacious house, don't you feel lonely?"

"Well, if I say I'm not lonely at all, it would be hypocrisy and a lie. Of course I was not determined to live by myself from the beginning, you know. Although I had married, I was confronted with the problem of having to live with people I couldn't agree with. Besides, my mother-in-law was so morbidly obsessed with her own son that she couldn't bear to see another woman live with him. So I found it a waste of time to live tormented that way, and realized that the reality of marriage was as frustrating as living in a small house. In addition to this, my love was not deep enough to get over the conflict that confronted me, since the marriage wasn't made out of love between me and my husband."

"In spite of the absence of love," Yun-hee responded, "I think many people are simply living together because they lack courage and are, most of all, not confident enough in terms of emotional stability to live by themselves. Also, since we live in a conventional society, women themselves consider divorce a kind of deficiency in their life. By the way, what have you done in the springtime of your life, without even a chance for love?"

Yun-hee looked up at the woman, feeling that here is another person to be pitied like herself. Han Min-wha briefly took her hand off the bamboo stick with which she had been stirring the skein of thread in the kettle, and said thoughtfully:

"Of course I got someone I liked and even thought of marrying him. But for no obvious reason I felt less and less confident and eventually kept avoiding him. I didn't feel like marrying him because I'd cherished him too much. In other words, whenever I have a meal I take the side dish I like most at the very last, because I don't feel like touching something precious in haste. After all, it's not to my taste to abuse something."

"You are an extraordinary person, Ms. Han."

"You mean I am a strange one?" Han Min-wha stopped stirring the thread and looked playfully at Yun-hee with her shining eyes.

After she had dissolved the salt evenly in the kettle five times and boiled the water to reduce its volume, the dyeing work was finished. Han Min-wha then took the skein of thread out of the kettle and put it into the washbasin. When she suggested they take the thread to the stream, Yun-hee followed her instantly, although by that time a light rain was falling.

Meanwhile Han Min-wha went back to the barn to bring a fresh bamboo stick. Picking up two big stones beside the stream, she put the bamboo stick through the skein of thread and held it across the stream. Then she weighed down both ends of the bamboo stick with the stones and rinsed the dyed skein of thread in the stream, turning the water a deep black. In the gray sky, with even the surrounding fields looking dark, the stream was suffused with the deep black color.

"By the way, did Mr. Hong go on a journey?" Han Min-wha idly asked Yun-hee.

"Of course. Because I've got no one to attend to now, I have even time to come and see you here."

Yun-hee suspected Han Min-wha already knew that Hee-jo had gone on a journey. Could it be then that Hee-jo had called on her that night when he put the jars on top of the kiln chamber to dry them? Yun-hee felt relieved that, at any rate, Han Min-wha had revealed what she knew about Hee-jo, even before being asked. Once the thread was washed out to some extent, Han Min-wha pulled it up and asked for more help. "It'll take a lot of time to wind all the thread I have dyed in the past few days. If you have time, will you come and help me wind the thread?"

Yun-hee granted this request willingly, supposing that Han Min-wha was trying to show her willingness to be close to her. Out of the instinct of a woman who had a husband, Yun-hee wondered about her, since Han Min-wha no longer hesitated to reveal her intentions.

It was a week after Hee-jo had left on his journey that Yi Sung-ju came to Yun-hee's house. Tan-bee, who was playing in the yard, ran to her mother, saying her poet uncle had come. Stepping into the yard, Yun-hee saw Ji-woon standing shyly behind the paulownia tree. Upon seeing Yun-hee, she smiled brightly in greeting, and Yun-hee, in turn, gave her a hearty welcome. Finding that Hee-jo was not home, Yi Sung-ju put on a drained look.

"Anyway it's me who asked you to come again, so I don't care whether Mr. Hong is home or not," said Yun-hee to Yi Sung-ju.

"How about us women getting together and sending the man away?" proposed Ji-woon joyfully.

"You must be afraid I won't serve you grain tea, Mr. Yi," Yun-hee joked.

As Ji-woon agreed with Yun-hee, Yi Sung-ju roared with laughter and entered the house. Although there was little to serve the guests, Yun-hee set a table in a moment with the fruit wine kept in the house, dried pollack, and a seasoned vegetable.

"If you had informed me of your visit in advance," said Yun-hee, "I would have treated you better."

"Don't mention it. We're close enough to make a visit any time we want." Yi Sung-ju replied.

As Yun-hee put the wine table before Yi Sung-ju, he revealed a more apologetic look than ever before. After pouring wine into Yun-hee's glass, he filled the glasses set before Ji-woon and himself. Ji-woon brought forward a book whose title Yun-hee saw was *The Decline of the American Indians*.

"You didn't forget your promise, Mr. Yi. Has your poetry collection also been published?" Yun-hee asked.

"The publication of *The Road to Kobu* was postponed for some time."

"You mean Chun Bong-jun's Kobu?"

"Right, it's the title of my poetry collection. I've collected some unpublished poems even while preparing for punishment, but I thought they were definitely subject to censorship, and that the publisher would also be in trouble. It might be well to distribute the poetry collection to the bookstores first to avoid censorship, but I'd rather keep silent until *The Literature of Liberation* is published."

"I suppose your work must have been too radical."

At Yun-hee's words Yi Sung-ju spoke with the glass in his hand. "I drink a glass of wine with this lonesome spring day as a side dish, and everything in the world looks pitiful. Ji-woon, recite the poem 'Go Away, Shell,' by Brother Tong-yup."

Leaning against the wall, Yi Sung-ju gazed into the air. Emptying her glass in silence, Ji-woon began to recite the poem in a low but forceful nasal voice:

Go away, shell,
Go away, April,
Leaving behind only its essence.

Go away, shell,
Leaving behind the outcry in the year
When the Donghak Revolution broke at Bear Ferry.

Then again
Go away, shell.
In this solemn place
Asadal and Asanyo, our founding father and mother,
Bow to each other shyly, exposing their bosoms and secret parts,
Before a wedding hall where there are no extreme forces.

Go away, shell,
From Mt. Halla to Mt. Paekdu.
Leaving behind a fragrant bosom smelling of the soil,
Go away, all you metal weapons.

The sound of Ji-woon's recitation of the poem seemed like the sound of water running in darkness. Clear yet somewhat sorrowful, her nasal voice increased the power of the poem, leaving behind a lingering effect. Yi Sung-ju, who had listened to Ji-woon with a gloomy face, gave her a piercing look and filled her glass. Yun-hee found it a boastful glance, a glance of mutual affection that only people who love each other can share.

On the white blouse Ji-woon wore glittered a golden crucifix on a chain. Finding it, Yun-hee asked her if she were a Catholic, suspecting that she belonged to the church. Then Ji-woon nodded, smiling.

"I used to go to church," Yun-hee said, "and I was also baptized."

"So? What's your baptismal name?"

"Magdalena, the sinful woman."

As Yun-hee pronounced the name dramatically, Yi Sung-ju suppressed an outburst of laughter. But Yun-hee continued: "I chose her as my patroness because her birthday happens to fall in the same month as mine. Anyhow her name has remained in my mind."

"Because she was a sinful woman, Magdalena gives us comfort," answered Ji-woon. "Because of this, no other people in the world are more sinful than those who claim to be blameless, I believe. Such people are liable to punish others, convinced that they're entitled to. Naturally, they're inhuman as a cold wall and drive us to despair."

Yun-hee was startled while listening to Ji-woon. Though being about ten years younger than Yun-hee, she seemed mature enough to make such a clear and paradoxical definition of sin. In fact, Yun-hee was herself one of those who insisted they were blameless. His curiosity aroused, Yi Sung-ju asked Ji-woon her baptismal name.

"Clara, the saint who fell in love with Saint Francis," she answered.

"Clara . . . As I'm an unbeliever, I'm always amused by such odd names as Stepano or Jacob or something, but the name 'Clara' sounds good. Well, then, I would choose the name 'Francis' if I ever became a disciple of Jesus Christ."

Looking up at Yi Sung-ju, who had spoken half-jokingly, Yun-hee laughed lightly. As Ji-woon got up and went out, Yi Sung-ju glanced at her through the window and confessed, "You know, she is the woman I love."

"Really? She looks romantic as a poet's lover, Mr. Yi, but she's too promising to be the lover of a person with a wife and children."

Yi Sung-ju remained silent for a moment and then informed Yun-hee of something she didn't know: "I'm told that three years ago when Ji-woon took the responsibility of keeping the document the Declaration of an Independent Democratic Country, she was taken to the police station and interrogated for a week. Although not tortured there, she was raped on the cement floor by the police investigator in charge just before she was released. Like a true

110

romantic, that scoundrel kept following her for some time afterward, insisting he loved her. True, there's no denying him the right to love somebody."

Listening to Yi Sung-ju, Yun-hee remembered that when she saw Ji-woon for the first time, she called to mind instantly the image of a martyr. Perhaps on account of the white dress the woman was wearing then, Yun-hee found in her a deepening sadness that was like a mark of hardship. Hadn't it been because of Ji-woon's pain that Yun-hee was drawn to her? In the meantime Tan-bee followed Ji-woon as she entered the room and asked if there might be something else she could do for her. This action, however, was not what Tan-bee would do when guests were around; normally, she never presented herself before them unless being called.

"Oh, thanks. Would you bring me some tea?" Feeling a need to ask the child to do something else for her, Ji-woon said she would like to have hot water. The wine was almost gone, and as the day was waning the evening glow blazed in the west. Tan-bee came back immediately with a bottle of boiled water on a tray, and as Yun-hee took out the teapots and poured water into them, the child sat next to Ji-woon and said, "How good-looking you are, Auntie! Besides, your recitation of the poem took possession of me."

"Oh, my! Thank you. But I think you're more beautiful than me."

Then Tan-bee stared at Ji-woon's big eyes as if searching for something about her, and looked dazzled by her. Amused at the child who didn't hide her own feelings at all, Yi Sung-ju showed her the book *The Decline of the American Indians*.

"Look, you might as well read this book. After reading it, you'll get to know how the whites, in settling the American continent, drove the peaceful Indians off their land and slaughtered and destroyed them. Then you'll realize why imperialism turns out evil."

Tan-bee cocked her head and took up the book quietly. In the meantime Yun-hee had poured the tea, but no one drank it. Urging them to drink the tea, Yun-hee expressed her feelings. "At last you teach your ideology even to my child. You're worth having here, Mr. Yi. You know, the person Tan-bee respects most is Yu Kwan-sun."

Tan-bee was eager to read the book Yi Sung-ju had brought, so Yun-hee read far into that night to finish it because Ji-woon was worried that some brutal scenes in the book might shock the child. The cruelty culminated in a scene in which the whites removed the scalps and cut off the private parts of the dead Indians in order to ornament their caps in combat:

What have we done to offend you? the Indians cried. All we did was move about the land where we were born, but wherever we went the whites kept chasing us.

The whites had made countless promises to us, but they only kept one: they pledged to take possession of our land and they swallowed it up.

I'm worn out. My heart is in torment and I'm overcome with grief. There will be no more fighting in this land as long as the sun keeps shining.

The dreams of a race with passionate, tender hearts died out that way. Yun-hee sighed deeply for the grief of the chieftains and cut out the pages on which the Massacre at Sand Creek was told, judging that even as a documentary, it was too cruel for a child to read. Getting home from school, Tan-bee sought out the book, not minding her homework. From childhood she had liked to read books, and once engaged in reading she would get so absorbed as to take the book even to the toilet with her.

After eating quickly, Tan-bee continued to read the book and twice had to wipe tears from her eyes. As Sae-bul stopped his homework and looked up at his sister's face, Tan-bee sniffled, saying, "Crazy Horse is so pitiful!" Crazy Horse was a genuine Indian who never lived on a reservation or was given food by the whites, and he was a brave chieftain never defeated in battle with enemy soldiers. He was captured by the whites and struggled to the end, only to be stabbed to death with a sword. At the age of thirty-five he was buried by the Wounded Knee River. Perhaps such scenes might touch the child deeply, Yun-hee thought.

After reading the book for two days in a row, Tan-bee told her brother about some legendary Indian chieftains. An old warrior of the Apache who, even after turning seventy, fought against enemy soldiers; a hook-nosed Cheyenne who, in his war bonnet with long feathers dragging the ground, galloped through the lines of the American soldiers; Red Cloud and Sitting Bull; Solitary Wolf and Small Crow—all of these were names of Indian chieftains. Telling of them and the battles they were involved in, Tan-bee asked her brother to choose the names he liked. She went on to say that in the calendar of the Indians there were the months called with such names as the month of the severest cold, the month when the wild geese return, and the month of strawberries. She was also delighted to find there was a month when the geese laid eggs—the name the Cheyenne used for April.

It had been nearly ten days since Hee-jo had left, and the azalea blossoms in the west fade quickly. Awaking late in the morning, Tan-bee drank milk for breakfast and murmured, "I suspect Father will come back today."

"You think so?"

As Yun-hee asked her, Tan-bee spoke of the dream she had had: "When I stopped studying and went into my room, I discovered a knapsack lying down. It's the one that Father would carry with him whenever he went on a journey."

Once before Tan-bee had guessed right, based on a dream, about a visit from her grandmother. Accepting the child's dream then, Yun-hee told her she would go to the market. Counting the days in her mind, she found that it happened to be a market day today. Finding Jae-chull's mother at work in the field in front of her house, Yun-hee asked her to watch the house and set off hurriedly. On most market days Yun-hee enjoyed looking around, but today she intended to drop by at Han Min-wha's house, remembering that the woman had asked her to help wind the thread.

As the market was always bustling, Yun-hee was inclined to look around here and there to see many things. Finding street peddlers lined up on the corner of the street where fresh-water fish were being sold, she stopped for a minute. In the water trough in front of the peddlers were fluttering snake fish, crucian carp, and eels. The pink carp as long as an arm looked sacred, and the turtle crawling idly in the narrow space was like a hermit under the water.

Some days before, accompanied by Hee-jo, Park Young-soo had bought a turtle without hesitation since he had a water pail at home. He said that while watching the turtle, he could take control of his life, which was often without serenity.

As a man came around her to buy a crucian carp for a side dish, Yun-hee advised him that it might be better to buy a mandarin fish because the crucian carp was too bony to eat, then set off toward the shops along the stream. While at leisure, she would look around at the medicinal plants sold on the street by the stream, and sometimes buy some dried mugwort.

On the country market day she would see such medicinal materials as a centipede, a mole, or even a dried weasel looking like the fossil of a young dinosaur. And now Yun-hee could find the various nameless herbs she was familiar with spread out in the street. As a child, she would poke around her grandfather's herb shop, so the smell of the herb brought back to her a kind of old memory. Her grandfather, Yun-hee recalled, was so stern as to use a whip even on his grandchildren, and while giving spending money to them, his hand was always permeated with the smell of herbs. He liked *sijo* so much that he would recite it once in a while. The sluggish tune he would make gave Yun-hee a feeling as if she were walking into a deep mountain, and it lingered in her mind. Also, she remembered the moment when, dying in bed of cancer, her grandfather was making a tremendous effort to suppress the pain. That moment revived in Yun-hee nearly twenty years afterwards whenever she faced hardship, and often taught her perseverance. Discovering the lingering effect of the memory, Yun-hee was startled again.

Staring dully at the medicinal things, Yun-hee bought some greens, wild garlic and fernbrake, and hurriedly walked toward the fish shop she had frequented. She ought to hurry as she was on the way to Han Min-wha's house. Fresh-looking young crabs wriggled in the buckets of the street peddlers, and though they were expensive, Yun-hee bought a few crabs filled with spawn and a flounder. Because of her family's unbalanced diet, she didn't fail to buy fish and a few shrimps as they caught her eye on the corner of the street, and she intended to give some of them to Han Min-wha. While Yun-hee was waiting to get her change, the woman shopkeeper said, putting on an apologetic look, "I'm sorry, Auntie. I can't take even a penny off although you buy many things here. You know, businessmen are meant to be shrewd."

"Don't mention it. You don't need to take a penny off since you always ask a fair price," Yun-hee responded cheerfully to the woman. The market was as animated as always, and so she could have a change of air even when she started out gloomy. Moreover, the sight of common folk who didn't make much profit in their businesses also impressed Yun-hee. Whenever she went to the meat shop, the shopkeeper made a pleasing remark to her: "Well, I think I'll be doing good business today. There're always many customers around whenever you visit."

There was also a young woman in a fruit shop who gave a small orange to Yun-hee whenever she brought some empty sacks back to the shop. To Yun-hee, all these people embodied the healthy side of the common folk. Looking at these people who, though lacking an ideology, didn't harm anybody as they went through daily life, Yun-hee felt sickened by the arrogance of some artists and intellectuals around her, let alone her husband Hee-jo. Yun-hee shuddered as if there was a kind of poison coming from their ideology. Each time she perceived this poison of exclusion from the people, who were believed to have their own ideology, Yun-hee was startled, and found it necessary to wash out the poison that seemed to permeate her while she was not conscious of it. After all, there is not a soul who can't teach us if we regard all the people in the world as mirrors of ourselves, Yun-hee judged.

It was just after noon that Yun-hee got off the bus at Han Min-wha's house. Han Min-wha was sitting leisurely in the field in front of her house after planting tomato seedlings. The woman, gazing at the mountains in the dazzling spring sun with a hoe in her hand, looked as if she was talking with the mountains. As Yun-hee drew near her making a sign of life, Han Min-wha turned around and recognized the visitor.

"Hi, you're at work now?" asked Yun-hee.

"Yes, I make a point of coming out to the field to enjoy the sun. I have no urge to work inside the house, since I'm tempted by the land."

"Absolutely! Who can resist this glorious spring day? I myself am tempted to look out the window while working in the kitchen."

"Are you on the way back from the market?" asked Han Min-wha, looking at the market bag. And Yun-hee said, taking out a sack of shrimp. "Since it looked so fresh, I bought some seafood at the market. Please have some of these shrimp I bought for you."

"Oh, no! You don't need to bother to bring them to me."

Han Min-wha at first declined to accept them, but, feeling apologetic, showed her gratitude. After helping Han Min-wha plant some more tomato seedlings, Yun-hee went into the house and the woman immediately began to prepare a snack. The room was bright with sunshine coming through the rice paper on the windows, and on the wall shelves hung all the colorful threads which, struggling for a new life, seemed lost in their dream. Some skeins of thread were piled in wooden bowls scattered around the room. Looking into one of the bowls close to her, Yun-hee discovered some bundles of gray thread that seemed to be ones the woman had dyed the last time Yun-hee had visited, and it appeared she had wound the thread all by herself.

When Han Min-wha brought in some strawberries, Yun-hee picked up the bright gray thread and asked, "Is this the thread you dyed when I was here before?"

"That's right. Have a close look at the threads over there and you'll find that, depending on the thread and dye materials, each piece gives a different effect." Then Han Min-wha took two bundles of thread out of one bowl and showed them to Yun-hee. They produced a thicker and heavier effect than the gray thread she held in her hand.

"These are all dyed with Chinese ink," she continued. "The thread that looks thick and glossy is an artificial silk, and the one that looks rough and nappy is a hemp thread. The thread you hold in your hand is the one dyed with the azalea root, and you'll find its gray color gives a cheerful air. Don't you think it looks jaunty?"

Everything was as Han Min-wha had explained. Interested, Yun-hee disclosed her impression that the use of the natural dyes gave a more subtle color. Taking a skein of thread in a mustard color out of a bowl in the corner of the room, Han Min-wha said:

"Whatever they are, I think things look better as they're closer to nature because they produce a more profound effect. So even the dried *ume* flower can be used as a dye. Don't you think its fragrance would permeate the textiles dyed with it? This piece was dyed with the onion skin. And in order to make it, I even went to the Chinese restaurant in town to ask them to save onion skins for me."

"It's not yet wound. Actually I came here today to help you wind the thread." Yun-hee was delighted to find something yet to be done as Han Min-wha arranged a yellow skein of thread around her hands.

"Thanks. In fact, I left this thread undone so I could work with you. It has a gorgeous color."

As Yun-hee put the skein of thread around both of her hands, Han Min-wha looked for the tangles to unravel them. Once in a while, sitting with Tan-bee at home, Yun-hee would wind thread, and doing it now, she recalled the time long before when she had untied thread sitting face-to-face with her mother. While at work they could face each other directly, and at times like that Yun-hee would indirectly ask her mother to do something she did not ask at other times, saying she wished to attend the dance studio, or she felt like staying late at her friend's house to study for an exam, or something. At such times Yun-hee was frustrated because her mother didn't give her answer readily and remained silent until they finished winding the thread. Thinking about it now, Yun-hee realized she had learned patience from such a mother, and so the way Han Min-wha wound the thread appeared to her anything but ordinary. Since the thread was tangled, Han Min-wha began to unlace the complex tangles, moving nimbly at untying the knotted parts.

"I guess it'll take quite a while to untie them by your hands alone," observed Yun-hee.

"I know. Although there is a machine to untie the knotted thread, I've worked until now only with my hands. By using such a machine, people are able to even make thread out of cotton or wool, but in contrast to that I find it rather simple to untie the tangled thread with my hands. Just as the very act of making the thread becomes creative work, so the act of untying is a creative process, I believe."

"If compared with the making of pots, I suppose, the work of untying the thread is the same as the making of a ball of clay by wedging the lump," responded Yun-hee.

"Maybe so. The knotted parts get more and more tangled as I try to pull them out of impatience," Han Min-wha went on. "I used to cut off the tangled parts, but as I got more experienced I stopped doing that. I'd feel unfulfilled until I had succeeded in untying it, so I'm trying not to yield to the thread. I've heard that people working with thread are naturally tenacious in their character. The raw silk in the body of the cocoon which is the source of silk is said to be as delicate as a cobweb. Nevertheless, people long ago learned to unwind it carefully so that they didn't need to cut it off because of unskillfulness. I imagine such training must be, above all, a time of painful endurance. In those days, I'm told, a young widow would try to forget her sorrow by losing herself in work with the loom, whereas woman peddlers would vent their spite by weaving far into the night to sell the next day. You know, in the beginning even my mother didn't allow me to do weaving, considering it a work done only by an ill-fated woman."

"Because of my childhood memories," remarked Yun-hee, "the thread gives me such a warm feeling. And when I saw it first in your room, it reminded me of my aunt. As I see you at work, I find the thread piled over there anything but ordinary."

"You think so? Some time ago when I happened to go by the shoe shop, I sighed deeply in spite of myself. The moment I saw the shop filled completely with the shoes, I was amazed to think how long the shopkeeper had been wandering in his former life and subsequently was fated to live with all those shoes in his shop. And looking at all the threads filling my room, I often feel I'm sentenced to live with them as things that should pay for my own sin. Naturally, I'm relieved whenever I untie the tangled thread."

"Indeed. I can imagine what a laborious work it is. That's why people would call the work itself 'making fate.'"

Recalling Hee-jo, who always said he felt burdened at the beginning of his work, Yun-hee was able to understand what Han Min-wha had said. In spite of the fate she must endure, however, there was nothing in Han Min-wha that weighed on her mind.

As Yun-hee was preparing to leave shortly after they finished winding the thread, Han Min-wha said she would get lunch ready. But Yun-hee declined without hesitation, adding there was nobody at home. "My husband will be back today or tomorrow, so there are many things to be done before the man I must attend to returns."

Hee-jo didn't return until Yun-hee had made a cucumber *kimchi,* stewed the crab she had bought at the market, and set the dinner table. She sprinkled water on the floor of the studio, which had been empty all this time, and cleaned it. Meanwhile Tan-bee picked a peony, which was beginning to bloom in the yard, and put it in the studio. The fresh blossom brought an air of spring into a place containing only empty, unfinished wares. Looking at the blossom, Yun-hee suddenly felt like putting on her traditional costume of pure silk. The fascinating color of the peony blossom would become fully alive next to the pure silk costume, she thought.

With the days getting warmer, the briquet was burning well, boiling the water on top of the fuel pit. Filling the kettle completely with water and putting it on the fuel pit before going to bed, Yun-hee intended to have her children take a bath. But Sae-bul was reluctant to have a bath, pretending he had too much homework. Although Hee-jo took him to the public baths every Sunday, Sae-bul didn't look with favor upon his mother's helping him take a bath. Growing children naturally try to get out of their mother's reach.

In the temporary bathroom behind the kitchen was a fuel pit for heating the *ondol* floor of the children's room. Since it was not warm enough to let the children have a bath there, Yun-hee built a fire in the oil stove in a room that was used as a barn in the winter. Yun-hee used it for storing food such as dried pumpkins, dried radish leaves, and other things, but with the days growing warm, she used it only as a bathroom, having sealed the mouse-holes.

After pouring the water into the rubber tub, Yun-hee called Tan-bee, even though the tub turned out so narrow the child could barely move in it. She pulled up the child's hair, which was in two braids, and splashed water all over her body. Tan-bee's yellowish skin, resembling Yun-hee's, was good to look at, like a fresh-baked loaf of bread, and her skinny, balanced body made the child look like a young dancer. Tan-bee rinsed the soap off her body and, getting into the rubber tub, splashed the water with her hands. The sight of the child who liked the water so much reminded Yun-hee of her own childhood, and she clicked her tongue inwardly.

The faint odor of tea was spreading through the water as Yun-hee put a gauze bag containing dried ground tea into the tub. Feeling as if her hands were getting soft with the odor of tea, Yun-hee splashed water over Tan-bee's body and touched her skin, only to find it was rough. Rubbing the child's arms, Yun-hee calmed her troubled mind—while growing up, Tan-bee's skin, unlike that of an infant, had grown rough and chapped, and now looked like the bark of a tree. Afraid that the child might be worried, Yun-hee hadn't even taken her to the clinic, but instead to the skin doctor, who was her friend. Though there turned out to be nothing seriously wrong with her skin, while living with her parents in a stuffy rented room where no wind passed through, Tan-bee had suffered from heat rash as an infant. With a vivid memory of that time Yun-hee often felt guilty, but her anxiety was even more increased as she reflected that the child's symptom might mean something serious.

There was no one on her side of the family who had rough skin, Yun-hee speculated. Into her mind came her husband's family, but it was no use to blame any of them for Tan-bee's skin. Tan-bee's classmates often called her the "slender-leg child," but, to Yun-hee's regret, she had skin barely worthy of attention.

As Yun-hee had the child stand to wash off, she said abruptly, "Mom, when I brought my homeroom teacher a class diary after class today, he asked me if I'd transfer to a school in Seoul."

"What did you say then?"

"I said I'll attend the school in this region."

Up till last year Yun-hee had been determined to send Tan-bee to her parents' home in Seoul so that the child could attend middle school there. In making such a decision she remembered a newspaper article of about two years before, which estimated that the total expense of out-of-school studies throughout the country reached an astronomical level of five hundred billion *won*. But Hee-jo didn't agree with her plan, suggesting it might not be too late to send Tan-bee to Seoul when the child began high school. Yun-hee, too, had no urge to send her daughter to a place with such fierce competition to enter college. It was Tan-bee herself, however, who decided not to transfer, worried that she couldn't make good progress in her studies were she to live alone cut off from her mother.

"Well, then, just do as you wish," Yun-hee said to Tan-bee. "You should be responsible for yourself and I'll watch how you grow to be a person of good promise."

"I wish I could live like an Indian," replied Tan-bee preposterously.

As Tan-bee remained standing, Yun-hee said, splashing water upon her body, "The Indians were a splendid race who settled on the American continent a long time ago, but they were destroyed by the whites, who were stronger. Likewise, you must build up your own strength to support yourself. And although your father and mother can protect you now, you must grow up and have your own strength. You know, it's in order to build your own strength that we ask you to study hard."

Tan-bee couldn't possibly understand what her mother felt toward her. Splashing water all over her body, she let her mother take care of her rough skin. Though she would be a middle school student next year, unlike many precocious children of these days, Tan-bee had not reached, and she was flat-chested. Finding that the pure body had not yet become maturely lovely, Yun-hee stroked the girl's secret part that looked like a low stony hill. As Tan-bee pushed aside her mother's hand, Yun-hee, suppressing a laugh, said what occurred to her. "Anyway, this is only my opinion, but wouldn't it be better for you to have 'Small Wolf' rather than 'Solitary Wolf' for your nickname?"

"Why?" asked Tan-bee.

Yun-hee had heard that after reading the book her children agreed to take one of the chieftains' names as each of their own. So Sae-bul had chosen the name "Red Cloud," while Tan-bee got "Solitary Wolf," and moreover Tan-bee had already sent a letter to her grandmother using that name. Sensing that the child was rather reluctant to adopt the name she had suggested, Yun-hee expressed what she had felt. "You know what? 'Small Wolf' sounds lovely, but 'Solitary Wolf' sounds somewhat pathetic. Why do you have to feel lonely while living close to your mother?"

Hee-jo returned late that night. As Yun-hee was about to light a fire in the living room after bathing Tan-bee, the goose hissed softly in the pen, which he always did when the children came home from school. Turning around to see the front gate, Yun-hee found it partly open, but the yard was quiet. She looked across at the fields in the darkness and then continued to burn dried twigs. Because it got chilly at night she needed to burn more wood for the room, and meanwhile she enjoyed sitting alone, watching the blazing wood.

Sparks flew up from the wood with a crackling sound. With the swaying flame casting a shadow over Yun-hee's face, the faintly blowing wind made the flame move inside. Seeing the fire in full flame made Yun-hee feel as if even the smallest particles of dust in her heart had been washed off. As a child she would go out to enjoy watching the fire when she heard the sound of a fire engine's siren, feeling fear and a strange excitement simultaneously. The fire would arouse ecstasy through the atmosphere to sacrifice itself thoroughly, and seemed to purify the human soul by this pathetic self-sacrifice. Obviously, Emperor Nero, who was said to have set fire to the city of Rome, then writing a poem of grief, must have been a lunatic. And Yun-hee wondered if it couldn't be that he embodied the perverse nature of humanity, inclined to be charmed by the act of making a fire.

Yun-hee heard the sound of the front gate opening as she put more wood into the pit to burn. She got up when Hee-jo was stepping into the house with an expression as ordinary as if he were just coming from town. So Yun-hee was momentarily amazed, standing as if hypnotized. Hee-jo spoke to her, approaching. "Nothing happened in the family?"

There was no sign of life inside until he opened the sliding door to the wooden floor, and the children all seemed asleep. Sae-bul had been occupying himself with assembling a model ship when Yun-hee went out to heat the room with wood, and Tan-bee had been drying her wet hair. Opening the door to the room, Yun-hee found Sae-bul falling asleep without putting on his sleeping clothes, and Tan-bee, weary after her bath, was also going to sleep with her hair wet.

Taking Sae-bul back to his room and covering him with his quilt, Yun-hee turned off the light. Leaving the room, she found that Hee-jo was taking a sketchbook and painting instruments out of his knapsack. What remained was a small bundle of laundry, which Yun-hee began to take outside to the bathroom, while Hee-jo rummaged in the knapsack again and took out a flat stone, comfortable to hold. Offering the stone to her, Hee-jo said, "I picked this stone up by the river. Its color is peculiar, like a sandy plain."

As Yun-hee carefully inspected the common, oval stone, she saw several faint gray lines against the faded jade-green, which looked like a coastline in many folds just before the dusk fell. They seemed to suit the name Hee-jo had given to it well, the sandy plain.

"You like this color, right?" Hee-jo asked swiftly as Yun-hee didn't remove her eyes from the stone, and then went into the room.

After the month when the geese laid eggs came a month when the peony started to bloom. Although Yun-hee had brought nearly twenty eggs to the hatchery, not a single egg hatched. Like a pot fired wrong in the kiln, it was a complete failure. Goose eggs and pottery were alike in terms that it was impossible to predict their results. However, the goose eggs brought Yun-hee the memory of Mr. Keichi, so she resolved not to tell Hee-jo about them, thinking that it was, after all, not wise to mention them in haste to the one who was about to resume his work after a journey.

Hee-jo seemed to have had a long period of rest during his absence; he confined himself to the studio from the day he returned. He got so haggard his face looked more pointed, but no longer affected by wine, he seemed to have recovered his spirits. Once involved in his work, Hee-jo would make Yun-hee feel strained to the point that she grew nervous; but now, like a person freed from an obsession, he seemed not to feel burdened at all. On the day after Hee-jo took up his work again, Wan-kyu came to him early in the morning with his things packed up. That night Hee-jo, sitting face-to-face with Wan-kyu, revealed what had been on his mind during his journey.

"This year I've finished not a single piece of work. Like a person who had suddenly lost his memory, I was overwhelmed in the presence of the clay, not knowing what to do, and was occupied with things past. I thought it was a retrogression, because even while I felt bound to march forward, I had an obsession that I had to accomplish something. In fact, this is the reason I took the journey. And in the temple I visited I made nearly thirty thousand bows to the statue of Buddha in order to empty my head. But in spite of this, I felt possessed by something, so I wandered about the mountains with trembling legs for several days. One day while I was sitting on a mountainside and looking vacantly at the valley below, I suddenly realized that, after all, the pattern in the pottery is no more than what it is. Now I must tell you, Wan-kyu, that from the beginning I remained conscious of the pattern and so struggled with what I felt ought to be the necessity of making pattern in the *punch'ong* ware. Then, all of a sudden, I was released from my obsession with pattern. Perhaps I might have been touched by the lines of nature as they really were, and now I'm released from the burden of having to do something. Despite its great significance, the pottery itself doesn't make a difference to me now because I'm not possessed by it anymore. With such an unburdened mind I can understand what it means to do things with clay. Now I know what it takes to be released from any obsession."

Hee-jo's face looked more serene than before—even if the serenity was confined to his work, the way he ceaselessly endeavored to go beyond his self-limitations was sincere. In spite of innumerable deficiencies in his character, it seemed, Yun-hee couldn't give him up, since he suffered so much in proportion to his limitations. She imagined that someday Hee-jo would turn into a different human being—one who was capable of doing whatever he wanted. That he brought his wife a jade green stone looking like a sandy plain . . . ! Yun-hee had never imagined such a thing before.

The next day Yun-hee happened to see Hee-jo's sketchbook and discovered that he had been to his mother's grave. On a big bowl shaped like a flower basin he drew a pattern in dotted lines and wrote next to it a phrase that read, "By my mother's grave at Puyeo."

An inventive idea as it transformed the grave into a bowl, Yun-hee thought. And its form gave a stable, serene feeling; rather than a repose as an end of life, it showed the fertile other world, which embraced death itself. The mother who had lived crouching in the narrow world like a snail and had been buried in the dark, damp ground . . . Perhaps Hee-jo might have intended to revive that pitiful old woman in the picture of the bowl. On the journey he seemed to have discovered other graves, since in a hilly spot where he could look down upon the Kum River he made a sketch of a monumental tombstone for people long dead, below which he scribbled:

Dolmen, menhir, tombstone . . . People seem to like to erect something. It's to give a meaning to their existence, or a struggle with the meaninglessness of life.

Hee-jo involved himself for two days in making a teapot as preparation for a large work, then lost no time in making the large piece. It was what he had attempted to accomplish before going on his journey. He concentrated on putting together the two pieces of the work that had been made separately, the result of which was to bring into being a shape he couldn't anticipate. Its neck, clearly distinguishable from the main part, aroused a sturdy feeling, like an earthenware vessel from the period of the Three Kingdoms. The year before, at an exhibition by a sculptor she knew, Yun-hee found herself dissatisfied with sculptures of women whose necks were omitted, and it was then that she realized each pot gave a different feeling, depending on the rim or foot.

As Yun-hee went to Hee-jo with a snack and looked into the vessel he had just finished throwing on the wheel, he told himself, "Well, I find it not to my taste to make a form that is already fixed . . ."

Wan-kyu had spent a full four days working with the clay, making plenty of balls of clay, and then began to make a plate. Since a plate is flat, it's necessary to force the clay down while throwing it on the wheel. But as Yun-hee realized, it's by no means easy to do such a thing because too much forcing down would destroy the shape. Since the relation of clay and force is best understood through this work, the principle of pottery is said to derive from it. As a result, the first thing Hee-jo would ask his students to do was to make a plate.

On the second night after he took up his work, Wan-kyu observed after dinner: "Before, I was instructed to make only a plate and teapot. At first I wondered why I'd been asked to do that process because even in class I was never asked to do so. But right now I'm gaining a little confidence in throwing the wares."

"As for the painters," answered Hee-jo, "the potter should first of all be a craftsman rather than an artist, which means he should learn something technical first. The art comes next, you know, since anyone can be a master when the art and the craft are intermingled with each other. Like the old saying goes, once you cross the river you don't need the raft anymore. As you know, the renowned Koryo celadons or Choson white porcelains are all products of professional potters. So it's quite natural that they could produce such impeccable pieces, since they had mastered the craft of their work. But I think it's a pity there are so many people nowadays proclaiming themselves as potters, who don't even know how to throw wares. In this sense, the first thing you must be is a professional potter."

As Hee-jo finished his words, Wan-kyu said without a pause: "I understand your argument. But I still have no idea why you make a ball of clay each time you begin a job, even while in the process losing your energy. Now that the kneading machine is getting to be used in the large mills, I suppose there will be no necessity to knead the clay in such a primitive way. I'm planning to buy that machine, too, once I get to my work in earnest."

"Well, you may remember I asked you only to pull weeds for a whole week when you came here first. But when I was learning pottery, I was asked to clear away garbage, not just pull weeds. After that I spent a whole month sieving powdered clay. While I was doing as my teacher instructed, I pitied myself and was skeptical of what I was supposed to do. But now, I don't think such work was all in vain, as I realize that I learned a lot in the process."

Then Hee-jo said no more, as he felt a generation gap between himself and Wan-kyu, who already enjoyed modern conveniences. Because he didn't like machines, Hee-jo was planning to make the living wares he intended to distribute by using the potter's wheel, which Yun-hee herself agreed with. Perhaps life in the countryside, where one could assimilate into nature, might lead him to pursue something more human.

On Children's Day Sae-bul and Tan-bee spent the whole day roaming about the fields on the bicycle, and on Sunday they went to the stream in the morning to bring back a fishing net. Since Children's Day was Saturday, they had a two-day holiday, and enjoyed their freedom to the fullest. In the net they had set out with Wan-kyu the previous night were hopping such fishes as a catfish, a minnow, and a mandarin fish with a yellow belly. As it was likely that people would visit her house, Yun-hee filled a bucket with water and put in the net full of fish, thinking of making a peppery stew with them. In the meantime Sae-bul had caught two prawns in the stream and put them into the bucket too.

Yun-hee looked for Tan-bee as she set out to gather some greens for a fish stew, and found her in the ginseng field in front of her yard. It seemed the child had been watching Chung-ki's mother set up tomato stakes. Seeing Yun-hee, Chung-ki's mother spoke loudly. "Look, the people who came here last night on a pleasure trip put up a tent by the stream, right? They took away a box containing some plants and stakes from the tomato field to use for fuel. Those stakes cost twenty *won* each, you know. Huh! How insensitive they are!"

"Probably it's because they're still young," replied Yun-hee.

"But the grown-ups are no better than the young ones. Some time ago an adult who came to my house with young ones kept asking for red pepper. Obviously he had no consideration for the farmers! Once before, I shouted at people from the city who had stolen watermelons from my field at night. I said they were impertinent enough to covet what the farmers had cultivated, while they themselves didn't share a sip of water with others. Once, fed up with farming, while I was peddling acorn jelly, I discovered people in the cities were so awful they didn't even give strangers a drink of water and turned them away."

With the passing of the lunar New Year things were getting busy in the countryside but, with the blooming of the wild flowers, people in the nearby cities came pouring into the suburbs. These idlers from the cities, who would arouse a sense of incongruity in the mind of country people, couldn't be welcomed. Yun-hee suggested to Chung-ki's mother, who was weary of her work, that on a busy day like this she must bring her son out to the field to help his mother work.

"When I told him yesterday to till the soil," the woman replied, "he got angry that he had been asked to work on Children's Day instead of amusing himself. Today he went to the study center pretending he must engage himself with his study. He usually makes good grades, ranking fourth or fifth in his class, but since he has no intention to be engaged in farming he wants to enter an engineering school. I really wish to pay school expenses for my children by selling young red pepper plants this season. In any event the farmers are so pitiable because, in spite of the laborious work, they can hardly afford to pay school expenses for their children. Besides, they're no longer satisfied with what they used to do, since all the living costs are soaring."

Yun-hee had no choice but to listen to the complaints of Chun-ki's mother, and then went to the ridge to gather greens. As soon as she had made the peppery stew, Chung In-ku came to her home as if by appointment. The husband of Yun-hee's friend Eun-kyong, Chung In-ku was a neurosurgeon and a lover of pottery who never failed to buy Hee-jo's works at the exhibition. Yun-hee was as delighted to see him as if she had met a friend by chance. "Hello! I expected someone would come, but I never imagined a medical doctor would visit in person. Why didn't you bring Eun-kyong with you?"

"Ah, I just escaped from the house. And in order to have a change of air while appreciating the pottery, I brought today two people I like, President Shin and his wife."

The couple who entered the living room with Chung In-ku seemed in their fifties. The man who introduced himself as President Shin had silver-gray hair, and his wife wore metal-framed glasses that gave her a cold air. Exchanging a greeting with Yun-hee, the woman offered Yun-hee a cake box, but Yun-hee was embarrased that a guest she didn't know had brought a present.

"Don't mind it. I just prepared it as I heard you were living in the country. That's all." Then the woman urged Yun-hee to take the cake.

"Thank you, anyway. I'll treat you just as we do in the country. This morning my children caught fish in a net, so I made a peppery stew."

Since it was a little past noon, Yun-hee intended to treat them to lunch, but the woman said she had had breakfast just before setting out and, moreover, she couldn't stay long because of a lunch appointment. As Yun-hee was about to prepare tea, Hee-jo asked her to set a wine table for the visitors. Setting a wine table before Hee-jo and Chung In-ku, Yun-hee urged the couple to have tea. Meanwhile President Shin looked carefully into a pot on the stationery chest. It was a work of art that transformed an antique flask into a square shape with a drawing on it, giving it a bold touch. Observing it, President Shin said, "Well, it's not suitable to hold flowers."

"You might keep it simply as a work of art," Chung In-ku replied. "If you insist on using it as a vase, you can put a dark rose blossom into it as well."

"If so, is the piece over there also a work of art?"

While exchanging words with Chung In-ku, President Shin pointed at an object on the chest in the corner of the room. An abstract sculpture rather than a pot, it awakened in him an image of a piece of stone wriggling or indulging in a dream.

"That's called an *object*—a work different from the conventional form," explained Chung In-ku. "In foreign countries, I heard there is no clear distinction between pottery and sculpture or pictures, so that a potter often holds an exhibition for pottery and sculpture at the same time."

"I'm not familiar with such work, but as far as pottery is concerned I couldn't think of anything but bowls or vases. By the way, how much is this one?" With this remark President Shin pointed at the square-shaped piece again.

Chung In-ku, who had been explaining the work like an artist, looked at Hee-jo already on his second glass, and with an expressionless look Hee-jo merely answered, "One million *won* might be enough." That price, however, was twice as much as what Yun-hee had thought it would be, and she instantly perceived he was not in a good mood.

"How much is the piece over there?" asked President Shin again.

"It's the same."

President Shin seemed to feel it was too expensive and, raising his eyes, he asked the price by pointing at the jar in the middle of the antique bookshelf. As Hee-jo responded, not even turning his glance, Yun-hee read the situation in a moment. It was in order to urge them to buy pots that Chung In-ku had brought President Shin and his wife. Meanwhile President Shin's wife seemed obsessed with the jar with the triangular pattern lurking like a light and continued to stare at it, cocking her head. "Well, I like that work of art, but . . ."

"Both of them belong to the large piece. The thing you saw first is bold and modern whereas the jar looks stable," Chung In-ku commented spiritedly.

"You'd better become a pottery expert, Mr. Chung."

President Shin remarked to Chung In-ku, who had spoken in excitement like a broker, then tapped on the square-shaped vessel with his finger. Hee-jo, who had been drinking wine without minding the people around him, glanced at it with his brows raised. Some time ago in his exhibition, when a spectator tapped on the pot with his hand, Hee-jo approached him and remarked, smiling, "You might as well touch it, but don't tap it because it's not a watermelon." However, this time he didn't have enough courage to make such a remark to his visitor.

After looking at each work one by one, President Shin asked his wife's opinion with a reluctant look. "Which would be better—this one or that one? Which do you prefer?"

But his wife just sat, not saying a word, weighed down by the high price. Moreover, she revealed her discontent openly, convinced that Hee-jo was turning a cold shoulder to people who came to buy his work. As President Shin, to save face, didn't complain about the price and looked at each piece hesitantly, Hee-jo spat out brusquely, "If it's so hard to select such a worthless piece of pottery, just toss a coin for it."

Yun-hee, who had been on edge all this time, sighed deeply to see President Shin and his wife grimace, and she thought everything had come to nothing. Although she didn't object to Hee-jo's work being sold, it was true these visitors with their imposing manner had irritated her. Though worried about making a living, she didn't have the slightest desire to sell the work, and even felt displeased with them. Also, Chung In-ku was at a loss since Hee-jo brought the meeting to an abrupt ending. Having been interested in painting ever since medical school, he still had an ardent desire to be a patron of the art. Looking at his watch, Chung In-ku concluded by saying delicately to President Shin: "Because of your lunch appointment, you must be in no mood to think over the work. Allow yourself more time to choose and I'll try to get the price reduced for you. At least as a broker, I'm sure I can have such an influence."

On Sundays, when visitors or weekenders kept pouring into the area where Yun-hee lived, she felt distracted, even staying at home, but when dusk spread those people hurriedly returned to their shelters. The aftermath of the day ebbing away, it now became more tranquil than ever before, and even the stream looked crystal clear. The small mountain peak, which had already turned green, threw its shadow over the mirror-like stream, deepening the color of the water.

Doing laundry in the stream for the first time in a long while, Yun-hee recalled the time when she had moved to Choha-ri as if it were only yesterday. In the beginning, fascinated with the stream she had found, Yun-hee had done her laundry there almost every day. No less than three or four years before, the water had been so clear that even its bottom was visible, and at times like that the minnows or dace, waiting to eat the suet, would swarm in when Yun-hee did laundry in the stream. Once in the stream, the soap itself washed away from the soaped blanket, and when her mind was troubled Yun-hee would seek the stream, even in the deep winter, to calm herself down by breaking the ice.

To Yun-hee, the stream had been a good friend beyond comparison, but now, polluted, its current was like foam, and it was

131

all occupied by the idlers from the nearby cities. Thinking that the stream had suffered too much, she made a point of not looking toward it on Sundays, but, nevertheless, an empty can or a scrap of paper scattered around the vacant stream would touch her like a close friend's wound.

The hard soap Yun-hee was now using didn't dissolve quickly in the water, so she scrubbed it over the soaked clothes repeatedly. The trousers Sae-bul had worn were all covered with the white soap, and as Yun-hee scrubbed the laundry forcibly against the stone, foam appeared all around it, making her feel unburdened. That was the soap she had exchanged at the peppery-stew restaurant in town for the President Shin's still-wrapped cake. Doing her laundry with this soap gave her a feeling as if she could shake off the uneasiness that had remained in her mind from President Shin's visit.

Yun-hee didn't usually do her laundry on a day like this, but it was something she wanted to do. And it washed off all her idle thoughts together with the foam she made. As she was about to rinse out the clothes, her friend Eun-kyong came suddenly to her mind. While her husband had been working as a professor in a medical school, Eun-kyong had ruthlessly turned away the requests of students who tried to bribe her husband, and was said to have confirmed her sense of participating in the real world. In college she had been such a bright student as to have the best academic record, not only in her department, but also in the graduate school she attended. But since it was not easy for a woman to get a professorship, she was merely wasting her talents. Yun-hee wondered if Eun-kyong got a sense of satisfaction from the self-confirmation she felt in turning away the bribes offered by her husband's students.

As Yun-hee, having finished doing the laundry, went to take a rest, she heard someone behind her. Turning around, she saw Wan-kyu approaching. "Are you looking for me?" said Yun-hee, but he asked her preposterously how to use the rice steamer.

"What for?"

"I washed the rice for lunch. I'm going to set at least the lunch table myself, because I feel uncomfortable eating meals you prepare."

"You don't have to say that again."

Actually Yun-hee was on the point of returning home to prepare lunch. Holding the washbasin full of laundry, however, she suggested they stay for a moment, indicating the ground with her eyes. Even on the stony ground she could feel the warmth of spring. With a gently surging ripple, the water looked like broken pieces of glass scattered in the sunshine.

"You're doing laundry out here because the day is warm," said Wan-kyu. "Your hands don't feel chilly now?"

"Not at all. As a matter of fact, I'm enjoying the fine weather as well as the stream. Obviously we can't get this kind of pleasure if we use a washing machine."

Turning toward Yun-hee, Wan-kyu said: "Well, it's amazing how you manage to take care of the household. I feel Mr. Hong must be very fortunate to have a good woman like you."

"Then you mean I'm not fortunate?" countered Yun-hee jokingly.

Wan-kyu remained silent a moment, then continued: "When I came here for the first time, I thought Mr. Hong was wealthy. As far as I know, there are many artists who have a second house as good as yours but don't even work as hard as Mr. Hong. I was startled to see an old-fashioned chest of drawers in your room."

"If we'd had enough money to spend, we could have bought an antique chest or other ornaments, but Mr. Hong doesn't like such things. Like an ascetic, he has been wearing the same necktie for nearly ten years."

Wan-kyu hesitated for a moment, then ventured as if something unexpected had occurred: "When I looked in the rice chest before coming down here, I found it almost empty. Mr. Hong seemed embarrassed to find it, you know."

"Oh, don't mind it. We still have another bag of rice in the barn. Though we're not rich, it's absurd to worry about rice now that we expect to make money at the exhibition."

Perhaps because of the empty rice chest, Yun-hee thought, Hee-jo might have regretted that he had turned a cold shoulder to the people who had come to buy his work yesterday. Had he known that the cake was already exchanged for soap, he would have been more reserved. Only then did Wan-kyu feel relieved, saying, "Before, I wondered why such a talented man as Mr. Hong didn't teach at the college, but now it gives me relief to know there is still an artist who lives in his own way."

"Nevertheless, I'm worried you're engaged in pottery, Wan-kyu, because making pottery is more difficult than is generally understood. As you know, there are only a few artists engaged in it while living alone, cut off from Seoul."

Wan-kyu seemed lost in thought for a moment, then got up to leave. "Anyway, it's what Mr. Hong is doing, so why should I be worried about making a living?"

Hee-jo had spent all day yesterday drinking with a friend who had come to see him for the first time in a long while, but today Yun-hee had discovered the thrown pots on the kiln chamber as usual. Wan-kyu, too, had been as intent upon his work as Hee-jo.

In the evening after dinner he spoke to Hee-jo with a flushed face. "As I reflected yesterday, I came to the conclusion that your way of making pottery using only your hands was right. Using a machine, I find, wouldn't give us the opportunity to contemplate, since we've got a chance to communicate with ourselves while kneading and mixing the clay."

"Can I tell you then an episode from the book of the Chinese philosopher, Changtzu?"

With a good spirit, Hee-jo urged even the children, who couldn't comprehend his story, to listen to him.

"On his journey," opened Hee-jo, "Tse Kung, one of Confucius' disciples, happened to meet an old man who was digging out a narrow path to make a ridge and carried water to pour into the patch. Feeling so much pity for the old man who, in spite of the laborious work, made little progress, Tse Kung told him of a machine that could supply water for a hundred ridges every single day. While listening to the explanation about the machine, the old man lost his temper but, soon recovering himself, said: 'According to my teacher, if people turn to a machine they become involuntarily involved in petty wiles. With such thoughts settled in the heart, their purity of mind is also destroyed, which in turn leads to the disturbance of mind. The disturbance of mind, then, prevents the way of thought from settling in the mind. Therefore, I don't use the machine, not because I don't know how to use it, but because I would feel ashamed to use it.' So the old man's remark awakened Tse Kung to a great extent. You must know that a machine is nothing more than an instrument for humans, but once we get accustomed to its convenience it can establish itself as a master of humans."

"I understand," said Wan-kyu. And Hee-jo, contented, went on:

"I have no idea what the way of thought means. But I feel certain I'll come up with something if—with purity of mind—I'm involved in my work without turning to petty wiles. Of course, in order to perceive the way of thought I've got to choose a course no one would want. And I wonder where I'll arrive after such wandering. Like a tree awaiting a timely rain, I'm looking forward to finding out something."

Since his return from the journey Hee-jo felt refreshed, and confined himself to the studio, ready for the work he had not done before. As soon as the thrown vessels had dried, he began to coat them with white slip. For that work, he had been in the habit of drinking *soju* to make bold strokes in drawing, but now he was different. To Wan-kyu, who felt somewhat dubious, Hee-jo said, ill at ease: "I used to drink wine, saying it was to make my drawings in a state of self-effacement. But I came to realize being drunk is anything but a self-effacement."

Hee-jo seemed more confident than before. Yun-hee entered the studio quietly through the back door to put firewood in the kiln chamber, and discovered that with the coating of the white slip finished, the white wares were scattered here and there around the studio. Finding Yun-hee, Hee-jo stopped her to show a teapot dipped into the white slip. The part by which he held it was not dipped and remained in the shape of a petal, so Yun-hee commented it looked like a pattern. Turning to Wan-kyu, Hee-jo explained: "If I tried to make it with a purpose in mind, the work wouldn't appear natural. In fact, this is a pleasure I discovered in the process of coating the ware with white slip."

After a few days Park Young-soo paid a visit to them. As Hee-jo spoke of how he had recently come back from his journey, Park Young-soo reported he had moved his studio to Namhansansung some days before. As soon as Hee-jo suggested they celebrate his moving to Namhansansung with wine, Park Young-soo took a bottle of western liquor out of an inside pocket of his working clothes and, looking at Yun-hee for a moment, gave it to her as an indication he trusted her. With steamed fresh *Aralia* shoots, she set a wine table. Park Young-soo handed her a glass first, but Yun-hee declined the glass, saying she didn't like strong western liquor, and brought herself some left-over *makkoli*. At the sight of this, Park Young-soo made fun of her. "Look at such a sly woman! Don't be sneaky anymore and set a wine table just for yourself."

As Yun-hee inquired about his new life in the countryside, Park Young-soo told about it, full of wonder:

"In the morning when I awaken to a bird's song rather than the noise of cars, the sunshine coming through the rice paper seems to stroke me like my mother's hand. Then, going out into the yard, I find the graceful mountains looking down upon me modestly, while all the plants in the ground are splendidly beginning to open their buds to exhibit their timely coming into being. Can you imagine how marvelous it is? It feels like the clear mountain air washes the taint of vanity from the lungs, so I leave my door open while I sleep. In moving to the countryside you had a great deal of hardship, Hee-jo, but you've got to know you must pay the price for what you get to enjoy. You might as well consider the money you'd paid for paving the road as your dues."

"Sounds great," Hee-jo rejoiced to hear Park Young-soo's words. "The only thing you have to do, then, is devote yourself to painting. That's what you can pay in return for enjoying life in the countryside."

As Hee-jo, living in the countryside till now, spoke to Park Young-soo like his senior, he, the painter, told them something they didn't know:

"By the way, Jung-dal and his family will be moving in tomorrow to live with me. At any rate the house I live in is too big for me alone. Jung-dal has supposedly been engaged in writing, so even now he doesn't have a house of his own. While living with me, he might feel settled, and I myself can enjoy his company. Since his field is different from mine and he is also my junior, I think we can get along pretty well together."

"So? How many family members does he have?" asked Yun-hee.

"There are three of them—including a small child at the prime age of cuteness."

Unlike Yun-hee who asked about Jung-dal rather worriedly, Hee-jo showed an obvious opposition to Park Young-soo. "Tut! Nevertheless he's going to depend upon his friend for a living?"

"Actually I suggested he live with me," replied Park Young-soo, "and he can be good company for me as I live in the countryside alone. In addition, we can stimulate each other while engaging in our own work in earnest. Even his being poor strikes me as refreshing. So, as long as we're living together, I'll make every effort to help him. But certainly there'll be much I can learn from him—something like his devotion to and concentration on literature, or the purity of his passion."

"Being poor is nothing to be ashamed of," Hee-jo declared, "but at the same time it's not a thing to be proud of. I detest those who, supposedly proclaiming themselves as devotees of art, single out their being poor as a symbol of their purity of mind, like a decoration, and take their dependence on others for granted. To be honest, they're no better than the pimps who get their income from women. So, whatever good works they're trying to produce, there can be no excuse for such people."

"Huh! You exaggerate my words too far."

At the hysterical response of Hee-jo, Park Young-soo was stunned. And when Yun-hee looked up at Hee-jo without a word, he merely emptied his glass, not even lifting his eyes. After a pause he continued: "I'll leave it at that, but you must keep in mind that any artist has a right to be alone, as well as a mission to be so. After all, you should not keep your friend living with you just out of compassion."

In early May the paulownia buds began to open one by one, and soon the purple blossoms were in full bloom, spreading their fragrance all over the garden. Yun-hee recalled vividly the time when she surrendered her body to Hee-jo under a paulownia tree and when, discovering the tree on her very first visit to this house, she had felt reassured about living here. It was a tall, straight tree whose soaring foliage was enough to cover all its face. The tree also reminded her of the maidenhood of an elderly lady when, with a spreading dense fragrance, it began to open its blossoms like a cloud.

On the day when the paulownia was in full bloom, Han Min-wha suddenly paid a visit to Yun-hee. She was wearing a thin blouse with a long, roughly woven shawl around her shoulders, holding a bundle of dropwort in her hand. Yun-hee greeted her with a startled look. "Hello, how could you turn up so gracefully?"

"Oh, thanks. I dropped by as I'm curious about you. On the way home after a lecture in Seoul yesterday, I bought some drop-wort from a street peddler. Because I have too much of it, I want to share it with you."

"Thank you for bringing it anyhow. Go and see Mr. Hong. He is now at work in his studio."

As Yun-hee pointed to the studio without hesitation, Han Min-wha turned around, smiling. There was no awkwardness in her manner, even though she had come to meet Hee-jo, and her spontaneity seemed to break down the barrier between Yun-hee and her. Han Min-wha stopped before the studio for a moment to look up at the paulownia tree, and the color of the shawl around her shoulders, so similar to that of the blossoms, suggested that the season of dreams was just around the corner.

While Yun-hee made fresh apple juice to treat her guest, the goose hissed in a low voice, and, looking out, she saw Sae-bul walking across the brook toward home whirling his lunch box. Making six cups of juice with her children in mind, Yun-hee contemplated scolding Sae-bul severely. That morning Yun-hee had prepared a present, asking Sae-bul to take it to his teacher. On Mother's Day when Sae-bul returned from school, he told his mother it happened to be his homeroom teacher's birthday. Telling her students about it, the teacher might have been amused at the coincidence; Yun-hee, after thinking it over for several days, had made up her mind, though late, to send a present to the teacher. So she prepared five pairs of stockings and three handkerchiefs, which she thought would be modest enough to give to a woman teacher in charge of her stubborn child, but nice enough to express her best wishes. Because she wanted Sae-bul to have a better relationship with his teacher in the future, Yun-hee had even enclosed a short letter in the present she prepared.

In spite of his mother's blandishments, Sae-bul had refused to take it to his teacher, making impertinent remarks. In the end, Yun-hee angrily stuffed the present into his schoolbag. But despite having sent him to school with such a struggle, Yun-hee had found the wrapped box thrown away in front of the goose pen when she stepped into the yard after her kitchen work.

"I'm home, Mom."

At the sound of the child's voice, Yun-hee stepped out onto the wooden floor to see Tan-bee coming in first. Then she told the child just taking her schoolbag back to her room to bring two cups of apple juice to the studio. Yun-hee pretended not to notice Sae-bul who, following Tan-bee, entered the room. Remembering the paper ship among the wooden wares in the stationery chest, she took it out. It was a present Sae-bul had made for her on Mother's Day, saying it was the tiniest ship in the world. And so it seemed miraculous that he could make such a ship as tiny as a fingernail.

In the room Yun-hee let Sae-bul sit face-to-face with her, then immediately asked him pointedly, "Did you take the present to your teacher?"

As Sae-bul dropped his eyes downward, Yun-hee said, showing him the tiny ship. "Listen, I like this paper ship you gave me so much and cherish it because it seems to express your true heart. A present to anyone is meant to be an expression of one's mind, so I prepared a present for your teacher to express my gratitude to her. If your teacher punishes you, it means she's concerned about you, you know. Despite that, you threw away the present containing your mother's sincerity in front of the goose pen. Did I ever tell you to take it to the geese?"

Yun-hee lowered her voice as Sae-bul remained silent, and went on.

"At any rate, if you have a pent-up emotion, you must resolve it, because if such an emotion accumulates, your mind will feel constantly troubled. As a mother I want you to grow up to be strong, so you must forget trifles and not be easily bothered by them. Don't you think you should be like that, since you have the name of such a brave chieftain as 'Red Cloud'?"

Yun-hee was slightly amused herself at the reference to "Red Cloud," even though Sae-bul remained silent. As Yun-hee was searching the child's face to know whether he understood her words or not, Han Min-wha stuck her head out through the open window.

"Oh, come in," said Yun-hee. "Why didn't you stay a little longer in the studio talking with Mr. Hong?"

"I've got nothing in particular to talk with him about. I must leave him alone so that I don't disturb his work."

Yun-hee couldn't hold the child anymore as Han Min-wha entered the room, so she spoke to Sae-bul appeasingly: "You think I'm wrong in telling you that? Or do you admit your mistake? Anyway I don't think I'm always right in my thinking, so tell me what you think when you don't agree with me."

"I won't do such a thing. . . ."

With this remark Sae-bul retreated, neither making an excuse nor admitting his mistake. As Yun-hee shook her head, fed up with the child's stubbornness, Han Min-wha asked what the matter was with her. Yun-hee told her the details, even showing the paper ship. Watching it, Han Min-wha said in wonder: "How wonderful! To make a gorgeous ship like this with such a tiny bit of paper that was no better than a scrap. . . ."

"Indeed, children are so wonderful," Yun-hee replied. "If the whole world were merely occupied by grown-ups, we'd be as fed up with it as with a table upon which only greasy food was set. That kind of world must be all unbalanced and grotesque."

"I suppose so. Actually I spare three or four days a month for playing with my young nephews and even cook food for them. Coming to the countryside, the children grow animated. And I, too, become alive because at that time I can go back to life itself."

"Oh, do you like children? Why don't you have a child of your own, then?" Yun-hee suggested to her, but, unlike the way she had been talking, Han Min-wha shook her head resolutely. "No, I don't have any desire to have a child of my own. Even if I were to marry again, I wouldn't have a child, I daresay. Life is so hard to manage, even by myself, that I don't have enough confidence to raise a child.

If there is something successful in my life, it is that I haven't had a child till now."

Han Min-wha spoke coldly and looked out the window. In the yard the children were playing, chasing a yellow butterfly. They are indeed adorable children, Yun-hee thought. On reflection, Yun-hee found that there had been no single occasion in the course of her arduous life since marriage when she had become cynical about her children's existence. It was not for her own sake, but for that of her children, that she once considered getting a divorce from Hee-jo. A good number of women, who depended on the patriarchal system, often used the tired excuse that they couldn't get a divorce because their children would become "children without a father," yet Yun-hee had a different idea.

It is those children who grow up with a couple not on good terms who are liable to lack the capacity for love, and consequently be dependent on others. One of Yun-hee's school friends, who grew up watching her mother frequently beaten by her father, ended up being beaten by her husband after marriage. That Hee-jo had been so filial to his mother might have come from his sympathy for her unhappiness. As for Yun-hee, however, she didn't want her children to grow to be as filial as Hee-jo.

While Yun-hee was lost in her thoughts, Han Min-wha arranged her shawl and got up to leave. Staring at her, Yun-hee said, "Why, that shawl looks good on you."

Hearing this, Han Min-wha gave a sudden, unexpected suggestion. "Do you like this kind of thing? I'd be glad to make one for you."

"Not at all. I don't need such a thing."

"It's not necessarily used only in the winter," asserted Han Min-wha. "Rather, it gives an effect like music. I imagine that whenever they went on an outing, many women long ago must have slipped on a shawl as if changing the air."

"You're right. It gives an effect like music."

As Yun-hee mollified her refusal, Han Min-wha asked her what color she liked. Yun-hee replied: "On the ceiling of the Buddhist temple I often see a jade-green that seems somewhat faded. And I like that color most from long ago."

"You're very peculiar to like such a color."

"Whenever I go to the temple, I look carefully at the ceiling. Staring at it for a moment arouses a feeling in me as if I'm in the world of the dead."

Then, all of a sudden, Yun-hee noticed the grayish jade-green stone in the square dish and showed it to Han Min-wha, saying, "This looks like a sandy plain, doesn't it?"

"I suppose so. Where did you pick it up?" asked Han Min-wha.

"At the Kum River."

It was Hee-jo who had picked it up, but Yun-hee said no more. Then Han Min-wha promised to make a shawl for Yun-hee, asking her to drop by at Eunti village a week later. And she left quietly, begging Yun-hee not to disturb Hee-jo. He was probably occupied with putting the precious wares into the kiln, as if putting goose eggs into an incubator. Tomorrow he'd put the kiln to use for the first time this year, and Yun-hee was so agitated she couldn't concentrate on anything. In the meantime she stuck the whole bunch of dropwort that Han Min-wha had brought into a *punch'ong* vase. A wildflower more exuberant than ordinary flowers, it gave a fresh air suited to the season. When Hee-jo came into the living room after closing the kiln and checking the burner, he was delighted to see the dropwort in the vase.

Early the next morning, when Yun-hee looked up at the sky through the paulownia blossoms after feeding the geese, a cloud was hanging in the boughs of the tree—as if birds had scattered their feathers. The sky was clear but, with a balmy wind beginning early in the morning, it was likely to get hot. Getting up in the morning, Hee-jo first checked the oil tank and started the kiln at seven-thirty. As the fan motor and the burner started simultaneously, the whole area around the house seemed like a small factory. The sound of the burner throwing its flame into the kiln sounded so lively, even from outside, that Yun-hee came near to enjoy it.

This morning she washed out the hemp cloth, which she had soaked in water overnight, and hung it out. After it had dried slowly for two hours, she began to fold the hemp cloth, and pressed it wrapped in poplin. Soon Wan-kyu came to her and asked for a book out of boredom, since he must keep watching the kiln all day long while it was in operation. Curious, Yun-hee asked him how the burner was working.

"On the left side of the burner," replied Wan-kyu, "a little oil is dripping. Since we checked it before setting the burner in operation, we don't mind it. I suppose it is nothing particular."

The expected useful life of the burner, Yun-hee had heard, was only three years, and so this old kiln was frequently out of order. The groundhog kiln fueled with brushwood had its own problems, both in the high cost of wood and in the high cost of hiring people to run it; naturally, many potters had turned to the modern convenience of using a gasoline kiln. The gasoline kiln Hee-jo used was a conventional type that had been in use since the time of Japanese rule. As an old one, it would produce irregular results, which, in turn, made Hee-jo feel more attached to it. As a result, the burner would suddenly stop and the electricity would also fail often. But Hee-jo had learned to keep the damper open when the electric heat control was set for the initial firing.

With the damper open, the outside air seeped into the kiln and prevented the heat inside from leaking through the pipe. During the fifty minutes when the electricity was off, the fire spread evenly into the kiln, steaming the wares thoroughly. Since the result of this method proved so satisfying, when doing the second firing Hee-jo made it a habit to turn off the burner to sustain the heat.

Yun-hee was worried that both sides of the bag wall looked unchanged even after seven hours of firing. But all the wares except those in the bottom left part were out of the soot, and soon the initial firing was finished in thirteen hours. That day Yun-hee pressed the hemp cloth from time to time and put it into the attic about the time the kiln was turned off. And the next day she sewed the four pieces of cloth together with fine stitches on the edges. In preparing a summer quilt for her children, she made a point of sewing them by hand, instead of using the sewing machine. In fact, the whole family had become so aware of the operation of the kiln that when the burner stopped the sudden stillness seemed unreal to them.

While Yun-hee finished the quilt, Hee-jo did the glazing. As long as the firing was done slowly, there was no great chance of failure, so in the kiln record book Hee-jo had written the words "extremely good," suggesting that the result of the current firing was successful. A few wares placed on the very bottom of the left side were completely stained with soot, but not even a single piece of a teapot, much less the large pieces, turned out useless. Hee-jo picked up a piece of a dish and broke it spiritedly so that he could use it for the test-piece in the second firing. That act, however, was a kind of ritual against a sense of self-satisfaction coming early.

More than twenty large pieces along with a hundred or so living wares moved like a small army, preparing to pass through another firing. It was not until late the next afternoon that the work of putting wares into the kiln was finished. Because the intensity of firing was somewhat different in each corner of the kiln, it was necessary to put the wares into the kiln carefully to make the heat spread evenly all through the kiln. In the bottom and central parts of the kiln were placed the living wares such as tea pots and earthen wares; in the upper parts, where the heat concentrated, were placed large pieces. But there was still enough space left to hold two small jars.

So Hee-jo, pondering, entered his studio and returned with a big bowl that he had sketched out while in the hospital and that he'd made soon after getting out of the hospital. Though he had made slip for the bowl, he hadn't taken it for the initial firing because of its size. Put into the kiln, the bowl seemed to fill the entire remaining space, and Hee-jo, satisfied, asked Wan-kyu to put the glaze on it.

"Will it be all right, since it wasn't in the initial firing?" Wan-kyu asked, cocking his head. But Hee-jo answered, convinced. "That's okay. I've already tried some pieces without the initial firing because there was once some space left. And it turned out unexpectedly satisfying. At the time, though the pieces were half-fired, the result was beyond comparison with normal firing using the same slip."

This incident, Yun-hee remembered, had happened one day the previous spring, when less than half of the works he tried were successful. At the time, Hee-jo had found a jar among the rest, which seemed, though half-fired, to have such a sophisticated feeling that he had cherished it for a long time before one of his friends bought it.

With Hee-jo's decision, the bowl was placed in the empty space and the next morning the second firing was done with the door of the kiln closed. As was usual before the final firing, he offered a sacrifice to spirits before a table set with a dried pollack and *soju*. All that humans could do by their own efforts was finished at this stage. Before, Hee-jo had customarily set the table for his offering with pork and *makkoli*. But then Monk Hyeo suggested he set the table with a purer food since the guardian spirits of the house might not like such greasy food, so Hee-jo changed the kind of food for the offering. It seemed quite natural to prepare clear food for an offering when he was going to send the products of a struggle with himself into the last tunnel of their life.

Once the sound of the burner started, Yun-hee relaxed and began her housework. She prepared dried slices of radish preserved in soy sauce with some fresh garlic she had got from Jae-chull's mother yesterday, and arranged the thick bowl of peony blossom so its root could grow well. Yun-hee planned to take Tan-bee to Seoul this Saturday after the second firing was done, so that she could drop by her parents' home as well as get Tan-bee an eye examination at an ophthalmologist's office. A few days before, Tan-bee had complained that she couldn't see the characters on the blackboard at school clearly. Thinking it over, Yun-hee decided that since Tan-bee was the only one in the family who was near-sighted, the child must simply have read too much.

While pickling cabbages, and reflecting on what she was going to do in Seoul, Yun-hee heard an ominous bursting noise from the direction of the studio. Though not loud, it sounded something like an explosion. Hastily finishing the cabbages and putting them into the pot, Yun-hee listened to the sound, feeling that the burner had stopped operating momentarily as the firing was interrupted. Out of curiosity, she stepped into the yard after washing her hands and saw two people walking impatiently about behind the open door of the studio. So she suspected there must be something wrong.

While Yun-hee stood motionless and watched the studio, Wan-kyu emerged with a look of surprise. He approached Yun-hee without a word and stopped before her.

"It seems the piece without an initial firing exploded inside the kiln," he said.

"What? You mean the bowl you mentioned a minute ago?"

As Yun-hee stood helplessly, Wan-kyu turned toward the house, murmuring, "Was the firing excessive?"

It had happened only three hours after the firing began. While eating lunch, Hee-jo deliberately tried to conceal his expression and acted as if nothing had happened but, overcome by his troubled mind, he went out instantly. Like any other time when he drank too much, he returned late at night and collapsed into a drunken sleep, but after eating a hangover-relieving soup the next morning he took to drinking again. Wan-kyu, at a loss, wandered about the yard, pulling weeds and sweeping. For her part, Yun-hee was impatient and her mind wandered from her work. Actually the kiln had been used for nearly six months—which was itself remarkable. In proportion to his expectations about the work, Hee-jo must have felt self-pity now that the result was totally different.

Around the time the initial firing had started, the faint scent of the paulownia blossoms had wafted about the yard, but by now the blossoms withered. With the sound of the burner stopped suddenly, the stillness weighed on Yun-hee's mind. In the afternoon of the day after the second firing stopped, Hee-jo asked Wan-kyu to open the door of the kiln, since he was himself afraid to see the broken wares. Previously, no one in the family would come around the kiln when the door of the kiln was opened, because they all felt extreme anxiety about the result. It was only after Hee-jo would break badly made wares into pieces that other people got to see the results. Sometimes Yun-hee found some wares too precious to be thrown away and would try to stop Hee-jo from breaking them. But on such occasions he always lost his temper.

While Wan-kyu was taking pots out of the kiln, Hee-jo confined himself to the studio where the potter's wheel was. Her curiosity aroused, Yun-hee wandered around the studio, but there was no response from inside. As she thought nearly an hour had passed, Hee-jo came out of the studio, and watching his expression, Yun-hee judged all had come to nothing. But it was not until Yun-hee stepped into the studio that she saw Wan-kyu looking into the kiln and sighing deeply.

The wares on the outer side in the kiln, Yun-hee found, had already been put together on the floor, while the wares on the inner side filled the heating space completely. After no more than three hours of firing, all the wares had got sooted; most of the large pieces were broken and their fragments scattered, with the glaze fallen away. Actually the fragments had spread in all directions until they spoiled even the wares in the bottom of the kiln. In spite of how small the explosion had been, however, the whole kiln looked like a ruin, with broken pieces looking like wounded spirits.

When Wan-kyu brought the still unfired wares into the yard in front of the studio, Hee-jo arrived with several bottles of *soju* in his hands. The wine he had already drunk this morning didn't seem to have improved his spirits, so he bought more wine. With a shrewd expression in his eyes, he looked at the fragmented pieces, which were not blessed with being born into a final product, and dropped to the ground. Taking a folding knife out of his pocket and opening a bottle with it, he poured wine into a tea pot scratched by the fragments and drank it straight out. Then he picked up a jar with a long neck and smashed it against the dividing fence. That unfinished jar clanked as it was mercilessly broken into pieces, and, after another drink, Hee-jo picked up a cylindrical piece and threw it against the dividing fence again. Each time he emptied his glass, he crushed the innocent wares one by one, repeating the process as if giving up his dreams.

It was a kind of self-degradation, Yun-hee felt. A hatred of himself for having happened to ruin his work in a moment of distraction—as if it were a sand castle. In fact, he had made wares with all his efforts in pursuit of a faint gleam like a spider's web. Yun-hee shuddered half in terror at hearing the wares break against the dividing fence. Hadn't Hee-jo, in search of his dream, regarded Yun-hee and other family members as a kind of sacrifice, like the failed fragmented wares? He seemed to have pursued a light through which he could achieve his goal and, in the process, to have considered the suffering of his family an inevitable consequence.

5

A Passing Storm

The house had been ghostly still for several days, as if swept by a typhoon. Making some excuse, Wan-kyu had fled to Seoul a few days before like a fugitive, and Hee-jo had either fallen asleep each afternoon in the backyard still strewn with the broken pieces of pots, or played the *changgi* game alone. He hadn't even spoken to his children of his thoughts, so there was an air of depressing silence around the house.

After having idled away nearly three days, Hee-jo went out one morning and came back at dusk, carrying two thick pine boards on his shoulders and a plank in one hand. As Yun-hee asked about it, he merely replied: "I happened to pass by the sawmill and bought them. The timber merchant said someone had ordered them to make a coffin but he didn't turn up." So Yun-hee asked no more, wondering why, of all woods, he'd bought boards intended for a coffin. All she could suspect was that he seemed about to do something with the wood, as he couldn't concentrate on his work.

The next day Hee-jo took out a saw and other tools and spent the whole day cutting and planing. It seemed he had borrowed a plane from the owner of the peppery-stew restaurant, who was a carpenter before. In three days Hee-jo finished cutting the small piece of oak with which he worked first, and turned it into a smart-looking mallet. At first Yun-hee thought of it as a tool for pottery; being so small and carved so elaborately, it didn't seem too rough to be used.

As the end of May approached, it got warmer and warmer. The papers had already predicted a long, sultry summer, and the children would return home from school stained with sweat. Yun-hee had planned to go to Seoul on the weekend of the second firing if it was successful, but went instead to Han Min-wha's house, remembering she had asked her to drop by in a week. Moreover, Yun-hee herself needed the company of a friend outside her family.

As it was time for the barley to ripen, the whole field was covered with green waves. The barley swaying above the Mother Earth—its grain covered by a sharp yet delicate crust seeming to let the sunshine and wind caress it—looked like a wild maiden. Yun-hee had learned to like the barley field as soon as she had moved to this countryside, since it gave her a feeling of a ripe, devoted and strong, if not splendid, life. She heard there were even artists who painted only barley fields; although she couldn't tell whether or not they painted them for their beauty of form, the wide, green barley field stretching ahead of her revived a healthy emotion in her.

From somewhere a cuckoo's song was likely to be heard, but Yun-hee could only hear the noise of a cultivator on a farm in the distance. Ho-ja's mother, who had been complaining of the drastic fall in the price of garlic, was sowing sesame seeds in the field. Soon the ripe barley plants would droop their heads like a defeated army, Yun-hee imagined. She hoped the barley would not ripen, so that it would always remain green—a wish that couldn't be justified to the farmer. A year seemed a long time as Yun-hee thought she would have to wait for next spring to see a green barley field again.

Han Min-wha was weaving in the living room with the window open, since it was a little hot. That living room, barely worthy of its name, was also used as a dining room, and had a cement floor. A piece of Han Min-wha's weaving was hanging beside the cup-board, and the loom stood beside a rice box. The loom was lined up with a rice pot and the cupboard with its hanging works of art, and the bamboo basket filled with weaving thread was on the table with a spoon case, so it was hard to distinguish her studio from her kitchen.

Han Min-wha was so deeply involved in her weaving that she didn't even notice Yun-hee watching her through the window. Shifting the treadles with her feet, she passed the shuttle between the spread warps and struck the weft into place with the beater. Throwing the shuttle alternately with each hand, she wove a tex-tured pattern. The warp was a mustard-colored thread dyed with onion skins, and the weft unwinding from the shuttle was wine colored. She seemed to have been working for a long time, since the front beam of the loom was thick with weaving, in which the two colors fit unexpectedly well. Sensing someone approaching as she was about to strike the beater, Han Min-wha turned around.

"Hi, I'm just standing here because I'm afraid to disturb you," Yun-hee said.

"Oh, come on in. I didn't notice you since you were standing there like a shadow."

As Yun-hee stepped onto the studio, Han Min-wha put a chair beside the loom for her. And Yun-hee said, "I've so enjoyed looking at the barley field on my way here. It's getting warmer."

"It'll be for the time being," replied Han Min-wha. "Up until last month I didn't make much progress in my work due to spring fever. That's why I began working only recently. For the last two days I've gone to bed with the sound of a church bell at dawn."

Looking carefully at the texture of the cloth on the loom, Yun-hee commented that the mixture of colors seemed to arouse a simple yet subtle feeling. At this remark Han Min-wha answered that she had planned to title it *A Poem by the Blind*. She then went on:

"Last year I taught weaving at a rehabilitation center for the blind run by a group of nuns. And what was peculiar to me about the weaving class was that all the students had become blind after sudden accidents—not at birth. Anyhow, when they were asking the nuns for a color they remembered, the nuns dyed the thread for them, but the blind hardly ever chose pale colors except strong ones. Since they'd had no experience in weaving, they usually chose red for the warp and blue for the weft. It seemed to me that they could feel the difference in thread dyed red with their fingertips because the dyeing ingredient was a little different from others. In any event they managed to weave, recalling color in the dark and mixing separate colors. I suppose those who were not interested in color might have no fun in this sort of work because they would simply repeat the mechanical function. For the blind, however, the color became a poem as well as a light."

Hearing Han Min-wha talk, Yun-hee came to understand what the mixture of colors meant. Aspiring to the memory of colors, those blind weavers must have worked in loneliness a pattern of memory in violet. "So, only the blind who have once known color are able to weave," replied Yun-hee. "I realize the amazing power of memory because, in a sense, we live only by means of memory itself."

"That's true. And I believe that what's called poetry surely comes from suffering and loneliness—a world of darkness we cannot see. The piece of work over there was woven when I was enduring tremendous suffering, so I like it very much."

With this remark Han Min-wha indicated with her eyes a frame above the kitchen table, which was four times the size of a postcard. It was made by putting together many textures woven as wide as a belt. With the warps hanging, wefts of such strong colors as deep purple, red, and green were wound upon them so that the color itself became a composition. In short, it looked like a painting made out of thread.

"That one is a hand-made work," explained Han Min-wha. "When I wove it, I hung the warp on a nail driven into a pillar. At the time I was at the height of my inner struggle, so I would awake even at midnight and carve the pillar of the house with a knife. I felt I would surely die. As I did nothing but weave to overcome myself, I felt as if my blood streamed even in the thread. Just so, the tapestry works in my exhibition last spring were all woven in such a way. That piece over there I named myself and hoped it wouldn't be sold. Fortunately it wasn't."

"What is its title, then?" asked Yun-hee.

"*A Martyr.* I believe martyrdom is not far away since our everyday life itself is a kind of martyrdom. In other words, to live is a martyrdom."

Yun-hee stopped drinking her tea and looked at Han Min-wha. Even if she didn't understand the suffering of creation, Yun-hee, too, had led her life as if suppressing an impulse to carve the pillar of her house, and spent each day overcoming herself. Wasn't such a life a martyrdom?

Feeling close to Han Min-wha for the first time, Yun-hee said. "Though I don't expect you to use strong colors, you actually use them, Ms. Han. I find that the colors you're using are different from other strong colors. Not flamboyant, they look as if springing out of darkness."

"You think so? Anyhow, a color is an expression of one's mind. I heard that as many as twelve thousand colors have been classified up to now, and so people can express their own mind in a different color."

As if suddenly called to mind, Han Min-wha got up and left the room, and presently returned with something wrapped in a light blue cloth. It was a shawl with a mountain-like pattern. She spread it with both hands and put it on Yun-hee's shoulders. "Look, it becomes you very well. I thought a single color would make it too monotonous, so I wove it by mixing jade-green and light blue. Its water-like color looks like a fine-textured ramie cloth."

The cotton thread made the scarf feel soft, while the mystical color gave the impression of moss in water. The shawl captured Yun-hee's attention at once. Although it was a burden to take a shawl made by Han Min-wha herself, Yun-hee, nevertheless, didn't hesitate to show her delight.

"Oh, my! I haven't had something like this for many years. Because there is no need to go out, I've never sought luxury. But, to tell the truth, I'm a woman who likes something like this better than anyone else."

"I'm glad you like it. In spite of its plain-looking color, it gives a polished air. I think that in many respects Mr. Hong has a good wife."

"Please don't say such a thing to him. He may be angry to hear it."

"Why? He may not."

Han Min-wha laughed and then went out to bring in some pine tea that she had made a few days ago. Feeling the aroma of pine resin spreading in her mouth, Yun-hee lowered her head idly, only to find a mallet under the loom. And she looked at it closely since it seemed familiar to her, then realized it was the oak mallet Hee-jo had made a few days before. Had he then gone out in the morning the day before yesterday to give Han Min-wha this mallet? Yun-hee spoke instinctively. "Mr. Hong has been here, right?"

"Yes, I asked him to do something for me."

Pausing in drinking her pine tea, Han Min-wha raised her head. After a while Yun-hee opened, "As you're living alone, don't hesitate to ask him to do anything hard. Actually Mr. Hong likes you, Ms. Han."

"Really? But I think I have a good friend. And I hope you'll understand our friendship. I know many people consider marriage possession of each other, so they're inclined to bind the other party in the name of the institution—without knowing that it's nothing more than a preoccupation. But since each human has limitations, even a couple or lovers can't communicate completely with each other. Besides, the human soul is by nature destined to be free. Just as we open windows to change the air, so those who need other souls are seeking people with whom they can communicate to fill their life. In any event, even if I had a husband, I might need a male friend, because he might give me a wider view of the world."

Leaning against the wall, Han Min-wha blinked her eyes like a wild animal. Yun-hee thought this was the first time the woman had shown such an attitude. Since Han Min-wha had spoken her thoughts resolutely, Yun-hee answered frankly:

"You've made a good point, Ms. Han. In fact, I've never regarded my husband as my possession till now—likewise I can't be his. That's true at least in my soul. In a Picasso painting, there's a man whose profile and front face are captured in the same perspective, and I think this explains a marriage relationship. We're often deceived into thinking we possess a man, but all we know in this instance is one side of his face. From the beginning I acknowledged the world of my husband, and I also understand he has a deep sense of intimacy for a person like you who leads a life similar to his. Because you and I are friends, Ms. Han, all I want from him is to speak candidly whatever is on his mind. Anyway, I don't know if I've got to let him know our talk like this."

"I think it's not like hiding something," returned Han Min-wha quietly, "since there are many inexplicable, if not secret, things in life. As I admire a person like you, Mrs. Hong, who always speaks out candidly, I think we can be good friends to each other. After all, to have someone to talk with is to enrich our life."

Could there be so strong a person in the world as to think he needs no friend at all? Yun-hee mused. If there existed such a person, he must be either cold-blooded or very religious. Even Hee-jo, who had decided without hesitation to live in the countryside in the belief that an artist ought to be lonely, would look blindly at the fields, feeling embarrassed at the sense of being cut off from the outside world. Not a hermit in seclusion, he often felt dissatisfied with the inherent limitations of having only an interior dialogue.

It was rather Yun-hee herself who had enjoyed loneliness. Her father, who had married off six of his daughters, stressed family ties so much that he used to bring together all of his grown-up children with their spouses, even on a grandchild's birthday, and only Yun-hee could be excused, because she lived in the countryside. Free from her parents' family and isolated from her friends, Yun-hee had had nothing to do but spend her time reading books. So when she got angry, she would go out to the stream to calm herself down. Had she lived alone like Han Min-wha, Yun-hee could not have found relief in such a way.

Into her mind came suddenly the memory of living alone as a country school teacher before her marriage. She remembered two particular scenes that embodied the life of a young woman living alone. One of them was when she turned on the radio to listen to part of a serial drama, whose story she no longer remembered. At the moment, overcome by a reasonless sorrow, Yun-hee burst into tears. And she, deeply lost in her sorrow, ended up burning the herbal medicine sent to her by her mother.

The other was when she had visited the school keeper in the same village one night in order to ask for something. When she got there a little past eight o'clock, Yun-hee had to wait for him a while in the next room, since he was eating dinner. It was a small room for only two persons to sleep in, with only a chest of drawers and its broken mirror occupying the whole space. Some bundles of shabby clothes were hanging on the wall; a frequently patched quilt was spread carelessly on the floor. A small bag that seemed to contain soybean malt was in a corner of the room, spreading a sickening smell.

Was it the smell of the soybean malt that made so shabby a room look lively and warm-hearted? Yun-hee tried to remember again. Compared with it, her room with plain white wallpaper seemed a lifeless thing; without even a tiny bit of dust, her clean room did not show a trace of living. On returning home that night, Yun-hee felt a strong impulse to tear off the white wallpaper as if she were suddenly suffocated by her inanimate room. All she wanted at the moment was to go out, and she missed her mother more than any other time. She spent all night crouching like a cockscomb, resolving in the middle of the curfew siren that she would go to Seoul at daybreak. However, the dark, deserted street at dawn gave her another kind of despair. Four years before Yun-hee happened to read a short poem titled *Longing,* which reminded her of that day.

Wandering in the deserted street at dawn,
What I long for is closed like a door.

❦

Now the acacia flowers were in full bloom along the lane overlooking the stream, and Yun-hee's children picked the bell-like young flowers on their way to and from school to bring them to their mother. Around the time when the fragrance was fading along with the flowers, Yi Sung-ju appeared with Ji-woon. She looked like a young girl in a white T-shirt and a skirt with a white teardrop pattern. Moreover, her short glossy hair made her look jaunty, but Yun-hee missed the air Ji-woon used to have with her cool, long hair.

Hee-jo, who had recovered his spirits to some extent, greeted Yi Sung-ju heartily. Informed of their previous visit, he led them to the bamboo bed and set himself a drinking table. The paulownia flowers had withered, with only the leaves beginning to come out. Bringing in a side dish, Yun-hee spoke regretfully, "You should have come when the paulownia flowers were in full bloom. Drinking under the trees would have given any beverage a better taste."

"Never mind," replied Yi Sung-ju. "My spirit gets revived in this place. I think this is what life should be."

"You're speaking just like a foreigner. I know you're living just around the corner," Yun-hee returned.

"I feel I'm destined to wander about, so I spend more time wandering than staying home. Though I live in the countryside, I've never been touched by a beautiful landscape. Have you ever met a poet like me with no poetic sentiment? I'm not so much a poet as a vagabond."

"What? Are you already tired of your mission as a revolutionary? Ji-woon, you'd better not hang around with him."

As Yun-hee clicked her tongue, Yi Sung-ju ventured, "Actually I came here to get something. I built a humble house at the outskirts of town for the workers' evening school, so I need some furnishings. It was Ji-woon who thought of your pots, Mr. Hong."

"We might readily use some cheap cups," added Ji-woon, "but after I saw your pots here I had a strong desire for them. I expect you to donate a dozen pots or so—whether poorly made or not, they'll be indispensable to us. If you think my demand is too much, you may say so."

"I've never given others even a small cup if it's poorly made. I must give you well made cups."

Since Hee-jo consented willingly, Ji-woon rejoiced. Then Yi Sung-ju said, looking at a *punch'ong* wine cup he just emptied: "To tell the truth, I believe you must make a lot of *punch'ong* wares and distribute them to the public, Mr. Hong. Of course, you must lower their price too. I know there are some people who, holding a mere stone in their hand, claim they've got a work of art, and even display it in an art exhibition. But I think the pottery that is so closely related to our national sentiment should be humbly assimilated to the need of a common folk, instead of being arrogantly called a work of art or something. After all, vessels or vases are no more than daily necessities."

While listening, Hee-jo quietly turned his cup around with his eyes cast down. In reality, it was not Yi Sung-ju alone who didn't regard pottery as a work of art in the belief that pottery was mere living ware. In the presence of such people Hee-jo would feel lonely as a pottery artist. Yun-hee, who had been observing how the greenwares turned into a pot, felt as frustrated as Hee-jo.

Discontented, Hee-jo stated: "Let me first ask you then. For instance, how can you distinguish what's literary from what's not? To my knowledge, it's a matter of spirit, because writing permeated with a spirit becomes a literary work. So, whether a pot can be art or not might be explained in the same way. Though the pottery had been used as living ware for a long period of time, the desire for something more beautiful led to the creation of Koryo celadons. Likewise, not all paintings on a wall can be works of art. An identification picture isn't a work of art, but if a picture is taken by a photographer with spirit, it can be artistic. It's a pity, I think, that there're so many people who instantly proclaim themselves as pottery artists by holding an exhibition of pots made with mere mechanical skill. There's no expert in this regard who has a discriminating sense of art."

As Hee-jo finished his words, Yi Sung-ju resumed: "I once met a senior architect who said flatly he was nothing more than a maid for capitalists. The self-scorn of the master shocked me. Since his words seemed to imply a facet of artistry in a capitalistic society, it aroused in me many thoughts. Don't you have any inner conflict, Mr. Hong, because only rich people can buy your work? I think literature at least is fair in this regard, since no one can possess language itself."

"It's true that only a limited class can possess not only a pot but also a work of art," Hee-jo answered. "No one can deny the conflict occurring in the trading process, but I don't see it merely as a negative class conflict. You must know that, from the beginning, art has been something dedicated to kings or nobles, and it's true in all ages and countries. Conversely speaking, it's owing to such sponsors that art could develop. For instance, King Ui-jong of the Koryo period is known to have led a fabulous life—loving poetry and seeking mundane pleasures. Though he ended up being deposed by the military protest of Chung Jung-boo, it was during his reign that the great Koryo celadons reached their peak. As is widely known, King Ui-jong had the luxury to build a new palace and completely cover the newly built Yangi Pavilion with celadon tiles. In the kilns where the celadon tiles had been made in those days were found many fragments of celadon tiles used for interior and exterior decorations. And among them were some inlaid celadons that suggest the luxurious life of the court. I remember that some folk historian had deplored the Koryo celadons in his book, asserting that their line evokes the intestines of the devastated common folk, while its jade green symbolizes the doomed fate of the dynasty. That historian even asked if we ever knew this fact hidden in the Koryo celadons, blaming our ignorance of a historical implication. Ultimately he showed his strong antipathy toward the Koryo celadons, suggesting we bury them deep in the ground rather than put them on the table. No matter how great his common folk philosophy is, it's something of an iron wall, I must say. Despite his argument, then, how can you explain the fact that the Koryo celadons were in those days regarded as the best even in China, representing our country?"

Hee-jo then stressed the idea of pottery as an embodiment of national imagination, saying it can't be a mere visible object of art. He went on to explain that things become abstract as they approach something absolute. Pottery, he added, resembles music in the sense that it begins in an abstract form and ends up being formulated into a concrete state. Yi Sung-ju, however, didn't seem to understand this explanation easily, and remained silent.

Indifferent to Yi Sung-ju, Hee-jo spoke. "Then the most important thing in pottery is the form itself. It's a kind of an image, so whenever I hit upon a good image I make a sketch even on the street. After it takes a concrete form in potter's clay and white slip, it makes a good combination with the two heterogeneous materials harmoniously yoked together."

"I understand pottery is a work of art in the abstract form," replied Yi Sung-ju. "But what in the world can modern pottery bring us? I know some people are trying to revive the tradition of our pottery in the belief that the traditional spirit has ceased to exist. But their effort, I think, will turn out to be nothing but an imitation unless accompanied by the spirit of our time."

"You're always concerned with the spirit in art," said Hee-jo to Yi Sung-ju. "As a matter of fact, you can find in pottery a spirit of our time—I mean a commercial spirit! In this regard you'd better remember the historical background. Since many potters today are trying to make our pots appeal to the taste of the Japanese, they have no choice but to make something like a Japanese pot. With the Hideyoshi invasion of Korea in 1592, the Japanese brought the Choson clay to their land and even attempted to make pottery in our country since they found our celadons so exquisite. Consequently they built their kiln and called it *Obonso*. But the pots made there were different from ours because, though looking similar, each type had a different touch. In contrast to this, the pots made by Koreans under a Japanese director during the Japanese rule were to have a completely Japanese style because there was no choice for Korean potters then. Nevertheless, we could tell the Japanese pottery from ours even until the middle of the seventies. During the past two or three years, however, our modern pottery has come to resemble that made by the Japanese in the old days. If there is something distinguishable, it's only that ours is rougher in technique. As a pottery artist, I'm really ashamed of this. Actually it's for this reason that I've regarded it as my duty to make and distribute to the public living wares that can be used on the meal table. Since even our living wares become more and more Japanized, I try to restore the wares containing the old innocent spirit of Koreans."

When Hee-jo's long statements were over, Yi Sung-ju remarked at once: "Indeed, a pottery artist like you, Mr. Hong, has all the more reason to mass-produce pots so that people can buy them without minding the price."

"Well, it's just in order to distribute as many pots as possible that I've attempted the vessels and other living wares. People can enjoy using the vessels instead of only keeping a work of art. As a matter of fact, the taste of wine is good in a *punch'ong* cup, you know. By the way, do you really think that life is fair enough to give even a tiny piece of ware to everyone equally? Never so! I dare say there's no utopia like that in this world. Life is never meant to be fair under any circumstances."

Ji-woon, listening silently to the conversation between the two men, stood up. Seeing her going out to the front yard, Yun-hee also got up and entered the kitchen. Because she'd put a bucket of laundry on the briquet fire before the visitors came, the water was boiling already. Rinsing the clothes and going into the yard to hang them out, Yun-hee found Ji-woon resting under the paulownia tree, looking vacantly toward the field. Approaching, Yun-hee saw a look of anxiety spread over her face.

"It's getting warm," said Yun-hee. "Why are you sitting in such a place without even a sunshade? You look a little pale in your short hair."

"I barely slept last night because of the mass at dawn. Now I feel more serene than any other time."

"It seems my prayer in the clear early morning can reach the sphere of God," said Yun-hee. "Sometimes I feel like going to a Buddhist temple so I can listen to the early morning ceremony."

"If you used to believe in God, how did you turn into an unbeliever? I know people have their own conflict and crisis. Tell me your story."

So Yun-hee revealed a secret that she hadn't told anybody. It was after her marriage that she had started to go to a cathedral. "Come to think of it, my married life was very hard to endure. I felt then that my whole being would fall down unless I depended on something omniscient. At the time I merely asked God to order me to do this or that. After I was baptized, I devoted myself to God for nearly three years as it gave me a great deal of ecstacy to sacrifice myself to Him. Then one day, during a mass, I suddenly felt the word 'resurrection' bouncing against my consciousness like a ball. Soon I doubted the resurrection itself. Of course the resurrection is not a thing to reason about because it is a basis of religion. But since I felt rejected in my consciousness, with the very basis of my belief shaken, I became skeptical about the almighty God and eventually stopped going to the cathedral."

"The life of Jesus Christ," replied Ji-woon, "shows that he achieved resurrection through death. Because of the resurrection, I believe his existence is eternal and free of any mortal restrictions. Naturally the resurrection shows another way to the light for our mortals who are ruthlessly driven to the cliff of death. I think our life should be guided by a principle of resurrection. In truth, if we believed in the resurrection, we'd be deprived of the right to despair. That's a little annoying."

"If so, have you never been driven to despair?" asked Yun-hee.

Shaking her short-haired head, Ji-woon answered. "To understand something with our head is one thing, and to accept it with our heart is another. So I've often fallen into a deep despair."

"As I come to think of it now," said Yun-hee, "my life must have been so hard that I regarded the resurrection as an uncertain hope. Perhaps I'm either a positivist or a nihilist."

"Because I believe in the resurrection, I've kept one lasting desire even in times of despair. Just as the Eternal Father took his son's life, so he may claim our life when we exhaust our time on earth. That belief gives me strong relief."

The leaves in the near mountains had already turned green before Yun-hee noticed. Looking at them, she wondered if life was such a burden to everyone. After a pause she said:

"After I moved here I learned the cycle of nature to replace the resurrection. But it's different from what we call metempsychosis. Everything in nature generates itself and goes back to the Mother Earth after it sacrifices itself completely—like a fertile sheaf of rice. I think this process will be repeated incessantly as long as the earth exists. No matter how great people may become, they're subject to this law of nature, and someday I myself will return to the earth, like the wind or the rain. If there's anything fair in life, it's just the existence of the cycle, I think."

☙

Like the waxing of the moon, the green barley plants in the field, which had seemed to pierce the wind, turned golden now and fell to the earth. In the harvested field farmers began to transplant rice seedlings, and Hee-jo also resumed a journey with the clay. Out of a pine board he made a long table and engraved an old poem of Chusa on it, just as he would paint on a pot.

Sitting serenely in a pavilion and drinking a half cup
of tea,
Its fragrance touches me as if for the first time.
With the moment of divine height the stream flows
And the flower blooms.

When could the moment of divine height come into a life immersed in habit and daily routine? Yun-hee wondered. How then would our life be transformed? Though she had no idea of what the divine moment would be like, Yun-hee seemed to glimpse a dim light, waiting vaguely for such a moment to come someday like the blooming of a flower.

The next day Wan-kyu returned and began working with the

clay. During the first half year he had lived in Yun-hee's house, Wan-kyu was not even allowed to touch the clay in the studio. Then he worked with the potter's wheel to make small tea cups and other dishes, and it was nearly a year before he was allowed to make his own work of art. On the first day Wan-kyu started the potter's wheel, Hee-jo, looking at the wares spread on the floor, pointed out the rim of a cup. As it is a sensitive spot equivalent to the lip of a person, usually the rim of the ware gives evidence of the handling of the potter's wheel in making the shape. The shape Wan-kyu had made in handling the potter's wheel was similar to Hee-jo's, but its rim was not so keen.

Observing it, Hee-jo spoke. "Whenever I look at works made by a technical potter, I find that the rims look all the same—no matter how different the shape is. While looking at the rim, I get to know the artistic sense of the person who makes the ware. Depending on the rim, therefore, each work gives a different feeling."

Watching Wan-kyu grind the rim at the foot of a piece after the clay had partially dried, Hee-jo pointed out again: "The foot rim is also an important part. Depending on the thickness of the foot rim, each piece gives a different feeling—just as we have no inclination for a beautiful woman with ugly feet."

Later, over lunch, Wan-kyu looked hard at Hee-jo's works in the living room and asked about them: "Whenever I see your brush strokes across the surface of the pot, I find they're all slanted upward. But isn't it common to stroke sideways sometimes?"

"That's true. People long ago made it a rule to stroke horizontally. But I usually stroke across the surface of the ware to create variety, then the work looks animated. You can develop such a skill if you think a little differently in your work."

There are so many interesting things to observe in the world of artisans, Yun-hee felt. What kind of significance does even a tiny part of the foot rim of the pot have in the mighty stream of history? Though it seemed insignificant to create a small piece of a rim or stroke a brush over the surface of a pot, that process could result in a single jar that is a microcosm, like a brook merging into a river. As Yun-hee believed, the truth lies not so much on its surface as in the soul inherent in it. So how many fragmented parts of truth would be simply wasted away while people didn't open their minds to each other?

Five days after Yi Sung-ju had left, his wife made an abrupt visit to Yun-hee's house. It was her first visit since she had asked Yun-hee to watch her house and brought, in return, a cake around the end of last year, when she had supposedly gone to her husband's parents' house. Not far away, Yi Sung-ju's village was at the edge of a town called Chidoo-ri, so there was virtually no chance for them to meet each other as long as Yun-hee didn't go on purpose to see her.

Yi Sung-ju's wife, who seemed on her way out somewhere, dropped by Yun-hee's house with a light makeup on her white face. Although the mother of two daughters, she always looked like a maiden with her short hair, and still preserved her maidenly beauty. However, she struck Yun-hee as a woman who seemed to be grasping something in her hands, and as Yun-hee realized later, it was the expression of a strong obsession—a tension in her mind.

When they had first moved to Chidoo-ri and had brought Yun-hee a rice cake after making a burnt sacrifice to the spirit of their new house, Yun-hee talked with the couple about one of Yi Sung-ju's columns in the paper, which she had read recently. Yun-hee had little memory now of what they had discussed, but apparently she gave the impression that she agreed with the column. As soon as Yun-hee finished talking then, Yi Sung-ju's wife interrupted: "As a matter of fact, every word of my husband's miscellaneous writings seems to be a waste of time. So I reject every request for my husband to write except poetry, but since he's unable to turn down all the requests, he occasionally writes some miscellaneous pieces."

Saying this, the woman revealed her deep affection for her husband, which made even Yi Sung-ju himself feel ill at ease. To Yun-hee, however, who made it a habit to bring any mail delivered for Hee-jo straight to him, such an attitude was anything but ordinary. All this suggested the different view of life each had; unlike Yi Sung-ju's wife, who mystified her husband, Yun-hee had always been skeptical about her position as the wife of an artist. Perhaps this would seem to make them unable to understand each other—despite having lived in the same village not far away from each other.

Upon looking at Yi Sung-ju's wife who visited her now, Yun-hee opened: "Oh, how have you been? It seems as if we never lived in the same neighborhood as it's been so long since you visited."

"That's how life goes. Anyhow I'm sorry for it."

"Please come in."

As Yun-hee greeted her with a bright smile, though speaking formally, Yi Sung-ju's wife replied briefly and stepped inside. Since Hee-jo was working in his studio, Yun-hee entertained her guest alone, suspecting that there must have been something ominous because Yi Sung-ju's wife didn't smile even slightly.

When Yun-hee brought a ground barley drink, the woman barely took a sip and began: "Listen, it's been several days since my husband left home. From the beginning of my marriage I've accepted his erratic lifestyle, you know. But yesterday Mr. Yang who came to repair the roof of my house said he'd seen Myong-ha's father. He informed me that my husband has been here with some woman. Is that right?"

"Yes, he was here five days ago," admitted Yun-hee.

Then Yi Sung-ju's wife reproached, raising her brows: "Why, then, didn't you even inform me of that? As a married woman, I think you're in a better position to understand me."

"But how can I interfere with the private matters of others? It's no such thing as reporting espionage agents. Besides, Mr. Yi Sung-ju was a guest in my house as well as a friend."

Yi Sung-ju's wife toned down her anger as Yun-hee expressed her position, and continued: "This sort of thing is not unusual to me since my husband has shown very wanton behavior. Before we moved here, he had a scandalous affair with some woman, so I even ventured to meet her."

"What did you ask her, then?"

"Of course I asked her to leave my husband, saying that since he was a flirt and a very compassionate person there were always many women around him. Besides, I told her he had been so involved in the common folk movement that this kind of scandal should be completely cleared away. He's a leader in that movement, you know. A leader ought to be morally scrupulous."

As Yi Sung-ju's wife expressed her opinion out of conviction, Yun-hee stared at her for a while. If Yun-hee herself had been in

164

her position, she, too, would have felt betrayed as much as she. Despite that, it seemed absurd to criticize a love affair in the name of the common folk movement. Living together, Yun-hee felt, Yi Sung-ju's wife must have been affected by the philosophy of her husband. Just as Hee-jo felt about Yi Sung-ju, so was Yun-hee repelled by the woman's discussion of leadership and so forth. Since there were so many people oppressed by the current dictatorship, many people in this country, no matter who they were, tried to justify their existence with something big or great—such as history, or the common folk.

Feeling like asking something, Yun-hee said, "Even so, doesn't it occur to you that Mr. Yi Sung-ju is morally corrupt?"

"That's not a point. I can imagine what kind of woman she is. I know her character very well since many of my school juniors informed me about her. If my husband ever comes here, please tell me. Anyway it's so hard to live with a man whom many women admire."

Looking at her, Yun-hee stated, "I envy you, Myong-ha's Mom, since you're living with respect for your husband. It's different for me."

As Yun-hee was about to accompany Yi Sung-ju's wife to the front gate, Hee-jo emerged out of his studio. With lunch time around he seemed so hungry that he didn't recognize Yi Sung-ju's wife at first glance.

"Myong-ha's Mom from Chidoo-ri came to see me," explained Yun-hee.

"Oh, I was wondering who you were. Why don't you stay longer since you haven't been here in such a long while?"

In spite of Hee-jo's greeting, Yi Sung-ju's wife set out hurriedly, saying she was going to Seoul. In preparing lunch, Yun-hee explained why the woman had visited her. "Mr. Yi Sung-ju has such nerve! How could he bring his mistress here three times when his house is so near at hand? I guess people become childish once they fall in love."

"A mistress? Don't be kidding. I think he has the right to come around with anyone he likes."

"It's what Mr. Yi Sung-ju himself revealed to me," said Yun-hee, looking at Hee-jo intently. She then added: "I wouldn't live like that since I wouldn't need such a man—however great he is. There's something more important than love, you know."

As Wan-kyu's work with white slip was finished, Hee-jo lined up the wares and looked at them with troubled eyes. To Yun-hee, they merely looked like Hee-jo's and even the cloud pattern was very similar. Sighing deeply, Hee-jo said:

"A pot should not look sharp, nor should it look arrogant or artful. Even for a polished piece, that is not recommended. A stable shape will do. Also, it has nothing to do with technique since art is, after all, a matter of spirit. Suppose we're making a pot in the shape of a wrapping cloth. Every technique will look miraculous if we don't know how to use it. But once we learn the technique, it all becomes very routine. I'm told that Japanese pottery artists disclose their own skill in a book once they establish themselves in their field. An imitation of a skill is a futile thing, you know, so keep in mind the axiom that once you acquire a skill you must discard it immediately. Do you know the old saying, 'Destroy Buddha and destroy your master'? It means; Destroy any authorities whether they're Buddha or your master. As a matter of fact, my work starts with such a process of destruction."

Then Hee-jo ordered Wan-kyu to break all the wares he had made, so Wan-kyu, looking at his works for a while, began to break each piece, one by one. Those wares, which might have been born with no meaning, returned to the world of nothingness, giving up their portion of time. If it were possible for humans to control their share of life perfectly as they did the wares, Yun-hee reflected, there would be no such thing as a wasted life.

That night after dinner, Hee-jo spoke to the despondent Wan-kyu as if appeasingly. "I remember, in fourth grade or so in elementary school, when I was asked to write about a liberation in commemoration of Liberation Day. When I was six years old I learned about Liberation Day, so I managed to write some piece in my own way. As my teacher read my writing to the other students and complimented me a lot, I flattered myself. Only then he told us his point, commenting that although it was well written there was no voice in my writing. He found out what was missing in my writing, and from then on his words have reverberated in my mind."

"I understand," said Wan-kyu. "Not all pots become works of art. While working with you, I end up imitating your style in spite of myself."

Resuming his work, Hee-jo had formed the habit of knitting his brows. The children seemed to feel strained with their father, who rarely spoke, and whenever Hee-jo was at home they would tiptoe on the wooden floor.

One day Hee-jo stopped working and entered the living room, smoking continuously. Yun-hee was rather curious to find he was still wearing his working clothes, but Hee-jo murmured to himself, "I must get Wan-kyu out of here."

As Yun-hee asked him anxiously about what had happened, Hee-jo said, running his hand nervously through his hair, "While I was working with the white slip, Wan-kyu dropped a tea pot in trying to put it on the shelf. As a result, the white slip was all scratched and I had to remake it because that piece became useless. What could be more troublesome than to keep him at my side all the time?"

"Anyone can make such a mistake, you know. How can you be called a teacher if you kick him out of here due to a small mistake like that? Once you accept him as your student, you must keep your promise and not think so little of him."

With Yun-hee's urging, Hee-jo replied: "What does he need a teacher for? At any rate, he's got to develop his skill all by himself now. Because of my preoccupation with my sense of duty as a teacher, I felt more burdened."

"Then let him do his own work. Since he has a good sense of what you've said, he'll manage to learn by himself whatever you do. If you stay conscious of his existence, how can you feel comfortable even for a day?"

Hee-jo said no more, but Yun-hee knew artists have a tendency to protect themselves like hedgehogs once they get absorbed in their own world. Thus the slightest attempt to get close to them makes them feel defensive, lest anyone interrupt their world. In fact, this sort of fierce self-protection of artists resembles a wild animal that has just borne its young. Artists are no more than another species ceaselessly giving rise to the dream of a revolt, even though such a dream may end up with mere self-confirmation.

The evening glow was unusually beautiful that day. The sky in the west was suffused with a rose color and surged momentarily like a wave. Tan-bee and Wan-kyu followed Yun-hee on a walk, strolling together along a stream that looked as if a bundle of flowers were pouring down upon it, because of the sunset.

"Mom, it looks like a pink net is spread over the entire stream," exclaimed Tan-bee, and from behind Wan-kyu picked up a pebble and threw it across the surface of the stream. The way he skipped the stone across the water was quite skillful.

"Was Mr. Hong very upset? He didn't talk at all—perhaps because of my blunder," Wan-kyu observed despondently. Actually Hee-jo hadn't said even a word at dinner, and it seemed a silent admonition to Wan-kyu.

"Don't worry," answered Yun-hee, "he can't even stand the dripping of tap water while his nerves are on edge. You must understand his way of treating you like a family member since he regards you as a student. That's a kind of teaching, you know."

"I understand. I discussed my future with my friends when I went to Seoul before. Most of my friends, however, seemed to make up their minds to make money first of all, simply because it was so demanding to endure all the procedures to become a potter. With such an opinion, they worried about me. And one of them went even so far as to assert that I unreasoningly chose a difficult course under the teaching of Mr. Hong, and pitied me. But I wasn't disturbed at all by such remarks. No doubt I'll soon be worried about making a living after school, but I got a different view of life from them. There are, I believe, two kinds of people in life—one group who struggle with themselves, the other group who put much value on money."

"You're right. If only you knew what it was to struggle with yourself, you wouldn't have to make an easy compromise. In any event, don't think too much of Mr. Hong."

"I don't think Mr. Hong is extraordinary. Anyway, that is the kind of life an artist should live, and he shows the universal way of life for an artist. Since there are few people living like him because of their secular desire, Mr. Hong looks greater. That's all."

Agreeing with Wan-kyu, Yun-hee then asked about his age.

"Because I attended a graduate school after my military service, I'm now twenty-eight."

"You might as well marry."

To these words Wan-kyu readily replied, "Why don't you find a good woman for me?"; then he abruptly inquired, "Who is the woman who came here a few days ago? She looks like a college student with her short hair."

"Ah, you mean Ji-woon? She works for a publishing company. I think she's about your age."

Wan-kyu seemed to pay much attention to Ji-woon, Yun-hee felt, yet she couldn't say anymore. It seemed Wan-kyu, smart and determined, would make a good match for Ji-woon, but it was no more than Yun-hee's imagination. As for Ji-woon, there was something in her that was somewhat adverse. Wasn't it proven by the fact that she'd chosen a love that caused her tremendous suffering, even in her glorious youth? On Yun-hee's mind flashed the face of Yi Sung-ju's wife, who had come to see her, and momentarily she felt compassion for the two women who were equally clinging to a hopeless love.

"Look, the evening glow is gone," Tan-bee exclaimed, pointing at the sky as she was sitting alone by the stream. "I wish it weren't erased like chalk."

In the meantime the pink net of the evening glow spread on the stream disappeared, making the last faint remnants of the waning glow in the southern sky vanish all at once. Perhaps the child couldn't realize that the evening glow was more beautiful as it was destined to wane. As the three of them were about to get up to leave, Sae-bul ran to them, calling out to Wan-kyu, "Father is looking all over for you for a *changgi* game."

Because she had an unusually large number of guests in her house over the weekend, Yun-hee had to drop by Han Min-wha's house on Monday. Her uncle from Puyeo had called at her house after a long absence and stayed the night. Moreover, Eun-kyong and her husband had visited Yun-hee with another couple to let

169

them buy Hee-jo's works of art, and after that the owner of a gallery in Seoul came to see Hee-jo to suggest an idea for an exhibition. Each visitor had brought a different present. As a result Yun-hee had three different kinds of western cakes, and so she decided to take a pound cake to Han Min-wha. In fact, Yun-hee hadn't given Han Min-wha anything in return for the water-colored shawl she had received from her; in addition, she wondered what had become of her.

When Yun-hee left the house, saying she would be back in about two hours, Hee-jo glanced at what she had in her hand. It was a long box with the cake in it, wrapped in a blue cloth. Because he knew that the cloth had been used to wrap the shawl, Hee-jo was sure to guess where Yun-hee was going now. Just as he hadn't said anything about the shawl, so he tried not to care about it. Maybe that was the only honest expression Hee-jo was able to convey, Yun-hee thought.

Han Min-wha was sitting in front of the loom working as she had been on Yun-hee's previous visit. She seemed used to working with the loom, passing the shuttle between the warps and immediately striking with the beater. As such, her action looked as light as air. Looking like a work she had just started, the warp thread on the loom had a tone of purple. As Yun-hee stepped in through the open door, Han Min-wha took her eyes away from the textile and greeted Yun-hee. Sitting on the chair by the window, Yun-hee urged her to continue to work.

"That's all right," replied Han Min-wha. "There's no point in working further with a guest here. I can stop now since I just began."

"The work you're engaged in must be laborious, but the sight of you weaving looks so idyllic."

"Do you think so? Perhaps it's because the loom is made of wood that you've got such an impression. Actually the loom is known as the oldest wooden device still in use today. Since it was the first machine invented, people in the West even use it for an interior decoration."

"Really? But it must strain your arm to keep on striking the beater in such a way. This work must be as demanding as making pottery, I suppose."

"Absolutely. But the hardest part is the process before I start to work at the loom. In accordance with my design and purpose, I prepare the thread, select and dye it, or sometimes wind and arrange it. Once I start weaving, however, I come to enjoy the process of weaving, watching how it develops. As a matter of fact, it's good exercise to move my neck, to move the beater with my arm, and to press the treadles with my feet. I heard that old women engaged in weaving are supposed to live long. Besides, even the loom itself can be used as an instrument for physical therapy in an orthopedic hospital. So I don't hesitate to recommend weaving to my friends who are wondering what to do for exercise, because it would make them feel concentrated and strong."

At the reference to the word "wondering" Han Min-wha smiled lightly. Then Yun-hee observed, "Unlike painting, weaving gives us an intimate feeling, since it's a tangible thing. Beyond that, it feels soft, too."

"In foreign countries," Han Min-wha continued, "architects often become textile artists. They are, as it were, transformed from something hard and solid to something soft and flexible. As you know, the Western-style loom was introduced very late in our country with the disappearance of the conventional loom as an outmoded means of production. As an art, weaving is still in its beginning stages, I'd say, because the history of weaving in the sphere of artistic creation is not very long. I learned that even such an avant-garde art as textile moulding has already been tried. Naturally, such an effort ends up creating an elastic piece of textile, making complete use of space available. In this instance, of course, they don't have to confine the weaving to the wall only. History is destined to march toward freedom, and I believe art is no exception in this respect. Although we're not yet liberated from the dark political situation, it's art itself that leads us forward."

After her words Han Min-wha brought in a handful of gorgeous-looking red cherries on a tray. Looking outside as she leaned against the window, Yun-hee saw in the early summer yard blooms of peonies and dappled flowers. Soon such flowers as four-o'clocks would yield seed, and wild lilies would come into full bloom.

Suddenly Han Min-wha rushed to a corner of the kitchen and took away a dried yellow corvina fish hanging on the wall. In front of the pump she threw it toward the vegetable garden; a black cat jumped out in time to snap it up and disappeared into the grove in a flash. Such actions of giving and taking seemed as customary as if the woman and the cat had promised to do it. Finding her action as nimble as the cat's, Yun-hee wondered when Han Min-wha had caught a glimpse of the cat.

"Oh, it must be a stray cat, isn't it?" asked Yun-hee.

"Right. I heard that cat belonged to a temple once. But when someone took it home with him, it ran away and continued to roam about like that."

"Do you like cats?" asked Yun-hee.

"No. I've no mind to keep a cat around me because it would surely give me a sense of obligation. All I like about the cats is their wild nature. A dog is nothing but livestock, but a cat doesn't look like that even when it stays around us. However tenderly we deal with a cat, it claws us if we treat it unkindly even once. There's something in a cat that we cannot tame, you know. I suppose it's this peculiarity of cats that many people dislike. We cannot control a cat as we wish."

It was actually Yun-hee herself who disliked cats, since she thought that, though regarded as a spiritual animal, a cat didn't seem to need the affection of people. Because of such feelings, there was something cold-hearted in a cat, yet it would be better to change the expression "cold-hearted" into "wild-natured."

Han Min-wha ate three slices of the cake as if she were hungry. The loose clothing she wore revealed the bones of her upper chest, so Yun-hee watched her anew. In truth, the woman seemed to have an untamed, wild nature, but nevertheless there was nothing neg-ligent about her. Staring at her, Yun-hee said, "By the way, Ms. Han, I just realized there's something in you that is like a cat. Something of coolness, I mean."

❧

The earth had seemed to burn as the weather grew hot with no rain. As predicted by the weather forecast, it had begun drizzling occasionally in the morning, but by the time childen got home from school the rain poured down vigorously for a long while, making a loud noise as it fell. Yun-hee made up her mind to go out to meet her children with umbrellas, but soon changed her mind. It would seem all right for her children to get wet in the early summer; moreover, she was curious to see how her children would behave in the rain.

In childhood there were always some children who, on rainy days, would make a point of roaming about barefoot. When Tan-bee was in second grade before they moved to the countryside, Yun-hee purposefully didn't give her bus fare for the trip home a couple of times to see how the child could cope with a difficult situation by herself. The first time Tan-bee had asked her home-room teacher to give her bus fare and returned home by bus. The second time, however, Tan-bee did not ask her teacher perhaps because she felt ashamed to ask for money again, and walked home. As Yun-hee was then worrying about the child being late, Tan-bee returned looking tired, her face flushed. Tan-bee, it turned out, was late because she had engaged in watching the street scene that she used to miss while coming home by bus. To Yun-hee the child enumerated one by one what she had seen on the way: a shop with an aquarium, a blind fortune-teller in the street, and movie posters on the wall. Obviously all these seemed miraculous to Tan-bee.

The scenes of unfamiliar street corners may have been a dream world to children. Yun-hee called to mind, as if in a picture, the time in her childhood when she had been to some relative's home by streetcar, leaning on her grandmother. At times like that she would lose her senses while watching the miraculous landscape outside and hearing the clanging of the streetcar bell, which seemed to have come from beyond the world of memory.

Reverberating in her memory were such places as the Ku-jung Silk Shop, next to the Poshin Pavilion in Chong-ro, where she once visited hand in hand with her mother; the majestic Whashin Department Store, which seemed proud of its newly installed elevator; and a formerly Japanese house at Ulchi-ro where her stylish aunt, then a college student, had lived. In her aunt's exotic room with a *tatami* floor, Yun-hee would smell the mystical odor of a manicure. And the bottle of nail polish looked like a present from heaven, or a magic bottle.

173

Into Yun-hee's mind came the wood-framed houses in the Chunggyechon area, which was crowded with poor people living clustered around like a straw rope, and the dyeing houses prospering at the East Gate Market, which specialized in dyeing worn-out military uniforms. She also remembered a familiar scene of children carrying a bottle full of minnows they had caught in a nearby stream. The vacant lot behind the Dong-A Daily Newspaper building where Chunggyechon ended was always full of children. In autumn, red dragonflies would fill the sky and make it all red, while joyful children would fly kites or play with straw ropes.

How fascinating, too, were the sweet shops in the street! Yun-hee marveled time and again. The honeyed-rice-cake shop she used to pass by made her mouth water without fail, and so she wished to occupy the empty shop all by herself if all the people were to retreat with another outbreak of war. Han Min-wha had once told Yun-hee about the blind who wove colorful cloth on the strength of their memory. Likewise, if each of the street scenes that was glanced at in childhood could be stored in a child's memory as vividly as the glow of fireflies, wasn't it possible that the glow could be revived someday, even in darkness, so that it could guide him in the course of life?

Despite Yun-hee's concern that her children might return all wet, Tan-bee came back wearing a pink raincoat she had brought, while Sae-bul came with one of his classmates, sharing an umbrella. His classmate was a girl living near Eunti village, and it seemed she passed by Satgol just to share her umbrella with Sae-bul. In spite of Yun-hee urging her to stay for a while, the girl declined, not even stepping into the house, saying she had to go home immediately. Though Yun-hee wanted to treat her to some snack, the girl merely repeated her thanks. And when she was gone, Yun-hee asked Sae-bul her name.

"Kim Kyong-mi," he answered, "she's the section chief in my class."

"She must be very considerate to take you home in the rain with her umbrella," said Yun-hee.

At this moment Tan-bee interrupted: "But Sae-bul often teases her, lifting up her skirt. As a matter of fact, that's the way he acts with his girlfriends in school."

Sae-bul was embarrassed at Tan-bee's unexpected remark. Surprised, Yun-hee countered, "What? You lift a girl's skirt?"

"That's not unusual among us children, you know."

As Sae-bul gave a sullen answer, Yun-hee said, looking at him sharply.

"How would you like it if someone lifted your shirt trying to see your bare back? Suppose Tan-bee's classmate tried to tease her just as you do. You must know you're not a man if you have no regard for girls. It's a shameful thing to afflict the weak. Compared with you, Kyong-mi is considerate enough to make you feel ashamed. She did just what you ought to have done."

It looked like the rain had stopped overnight, and the next morning the sky revealed a blue face without any trace of rain. As if regretfully, Tan-bee replaced her raincoat, and Sae-bul, taking out the bicycle, put his schoolbag on it. In going to school with his sister Sae-bul usually didn't take his bicycle, so Yun-hee was curious why he had brought out his bicycle this time.

Meanwhile Wan-kyu had already brought out a bucket full of a white slip, so Yun-hee suspected they were about to resume the slip work. It seemed they intended to dry the white slip in the sunshine, but the slip looked rather thin for that purpose. Hee-jo had barely finished his lunch, making preparations for the slip work, when he took out two bottles of *soju* from somewhere. He seemed to arrange his thoughts by looking at his sketch before moving on to the slip work. Since his return from the earlier trip to the temple, Hee-jo had planned the slip work with a clear mind. Out of anxiety for the work he had begun, however, he had taken to drinking several bottles of *soju* again.

By the time Hee-jo had nearly finished his work, Park Young-soo dropped by with Yi Jung-dal. Greeting them, Hee-jo urged them to move into the room first and continued the slip work he had just done for two of the last remaining greenwares. So the visitors had no choice but to go into the room without Hee-jo, for there was no denying they interrupted his work. The good-natured Park Young-soo brought six bottles of *makkoli* hung on straw ropes, and it seemed he'd bought them at a shop in the neighborhood, remembering that Yun-hee had drunk it before. In spite of his good intentions, Yun-hee was not inwardly grateful, since she

175

was worried about Hee-jo's work above all, but without betraying her emotions she set a drinking table for them.

Though meeting Park Young-soo for the first time in nearly two months, she inquired first of all about Yi Jung-dal, because his visits were far less frequent: "Well, I heard you're now living with Mr. Park. How do you like living in the countryside?"

"I'm impressed with the fresh air. I feel like becoming a hermit all of a sudden as I think I lost reality," Jung-dal asserted.

"Despite that, you can keep reality in your head. Isn't it enough?" Park Young-soo said, half-jokingly.

"A writer is supposed to have inspiration from his contact with reality," replied Jung-dal, "so I believe it's important to be closely in touch with the actual scene. I heard that even such a writer as Sartre didn't get inspiration from nature at all."

Indifferent to Park Young-soo's words, Jung-dal kept insisting on the importance of being in touch with reality. Though living in the countryside thanks to the goodwill of his friend, he didn't seem to enjoy his life that much.

Just then Hee-jo entered and Yun-hee suggested to Jung-dal: "You may write a masterpiece if you think of yourself as being in exile like such old masters as Chusa or Chung Yak-yong. You may even get inspiration from the Namhansansung site."

"Huh, shall I have to try a historical novel?"

Jung-dal responded in a casual way as if he had no interest in the new environment. Feeling displeased, Yun-hee considered Jung-dal lacking in sincerity. To Park Young-soo, then, Hee-jo expressed his admiration for the new place, making Yun-hee wonder when he had been there: "The bosom of the mountains seems very broad. Not looking wild, that place has a sacred air. I assure you that your painting will be much improved from now on."

"I envy the painters," said Jung-dal, "since they paint nature like a hermit. I think the painters are the real artists, as they get inspiration from the landscape, which is itself no different from a still life."

"They say that only people who can communicate with the leaves of grass can become poets. In other words, those who have an open mind can get inspiration wherever they are."

Hee-jo responded unenthusiastically, emptying the glass before him. He had already drunk *soju,* and with the influence of wine he seemed intoxicated tonight. As Yun-hee asked Park Young-soo where the two housemates were headed for, he replied, "We're going to Seoul to do some business early tomorrow morning. Besides, one of my friends who runs a theatre will be presenting his first work on stage tonight. We came to know each other since he's Jung-dal's college senior."

"If you're going all the way to Seoul to see a play, it must be a good play, I suppose," observed Yun-hee.

"I heard it's a modern version of *The Tale of Shim Ch'ong.* But the real purpose of our visit is to have a drink together after the performance, you know," Jung-dal said, smiling.

Then Yun-hee asked Jung-dal, "Isn't that a play by the poet Ahn Ki-sun, which was published in a literary magazine this spring?"

As Jung-dal answered it was the same one, Yun-hee revealed her impression that it was original. In truth, she liked the poet, who had recently put the religious motives inherent in traditional Korean myth or folklore into a play full of poetic tension. Unlike the figure of Shim Ch'ong in folklore, however, the protagonist Shim Ch'ong in this play was depicted as a person who had been sold to a Chinese sailor, driven to a brothel, and finally returned home completely wrecked. The play captured in its condensed dialogue, as if in an epic, the ordeal of initiation that the protagonist had gone through.

"As a matter of fact, I like the poetry of Ahn Ki-sun, too," asserted Jung-dal, "but the play itself is not to my taste. I think his play degrades the image of the filial girl Shim Ch'ong, who embodies the feeling and aspiration of all Koreans, into a mere prostitute, in a way that seems to deprive us of our cherished dream. Of course I admit Shim Ch'ong's sacrifice can be interpreted in such a way in a modern perspective, but the way of making it tragic even to the very end reminds me of the ancient Greek drama. Indeed, it looks like Shim Ch'ong is in a lost land."

"I don't think so," Yun-hee responded immediately. "In folklore we can find a dream that enables us to reject the ideological principle of causation supported by the upper class *yangban,* and hence to overcome the agony of life. But although they emphasize Taoism or something similar, the ideal expressed in folklore ends up failing to raise a serious question by simply bringing up a dream that is impossible to realize in the real world. The filial duty of Shim Ch'ong, which is, of course, the supposed subject of the folk tale, was merely invented by the Confucian ideal. In contrast to this, the futile dream of the common folk is excluded in Ahn Ki-sun's play. That is, by making the story of Shim Ch'ong a tragedy to the end, it awakens us to the futility of Confucian ideals such as loyalty or filial duty. Obviously, the saint-prostitute Shim Ch'ong is a victim of Confucian society. I believe that if a common folk literature should ever exist, this is the kind of work they should write."

That Yun-hee had no mind to idealize the figure of Shim Ch'ong may be attributed to the fact that she had another side in her that was inclined to revolt against herself—though she had been tamed by the Confucian ideal. She remembered, in particular, how the virtue of Chun-hyang, which was praised by the patriarchal society, had resulted in implanting the so-called "Chun-hyang complex" in the minds of countless Korean women. To Yun-hee's mind, therefore, Jung-dal's insistence on keeping the original version of the story of Shim Ch'ong was simple and, above all, banal.

When Yun-hee was about to leave, disappointed, Park Young-soo opened the third bottle of *makkoli*. Filling Yun-hee's glass, he asked. "By the way, has Yi Sung-ju visited here once in a while? I haven't seen him at all these days."

"I heard he's living in this neighborhood," interposed Jung-dal. "Last year I happened to have a drink with him. At the time he seemed to be dating a woman."

"Who are you talking about?"

As Yun-hee became attentive, Jung-dal uttered Ji-woon's name without hesitation and continued. "She's a woman working for a publishing company. I don't know her very well, but I was slightly acquainted with her younger sister. She's an aspiring poet as well as a woman reporter for a weekly paper published by a welfare organization. Each of the sisters has an air of her own, not restricted to anything."

"What do you mean?" demanded Yun-hee.

Grinning at her question, Jung-dal emptied his glass. When Hee-jo emptied his glass, Jung-dal filled it and began. He remarked that one day he had gone to the publishing company to deliver a commissioned manuscript and had drunk far into the night with Ji-woon's sister, who was then in charge of handling the manuscript.

"So when I complained about the delay of the manuscript fee that day," Jung-dal went on, "she became apologetic and told me she would give me her own money instead. She even offered to buy me a drink. I was then driven to anger, since I was obliged to be indebted to a woman for such loose change—and I despised myself as a poor writer who barely managed to make a living from manuscript fees. At any rate I drank to my limit that day and, drunk, with no idea of the time, went out about thirty minutes before curfew. Naturally I failed to get a taxi for Ahnyang, where I then lived, and staggered down the road off balance. Then I strode to the elevated road trying vainly to walk home to Ahnyang. But I couldn't remember what had happened after that—except that she had taken me to her home. It seemed her mother had opened the gate for us while her brother, who had been sleeping, allowed me to use his room. That's how I happened to stay a night in her house—as if it were my wife's parents' home. Now come to think of it, I took her by the wrist with rapture under the influence of wine, but she left me in anger. How strange these women are! I thought she loved me because she'd even taken me to her home, you know. Anyhow it was at the breakfast table the next morning that I encountered her older sister for the first time. It turned out she was so kind as to serve breakfast to a stranger her sister had brought home. In addition, I borrowed bus fare from her. They all looked good-natured, but it was hard to figure them out."

As a woman, Yun-hee found Jung-dal's attitude impudent. Displeased, she spat out: "Listen, it seems obvious she took you to her house because yours was too far, and she couldn't leave you alone at curfew time. In a circumstance like that I wouldn't have cared about you at all. Perhaps Ji-woon's sister is either an angel or an idiot because she gave you a hand as if she were doing welfare work. Obviously there's no point in feeling strange toward her since you're in a position to thank her, at least. I believe Ji-woon's sister had no eyes for men!"

Yun-hee thought that the innocence and goodwill of Ji-woon's sister had been deformed in a shabby way by the unworthiness of Jung-dal—just like a pearl thrown to a pig.

However, Park Young-soo smiled at this unexpected episode. "Tut! Though I myself was often overcome with wine day and night, there was not a single occasion when I failed to return home. To all appearances, it seemed you pretended to be drunk because of some wicked intention."

"Don't be silly. At any rate it's so hard to figure these women out. I don't know if it can be called maternal affection or something."

Jung-dal glossed over the whole thing, saying no more. But Yun-hee thought that Jung-dal had gone too far in making such an awful joke. In fact, she had often heard such idle talk among men who have only to spend time idly, so she ventured: "If you feel even a bit grateful for the goodwill of others, don't ever exaggerate what happened, because it'll make those women misunderstood. It's so ungentlemanly, you know."

At Yun-hee's reproach, Jung-dal merely said: "There should be no room to be misunderstood or anything. All is an empty dream."

"Damn it! Stop such ludicrous talk."

No sooner had Jung-dal replied to Yun-hee's words than Hee-jo bolted up, a strange look in his bloodshot eyes. Suddenly, a stream of liquid poured down Jung-dal's face across the table. Looking up in surprise, Yun-hee saw Hee-jo urinating on him. In a totally defenseless position Jung-dal tried in vain to protect his face with his hands and at the same time Yun-hee shrieked at Hee-jo: "Stop it! What do you think you're doing? You're no different from him!"

As soon as Yun-hee rose to stop him, Hee-jo pushed her aside with one hand. His power, appearing as though from nowhere, was so overwhelmeing that Yun-hee's small body was hurled into the corner of the room and crumpled like paper. She remained motionless, with her eyes shut, seeing flaming stars. She heard the windows smashed to pieces one by one with a noise that seemed to penetrate. Apparently that was the response from Jung-dal himself.

Appalled at Hee-jo's action, Park Young-soo went away with Jung-dal hurriedly without even saying good-by. With the waning sun flaming its last rays, the sight of the fragments of broken glasses scattered on the drinking table looked like a surrealistic still life.

It was not until Sae-bul returned, pushing his bicycle, that Yun-hee roughly cleared the room. He had come home nearly two hours later than usual, but Yun-hee had no time to worry about him because of the drinking incident. In fact, it was fortunate the child hadn't witnessed the ugly behavior of the grown-ups.

"Why are you so late?" asked Yun-hee. "I was worried about you all the time, since you didn't say a word in advance."

At this instance Tan-bee explained on behalf of Sae-bul: "You see, Sae-bul carried the schoolbags of his girl classmates on his bicycle. He even saw Kyong-mi home and stayed there eating potatoes."

Then Yun-hee came to realize why Sae-bul had gone to school with the bicycle this morning. Sae-bul must have reflected by himself after having been scolded by his mother the previous day; remembering that his mother had told him to show a tender regard for girls, he had carried the girls' schoolbags on his bicycle. With this thought Yun-hee embraced Sae-bul tightly to her bosom. Truly, children are sometimes better than grown-ups, she said to herself.

Hee-jo went to his studio with a bottle of liquor without even eating dinner, and confined himself there until nine o'clock. Frowning, still he seemed angry. Looking for a book on the bookshelves, Hee-jo happened to find a collection of Jung-dal's poetry and uttered sarcastically to Yun-hee who just entered the studio, "Hmm! He must build his character first before writing anything else."

"Whether writing or pottery," Yun-hee responded quickly, "it's the same. Do you think you're perfect enough to make pottery? Even if people are not fully mature, they're able to write or make pottery. Isn't it true you're trying to discipline yourself through your work precisely because you're imperfect? Even if you identify yourself with your work, it is, as you always said, only a trace of yourself when you approach God. You're no better than other ordinary human beings with many faults, you know, although you seek to make your soul sublime through the art of pottery. You're childish and arrogant, so don't pretend you're better than the rest of the world. After all, you're trapped in your own myth, living like a snail!"

Yun-hee had lost her temper and even prepared for Hee-jo to throw a bottle of wine at her, but instead he kept silent. Now his eyes, directed toward her, looked embarrassed and hollow. Had he thought of her as his ardent follower to the extent that she might endure whatever he did? In the presence of his wife, Hee-jo now seemed to witness his poor self, deprived of the clothes of his sanctuary as an artist.

However, Yun-hee's words came from deep in her heart. She had longed for marriage with a person she could respect, but since her marriage, she had respected Hee-jo only as an artist. As a man, Hee-jo was nothing but an ordinary husband indulging in patriarchal authority. Believing that a wife should be obedient on all occasions, he revealed his hostility whenever he felt his sanctuary violated. Just as one's personality has nothing to do with one's learning, so it's certain that one's personality alone, though perfect, isn't enough to make anyone an artist. Yun-hee believed artists were supposed to be people who struggle ceaselessly to better themselves through art. Admitting it, she respected their will to elevate themselves.

Even so, not all artists are entitled to ascend the ladder of light. Once before, Yun-hee had been deeply disappointed to see a large-scale group exhibition. Only a few works among them were imbued with a sublime soul, while all the other works were merely like scribblings on the back wall, having neither meaning nor life force. Looking like the secretion of futile gestures without any trace of artistic technique, those meaningless works reminded Yun-hee of the existence of a drifting god in Buddhism. In Buddhism, it is believed, a drifting god called *Jungeum-shin* exists in the state of a soul before it's given a new life in the world beyond, so the Forty-Nine Rememberances Rite for the deceased in Buddhism becomes a rite of prayer that this drifting god may enter Nirvana. Yun-hee felt that those deluded artists in the exhibition who cherished a chaotic dream were like the drifting god—alive but imprisoned within their own crust, and unable to discover the light.

Meanwhile Yun-hee replaced the broken glass with new panes, and then dug potatoes, a job that she had intended to do for the past few days because the day after tomorrow would mark the beginning of summer. In the afternoon she brought some steamed potatoes to the studio, since Hee-jo still looked angry, and hadn't said a word. The wares on which Hee-jo had put slip the previous day, while drunk, were scattered in pieces on the floor. He had taken to drinking while working, asserting it made him feel liberated; nevertheless, once he stopped drinking he would feel more liberated, with a sense of creativity. So it was when Hee-jo stopped drinking for some time the previous autumn that he attempted an *object*. In any event, though drinking couldn't become his companion, it still seemed difficult for Hee-jo to stop his habit.

Hee-jo went out somewhere after dinner. Because it was summer, it was as bright as broad daylight even in the evening, as if time seemed to stand still, and Yun-hee too tried to adjust herself to it. The daytime is a time of devotion, while the night is a reward for it, bringing a certain comfort. But as the sun lingered far into the evening, she couldn't rest as she wished.

It was after her children had fallen asleep and Yun-hee too was going to bed that Hee-jo returned. As his face was flushed, he must have been drunk; Yun-hee saw instantaneously that his eyes were bloodshot. From his bloodshot and swollen eyes, she could tell he'd wept, but Hee-jo went to bed immediately though it was only a little past ten. After that she could only hear his breathing, since he hid his face in the dark. Hee-jo sighed deeply as if enduring torture, then rolled over on his side. His hand traced a dim outline of his feature as he seemed to wipe his tears away silently.

Yun-hee pretended to sleep, fearing that Hee-jo might feel embarrassed. However, she knew that his tears didn't need other people's consolation, nor were they the tears of anger he had shed when throwing away broken wares; rather, they were tears of a deep regret that was beyond his grasp. This caused Yun-hee to be reminded of the day when, in his first athletic meeting in elementary school, Sae-bul had come home weeping, having lost one of his new running shoes. But what had Hee-jo lost? Yun-hee wondered. She wished she could restore what he'd lost, feeling sorry for what had happened the previous day, and sympathizing with his child-like sorrow as well. Turning her head toward him quietly, Yun-hee could see his hunched back. It was a wall of solitude that no one could approach, she realized. Watching Hee-jo shed tears alone in the darkness, Yun-hee, too, felt a deep loneliness.

The earth that teaches a cycle of life was beginning to yield its fruit on the threshold of summer. Nature is impartial without fail in distributing the seeds that it received in spring in proportion to the sweat of one's labor. When Yun-hee brought Han Min-wha the potatoes she'd dug up, she found her gathering tomatoes in the garden patch. The earliest bearing strawberries now visible in the patch, Han Min-wha gathered two full baskets of tomatoes and handed a well ripened one to Yun-hee. Sitting barefoot on the edge of the tomato patch, Han Min-wha looked like a real farm woman. Then Yun-hee handed the potatoes to Han Min-wha, saying she'd dug them herself, and sat beside her. Disregarding the hot sunshine, Han Min-wha looked contentedly around the scene.

"Did you also have a heavy wind at your place?" she asked. "I took down the wind-bell last night while I was sleeping because it was ringing so violently in the wind, as if shaken by someone."

Only then did Yun-hee remember she'd heard the sound of the wind-bell once in a while, but she hadn't noticed its sound consciously, feeling the wind blowing in her heart first.

"So you must have been frightened alone," observed Yun-hee.

"Probably it was a reflection of my mind. In fact, I don't feel horrified by nature unless it's a natural disaster. People have often asked me if I'm not afraid to live alone in the countryside, but each time, I'm convinced that this is just what I've longed for. What I've yearned for is not, so to speak, the bosom of a human being, but that of nature."

As Han Min-wha took a bite of a tomato she had just picked, a woman's cracked voice was heard from the road: "Hmm! You're going to meet Young-i's Mom? You seem to have a good excuse, eh, but I know it's only a pretense to go to work in the field. I once saw you two coming out of the wheat field after making love. Am I right, eh?"

With this remark another voice was heard: "Damn it! That wretched woman is eager to make love even in the daylight. How about openly chasing men wherever they go?"

Though, upon hearing this dialogue, Yun-hee laughed face-to-face with Han Min-wha, she didn't feel comfortable as she recalled how Hee-jo had returned the previous night with the tear marks on his face. Thinking that Han Min-wha might have a clue, Yun-hee, who had a habit of arranging her thoughts, made up her mind to solve the question.

At this moment Han Min-wha spoke: "You know, these country people have nothing to enjoy except intercourse, so they cannot understand my way of living. That's why I would tell them my husband lives in a foreign country. Actually they're not alone in this regard. Even my mother pities me, thinking that I failed in my marriage—even though she herself has led a superficial life all along with no good relations with my father. I believe it's a failure if people continue to live together while they don't like each other. Why is it called a failure to choose a different way of life? I'd say our Korean people don't know what it is to lead a life. Because they get few occasions to live outside the boundaries of an institution, they simply worship the institution itself."

As Han Min-wha finished her words, Yun-hee stared at her, surprised, since she'd never heard such a bold assertion. Was it true, then, that she too had lived up to now within the cage of marriage, conscious of the institution? Certainly not. Rather, what was wriggling quietly in her inner self was resistance against the institution.

After a while Yun-hee said: "If I could afford to lead my life alone, I'd live just by myself. How wonderous it would be to live in freedom!"

"Freedom?" countered Han Min-wha. "How overwhelming it is! You've got to deal with everything in this vast world just for yourself—whether it is truth or life. The vastness of freedom looks glorious, but it's difficult to cope with as well. Because of the boundlessness of freedom, I think many people seem to bind themselves by inescapable ties to each other and turn to the protection of institutions."

"Even so, couldn't it be a solution?" responded Yun-hee. "Because of their loneliness people depend on each other, yet no one can provide perfect satisfaction."

"In the Bible there's a story of a thirsty Samaritan woman. To the woman who, even with five husbands, kept coming for water out of thirst for a secular desire, Jesus said, 'Whoever drinks of the water that I shall give him will never thirst.' So I believe the weakness of human beings may give rise to the desire for religion. By the way, I made the same remark to Mr. Hong who dropped by my house yesterday."

Han Min-wha's abrupt mention of Hee-jo took Yun-hee by surprise. Nonetheless she responded reservedly, "I guess he must have drunk too much."

"Quite so. But there was another visitor in my house then, so we drank together. As he's a man I'm friendly with, he used to visit here about once a week. As a matter of fact, he loves this place as much as I do."

"Oh, really? Can I ask if he is the man you're going to marry?" Yun-hee ventured.

"No, I've never considered it. On the whole, I don't speculate about such a possibility when I meet people. We meet because we're both single and can communicate with each other. That's all. Fortunately, Mr. Hong came here just in time, so I introduced them to each other to make them friends over a drink."

As Han Min-wha spoke without much thought, Yun-hee felt her face harden in spite of herself. Now the puzzle was solved about why Hee-jo had returned with his eyes badly swollen from crying. Her jealousy surging instinctively, a thousand threads of emotion rapidly became entangled in her heart.

"At seeing Mr. Hong," Han Min-wha went on, "the man said he was reminded of a stubborn old friend from elementary school. He liked Mr. Hong's disposition to rebel, but was against his inclination to take things too seriously."

"True, he's too serious about everything," admitted Yun-hee.

In a moment Yun-hee's eyes met Han Min-wha's, which seemed to read her mind. On other occasions Yun-hee would have been faithful to her feelings, but this time she hid her face with her hand trying to block the sunlight, for fear that her inner turmoil would be revealed. Just then Han Min-wha suggested, "Oh, you feel hot? Let's go inside now. I'm accustomed to being outside like this."

"No, not at all. I've got to go back now."

Making the excuse that it was time for her children to return, Yun-hee prepared to leave. Then Han Min-wha gave her a full sack of tomatoes. As Yun-hee declined it, finding it burdensome to her,

Han Min-wha repeatedly urged her to take it, thanking her for the potatoes. Leaving the house, Yun-hee walked aimlessly along the stream through the field until she saw a corner of a mountain thickened with pine trees. Just by turning the corner, Yun-hee could enter Satgol where her village was, but she had no urge to go home now.

As soon as Yun-hee sat down under a tree overlooking the stream below, a gush of heat from inside her body took possession of her, and she feebly pushed aside the sack of tomatoes. A while before when she passed along this road, Yun-hee felt as if she were going to consult a friend on an important matter. But her way homeward after resolving all her suspicions was empty, and she didn't even notice the scenery. The moment she realized why Hee-jo had returned with a trace of tears, jealousy had flushed in her heart. But as the jealousy vanished like a foam, she was overcome by a sense of emptiness.

It had been some time since she had sensed that Hee-jo liked Han Min-wha, and for her part, Yun-hee accepted it rationally. But the sight of Hee-jo hurt by the appearance of Han Min-wha's male friend gave her self-respect a deep wound—a sense of being betrayed. Indeed, that was a precise description of her mind now. Hee-jo, it seemed, had disguised his deep love for the other woman so that even Yun-hee, who had already learned of their liking for each other, was led to think of their relationship as nothing more than an ideal friendship. All Hee-jo had done up to now was to be reticent about their real relationship. Perhaps he didn't mind Yun-hee's knowing, thinking that their relationship was platonic, so he had nothing to feel guilty about with his wife. Given this, however, was it moral? Yun-hee asked herself, looking down the stream through the pine tree and shaking her head gently.

It was, Yun-hee remembered, when Han Min-wha had visited her house for the third time in the spring of the previous year. At the time Hee-jo had seemed so pleased to see her, and from the way they looked at each other then Yun-hee had got a sense of something more than mere curiosity—and subsequently felt awkward herself. To give it a correct expression now, it was emotional intercourse!

To Yun-hee's mind, Hee-jo was the very coward who couldn't

even take a step away from the boundary of the institution of marriage. It seemed to be rather Yi Sung-ju himself who was more faithful to love. Had Hee-jo revealed his obvious interest in love as frankly as Yi Sung-ju, Yun-hee herself would have suggested a divorce wthout any hesitation. Despite his having been her companion for nearly thirteen years, Yun-hee had no intention of making an effort to change his mind simply out of self-pity. Nor did Yun-hee have the slightest idea of meeting the woman who took her husband away and insisting on her privilege just as Yi Sung-ju's wife did, for she had little mind to act like the heroine of a soap opera. After all, she was not so foolish as to be ignorant of the fact that the attraction of a human heart is more powerful than the legal rights of a wife.

Not being concious of the passage of time, Yun-hee sensed that all the sweat on her back had dried, making her feel cold. While the rays of the setting sun slanted through the pine tree and poured over the stream, she began to feel weary as her strain relaxed. By only stretching her arm from the shade she was in, Yun-hee could almost reach the sunshine. Then, finding a place flat enough to lie on, she moved toward it and put her palm on the ground. Pressing the ground as gently as she repressed her emotions, Yun-hee felt the heat of the earth like a human heart. The earth is always cozy, she thought. Like a priest who devoted himself to a shrine of God, Yun-hee lay flat on the ground with both of her arms stretched out and said to herself: Oh, Good Earth who conceives and embraces everything! Please govern this confused soul. Give me peace so I can escape this confusion. . . .

While tranquilly lying flat on the ground, Yun-hee fancied that a warm hand was caressing her back. It seemed like a familiar hand. Trying to remember whose hand it was, Yun-hee was, all of a sudden, reminded of Farmer Marei whom she'd forgotten completely.

It was not until the sun had set down completely, with the outdoor lamp already turned on, that Yun-hee returned home. Two geese honked harshly in the grass in front of the front gate as if they'd been waiting for her. Yun-hee caressed the long neck of one goose and drove the two into their cage. At the sound of the geese, Tan-bee looked out and ran into the yard to see her mother.

"Mom, where have you been?" she asked. "Father has been looking for you all this time."

"Haven't you had your dinner yet?"

"No, Brother fixed dinner for us. But I didn't eat so I could eat with you."

By Brother she meant Wan-kyu. Asking Tan-bee to take the tomatoes to the kitchen, Yun-hee entered the room to find Hee-jo pacing back and forth in front of the door. Smelling of wine, he burst into anger as soon as he saw Yun-hee. "Where the devil have you been?" he demanded.

At Hee-jo's shouting Yun-hee raised her hand instantaneously to slap him across the cheek. While she stared at him in anger, Hee-jo stood as if he'd lost his senses. Just a day before he returned home with his eyes swollen from crying for the love he couldn't attain. So how could he wait impatiently tonight for his wife who came late?

In the meantime Yun-hee cleaned up the kitchen and ironed until her children were asleep, then went to her room and found Hee-jo already lying in the dark. She worked purposefully far into the night, being in no mood to sit face-to-face with Hee-jo. Through the open sliding door to the outside, she could watch the moonlight pouring down into the room. The yard had been illuminated by the full moon a few days before, but since then the moon began to wane, throwing only a dim light.

Hee-jo was lying with his eyes closed, but he didn't seem to be asleep. He swallowed a sigh as if nervous at hearing Yun-hee enter and lie down beside him. So Yun-hee wondered if he knew why his wife had shown such an aggressive attitude toward him. Perhaps he was able to suspect at least that she'd visited Han Min-wha; nevertheless, he didn't seem to perceive the specific circumstances. At the moment Yun-hee saw Hee-jo, who had been waiting for her, she burst into anger. But now she had no anger left. Though Yun-hee had slapped him without stopping to think about it, she was far from satisfied. Wasn't it Yun-hee herself who always hated an act of violence, however trivial it was?

Turning her face toward him, Yun-hee said: "I'm sorry. Let's hold hands together so we can be reconciled with each other."

Hee-jo, however, didn't respond at all to Yun-hee's suggestion, so she gently took his skinny hand, which was lying outside of the quilt. Letting his wife take his hand, Hee-jo looked relaxed, feeling the warmth of the contact. Indeed, she felt, the hand is more than anything else the expression of a sincere mind. After a while Yun-hee spoke as though taking an oath as a believer:

"Yesterday I suddenly realized we hadn't talked with each other for so long that we don't know each other's minds. I've come to believe that it's not a real life just to live like hard-working ants. Now it's necessary to have a chance to talk to examine our real minds. Tell me honestly. You can live without me, right? Actually I haven't the slightest idea of changing your mind which, I think, is already turned toward another woman. Neither do I intend to use my children as a shield to make our home a sanctuary. Although most women consider it a primary aim in life to maintain peace in the family, I've been skeptical of my position while I've been living with you. So, if I'm allowed to choose another path of life, I'm willing to take it."

At Yun-hee's words Hee-jo sighed deeply, his hands trembling convulsively. After a pause he spoke:

"Now I can't do even the tiniest thing without you since I came to realize I've lived with too much dependence on you. To this day you've acted like a vanguard who paves the way for me, and watched my way constantly at my side like a shadow. As I remember, you would cherish every tiny bit of clay, prepare kindling wood for the kiln chamber so devotedly, and smile deeply and considerately before a well made work. And working as laboriously as a bee, you also know how to enjoy the moonlight while the earth rests. After all, I've been so dependent on you that I notice your every gesture, or your turning the pages of a book. I'd say your existence is as invisible as air, yet I can't even hit a nail without you."

"Your whole remark simply proves that you have no courage at all," sighed Yun-hee feebly.

Soon Hee-jo's hand was getting hot as he turned to Yun-hee, who stared at the ceiling with a hollow heart. No other compliment could make her feel delighted or proud. In truth, she was well aware that her mental structure was not so simple as to love such a chaotic soul as Hee-jo blindly. Even Hee-jo, too, might be thinking that Yun-hee was neither a woman to be easily dealt with like a chicken in one's bosom, nor a woman with whom he could feel comfortable, as one does in one's native country.

Hee-jo must have been convinced of their course of life together from the fact that he was accustomed to her. But wasn't it Yun-hee herself who was accustomed to the life they'd led together? In the moment when, even in the midst of the conflicts succeeding each other in her mind, she found herself in the presence of a beautiful pot Hee-jo had made, Yun-hee would be momentarily overcome with ecstasy. Even Hee-jo's struggles with himself would become a mirror to Yun-hee through which she attained the opportunity to reflect upon herself. Moreover, who else would bring a flower for her to show his love? If separated from Hee-jo, she wouldn't have a chance to see his slender necktie, which was strangely suited to him, around his plantlike neck anymore. Maybe Yun-hee was even accustomed to his spasmodic, pitiful destructiveness.

Yun-hee turned her head toward the window as the misty moonlight shone on the wall. Looking out, she found the waning moon, which seemed to saunter alone looking at the world below, roaming about the open field. And the wind blowing spasmodically in the midst of tranquility was ringing the wind-bell. Its clear metallic sound seemed to purge her mind, and presently Hee-jo's searching hands began to entangle with Yun-hee's fingers like the root of a plant moving into the ground. Though wandering through the air like a dandelion seed, your soul cannot help but be interwoven with me in the dark, Yun-hee groaned silently. The dense darkness was a shield for human loneliness, solidifying an inescapable tie between souls, and your tired, wandering soul sought root in the soil of a family. Both you and I have no choice but to make a compromise with each other, which is an instinct to survive. In the soil where people are destined to rely on each other, she imagined, no one can recklessly deny the root of life.

In the last weekend of June, Yun-hee went to Seoul with Tan-bee without telling anybody. Although she lived within about a two-hour bus ride from Seoul, her visits there had become less and less frequent since she had moved to the countryside. In the city, where big buildings were thriving and people seemed blessed with a variety of cultural activities, the polluted air made her eyes sore.

Looking at people who were moving so busily that even their souls might be lost, Yun-hee was able to detect in their rapidly moving feet an air of greed, an air of grasping, and taking something away from each other. In proportion to the construction of countless buildings, the destruction of humanity was deeply felt—a symptom that society was being poisoned by the military regime, which ignored human life by its repeated use of the authoritarian Emergency Acts.

That happened to be the day when U.S. President Jimmy Carter visited Korea, so the national flags of both Korea and the U.S. were fluttering on every street corner. The successive visits of U.S. Presidents to Korea since Eisenhower had only been an outcome of the Korean War, Yun-hee had learned. But until Carter had declared the plan to withdraw the U.S. forces from Korea, no one in Korea had ever shouted "Yankee, go home!" except those comfort girls around the U.S. military camps who had begun to worry about making a living. So the Stars and Stripes were fluttering majestically under the sky of Seoul. Even the figure of Carter with his blond hair on the television screen looked composed enough to overshadow the rigid-looking Korean dictator, with his small body. A politician who defended human rights, Carter seemed to receive a hearty welcome from Korean people, and his bright smile alone was enough to make people feel certain that he was indeed from a blessed country.

Meanwhile Tan-bee's eye test showed she was extremely nearsighted. In fact, she had been complaining these past few days that when exposed to the sunshine, her eyes would fill with tears as if some dust had gotten in them. There seemed no doubt her eyesight had become very weak. Around the end of the previous year, when Tan-bee had taken an eye test, her eyesight had been all right, so Yun-hee felt regret for not having brought her daughter to the oculist a little earlier. In spite of all this, Tan-bee was calm, even while Yun-hee was thinking regretfully that the child had to wear glasses on her face no bigger than a fist. Even in a bakery they visited, Yun-hee looked into Tan-bee's face, imagining how she would look wearing glasses.

Stopping while eating a red bean sherbet, Tan-bee asked, looking at her mother.

"Mom, are we going to stay at Grandmother's tonight?"

"Do you want to?" asked Yun-hee.

But not responding to her question directly, Tan-bee said, "Don't be so worried, Mom."

Then Tan-bee raised her eyes as if reading Yun-hee's mind. Three days earlier the windows at home had been broken to pieces, and at the sight of Yun-hee, who returned home late the previous day, and her angry father, the child seemed to suspect that something serious had happened in her home. Though feeling gloomy that her daughter occasionally had to witness such incidents, Yun-hee said calmly:

"Tan-bee, you must understand that your father and mother get mad and quarrel once in a while, because they're human. You know, even twins can't always agree with each other. The fact that every human is different from every other makes us uncomfortable, but it gives us a chance to be curious about each other and try to understand as well. In this way we can learn how to overcome the differences between people."

"What aspect of Father did you like before you married him?"

At Tan-bee's question Yun-hee reflexively recalled the time when she had taught at school before her marriage. It was a Christian school where smoking was strictly forbidden, but Hee-jo boldly offered his studio as a smoking room for his fellow teachers, even hanging on its door a plaque with the mark "Ongdalsam," meaning a small spring. The principal had then felt very displeased with it but, soon giving up, had presented Hee-jo with an ashtray that he himself had been given. What Yun-hee had felt attracted to was the perversity of his character. That was the beginning of tragedy, Yun-hee joked to herself.

With a fleeting smile Yun-hee told Tan-bee another story. "You know, Father has no desire but to make a good work of art. He doesn't like to be pompous either. For my part, I want to decorate our house prettily, but your father feels uncomfortable with such an idea, as he thinks a well decorated house would arouse in his students' minds a desire to make their house like it in the future. I believe that is a real virtue in your father."

"How did Father come to love you?" Tan-bee winked her eye, wishing to hear the old story.

"He said he felt inclined to me because I always liked reading. Although I taught mathematics in school, I aspired to be a novelist."

"Really? Why didn't you write a novel, then?"

"Well, it was just a dream of my youth. And we can all have a dream whatever it is. Even if I'd written a novel, it couldn't surpass the sort of writing you've done."

Yun-hee invented her dream to be a novelist on the spot because she needed another story to impress her young daughter with. Tan-bee seemed amazed at what she had heard, and even looked proud. Then she asked abruptly, "Mom, why should I have to be Hong Tan-bee, instead of Park Tan-bee?"

"Because you've got to follow your father's name."

"Why should I have Father's last name? I prefer Park Tan-bee."

Then Yun-hee figured out the implications of her daughter's remark. It was, she thought, an expression of affection toward her mother as well as an impartial, innocent question about the social custom. So Yun-hee told the child she could have her mother's last name if she had no father, then went on:

"You know what? It's in order to preserve family identity that you take your father's last name. If the last names of your father and mother were mixed with each other, wouldn't it be difficult and confusing to set up a family tree? Think of it this way. If women are compared to a field, men assume the role of sowing seeds, and that is why men are given the privilege. But who knows if the children born in the far future might have their mother's last name? Take you for instance, Tan-bee. Who will deny you the right to have the name Park Tan-bee some day? If you grow up to have an occupation like a writer, you'll be able to have a pen name. Then you may use my last name too."

Tan-bee looked up, smiling. It seemed she thought her mother's hope funny as well as awkward. As Yun-hee asked the child what she wanted to be in the future, Tan-bee shook her head and answered she had no idea yet. However, Yun-hee could dimly perceive the course of life the child would take—a life of loneliness like a bird.

Since Tan-bee was anxious about her father, Yun-hee returned home by the last bus after stopping by her parents' home and finishing the other things she had to do. That day Tan-bee, who would soon wear glasses, bought five books, and Yun-hee watched an exorcism dance performance with her daughter. From the moment she learned of that performance in the newspaper, Yun-hee was determined to see it. Called *Relieving the Agony of Flesh,* it was a kind of traditional dance Yun-hee had been wanting to see for a long time. A dancer in white *chima* and *chogori,* who moved like a shadow, carrying a silk cloth, seemed to absorb her from the first. The cloth whirling in the empty air in time to the slow rhythm of a shaman song looked like the beckoning of God, who relieved the suffering accumulated in this world. The dancer took her steps one by one as lightly as air and threw the cloth upward, as if soaring, and caught it again softly in her hand.

Looking earnestly at the cloth as it folded and then unfolded, Yun-hee found that the dancer's face was expressionless, without any feeling of joy or sorrow. It looked like the dance of a soul that had exhausted itself completely in the midst of a harsh life, a soul finally liberated from mundane life, and now in meditation.

Watching the dancer move like a mountain spirit, Yun-hee wished she could do such an exorcism dance in ecstasy some day in her own life. Perhaps she might dance such a dance with no border between life and death, once she could dissolve her mind and consciousness like some agony and cast off all worldly things. Wouldn't that be a moment when she could achieve the state of divine height?

6

The Rainy Season

As deep summer had set in, the seasonal rain front had already reached the west coast. As if caring about the minds of farmers who wished to finish the harvest before the rainy season started, various fruits such as watermelons and muskmelons matured in the fields of Choha-ri under the gentle hand of nature. In preparation for the rainy days, Hee-jo began to prepare the kiln, and soon greenwares were heaped in the studio, waiting for the last ordeal of fire. Dedicating himself to his work again, Hee-jo put aside his painful feelings; as to any other artist, the making of pottery was to him a path to get over every weakness as a human being.

Because of what had happened to her, Yun-hee's loneliness deepened in the valley of her heart, but at the same time she felt more serene than ever before. Regaining her usual calm after the gust of storm had passed in her heart, Yun-hee would wake up early in the morning to greet the rising sun with all her heart and at sunset get a taste of a slightly gloomy and dense melancholy. As nature gently caressed her wounded mind, she sent a prayer of deep gratitude to God.

On the day Hee-jo finished making slip for the wares, Monk Hyeo turned up as their first visitor of July. Though his face had become thin, his eyes looked so clear, shining with a bluish tint, that Yun-hee momentarily forgot to lead him into the house. Even Hee-jo, who usually made it a rule not to meet visitors while working, rushed out of his studio, recognizing the voice of someone he liked. Perhaps in communication with Hyeo through his mind, Hee-jo bowed with his hands clasped. At the sight of him Yun-hee was reminded of the phrase, "A visitor coming like a green grape," a line from a poem by Yuksa. In the meantime Yun-hee squeezed the juice out of the fresh tomatoes she'd picked before they got too ripe. And when she entered the room with cups of juice, Hee-jo was about to leave with the excuse that he had something urgent to do.

"Once involved in the making of *punch'ong* wares," Hee-jo said, "I should not be lazy, because the slip makes the drying process rather difficult. In the process of throwing a pot, the foot rim usually dries first, but the compactness of the wares comes from the drying of all parts evenly."

"The making of *punch'ong* is really miraculous, as it seems delicate yet tough."

With this appropriate remark about Hee-jo's work, Hyeo urged him to go back to the studio, saying he would be staying a long time. Like a child assuring himself of his guardian, Hee-jo gave one more glance at Hyeo through the window from outside and entered his studio. Then Yun-hee asked Hyeo about his health first.

"I've been ill," he replied. "Now I'm feeling as light as a feather in the air. Isn't there a saying that without hardships in the course of living people are apt to despise others? For this reason we must not simply hope for no hardship in life. And my illness turned out a good medicine for me. As long as people have the ability to manage themselves, any kind of hardships can give rise to self-improvement instead."

"But not all people can hope for such ability. For instance, I'm always afflicted with difficulty in getting over any hardship whatsoever."

"Well, your complexion looks better than ever before." With this remark Hyeo uttered Buddha's teachings as if he'd already penetrated the conflict Yun-hee had gone through.

"No one in the world wants any kind of hardship," he began, "still it's hardship itself that brings us to wisdom. Only with hardship around us are we able to learn how to endure it. Happiness blinds our eyes and ears, because, living in happiness and comfort, we're liable to lose prudence. A philosopher once said he'd rather be a hungry Socrates than a well-fed pig, so you'd better be aware that the best way to self-improvement is to go through hardships in the endless flow of time, since you cannot help but be restless when things are going well. Along with this, you must not even expect others to obey your will, either, because you're likely to be arrogant when others simply follow your will. Therefore, you must take as your masters the people who do not conform to your will. That's the teaching of Buddha."

"Then the man over in the studio is my master," spoke Yun-hee, pointing to where Hee-jo was working.

"Indeed. When we simply say in the presence of some object, 'That's the way it is,' over again and again, there'll be no need to put more words to the object. If our heart genuinely understands everything, it doesn't attach itself to anything anymore. For the same reason we don't hate children when they keep after us for something, because we've accepted the way of children. In other words, in dealing with children we change our way of thinking and accept their behavior as it is."

"Exactly," agreed Yun-hee. "I've always thought I'm perfect and innocent, only hoping that the man I'm living with will change someday. In fact, it's I who am not willing to change."

"In the former world you two might have been beings indifferent to each other. So you're destined to be a couple to gain the meaning of life together in this world."

Yun-hee put on a bitter smile at hearing Hyeo's words, which touched her heart. It occurred to Yun-hee that had she lived with an ordinary person, she would have settled in the normal happiness of life and consequently wouldn't have grown anymore in her mind. Looking at a *punch'ong* vessel on which Hee-jo had engraved the Buddhist scripture *Prajna-paramita-sutra,* Hyeo told himself, Surely, this inscription is not tainted with anything secular.

Just as all roads lead to Rome, so all roads to truth must lead to the core of pain, Yun-hee realized. Two days after Hyeo had left after praising the value of pain, President Choi of the Dawool Gallery paid a visit to her house after a long absence. President Choi said he'd been very busy changing the interior design of the gallery, and without further words suggested to Hee-jo an invitational exhibition for the coming autumn. Yun-hee judged that, even though Hee-jo had produced no successful works last spring, it was not impossible to open an exhibition if only he would hurry from now on.

As Hee-jo didn't give his answer readily, Yun-hee tried to persuade him: "It's timely, you know. You had an exhibition of living wares last year, so you may as well have one for your works this year. Of course you can put it off forever. But it seems not bad to arrange what you'll accomplish as time passes."

"I've no urge this year, though," replied Hee-jo. "For no obvious reason, since spring began I haven't been able to work as I used to. People at other galleries offered me such suggestions, but I couldn't accept them."

"Let's do it this time," urged President Choi. "There are no artists who plan to have an exhibition after their works are piled up. Once started, you can manage it. And you must also remember that no artist can work only with his craft. Heaven must help us to see the beautiful *punch'ong* wares."

"After this exhibition, please buy me a traditional costume of pure silk. I'd like to have one in peony red."

As Yun-hee spoke words that she did not intend to say, Hee-jo nodded his head slowly. "All right, let's do it around the middle of November."

"As far as the exhibition is concerned, October is the best month, because there are many holidays in a row. In November many customers would be restless, since the season for the college entrance examination comes near."

To President Choi's words, Hee-jo finally responded: "Let's do it in early November then. I want to have as much time as possible. Besides, I want to do it this time in the month I like best—when autumn leaves fall, and the woods become suffused with autumn color. It'll be good to take a trip after the exhibition."

"Ha, ha! I'm no better than a mere merchant. While you think about the autumn woods, Mr. Hong, I'm only thinking about how to sell the works. You must admit, though, that I, too, have a Burberry coat in which to walk in the autumn winds. I'm not far from being romantic myself—though I may not look so."

Joking, President Choi agreed to open the exhibition on the second day of November. At first he seemed somewhat reluctant, but as his proposal itself was an abrupt one, he couldn't insist anymore. With the agreement between the two made, they sat down at a drinking table. Hee-jo, who had finished making the slip for wares yesterday and had to wait for them to dry, was able to take his time to enjoy drinking. President Choi opened by mentioning the recent depression in the antique market.

"Like other markets, antique trading is now experiencing a severe depression, with the oil crisis and the soaring cost of living.

The fortune-hunting ladies, I heard, had swarmed to even the small shops to grab up every antique they could find, then started businesses of their own at home. In addition to this, many antique shops have been closed since the value-added tax was passed. As you know, the highest tax rate applies to antiques now that they don't belong to the category of industrial products. Perhaps this is the only country in the world that regards artistic works as luxuries, you know. Such a misconception may change some day when our country's economy is in better shape. But right now our Insa-dong street of antique trading is especially restless, since one couple who run a shop are missing."

"I read the story in the paper. You mean the accident about the Kumdang Shop?" interposed Yun-hee. After a phone call from her husband, the paper said, the wife had gone out with money accompanied by their chauffeur, but none of them returned.

As Yun-hee showed her interest, President Choi put on a grave look.

"As is shown in this case," he said, "there's no denying that there always exists the possibility of a carefully planned kidnapping in the antiques market, because the dealers often deal directly with grave robbers on the spot, without mediation by brokers. This is, of course, not only illegal but dangerous indeed. Even my uncle, who had run a big antique shop with my father, was once robbed and barely escaped with his life after going to the spot. After that he had to ask people who wanted to sell or buy to come to his shop and make the deal there. In truth, this is the golden rule of a store-keeping merchant in the antiques market. I heard Mr. Chung of the Kumdang Shop was not in the habit of going out with money to buy merchandise."

"I guess he must have found a very rare antique," observed Yun-hee.

"Maybe so. Sometimes antique traders risk an adventure in order to get valuable antiquities. So they'd be excited by the presence of rare pieces even though they're not able to possess them, and even think about them in their sleep. Mr. Chung's wife supposedly went to Suwon, but the mere mention of such old cities as Suwon or Kyongju stirs our mind, because they're places where the shady trading of antiquities prevails. The thing is, antique merchants experience a sheer pleasure of their own that no one else can easily feel. Although I became an antique merchant under the influence of my father, I realize it's rather the antique work itself that gives me a lesson in life."

As the talk deepened, President Choi listed three maxims that he said he'd learned from antiquities: "First, we learn through pain," he stated, then told a story about a merchant who had worked hard as a helper in an antique shop called Gochukyo and eventually inherited it from its owner:

"Since he'd seen so many times how his boss dealt with antiquities and also stored up some knowledge for himself, the young merchant collected all the money he had saved and, soon after taking over the shop, went to buy some work from a Chinese trader whom his boss had dealt with. As an honest and diligent man, this young merchant might have thought he was doing the right thing. However, in the eyes of the Chinese trader, he was no more than another rookie, so eventually the trader sold him a fake. After he got back, the young merchant realized he was cheated, and so his heart was much hurt. But he began to save money and went to the trader again years later. Since he had got a valuable experience with the trader before, the merchant prepared a present this time and told the trader that he'd learned a great lesson before. This time the Chinese trader felt sorry and thought the man was now prepared to have rare antiquities. So the trader guided him to the basement and gave him a genuine work of enormous value, saying he could pay for it later. That work was so precious that the money the merchant had saved was not at all sufficient to cover it. As a result, the Chinese trader compensated him for his previous loss. Making enough money to pay for that piece in time, and becoming rich again, the merchant visited Osaka some time later to buy a very expensive piece of china worth half of his whole fortune. Like other valuable rarities, the work he hoped to buy was kept in the deepest place of the shop. The antique dealer took it out of the secret place and gave it to the merchant wrapped in many layers of paper. As is usual for rare works, it's not customary to take its picture or tear open the wrapping paper, so that the pleasure and expectation can be preserved in the mind. After he returned, however, the merchant found he'd bought a fake. Just imagine how painful his heart must have been! With extreme pain in his heart he crushed the work to pieces, lest any other person should be lured and experience the same pain as he had. If he hadn't had the pain of being cheated, the merchant would have remained a mere antique trader, I believe. After all, he came to realize the road of a merchant through pain."

As Yun-hee sat motionless, fascinated by the lesson of pain, President Choi suddenly picked up the jade-gray stone from the stationery chest and continued:

"The second lesson is to find something extraordinary in the commonplace. At first people merely look for expensive works, thinking that only the most expensive piece is best. But the more they become experienced in collecting, the more they come to learn the beauty of the commonplace. For instance, the stone here is nothing special in the view of others, but it's breathing here, as it has the story of someone who picked it up."

Then, taking an episode of an unmarried woman painter who had once bought a sculpture of a lonely wild goose, President Choi counted the third lesson on his fingers: "The third we learn from antiquities is renunciation."

"You mean not having too much desire even though you want something?" commented Yun-hee.

"Exactly. But, besides that, I include a sharing of delight. When lust blinds your eyes, you want to possess every article you're dying for. But once your love for antiquities deepens, you're even willing to hand them to others so that more people are able to appreciate them. It's a kind of release from the desire for possession."

President Choi finished his story and took a drink of wine to moisten his lips. The three maxims he'd learned from antiquities can be applied to life itself, Yun-hee realized, since truth is always the same no matter what direction we take. What lingered especially in her mind was the word "renunciation." Actually, Yun-hee had consoled herself up to now that she had no attachment to anything, not even love or honor. But wasn't it true that in the course of life she grabbed something in spite of herself? Yun-hee countered to herself that if she were really liberated from a sense of possession, she would give up for others something she cherished.

When President Choi offered Yun-hee a drink, she marveled at him, "Oh, you're such a story-teller to have moved me so deeply."

"Oh, not at all. I suppose that anyone who has lived in pursuit of something is able to tell a story like this. You may have a more sincere story than mine, Mrs. Hong. A story of your own is also proof of your struggle in life."

⋖❧

The scent of paulownia flowers had wafted about in the air when the firing in the kiln had started last spring. On the day the firing in the kiln had started for the second time this year, a bunch of evening primrose bloomed by the wall. Perhaps because of the cloudy sky, the flowers, which usually bloomed only at night, seemed to greet Yun-hee in full bloom even until the next morning. It seemed as if the flowers themselves were eager to watch the kiln, so Yun-hee concealed her anticipation of good results deep in her heart for fear that such a feeling might disappear.

In time Hee-jo started a fire in the kiln. With the clouds completely dissipated, the sun began to blaze at about ten o'clock in the morning. Wan-kyu was dressed loosely in a sleeveless running shirt; Hee-jo, who didn't take off his thick, long-sleeved working clothes, kept wiping off his dripping sweat with a towel. Obviously Hee-jo was strained after promising to have an exhibition. Looking at him, Yun-hee called to mind a scene of three years before when Hee-jo, indulging in his work, wore a turtle-neck sweater all through the summer, since it was difficult for him to control his passion. The road that an artist takes in order to reach the essence of art is no different from that of an ascetic, and Hee-jo at the time had seemed to choose the way of asceticism in his work. Hee-jo, Yun-hee thought, would have been a Buddhist monk or a priest by now if he had not become a potter.

Five hours after the initial firing started, a loud scraping was heard in the left burner. Immediately turning off the burner, Hee-jo took it apart only to find that it was malfunctioning. Since it had happened frequently before, it was nothing to be surprised about, but it seemed an effort to have to repair the machine in the middle of firing. When Yun-hee had once suggested that Hee-jo replace it

203

with a new burner, he had spoken nonchalantly wiping away sweat, his face stained with oil: "Anyway I can fix it up. It's running all right." Hee-jo had then jokingly told Wan-kyu that he had no money to buy a new one, but Yun-hee was to learn it was not at all because of money that he insisted on using the old burner.

After repairing the machine, Hee-jo explained to Wan-kyu: "You see, I don't use a thermometer in the kiln because I want to concentrate more thoroughly upon the fire. If I use a thermometer, the process of working may be more accurate, but you must, in turn, rely on science. I know kilns have now been developed to prevent the possibility of burner failure, but it doesn't matter to me whether such a possibility is high or not. What I want is not the accuracy or logic of machinery, you know. I want above all to encounter a mystery that has never been thought of before, and that's why I stick to such an unreliable kiln."

What Hee-jo had strived to encounter in firing, Yun-hee realized, was a mystery itself. It is likely that one could reap in proportion to one's effort to earn; yet in the realm beyond the reach of humans a mysterious power works through human hands. Even Mozart's music, regarded as belonging to the realm of heaven, was supposedly helped by the power of God, so what happens beyond the horizon clearly belongs to God.

Though the soot appearing in the right bag wall was cleared away too late, the initial firing was finished in twelve hours. After cooling the kiln down for one day, the greenwares were pulled out. It turned out the large pieces on the upper side of the back wall were a little sooty, but on the whole the soot was cleared away on the lower part. If the results were as successful as the initial firing last time, Hee-jo would have to break a plate according to his custom. This time, however, his ritual was not necessary, because out of more than twenty large pieces six were already broken. Concluding that he had made the wares too thick to begin with, Hee-jo calmly admitted his mistake. Actually there was a time when more than half of the large pieces had been broken during the second firing. Looking at them, Tan-bee then consoled her father, saying, "Isn't it better to break them after the initial firing— rather than after the second?" Though it was a childlike idea,

Tan-bee only served to teach her father in her own way how to see the bright side of things.

After putting glaze on the greenwares that had passed the first phase of the test, and taking care of the melting trace of the glaze, Hee-jo placed them in the kiln tenderly for the second firing. Because of the weather forecast that the rain front was moving up to the central region of the country, he had to work with the wares far into the night before the firing. It was past midnight when the door of the kiln was closed with his work finished, and the next morning the oil tank was filled up.

Having offered a humble sacrifice to the spirits for a successful firing, Hee-jo started the fire with a cotton-tipped torch, and immediately the motor began to run loudly. Since the electricity had been off for a while the previous day, Yun-hee had called the electric company to check if there would be no more interruptions. It would be very frustrating if the electricity went off after the glaze started to melt, so she had to ask if there would be another cutoff of electricity during the second firing.

Yun-hee heard the burner going all day long, but at about four o'clock in the afternoon the machine stopped suddenly. As she was about to take Hee-jo an iced drink made with ground barley and some freshly boiled potatoes, Yun-hee simply imagined that the soot in the bag wall was being cleaned off. In fact, it had been Hee-jo's method to turn off the burner and put out the fire in the kiln so that the inside temperature would rise properly. Feeling hot, Wan-kyu then walked out of the studio and stood in front of the bamboo bed in the yard, and soon Hee-jo walked down to the pump to wash himself. Taking a tray from Yun-hee, Wan-kyu asked himself, "Isn't it too quiet?"

Wan-kyu seemed to feel numb at the sudden silence after the burner had stopped. Now, evening primroses as tall as the geese were sleeping under the summer sun; a goose, dipping its beak into the water pail, strolled alone in the backyard in the blazing sun as if stirring up the calm silence. As the goose walked toward the barn at the back of the studio where the chimney of the kiln protruded above the roof, Yun-hee set off toward it. It occurred to her that the slate had been installed from the roof of the studio to the top of the back wall, providing space for storing briquets in the winter. The slate was once damaged by a heavy snow about two years before, and though it was soon repaired, Yun-hee became a little worried as the rainy season came near. So she moved closer to look it over.

Approaching, Yun-hee found the heat from the chimney quite excessive and turned back hurriedly without examining it thoroughly. Yun-hee could tell the heat was escaping from the kiln as she happened to look at the insulating brick of the kiln and discovered it was now open just enough for a hand to be put in. As far as she knew, the insulating brick should be opened as wide as possible to increase the heat as well as to make the fire spread evenly inside the kiln. So Yun-hee went out to the yard and found Hee-jo drinking the barley tea on the bamboo bed. When she asked Hee-jo if he knew the insulating brick had been opened a little, he put down the bowl and exclaimed with a surprised look, "What're you talking about?"

At Hee-jo's words Wan-kyu answered with a trembling voice that he had opened the insulating brick about four centimeters. Then Hee-jo quickly stood up, walked to the barn, and came back trying to restrain his anger. Without even looking at Wan-kyu, Hee-jo ordered him, in a low voice, to turn the burner on immediately. Hardly ten minutes had passed before the burner began to rattle again. As the controlling of fire in the kiln was not an absolute necessity, it had only to be omitted this time. It was a relief, though, to learn early that the insulating brick had not been opened far enough. Despite that, the loss of the heat had been so great that Hee-jo grumbled, going out to the yard:

"Instead of letting the heat spread evenly inside the kiln, I let it be lost evenly. Damn it! How foolish that was!"

"Sorry, I was mistaken," apologized Wan-kyu. "Last year I noticed a line in the check list of the kiln, 'an insulation brick four centimeters,' under the heading of fire control. So I merely regarded it as an indication that in turning on the burner again I must open the insulation brick about four centimeters—just as I did this time . . ."

"What? I thought you were quite skillful in handling the kiln when you said you would open the insulation brick yourself. Give up pottery training if you go on like this!"

"I'm sorry. I think I was possessed by something."

As Wan-kyu reproached himself repeatedly, Hee-jo said, easing down his anger: "You should have done firing two or three hours longer than the previous time. Now you'll never forget how to handle the insulation brick."

During the second firing, when utmost care was needed, both Hee-jo and Wan-kyu were not to leave the studio, so they had to eat dinner on the bamboo bed. If the firing lasted late into the night, they might have had to sit up on the table through the night with mosquitoes swarming around them. But eleven hours after the firing started, a pyrometric cone on the left bag wall began to bend down—a signal that the glaze was about to melt. While the pyrometric cones on both sides of the bag walls with their fire holes and on the upper and lower shelves were beginning to bend down, flame as red as a well ripened persimmon was seen dancing wildly inside the kiln. In fact, the flame sweeping like a wind among the many pieces of greenwares looked like a ghostly magic spell of life, and as such, the long journey through the flame felt like a solemn ritual of final completion. Watching even a tiny ware be born through such a severe trial, Yun-hee momentarily got a curious yet shameful feeling about her own existence.

It took almost five hours for all the cones inside the kiln to bend down. Just before midnight, barely able to sleep during the firing, Wan-kyu came down to the living room to call Yun-hee, who was reading. As Wan-kyu asked her to hold a lantern while pouring oil into the tank, Yun-hee consented without hesitation. In the starlight he hurried to fill up a bucket with the oil remaining in the drum and climbed up the ladder to pour it into the tank. Repeating the task, Wan-kyu said to Yun-hee without a trace of fatigue: "My, if the insulation brick had not been opened immediately, more oil would have been needed. At any rate we spent more oil today simply because of my mistake. Luckily, we have some oil left."

The firing usually took two and one-half drums of oil, and since it had required only three drums this time Wan-kyu looked relieved. Telling him not to worry about the oil, Yun-hee held the lantern up for him, so he wouldn't slip on the steps. At this moment she remembered Mr. Yang, a villager, who once fell as he was dozing beside the oil tank while working with Hee-jo.

"When I called him out," said Yun-hee, "he was startled awake from having dozed off and fell off the tank. He must be a very drowsy man, since, on another occasion, he began to doze off and eventually spilled oil all over the tank."

Hearing this, Wan-kyu spilled some oil, chuckling. So Yun-hee clicked her tongue, "Tut! You even spilled oil without dozing off!"

Yun-hee looked up at the sky where the Great Bear attracted her eyes. She recalled her high school days when she would sit on a bamboo bed in the summer and stare up into the night sky, searching for exotic constellations such as Orion or Scorpion. Just as some stars drew maps of their own in the sky, so some people on earth spent the mesmeric night getting closer to the starlight. The sight of Wan-kyu, who lit the lantern and poured oil into the tank in the pitch-black night, looked more stable than ever before. And even Yun-hee, who usually went to sleep early at night, kept a vigil this night like the glow of a firefly.

After taking out all the wares, including the test pieces in the bottom of the kiln, they turned off the burner around two o'clock in the morning. It had been raining since midnight, and the rain continued all day long while Hee-jo and Wan-kyu played the *changgi* game. The rain stopped for a while in the evening, then turned back into a drizzle early the next morning. It was clearly a rainy season.

The sky was gray on the day the kiln was opened. Taking tea, Hee-jo looked out for a while, then entered the studio without a word. He would sustain his expectation for the wares before opening his kiln, but at the moment like this he had no other choice but to submit to the result of the firing.

While they were opening the kiln, Yun-hee made young radish-and-leek *kimchi* and put salt into a pickle pot full of cucumbers brought from a patch in the village the previous day. After that she decided to prepare hand-made noodles for lunch and patted the dough thin. After chopping a squash, while boiling some anchovy soup, Yun-hee went quietly to the studio to see the results. From Hee-jo's satisfied look as he smoked a cigarette in front of the door, she was able to infer that the results had been satisfactory. The floor of the studio was thickly covered with wares, not even leaving space to walk, and about twenty tea cups and bowls were heaped up in one corner. Four of the large pieces were broken, Yun-hee found, while the wares that had endured the test of firing, though stained with some smoke here and there, gleamed with a light brown color from the oxidizing fire. As such, it seemed still hot inside the kiln.

Removing his gloves and lighting a cigarette, Wan-kyu reported to Hee-jo: "Look, those from the left side of the middle shelf are a little over-fired. As a result, the firing in this kiln is strong on the left side."

"Perhaps so," Hee-jo replied. "Those from the right side of the upper shelf are a little less fired. Nevertheless, they look fine."

Because there had been a mistake in the process of firing, Yun-hee had already prepared herself for a failure. To her surprise, however, the results were extraordinary: with more than ten large pieces surviving, the firing this time had turned out a success. Hee-jo then took the four broken large pieces and other ruined works out to the yard and broke them to pieces one by one under the fence of the house. Perhaps it was because of the serenity of his mind that Hee-jo did not look pitiful at all even while breaking his own works to pieces in the drizzling rain. No doubt the result had made him happy, since he didn't immediately break up some works that left a little to be desired in technique. The previous spring, all the greenwares on the upper and lower shelves had been overheated; consequently they were fated to be smashed to pieces. Finding some of the pieces too valuable to be discarded, Yun-hee at the time had asked Hee-jo to spare them, saying it wouldn't be too late to break them later. At last she had taken a large bowl almost forcefully from his hands to use for cultivating an orchid. The bowl had since made a good water bed for the wild orchid.

Out of many successful large pieces in the present firing, Hee-jo arrayed seven of the wares in the living room. In the past he would destroy his works if not pleased with them later, but this time he found it admirable that the wares had passed the ordeal of firing. It made Yun-hee's mind peaceful, too, to look at the light brown pieces, because of the warm feeling they aroused. Moreover, the rough strokes of the brush across the wall of the pot filled her heart with liveliness. One design made with a fingernail looked like an elegant maiden, while the other, scrolled like a whirlwind, revealed a nervous sensitivity harmonized with a healthy mind. What captured Yun-hee's eyes in particular was a square bottle with rounded corners. The thick-layered slip in it felt rather strong, yet the drawing made by the thumb evoked the image of an orchid, even arousing in Yun-hee a sense of nobility, or the way of thought itself.

However, there was no time to appreciate the pots at leisure, since news of an oil price increase of fifty-nine percent had suddenly been announced. Along with it came an increase in other prices, such as electricity, transportation, rice, etc.—all jumped up so high that it was as chilling as throwing cold water onto the body. The previous March, the oil price had been raised, and it was hardly three months since the government had announced there would be no more price hikes this year. Even if she'd been unable to afford to store up oil before now, Yun-hee regretted not having prepared even one drum of oil before the price hike, because two more firings had to be done soon. When she had been a child, her mother would store fresh rice in the barn and eat wormy rice after drying it. It was, Yun-hee reflected, her wisdom of life, not a mere habit.

As Yun-hee was hanging up washed clothes in the bathroom, worrying about how to manage the household until the exhibition, Hee-jo called her. Entering the room, Yun-hee found Yi Sung-ju sitting inside—a guest she had not expected. Since it had rained hard to the extent that nothing was visible, the bottoms of his trousers were completely soaked.

"Oh, what brought you here in this heavy rain?" asked Yun-hee, handing Yi Sung-ju a towel.

"Thank you. I slept at my house last night, and now I'm going out again. Because of some urgent matters lately, I've hardly been home."

"By the way, your wife is anything but ordinary," remarked Yun-hee reservedly.

Thinking that she would tell Yi Sung-ju about his wife's visit the other day, Yun-hee brought up the recent price hike. She judged it was of no use to complain about such things to Hee-jo.

"I heard," Yun-hee began, "that there's a panicky hoarding of commodities going on in Seoul these days. Yet I don't know what I should do in these circumstances. A country like Japan, which imports oil just as we do, is said to have settled the oil crisis by raising its price only twenty percent. But why, then, must the oil price rise nearly three times as much in this country? I think we deserve a certain compensation in proportion to the high price of oil we have to pay. If we raise the price of pottery, which is already considered too high, many people might think we're cheating them, and assert they don't need pottery as much as oil."

"That's true," returned Yi Sung-ju. "But what's more serious than the mere number of fifty-nine percent in the price hike is the anxieties of people themselves. I heard that some supermarkets in the Kangnam region ran out of commodities because the wealthy are sweeping up everything, even toothpaste. Meanwhile, those who cannot afford things feel more and more anxious and miserable. Because of the uncertain political situation, which causes an unstable life for ordinary people now, I believe women in particular tend to manage the life of the entire family with their own hands. But such a mind, in turn, gives birth to the greed of the people and eventually produces fortune-hunting ladies, who grab up antiques and even dare to store up commodities—accelerating the turbulence of society. In any event I don't understand why the prices keep rising like this. Probably too many development plans, which lead to speculative investment, cause the prices to keep soaring. Anyhow I find it deplorable that, in the face of an urgent situation like today, people are only trying to save themselves by fighting against each other—instead of thinking about how to solve the problem through cooperative efforts. It all seems disgusting. I heard that once before, when the prices started to rise without notice in America, housewives put on a boycott campaign and eventually reduced the prices. Why, then, can't it happen in this country? No doubt the future of a country depends on women themselves."

"You're right," Yun-hee agreed with Yi Sung-ju. "Just before the Japanese annexation of Korea, in the midst of a national campaign to pay off our declining country's national debt, many women had dedicated themselves to the campaign wholeheart-

211

edly—surrendering everything they had, including such things as their rings and hairpins. Then it's proof of the avarice of this age that people get engulfed in materialism. And I think women are no exception in this regard. Although many people have asserted the necessity of saving nowadays, I realize that only the people who have nothing more to save are obliged to do it."

"No doubt about it," spoke Yi Sung-ju. "As the depression continues, I'm told, many companies are rushing to fire their employees. What a shameful and inhuman idea it is! I feel they must above all ask to whom they owe the success of their business in the past, since it's nothing more than the blood and sweat of the employees who made those companies thrive. Now they're kicking out the laborers who have been toiling in the shadow of a growing economy, simply because the profit level is going down. So I cannot side with those who have because I cannot help but love those who have not."

Yi Sung-ju then directed his criticism against the current regime, adding something Yun-hee did not know. "On leaving Seoul, U.S. President Carter was said to have advised President Park Jung-hee to be a Christian."

"Is that so? It hurts our pride," answered Yun-hee.

"That's because he already knew the severe oppression of such dissidents as Kim Dae-jung or Kim Ji-ha. Where do you suppose such severity comes from? Perhaps Carter thought that President Park lacked a spiritual basis as a leader. Do you also know that at the time of Carter's visit to Korea many dissidents were either imprisoned or confined to their houses?"

"Really? It seems we're living comfortably here—not caring about what's really going outside," said Yun-hee, a bit surprised.

"In an age like this, no one—not even a potter—is supposed to live looking only up at the sky."

Yi Sung-ju made a sarcastic remark to Hee-jo who had been listening quietly, then asked Yun-hee if any mail had arrived for him. As Yun-hee said as if surprised, "At my house?" he said no more. When Hee-jo went out for a while, she inquired about Ji-woon.

"I haven't seen her lately. Now that I have something extremely urgent, I haven't been in touch with her. Anyhow I'm so anxious to see her . . ."

"Since your last visit here with Ji-woon, your wife came to us. Has she told you about that?"

As Yun-hee informed him, Yi Sung-ju shook his head, not surprised. Then she continued. "She reproached me for being silent, you know. You're bold enough to come here with Ji-woon, but you don't have the courage to tell your wife about her."

"Mmm, she knows a little about her."

"But your wife accused you of your wanton behavior. Is it all right to be accused like that by your wife?" Yun-hee said reproachfully.

"No, I've never been such a wanton person. What I've done is a little courting. That's all."

As Yi Sung-ju answered cynically, Yun-hee felt sorry, realizing she was interfering with the privacy of others. So she said, "I understand you're free to love someone else, but doesn't it occur to you that you might end up hurting both women? You must remember that you're in a society where traditional morality dominates. Your continued courtship will only cause a scandal."

"What's wrong with a scandal? That's life anyway."

As Yi Sung-ju replied curtly, Yun-hee grinned helplessly because, nonchalant as they might be, his words sounded appealing. As implied by his remark, life is not something contained by an institution, or a conventional morality arrayed like ready-made bricks. Rather, it's inherent in the glances exchanged secretly outside the door, in the tear drops Hee-jo had shed in the dark, or in scribblings in a back alley. Dreaming of rebellion, people resist being molded into a certain form and ridicule solemn immobility.

After a pause Yi Sung-ju muttered, "A wanderer like me should not have married. Living tied to one woman is against my nature."

"You cannot say you're a man tied to something now that you have another woman."

"Nevertheless I'm far from free. I'd thought about divorce several times, but women cannot live without a husband—at least in name."

Then Yi Sung-ju sighed deeply and lit a cigarette. Was this what his wife once called compassion? Yun-hee asked herself. If Yun-hee were in her shoes, she would not seek such compassion from her husband, no matter how it might look like human weakness. In a moment Hee-jo entered with a drinking table and offered Yi Sung-ju a drink. Looking at the green stream through the window, Yun-hee stated, conscious of Hee-jo: "The important thing is how much a husband and wife respect each other. One-sided affection is as fragile as a building on sand. There's nothing like an eternal shelter—though I myself am not sure of the existence of eternity."

❧

It must have been the long spell of rain that had made Yun-hee gloomy for the past few days. Such a mood was not so much an emotion as a feeling, she thought, and had to be left alone like a stream of water. Regardless of the weather, Yun-hee put a handful of oak leaves into the refrigerator to prevent dampness, boiled the dish cloth, and dried it on the kettle lid. Also, she had to heat the *ondol* floor every two days to remove sticky dampness. The history of mankind's struggle against dampness, Yun-hee reflected, dates back more than one hundred thousand years. Examination of the bones of the Neanderthal men who had inhabited the globe at the time showed that most of them had suffered from rheumatism. Naturally, their dwelling in the dampness of a cave was thought to have hurt their joints, so the idea that the same dampness had haunted mankind for such a long time made Yun-hee feel attached to the existence of dampness itself.

The rain, which had continued for five days, started pouring this morning. Rejoicing, Tan-bee wore a raincoat and high boots, but Sae-bul had no raincoat of his own. Worrying that Sae-bul would get soaked if he went out without a raincoat, Yun-hee took out a yellow raincoat handed down from his cousin, now a middle school student. Though it was too large for him, Yun-hee judged, Sae-bul would look all right in the coat with the cuffs rolled up twice. However, Sae-bul ran away with only an umbrella, saying he might look like a policeman in the coat.

Yun-hee had dug a ditch in the front yard the previous day to drain the water, but the water was already knee-high by noon. If the water were not drained off pretty soon, it would overflow into the barn where the wares were stored. So, arming herself with a raincoat, Yun-hee bailed the water with a basin, assisted by Hee-jo. When they had managed to drain off the water by digging a wide furrow in the yard, the stream gushing beside the house made a swift current as it ran in a curve in one corner. Apparently the curve had made by the gushing stream sweeping stones along with it. If the water kept rising in only one corner, Yun-hee suspected, the stream would destroy the stakes along the boundary of the yard and flood the house.

At last, Hee-jo walked into the stream again, not even changing his wet clothes. He pushed big stones into the stream to fill up the hollow of the curve so that, with the curve removed, the stream could slow down. With the water further up the stream increased by the continued rain, Hee-jo's work was retarded, so Yun-hee joined to fill up the stream, only with smaller stones. Then, watching the geese strolling by the stream, she waved them back to the house and soon found that the clever grandfather goose was standing in the rain beside a stake, looking over the current.

Making the curve more moderate, Yun-hee had nearly finished her task when Kwang-ho walked along the ginseng field across the stream. They'd not seen each other till now, due to the trouble caused by the building of the henhouse early the previous spring. Judging by his raincoat and high boots, Kwang-ho seemed to be coming back from the rice paddies. Coming to the stream, he called out to Hee-jo: "Yo, dude! How dare you throw stones into the stream without my approval? Will you take full responsibility if the water floods into my field, eh? Don't you dare touch even the smallest stone on my side, remember?"

Hee-jo, dumbfound, merely stared at Kwang-ho. In fact, Kwang-ho had no right or reason to interfere, since it did not make sense to assume that a few stones thrown into the stream would make the water flood into his field. So Hee-jo returned coldly, "Look, take a nap if you've nothing else to do, or help me in my work."

"What? I told you not to move the stones. If you ignore my warning, I'll take the stones out of the stream with a crane right now."

As Kwang-ho threatened, Hee-jo picked up a big stone and got ready to throw it at him, but Kwang-ho urinated into the stream and walked away. Everything he'd done was so out of proportion that Hee-jo lost interest in fighting him. Shaking his head, Hee-jo sighed, "Damn! It has rained so long as to make even a tadpole scream."

The rain had continued for so long that the roof of the children's room had started leaking. Soon Tan-bee ran up to her mother to show her the raindrops on the notebook in which she'd been doing her homework. So Yun-hee immediately pulled the fuse in the box, cutting off the current to the fluorescent light in order to prevent a short circuit. It was the very first time the roof of her house had begun to leak.

Sae-bul, delighted with the expectation of candlelight tonight, went out to the yard after dinner, only to return and call his mother outside. Looking out into the yard, Yun-hee saw the child pointing at the goose cage, saying that Gu-chul, the grandfather goose, had disappeared. Then Sae-bul said in a half-crying voice, "My, where did he go in this heavy rain? I drove the other three into the cage, but not Gu-chul."

Sae-bul looked around with an anxious face, and Yun-hee asked him to search for the missing goose. Since it was not fully dark yet, there was still time to look around the house. In a moment Sae-bul put on the yellow raincoat he had thrown off in the morning and went outside. As Tan-bee stood up to follow him, Yun-hee cautioned her not to get near the stream. It was not the first time that the geese hadn't come back, so Yun-hee was not that worried. During the early years she'd lived in this house, Yun-hee had kept a dog for some time, but one day the dog had disappeared in the night and never come back. Because the chain had been cut, she guessed a dog-dealer must have stolen it. To her knowledge, however, there'd been nobody yet who had stolen a goose.

When Yun-hee was about to light a fire of dried twigs in the fuel pit, Tan-bee ran to her, shouting, "Mom, go over there! The goose is lying still."

"Where?"

"By the stream. He's dead."

Yun-hee pushed the paper she was holding into the fuel pit and followed Tan-bee immediately. In her hurry, Yun-hee had forgotten to bring an umbrella with her, and as soon as she left the house her hair was soaked. Following Tan-bee, she walked through the muddy lane along the stream beside the ginseng field and instantly caught sight of Sae-bul crouching in the stony field. It was near the point where the brook joined the stream, and Yun-hee, walking down, found the goose dead with his long neck stretched out on the ground. Seeing his mother, Sae-bul said, wiping away his tears, "Look here, Mom. He must have been swept away by the current."

Judging from the big stone beside the goose, it seemed likely that the current had swept the goose away and rammed it into the stone. The goose must have drifted to the bank after having hit the stone. While looking at the scar on the goose's head, Yun-hee was suddenly reminded of Kwang-ho and thought he might have thrown the stone at the goose for revenge in a fit of anger. Although there was no denying such a possibility, it was of no use now, she felt.

But Sae-bul was mournful, blaming himself: "I should have put him into the cage myself, instead of having dinner. If I had, he wouldn't have died."

There was something appealing in Sae-bul's sorrow and Yun-hee, feeling sorry, tried to console him. "It's not your fault, since everything is subject to something unexpected. Perhaps the goose liked strolling outside, or wanted to be left alone to move about freely in the rain."

Meanwhile Tan-bee started to pick the goose up by herself. Sae-bul helped her carry the goose to the house before Yun-hee could persuade them not to, since Hee-jo had promised to bury the goose the next day. Because of the continued rain, they could not leave the goose in the yard, and as Yun-hee was about to spread a straw mat over the goose in the barn, Sae-bul begged her to put the goose in his room just for tonight. But Yun-hee didn't agree: even granting Sae-bul's sorrow, she couldn't allow the dead body of a goose in his room.

His eyes almost overflowing, Sae-bul said, "I can't see the goose anymore after tonight. He'll be buried in the dark earth tomorrow."

"You know, no one can escape from parting," Yun-hee soothed him, "so let him pass away quietly."

The next day the grandfather goose was buried on the hill behind the house, with the stream visible below. Sae-bul buried a *punch'ong* cup filled with feed along with the goose and Tan-bee put a cross she had made on the small grave. The previous night Tan-bee had fallen asleep with a lighted candle, making a wooden cross. From the church at the entrance to the village, she had learned what a cross was used for. Going back down to their house, the children hurried to avoid being late for school. Seeing them, Hee-jo chuckled to himself.

"Sae-bul did it innocently," he said to Yun-hee. "But isn't it funny that the cup he buried along with the goose may be dug up by someone hundreds of years from now and treated as a valuable antique? Regardless of age, ancient or modern, the ideas of mankind are basically the same. As you know, food like acorns is found in the graves of primitive men. Nevertheless, when I think of the mummies in the Egyptian graves, I feel horrified at the ugliness of the human desire for eternity."

"What is your idea, then?" asked Yun-hee, wanting to hear something from Hee-jo, who had managed to survive his relentless self-reproach.

"Well, I'll live until I have a spirit for doing my work. Then I want to be buried next to your tomb—that's all."

As he mumbled, staring at the green fields, Yun-hee replied, "If I should die first, burn my body to ashes."

Hee-jo turned to her a moment after a pause. "Still, you'd better keep in mind that I like you better than you've ever liked me."

The rain stopped for a while in the morning, but it soon turned into a drizzle. As Hee-jo went to his studio with a book in his hand, Yun-hee covered the inside of the lamps in the kitchen and the wooden floor with shiny silver paper and replaced the sixty-watt light bulbs with thirty-watt ones. After the oil price hike, the newspaper said, the ever-bustling street of Myong-dong in Seoul had lost its vigor; the number of public disturbances in Pusan was reported to have decreased from about one hundred a day to twenty or so. In Tan-bee's school, teachers wrote questions on the blackboard to avoid having to use paper for their tests. There were even some parents in the countryside who had asked their children not to space their words—simply to save notebook paper.

Checking Tan-bee's clothes for the first time in a long while, Yun-hee discovered that many of them had become too short for her. In her prime, Tan-bee had grown as fast as corn, so Yun-hee took some of her own old clothes from the chest of drawers and examined how to alter them to fit her daughter. Though it seemed like no easy work, Yun-hee figured out the general shape so as to let the mending shop in town take care of the rest. There were half a dozen suits that Tan-bee hadn't worn for several years, and Yun-hee chose two one-piece suits with a check pattern that would be easy to alter and would look good on the child. Growing older, Yun-hee was beginning to favor flower patterns, although she had at one time had an extreme liking for a check pattern. The geometric check pattern once reminded her somewhat of a logical and mysterious feeling, so she had kept lots of clothes in the same pattern—ranging from shirts to suits. Even the curtains in her room were still in check pattern—her friends often joked she was too much of a mathematics teacher.

"Anybody home?"

Hearing a familiar voice outside, Yun-hee looked out to find Han Min-wha stepping into the yard and smiling at her. Surprised at Han Min-wha's sudden visit, Yun-hee threw open the sliding door to the wooden floor.

"Oh, please come in," invited Yun-hee. "You must have had a lot of trouble coming here on a day like this. Isn't the lane muddy?"

"Not terribly. I finished my lectures, so I need not go to Seoul every week. I usually stay home on rainy days like this. But since there's little rain today, I ventured to come out in a pair of boots."

With this remark Han Min-wha indicated her white boots with her eyes. Remembering the night when Hee-jo had returned with the tear marks on his face, Yun-hee was troubled in her mind but, not revealing her mind, urged Han Min-wha to enter the room. Noticing the old sewing machine in the living room, Han Min-wha said in amazement, "Oh, dear! It's an antique."

"Exactly. I've not used it for a long time," replied Yun-hee. "I take it out once in a while to get it lubricated as it's the rainy season. Actually it had been my mother's, but I brought it with me from my parents' home when I moved to this countryside. Since my father first bought it for my mother, even during the War she stayed home alone for fear of losing it. In the Great Retreat, however, she had no choice but to flee—holding the machine tightly. Can you imagine that?"

Han Min-wha nodded her head, saying, "Indeed, people in my mother's generation cherished their household things as if they were their own children."

"Because they were everything in their life. Whoever could do weaving or painting in those days except a few enlightened women?"

"Although women in our age have come to enjoy a more affluent life compared with their mothers," resumed Han Min-wha, "they, in turn, end up losing many valuable things in their lives. Many people say it's no longer possible these days to see the beauty of middle-aged women. Once an old painter I admire expressed his regret about it. He said that in the old days the sight of a middle-aged woman in traditional costume, coming out of a modest looking tile-roofed house, was so beautiful to look at. With a remark that he would notice modest- but noble-looking middle-aged women in the street, the old painter told me he doubted himself why he could not see such women anymore. When I agreed and asked his opinion, he answered that women in the old days had had a sort of sanctuary in their life. For instance, they'd kept the keys to the barns and had other household rights, regarding them as their inborn duties. I suppose this provided them with a certain dignity."

"True," returned Yun-hee. "Actually women in those days made a sanctuary within the limited space of housekeeping assigned by the conventional society, and then worshipped what was given to them as their fate. Since their life was rooted in such an attitude, they were spontaneously led to a life of dignity. But in an industrial society like today, no one is able to lead a life of serenity, I think. What's more, men and women nowadays cannot maintain such middle-aged beauty because they're immersed in a luxury of life—driven by materialism, and preoccupied with a strong sense of self-consciousness. And this seems to me entirely misguided. In short, their way of life is a reflection of themselves as well as their identity. If you were born in the old days, Ms. Han, I think you'd have led such a life."

"Maybe. I'd have been happier then."

Yun-hee did not expect Han Min-wha to agree willingly with the picture of traditional women. Then Han Min-wha turned her glance toward the large pieces lined up in the corner of the room. As Yun-hee explained they were the results of the firing a few days before, Han Min-wha answered that they evoked the atmosphere of a Buddhist temple.

"His works seem to be getting better," she commented. "Like a person who has cultivated himself to a great extent, Mr. Hong has made his works look pure and clear."

"Because he always has a fierce struggle with himself," answered Yun-hee.

"I suppose so. Art may be an act of humans who try to discover the greatest light of their age and make their way toward it. From the image of Buddha in the Paekche era through the pottery of the Yi Dynasty, I would think all art must be the culmination of such an effort."

"Precisely. By the way, Ms. Han, Mr. Hong is in his studio now. Go and encourage him."

At Yun-hee's suggestion Han Min-wha rose with no hesitation and went out promptly. It seemed Hee-jo had not visited Han Min-wha since encountering Han Min-wha's male friend at her house. Though he had engaged himself in firing in the kiln with the start of the rainy season, Hee-jo must have been turbulent in his mind all this time—seemingly letting the time pass so he could arrange his thoughts.

It was certain, Yun-hee felt instinctively, that Han Min-wha had read Hee-jo's mind, and come to resume her relationship with him. Sensing Hee-jo's wound, she was now trying to extend her hand in friendship again. After all, they regarded each other so seriously that the two, living in purity of mind, had become ideal partners by exchanging their views of life, just as they had done before.

As Yun-hee, after arranging her old clothes, was smoking her first cigarette in a long while, Han Min-wha appeared, tapping on the window of the room. In spite of Yun-hee urging her to have tea in the room, Han Min-wha waved her hands and merely said she hoped Yun-hee would visit her house in Eunti soon.

As Yun-hee walked out of the house to see Han Min-wha off, a villager was passing by with a baby on her back. Since his whole face was covered with pink powder, Yun-hee thought the baby must be suffering from chicken pox. And recalling Sae-bul who had suffered from it a long time before, she cast a pitiful glance at the mother and baby. At the sight of them, however, Han Min-wha muttered to herself, "Surely, it's really a life of drudgery."

At this sudden remark Yun-hee was taken aback for a moment. Actually the look of Han Min-wha seemed so far from the ordinary course of human life that it appeared almost inhuman. Her remark was by no means an expression of pity but was closer to antipathy. As Han Min-wha hurried off, entreating Yun-hee not to follow further, Yun-hee stopped. In contrast to Han Min-wha, who walked so lightly, the mother with the baby on her back looked burdened. As an individual soul, Yun-hee thought, the baby was to the mother no more than a present from God. No doubt the ordinary people who bear a heavy load of *karma* on their shoulders must be going through a life of drudgery. Yet, who could deny the small happiness of humans, sharing their pain in this life? All of a sudden, Yun-hee was reminded of a poet who, expelled from his society for the fateful disease of leprosy, said, "Oh, I miss the everyday life of humanity, but all I can do now is blow a horn. . . ."

Though it was still in the rainy season, sunshine and showers took turns unfolding a picturesque summer scene. The sky had cleared up the previous night, and the sun was shining brightly on market day today. Because she had missed one market day because of the rain, Yun-hee felt as if a long time had passed since she went to the market. The fields were littered with various fruits matured by the spirit of the sun, so in the market were heaped not only enormous, fresh watermelons with green stripes, but also fresh ears of corn, whose tightly packed yellow kernels looked like teeth.

The long squash were out of season now, but since the young

green squash were at the peak of their taste, Yun-hee picked one up and held it in her hand. In the summer she had made basic side dishes of squash by seasoning or frying it. This year, while busy with other things, she forgot to raise them in her kitchen garden. After Tan-bee's birth, Yun-hee had eaten a soup of aged squash frosted with honey to ensure a prompt recovery. As a matter of fact, squash made a wonderful food in summer, including even its rough leaves, so that with sliced fresh green peppers added with the boiled squash leaves, bean paste stew became so tasty as to make other dishes unnecessary. It turned out that squash was a vegetable that gave itself away to others with no reserve. Also, rice eaten with boiled cabbage gave a good appetite, while it made a taste of summer even more palatable to eat boiled rice with other cereals in cold water, along with fresh green peppers and bean paste.

In the market Yun-hee bought a chicken to cook with gruel. As it was a season when people would easily feel hot and tired, many health foods appeared in the market, including ginseng and a fresh-looking hairtail fish that attracted her eyes. When Yun-hee was about to set off with her hands full of the corn her children liked, a villager happened to pass by her.

"You bought something?" asked Yun-hee, walking toward him.

Just then Mr. Yi lifted a duck in his hand, whose wings were tied with a rope. "My wife is suffering from high blood pressure," he answered. "Since the doctor did not allow her to eat any meat except this, I must have her eat this at least twice a month."

Mr. Yi was still under fifty, but his caring for his wife moved Yun-hee's heart. Envying the couple's exchange of mutual affection, Yun-hee was about to leave the marketplace when she noticed some tiny brooms made of short branches of bush clover. It was possible Hee-jo could use them for painting slip inside small wares, so Yun-hee bought them with no more hesitation than when she found something very precious.

Having unpacked her shopping basket at home, and entering the room, Yun-hee saw a piece of mail on the floor. On the hand-made green envelope was written "Forwarded to Mr. Yi Sung-ju," and the return address was merely marked "The Samnamu Company," with no other name specified. So Yun-hee immediately went to the studio and asked Hee-jo about the mail, but he replied he didn't know about it at all. It might be Yi Sung-ju himself who had told the sender Yun-hee's address, since he had inquired of her if there'd been any mail for him when he visited her house the previous time. Perhaps it was a letter connected with a dissident movement, Yun-hee suspected. As a person who had been constantly watched by the police lately, Yi Sung-ju might choose Yun-hee's house as a liaison address for fear of censorship of his letter. Hee-jo agreed with her opinion, adding no more.

Recalling that Yi Sung-ju had said that he'd become extremely careful lately, Yun-hee said, "Even so, he should have asked for our understanding beforehand—if the letter is serious enough to cause him to worry about censorship."

"There's no need to worry about it," responded Hee-jo, "because he's not so foolish as to send a confidential letter openly to this address. As soon as Sae-bul gets back, ask him to deliver this letter."

Reluctantly Yun-hee asked Sae-bul to do so when he returned from school. As the sun came out of the clouds, she had her children take a bath, but the next day it rained again. Discovering in the morning that she had forgotten to close the lid of a soy sauce jar the previous day, Yun-hee boiled the sauce that had been diluted by rain all over again. While she was cleaning the house, with all the doors and windows wide open, Yi Sung-ju's wife came to see her.

While exchanging a greeting with Yun-hee, Yi Sung-ju's wife did not even smile, her eyes full of anger. Feeling instinctively that something had come up with her, Yun-hee asked first of all if she received the letter the previous day. The woman dropped onto the edge of the wooden floor and said, "Yes, I did. Actually it's about the letter that I came here."

Then Yi Sung-ju's wife showed Yun-hee the green envelope in her hand and asked her who had sent it. The envelope was already torn open, and only then was Yun-hee reminded of Ji-woon. Instantly the woman said in anger, "I heard my husband once came here with that woman. This letter came from her!"

"Oh, is it about something urgent?"

At Yun-hee's cautious question Yi Sung-ju's wife put on a look of anger and replied in indignation: "How dare she do this? What kind of woman is she to boldly send this kind of letter to a man with a wife and children? If she wanted to send a letter, why didn't she send it directly to my address, instead of to yours?"

"Mr. Yi Sung-ju must have told her this address so that she could send her letter here, I suppose."

Feeling uneasy about interfering with other people's private matters, Yun-hee put the blame indirectly on Yi Sung-ju, lest his wife be hurt any further. But she didn't say that Yi Sung-ju had come looking for a letter.

Indifferent to Yun-hee's emotion, however, Yi Sung-ju's wife went on. "I've lived like this till now. You know, I've already torn up love letters like this several times. I feel so insulted!"

"Oh, my! I admire you, Myong-ha's Mom. If I were you, I simply couldn't endure things like this."

Despite Yun-hee's attempt to comfort her, the woman's anger intensified: "You can easily imagine that as a woman I'd even thought about divorce."

"I know you've been more considerate to Myong-ha's father than anybody else. Besides, you're his fervent admirer, so how can you possibly divorce such a husband?"

Then Yi Sung-ju's wife sighed deeply, shaking her head. "I still have not the least idea why we should be living in this miserable state. Who else wouldn't like to flirt with others?"

"Mr. Yi Sung-ju is not merely as wanton as the wind," Yun-hee said calmly. "He's the wind itself since he keeps moving toward other women."

It seemed Yi Sung-ju's wife had tried to hold the wind in her hand till now. Because the wind cannot by nature be possessed by anyone, Yun-hee thought, the only way to care truly about it is either to let it go, or to wait as steadily as a rock for it to return. In truth, the wind seemed to whirl around Yi Sung-ju's wife, perhaps because she'd lived with a man as whirling as the wind.

Looking out to the field, the woman got up to leave. "If I'd been in Seoul yesterday," she said, "I might have gone to see her on the spot. But not being able to do so, I wrote a letter instead out of anger. I'm going to send it to her now."

"Well, your indignation is fully justified, Myong-ha's Mom. But at the same time you must know that you can't solve this matter with only hatred against your husband's woman, because it is a problem between you two—husband and wife. You must also remember that it's not the woman, but Mr. Yi Sung-ju himself, who swore the vow of marriage. After all, she's no more than a third party."

"But I'm not as logical as you, Tan-bee's Mom," the woman responded shortly and, presently opening her umbrella, went down into the front yard. All Yun-hee had tried to do was advise her to solve the problem from the bottom yet, with a troubled mind over her lost love, the woman didn't seem to listen to Yun-hee's words. Perhaps she might be a mirror of Yun-hee herself, thought Yun-hee gloomily as she watched the woman disappear.

In spite of a weather forecast that predicted torrential rain, the rainy season this year seemed to end quietly with a blazing sun at the height of summer. With the continued rain like the temper of summer retreating, the field was surging with green waves. Even the green seemed to flood into the human body, so that if Yun-hee could see into her heart it was likely to look green.

The rice in the field had grown to form rolling waves of green, while its kernels began to ripen under the sunlight. As a living thing of its own, each rice plant had the inherent rhythm of life. Some time before, Yun-hee had read an article in the paper about a farmer who had sued the army camps for hindering the rice's sleep with their search lights. Even if no actual damage had been done, the right of the rice to sleep should be protected as well if people knew that plants, too, had a spirit of their own, Yun-hee felt.

As Yun-hee moved toward the hill through winding lanes in the field, she saw Nam-ui's father walking toward her. Since she had seen him mending the banks of rice paddies and draining the water off the field, Yun-hee asked him if everything was all right during the rainy season.

"This year we've got a fair amount of rain," he answered. "Actually we can do nothing in the face of heavy rain—farming is done by man and Heaven together, you know."

Though talking about Heaven's will, he seemed to have no other remedy in farming than a spray of agricultural chemicals against damage by harmful insects. Yun-hee remembered having read that the resistive power of harmful insects increases in proportion to the amount of agricultural chemicals used. In truth, it's the same with the gradual strengthening of antibiotic medicines to cure venereal disease, which in turn gets stronger. When agricultural chemicals kill the bacteria in the earth, straw buried in the ground do not rot, thereby negating the cycle of nature. So, when people are oblivious to the fact that farming deals above all with life itself, the harm ultimately returns to the people themselves. With no professional knowledge of this process, Yu-hee could do no better than watch the violation of the natural cycle with an anxious mind. It occurred to her that what she'd done up to now in this world was no more than caring for her own family.

When Yun-hee arrived at Han Min-wha's house, the window was open wide, but the woman was not visible. On the loom were threads of violet, thick crimson, yellow, and black, and the woven textile looked splendid. While observing them, Yun-hee felt her mind turn bright, because she had been troubled ever since Yi Sung-ju's wife had visited her.

It seemed Han Min-wha had not been gone long, judging from a half cup of soy milk left on the chair. Thinking that Han Min-wha would soon be back, Yun-hee sat on a chair by the window. Then, noticing a violet bowl on the table, she realized it was a celadon of dark violet outside and light violet inside. Han Min-wha, she remembered, had used violet heavily in her works and, looking at the violet bowl, Yun-hee decided it must be her favorite color.

The dark violet outside evoked a sense of cool nobility, while the light violet inside looked mild and gentle. The former looked like the shadow of an empress living in solitude in the heart of a palace; the latter was like the flowers which a young girl picked in the deep mountains. Being of the same hue of violet, the two colors gave a different feeling in accordance with their intensity, and as a result the bowl itself aroused in Yun-hee a complex feeling with its splendid yet lonely look. Then Yun-hee realized for the first time that the emotion evoked by violet was loneliness itself.

Since the door to the room was open, Yun-hee looked inside to find a familiar work on the wall. It was the work whose blue-violet mountains in the darkness suggested a valley in the night, enabling Yun-hee to remember how Sae-bul had once expressed his feeling that Han Min-wha's work looked sad and lonely. Perhaps the sadness the child had felt at the time came from the atmosphere of loneliness lurking in the canvas, Yun-hee concluded.

"Ah, when did you come?"

At the sudden remark Yun-hee turned back to see Han Min-wha putting down a big paper bag and wiping off her sweat. Pointing at the bag, Han Min-wha said she'd bought nine liters of rice on her way back from visiting her friend in Ichon.

"Hi! Do you usually leave the window open that wide when you go so far?" inquired Yun-hee as soon as she saw Han Min-wha.

"Of course. I leave it open whenever I go out so that the smell of the earth can fill the room. And villagers passing by can take a rest here, too. In the early days of my living here, I made a point of doing it—lest villagers have unnecessary curiosity about my life."

"How fascinating! It's not necessary to lock the door when there's actually little to be stolen. I, too, occasionally leave my house open so that I can realize the blessing of possessing little."

While exchanging words with Han Min-wha, Yun-hee looked around the room. Except for skeins of thread heaped in the room as in a futile dream, there was virtually nothing in her house; not even a television set. Glancing at the kitchen table for a while, Han Min-wha brought a bowl filled with green beans. "Look, this is a present from the open window. A farmer must have brought it here while I was away."

The green beans were in the center of the table but, being attracted to the violet bowl, Yun-hee was barely able to see them. Han Min-wha filled the bowl with beans and then took a bottle out of the square refrigerator. After pouring a milky fluid from the bottle into the empty bowls, she handed one of them to Yun-hee. And the fluid turned out to be soy bean juice. Han Min-wha went out with another bowl and came back soon, saying she'd given it to a villager working in the field. Relating that she drank it in the summer when thirsty, Han Min-wha asked if Yun-hee liked it.

"I made noodles and soy bean juice yesterday, since the rainy season seemed over," Yun-hee replied. "It made an excellent summer meal."

"The farmers are very pleased to have it while working. That soy bean juice easily chases hunger away, you know."

"You get along well with your neighbors, I suppose. As a matter of fact, I was wondering how you manage to live by yourself, since people around here generally don't like city people."

In a moment Han Min-wha moved the loom to the inside corner of the room and then praised nature with a wondrous look:

"Except for the owner of the lot this house is on, who used to be a landlord in the village, every farmer is quite friendly. Since I've lived here in a deep trust of land and farmer, I feel I'm getting cured of my self-righteousness and selfishness. So, when I wake from sleep early in the morning, I feel a great consolation from the sound of the farmer working in the field. And as the grove comes into my view through the open window, the fresh smell of the freshly plowed ground brings a miraculous tranquility to me. Once I envied the perfect harmony of ox, farmer, and land, but soon realized I was no more than a meaningless fragment of the city—a drifting, corrupt soul of this age, full of unfulfilled desire and anxiety. After that I'd just look at the grove all day long, opening the window as if washing away the contamination in my heart. On a day when I felt like wandering, I'd walk deep into the grove and move about, smelling the odor of damp, rotten leaves. At such times I'd feel gradually stripped of the stink of the city. It's such a wonder that a heaven like this exists in a place just one hour's distance from the city. In the grove there's always the religion and music that I craved so much. In contrast to this, the city is nothing more than a gigantic psychiatric ward. Now I'm lucky to be treated here by the best therapy ever imagined."

Hearing what Han Min-wha said, Yun-hee found she could not find better words about nature than hers, even though she herself thought she had received great bliss from nature. So Yun-hee expressed her amazement. "The grove and the smell of the ground turned you into a poet, Ms. Han."

"As a person born in the city," returned Han Min-wha, "I sometimes feel sad at my sense of separation from nature. At such times I feel that nature and I can never be fully joined to each other. In fact, such a sense of separation horrifies me. When I'm visited by a sudden pain on returning to my home at dusk, nature becomes nothing more to me than an indifferent object."

Stopping her words, Han Min-wha stared at the field through the kitchen window. As silence fell on them suddenly, Yun-hee asked her, "What are you thinking?"

"Farmer Marei," Han Min-wha replied with a calm expression.

Instead of smiling, Yun-hee was surprised at the coincidence of their feelings, which involuntarily sought the warm hand of the farmer like a child. In truth, it was a yearning for the root of love.

Pointing at the violet bowl filled with green beans, Yun-hee asked, "Where did you get that piece?"

"An American potter who visited Korea presented it to me. When I was invited to his house, I kept staring at that bowl and paid no attention to other works, so in the end he gave it to me. It's the color of happiness."

The happiness spreading out of a lonely woman momentarily made ripples in Yun-hee's heart. To hold loneliness in her heart as happiness . . . Indeed it may be a depth that only a truly lonely being may reach.

7

A Blazing Sun

The rainy season was over, and the heat wave of summer had begun to roar, making children flock to the river naked. Humans first begin their life in the amniotic fluid of their mothers, so water is a sort of eternal home for them. Especially in the summer, when the sun continued to blaze, Yun-hee felt tempted to submerge herself naked in the cool, gentle water. Though supposedly talking about immediate problems such as the energy crisis, people really yearned for the wild sea to forget the bustling city life as the still exotic word *vacances* was making a colorful appearance in the newspaper.

The children were no exception to the excitement about summer. Tan-bee showed Yun-hee a mountain flower that she got in a letter from a friend. Her friend, who had moved to an east coast city in the previous spring, wrote to invite Tan-bee to visit her in summer. The pale flower, often called edelweiss, was one of the most noted plants of Mt. Sorak. In floral language it is said to mean "eternal love." How wondrous it was, Yun-hee grinned to herself, that children, who did not even know what love is, were speaking about eternal love! But she didn't give an immediate answer to Tan-bee, who insisted on going to both Mt. Sorak and the east coast during the coming summer vacation.

For his part, Sae-bul was looking forward to visiting his grandmother in Seoul, counting the remaining days on his fingers. He was buoyant with anticipation of the animated movies pouring out for children with the start of the summer vacation, and also expected to have glasses of his own. Since Tan-bee had begun to wear glasses, Sae-bul had begged several times to try her glasses himself, saying he could not see things clearly. He would stare and squint his eyes when called by someone and rub his eyes often, as Tan-bee had done before. It might be a symptom of conjunctivitis, which had been prevalent lately, and Yun-hee was worried, but fortunately there was no evidence of it in Sae-bul's case.

While Hee-jo was off work, Yun-hee went to Seoul with her children. She first dropped by an oculist to check Sae-bul's eyesight, when the child, shaking his head, insisted he couldn't see any letters except those on the first line. The doctor, who had examined Tan-bee's eyesight before, cocked his head and then asked Sae-bul, pointing at a small letter in the lower part, "Dear, you can read this, right?"

At this remark Sae-bul made a C in the air with his hand, so Yun-hee was puzzled. Pointing at a letter in an upper line, the doctor asked again, as if to coax the child, "This is much easier, right?" and Sae-bul said yes cheerfully.

After the eye test was over, the doctor called Tan-bee to come and sat himself near Sae-bul. "You've a good eyesight," he said to Sae-bul gently, "then, why do you insist you can't see clearly? Tell me frankly. You want to wear glasses like your sister, don't you?"

Then Sae-bul shook his head with a blush. Embarrassed, he looked at his sister, trying to avoid the doctor's eyes as his scheme to deceive him had ended in vain on account of his childish simplicity. Only then did Yun-hee realize Sae-bul's intention and clicked her tongue. "Tut! I thought it was strange myself!"

Yun-hee had not announced her visit to her parents in advance, but when she arrived with her children, her mother was sprinkling the yard as if she were expecting them. Since it was so hot, the water in the yard soon dried up, but the red cockscomb flowers, which were her mother's favorite, were in full bloom along the fence. The shape of the flowers, resembling the head ornament of a cock, was somewhat grotesque, but the rough, wild shape, unlike the common type of flower, seemed to have drawn her mother. If she got her ears closer to the heart of that flower, Yun-hee imagined, she might hear the beating of the blazing sun.

Besides the cockscombs, the garden was blooming with crêpe myrtles and roses and branches of the purple magnolia with their exuberant leaves, which Yun-hee had transplanted before moving out to the countryside. Yun-hee had presented them to her mother, who preferred the purple magnolia to the white one. In truth, her mother preferred flowering trees, and although the garden was not spacious, flowers of various colors bloomed every season. At the old house where Yun-hee had lived in her elementary school days there was a persimmon tree, and when its flowers began to fall, her mother would pick them up to make a necklace for her children. Although Hee-jo did not like Madame Shin, regarding her as a cold soul, her inner world was to Yun-hee's eyes in full bloom with a variety of flowers like her little garden.

Meanwhile Madame Shin gave a hearty welcome to Yun-hee's children. On entering the room, she opened the chest of drawers to take out a suit of summer clothes for Sae-bul and an elegant one-piece dress with buttons down the back for Tan-bee, making Yun-hee wonder how her mother had prepared them on time for the children. The dress for Tan-bee was blue with white polka dots and some narrow lace on the front. As such, it was Tan-bee's first new dress all year, because she had been wearing Yun-hee's old clothes altered to fit her. Tan-bee was so happy that she changed into the new dress immediately to show her gratitude to her grandmother. Looking at the glasses that Tan-bee was wearing, Madame Shin put on a pitying expression and brought a snack for the children.

It was a steamed ground barley cake, with a crisp, sweet taste, having carrots in it. Tan-bee, who loved steamed cakes, emptied her dish without leaving any crumbs, while Yun-hee marveled again at her mother's cooking skill. Madame Shin said, "The barley is doing very well this year. But I heard the farmers will get nothing because the government's purchasing price is so low."

As a matter of fact, the newspaper said, barley farmers were experiencing hard times: the abundant stock of barley did not match the negligible spending level. In some regions, the paper went on, public officials were to take a certain amount of barley at home in order to increase the spending. Since Madame Shin belonged to a generation that had suffered from a constant lack of food, she seriously regretted the barley thrown away. Only ten days before, Madame Shin told Yun-hee, she had made a sweet punch from barley grain for her oldest grandson's birthday, adding that it was thick yet palatable—though it didn't taste as clean as a punch made of rice. In the garden the cockscomb flowers seemed to be burning silently in the blazing sun. Fanning herself while talking in the midday with her mother about household things, Yun-hee realized how much time had passed since she had been a girl.

In the evening Yun-hee's father returned from a fishing trip with her brother Sung-ho. The youngest of Yun-hee's seven brothers and sisters and also a graduate student majoring in architecture, he was the only one still living with his parents. Yun-hee used to carry Sung-ho on her back when he was a baby, and even took him to the opening day of elementary school on behalf of her mother. And Sung-ho, who liked Yun-hee's children more than any other, would give his unsparing love to them. Upon seeing Tan-bee and Sae-bul, he hugged and lifted them up to the ceiling.

"Well, are they on vacation?" With this remark Yun-hee's father said no more, only smiling at his grandchildren's laughing voices. Having retired from the bank where he had spent most of his life, Yun-hee's father now led a busier life in his old age than he ever led before, climbing the nearby mountains early every morning to bring home mineral water, spending time with his many visitors, and pursuing his hobbies. The way he spent his retirement in good health was good to see, yet Yun-hee worried about how her parents entertained so many visitors after learning that her mother's rheumatism had worsened. Madame Shin, however, merely replied that fewer visitors were the sign of a decline in the family fortune.

In the meantime the dinner table was set with a raw fish dish made from a gray mullet Yun-hee's father had caught—a dinner such as Yun-hee had had with her family long before. Madame Shin made it a habit to have Yun-hee take a silver spoon she had used before her marriage, and even gave Tan-bee a little round silver spoon that Yun-hee had used as a child.

A soup made of conches Yun-hee's father had bought, boiled with green leeks, made a good appetizer. Yun-hee's children ate more than they were used to, and Sae-bul, who had been looking forward to coming to his grandmother's, repeated several times how much he was enjoying the meal. After dinner they spent a leisurely summer night, helping themselves to sweet watermelon.

Sung-ho said jokingly he had ended up becoming a graduate student, thanks to his father's advice that he should not be ahead of others were he to participate in the antigovernment demonstrations. While telling other interesting news to Yun-hee, including the turbulent political situation of the day, Sung-ho mentioned that his older sister Myong-hee, who had been to Europe recently, had sent home some pictures of her trip. A younger sister of Yun-hee's, Myong-hee left Seoul the previous winter to go to Canada with her husband, who was assigned to a branch office there. Regarding letter-writing as a great effort, Myong-hee, in spite of its high cost, had used the telephone whenever she had something to say. And her sending pictures would imply that no news is good news.

The pictures Sung-ho showed to Yun-hee included some taken in European countries: the remains of Pompeii after it had been destroyed by a volcanic eruption; the renowned Arc de Tríomphe in Paris; and the Schwabing district in Munich, made famous by the late writer Chun Hye-rin. As Yun-hee had also once enjoyed Chun Hye-rin's writings, she thought Myong-hee must have visited the city to look back on her old days when she had been fascinated by the genius woman writer. To Yun-hee's sense, most women had been once in their life absorbed by Chun Hye-rin, but wasn't it because the rebellious self-consciousness of that writer represented their inner yearning that cannot be named clearly?

Looking through the pictures, Yun-hee was amazed to see a picture in which two men with guitars seemed to be singing in a plaza. In the picture people were gathered around the two singing men, but what really attracted Yun-hee's eyes was four young women—perhaps travelers—lying on their rucksacks in the street, enjoying the singing. Obviously this was a scene not easily imagined for a woman like Yun-hee, who had grown up in a conventional society. Even on the beautiful campus of the women's college she had attended, Yun-hee could not feel free to lie on her back and gaze at the blue sky. The then president of the women's college would shout at students who were merrily chatting with each other, lying on their backs on the fresh green campus, "How dare women lie outdoors?"

To Yun-hee's eyes, the sight of the women lying on their rucksacks in the Place de Concorde was all bright and peaceful. No one interfering with them, they made a natural street scene. "Look, this teaches us what genuine living is," Yun-hee mumbled without being aware of it. "I suppose this is where real human beings live."

As Yun-hee's eyes met her father's, she handed the picture to him and said, "Father, you trained me thoroughly as a woman, but I don't want Tan-bee to be so. I suppose man and woman are

235

naturally distinguished as they grow older. So, regardless of her sex, I'll bring my child up to be a free soul. It'll be the same with Sae-bul."

"But you must remember we're living in a country with a totally different culture," her father replied. "Each country has its own unique customs that make the basis of living. What if you teach your children the customs of other countries—just because they look better? Moreover, how can you expect them to live their life when they grow up?"

"I believe," Yun-hee responded calmly, "that there are no absolutes with regard to culture, because people keep up with the progress of the age. Looking one step further just makes us advance that much faster. I don't think that being a common housewife like Mother is my vocation, nor do I have a clear idea of what kind of being I want to become. Maybe it's because I haven't pursued a definite goal in my life."

"As for women, being ordinary is the best way to be happy. At any rate I'm convinced I've brought my daughters up to let them lead a happy life in this society, so I never thought my way was anything but right."

Yun-hee said no more, feeling that her father's words demonstrated his paternalistic belief, as well as the generation gap. At this moment her mother, who had merely been listening so far, joined while untying Tan-bee's braided hair. "As a child you would come home crying because your teacher designated a boy you thought inferior to yourself as a class monitor. In fact, you've never been an easy one, although such an attitude was much softened in raising two children."

While in Seoul, Yun-hee would rarely meet her friends, since she always had to hurry back home. Staying at her parents' house for the night this time, she called up two of her friends the next morning. Since her marriage, Yun-hee had seldom been in touch with some of her friends who were contentedly absorbed in their own domestic life, thinking that the kind of life they led was totally different from her own. Such relationships as might hurt both parties or seemed to be on a superficial, insincere level naturally had ended. Therefore, the two close friends remaining to Yun-hee up to now felt like her sisters.

Eun-kyong was not home in the morning when Yun-hee called her, and her child, who answered the phone, said her mother had gone to a German language institute to study. Though her dream of being a professor had been thwarted a long time before, Eun-kyong did not seem to give up her studies, which always made Yun-hee marvel at her earnestness. Yun-hee then called the hospital where Eun-kyong's husband was working to send him Hee-jo's regards. "How about coming to my house so your children can enjoy swimming in the stream?" she urged. And Eun-kyong's husband accepted her offer gladly, saying he would visit around mid-August, because his children were already eager to go. During the time he had brought his friends to Yun-hee's home twice to let them buy Hee-jo's works; Hee-jo, in gratitude, had prepared a set of teacups with the couple's names on them.

Earlier, when Yun-hee had been in Seoul to buy glasses for Tan-bee, she had been unable to contact Young-ae except for one chance to call her on the phone. This time, she learned, Young-ae was busy preparing for the remembrance rite for her grandfather-in-law. It was hard to believe that Young-ae, who had sent Yun-hee a copy of *Fear of Flying,* was now preparing for the family event, but at any rate it was the reality of her life. Astonished, Yun-hee mournfully remarked: "Good Lord! I hoped to see your face with beautiful makeup. Now I'm obliged to put it off."

As Yun-hee expressed her regret, Young-ae answered in a low, calm voice that she did not wear makeup anymore. But Yun-hee thought it rather surprising, since Young-ae had been renowned for her vivid makeup, even in her college days. Depending on her mood, Young-ae had painted a mysterious shadow on her eye lids in deep blue, white, or light green; naturally she seemed to be born anew each time she finished her makeup, with the touch of lipstick on her lips, as if constructing the summit of a tower. Yun-hee still had a vivid memory of the color of winter red—Young-ae's favorite lipstick—and her makeup seemed so bold as to be a revolt against convention. Thinking of it, Yun-hee commented in a half-joking tone, "So? You're already acting like an old woman. Anyhow it sounds quite settled, you're preparing for a rite for your grandfa-ther-in-law."

With this remark Yun-hee made up her mind to acknowledge

her friend's changed condition. But Young-ae retorted instantaneously as if an animal feigning death had struck back again. "Settled? Not at all—it's against my fashion!"

Then Yun-hee smiled, holding the phone to her ear. "Right, you're always alive and brave. That's you."

The day after Yun-hee got back home, leaving both of her children at her parents' house, a thunderstorm began early in the morning. Even as people complained about the sultry weather, thinking the rainy season was over, a gust of rainstorms swept across the country again. In Pyongchang, Kangwon-do Province, eight inches of rain reportedly fell within two hours, killing thirteen members of a family as they slept. Moreover, in the area of Kunsan, Cholla-do Province, about fifteen hundred houses were submerged in water, all the farmland flooded.

There was even a family crushed to death while sitting at the breakfast table when the hill behind their house collapsed on top of the house. The newspaper report of a girl crushed while putting on her makeup to go to see her fiancé was as vivid as makeup itself, and Yun-hee could not wipe it out of her mind. The rain pouring down all at once as if dumped from a metal bucket! Like any storm in life, such a disaster could not be avoided by taking precautions— it was final as a flower that had fallen to the ground. Since there was a hill behind Yun-hee's house, she'd been anxious during the rain, but fortunately the rain stopped after a burst of heavy downpour. The next day the weather cleared up again.

Since Choha-ri was located on higher ground, the rice paddies around the area had escaped the storm. However, as the nearby region around the Kum River remained under water for two days, the harvest would surely be harmed in the fall. Also, the fields in front of Yun-hee's house were littered with broken pieces of yellow melons which were crushed during the rainfall and wounded like weak soldiers in a war, and the yellow green river gushing angrily through the fields no longer looked like the friend of farmers it had seemed before.

A heavy rainfall was reported in Seoul early that day, too. Hearing that houses on low ground were flooded, Yun-hee went to the peppery-stew restaurant to call her mother. Though there was nothing particular to say, she, feeling agitated, intended to assure her mother that everything was normal. Upon answering the phone, her mother asked first of all if she was all right. Yun-hee answered that she was fortunate to have left her children in Seoul because the thunder had been roaring throughout the early morning. She intended to tell her mother to send the children back home immediately if they bothered her, but her mother replied she would let the children stay as long as they wanted.

"By the way, I forgot to give you the dried corbina fish when you left," said her mother. "I had bought a bunch of them for a side dish during the rainy season."

"Oh, don't worry about such things, Mother. When you send the children home, come with them and stay a few days."

Her mother was silent for a while and then merely answered that she'd bring the children home herself. As Yun-hee hurried back home with some bean curd she had bought in the peppery-stew restaurant, she found a woman pacing up and down by the melon patch. Judging by her appearance in a black suit, it was the woman from Seoul. Approaching, Yun-hee was able to recognize by her profile that the woman was Ji-woon.

Ji-woon was staring aimlessly at the melon patch until Yun-hee came closer to her, and her eyes, while looking at the melons crushed by the storm, were filled with grief. As Yun-hee called to her in a low voice, Ji-woon, startled, looked back and barely managed to say hello to Yun-hee. Ji-woon looked beautiful with her short hair, now grown down to her shoulders, but she didn't seem to have the energy to put on a smile.

Looking at Yun-hee, she stammered: "Since I saw you slip out this way some time ago, I've been waiting for you here. It doesn't seem you went out for long."

"I went out to make a phone call to Seoul," replied Yun-hee, wondering why Ji-woon had turned up so unexpectedly.

Ji-woon silently followed Yun-hee toward the house and stopped before the front gate. Then she said she wanted to go to the stream to talk about something privately, to which Yun-hee willingly consented. With the heavy rain gone, no one was visible on the bank. The stony fields washed by the rain looked incredibly clean, while the blazing sun heated them white-hot. And the stream flowed on, as if denying the traces of the past moment by moment.

Staring at the stream, Ji-woon opened gravely. "You know, it's been a long time since I saw Mr. Yi Sung-ju. . . ."

"Really?" returned Yun-hee. "About two weeks or so ago, during the rainy season, he visited here. He was looking for a letter—presumably from you."

"Ah, my letter must have arrived later, then," Ji-woon said as if arguing.

"There was no name on the envelope, so I didn't know at first it was from you."

"I'm sorry. I recently went to work at another publishing company."

Since Yun-hee spoke stiffly, as if scolding, Ji-woon dropped her eyes to the ground and picked up a pebble. Feeling a need to explain how things had gone, Yun-hee told Ji-woon that she had had her child deliver the letter to Yi Sung-ju's house and that Yi Sung-ju's wife had come to see her shortly afterwards. "She opened the letter herself," she added.

At Yun-hee's words Ji-woon closed her eyes for a moment with a look of deep pain. "It's so mortifying—myself and the things around me . . . His wife sent me a letter. It was so insulting I can't bear it even for a minute."

"Just try to understand how his wife felt," Yun-hee comforted her. "It seemed she had enough reason to be indignant about such a letter being sent to her neighbor. Naturally, married people think of their spouse as a kind of possession."

"I know. Who would not be hurt if the husband of any woman were in love with another woman? But should she send such an insulting letter to me, though? Did I seduce a holy man like Jesus Christ? Did I also recklessly fall into flirting with a man who loves his wife? Am I blindly following, out of vanity, a great poet and leader of people? If not, shouldn't she try to talk to her husband first before she starts to blame the other woman?"

With this fierce remark Ji-woon dropped her head as if she was about to burst into tears. After a while she continued, shaking her head.

"As a matter of fact, I've never asked him to divorce his wife. I'd be satisfied with merely sharing our suffering together. That's all. Tell me why I should ask society's permission to keep my love.

Only love in marriage is allowed in this society, while every other love is sinful and immoral! Is this what you're talking about?"

At Ji-woon's vehement statements, Yun-hee felt embarrassed momentarily, but soon recovering herself, said: "I think there's no harm in loving somebody. But marriage is a promise, you know. Once married, the couple should make every effort to respect each other's personalities. And divorce comes when such an effort does not exist anymore. I believe Mr. Yi Sung-ju should have either chosen a divorce or given up his love for you. If I were in your position, I'd ask him to get a divorce first. In our conventional society, marriage is a kind of establishment, and naturally a woman in your position is regarded as a heretic. Like it or not, this is the deep-rooted morality of our society."

Regardless of Yun-hee's persuasive statements to soothe her, Ji-woon looked scornful of the morality of this society, which was as stubborn as an iron wall. Her voice was already weak, but her stature, firmly fixed like a post on a pebbled shore, seemed to declare her resolution not to back off even a step.

In a moment Ji-woon replied: "I believe such a principle exists above all for the sake of human beings—not vice versa. People are always talking about morality, but there's nothing more immoral than judging people by their morality!"

Though she was ten years younger than Yun-hee, the way Ji-woon had lived seemed by no means simple. So Yun-hee gave advice to Ji-woon as an equal.

"Ji-woon, forget about all these things. Just think you've been caught in a shower and start on your way again. Think what a beautiful age you're now at and try to catch bright and healthy things. Love does not exist only for one man, so the more you open your arms wide, the more you'll be able to meet people to love. There's no absoluteness in this world, you know. There are many women who worship men as gods, but once they discover the wonder of the world, no woman will do such a thing. After all, Mr. Yi Sung-ju is part of the love you've met till now. In time he'll become far from a perfect, absolute love for you."

"What I've in mind right now is not such a thing," responded Ji-woon immediately. "If love is defined as a thing that transcends pride, perhaps I don't deserve to love anyone. In fact, what I'm tormented by is not the fear I may lose love, but my own wounded pride! If I could forget this indescribable insult, I'd do anything in return. If I could take out this deeply wounded pride from my heart, I'd willingly smash my head against a wall. To live like this is no more than pain to me!"

In her agony Ji-woon suddenly fell to the ground and sobbed quietly, her forehead on the pebbled bank. While the sun was blazing down dazzlingly, she lay like a sacrificial offering, burning her heart. Looking at the grandly flowing stream that seemed to ask Ji-woon to forget everything, Yun-hee held her in her arms to soothe her, but couldn't utter even a word herself. No one, she thought, can aspire to give consolation to the despairing, and even a god might offend the deprived.

Ji-woon departed that day, leaving a letter with Yun-hee. She said it was the second letter she'd intended to mail to Mr. Yi Sung-ju using Yun-hee's address, and added she didn't send it because of a premonition. "If I keep this letter to myself," she said, "it will keep echoing through my heart. So I want you to destroy this letter on my behalf. Please burn it to ashes."

On receiving her letter, Yun-hee asked with a look of curiosity why she had chosen her to do it. Looking Yun-hee in the face, not hiding her bloodshot eyes, Ji-woon said: "Because you're the only woman who didn't show any animosity toward me, even when I visited your house with Mr. Yi Sung-ju. For the most part, married women regard a woman like me as their enemy, since we live in a conventional society."

Ji-woon continued that from now on she would arrange to get over her feelings. She said that was why she had asked Yun-hee to burn her letter, adding that Yun-hee had become a witness to her resolution. "So you may read my letter. There's nothing more for me to hide."

After seeing Ji-woon off, Yun-hee didn't return immediately to her house. She walked toward the stream again to read Ji-woon's letter, which she had accepted as her burden. As Yun-hee opened the envelope, the scribbled handwriting drew her eyes at once.

I went to the Taegu prison to see my younger brother, Ji-su, and came back to Chinju late at night. I took a room at a

242

small inn, but hardly slept that night. It was an inn in a residential area Ji-su's friend had told me about—a place like a whorehouse in the novels of the nineteen thirties. In a narrow corridor through which people could barely pass, rooms were lined up on both sides with a dim red light. I wanted to get out of the inn, but decided to stay there, knowing that Ji-su had stayed two nights at this place before being caught by the police.

The room was so small that my head and toes could touch the walls when I lay down, and moreover the window was blocked by a wall. While I sat vacantly, a group of drunken men rushed into the inn around midnight, shouting to the landlady to fetch comfort girls. Then I was startled by the commotion. A girl from somewhere was called into the room opposite mine, the door of which I could touch with my hand. I had no choice but to remain helplessly in my room because I could not go out during the curfew. Crouching like an animal, I put both hands over my ears and tried to think about Ji-su. Having been chased to this remote city, what did he think of being confined to the small room like a cell, hearing the coarse doings?

When, through the glass barrier separating us, I saw the gaunt face of Ji-su at the prison, I thought of the poor-quality apples displayed on a shelf of the prison store. Taegu is of course a city famous for apples, but those apples in the prison store were so misshapen that they didn't seem to have been blessed by the sunlight.

I don't believe life is fair to everyone. Nonetheless, should only such misshapen apples be available to the prisoners? What crime on earth did Ji-su commit? He turned into a radical student in the face of his sister's suffering, but before that he was so tender-minded as not to even catch a butterfly. I remembered you once said that you wrote poetry because of your accumulated sin. What is your sin? And what is my sin, too? What sin has torn and battered my life against my will?

As if fainting, I momentarily fell asleep in the hellish small room and soon woke up to the sound of a bell ringing imperatively. Instinctively I was convinced it must be a call from you. However, feeling the sticky sweat and the presence of the wall touching my head, along with the grumbling of the landlady at a wrong number at midnight, I discovered I was dreaming. The place where I was staying was a cheap inn in a remote southern city, and I found myself lying alone in a grave-like room. Feeling as if weighed down by something, I rose and turned on the light. Looking at my fingernails, which I had colored a few days ago with withered balsam flowers as if they were a talisman, I tried to calm myself down. I wondered if we could meet again by the time the red on my fingernails began to fade away.

I read a diary written in prison by an Iranian poetess, which you had given me the last time we met. Even in the midst of such ruthless torture, she seemed to think of the pride of her nation overcoming her suffering; the dignified attitude she demonstrated made me feel shrunken, because I can never be such a brave woman. Though I had an antipathy against the age we were in, I was such a feeble being as to feel compassion for a foreign priest with exotic eyes who walked through the field with children.

When I told you that perhaps you didn't like this part of me, you mentioned the story of Russian revolutionary poets, Esenin and Mayakovski, who both committed suicide. Even though they were deeply involved in the revolution, they were above all artists, you told me. At the time you took hold of my hands with a tender expression, saying we were no different from them.

As the sound of passing cars outdoors began to be heard, I went hurriedly out to the streets, only to come right back. I felt a sudden dread inside, not knowing where to go in the surrounding darkness. If I knew where you were, I would feel a gleam in my heart . . . Where did you rest in this darkness? Though I had sent my letter to Choha-ri, I felt restless, not being able to hear anything from you. The love I chose for you was all agony—now I don't know how to get over it.

What is going to happen to us now? But I don't care what

happens to us. Now extremely exhausted, I don't care about anything at all. All I hope is we will be able to meet again before the color of my fingernails fades. I pray my hope will not be in vain.

God, forgive my love.

Your Sorrowful Ji-woon
at dawn, July 30, 1979.

P.S.: As I slipped out of the inn, I saw the fat landlady walking around by the door for a change. I complained to her that I couldn't sleep at all because of the commotion. But she replied indifferently, fanning herself, "I thought that at your age everything in life is taken for granted. I supposed you knew what it takes to live."

I will never forget this city for the rest of my life.

After reading the letter, Yun-hee continued to sit vacantly on the bank. Apparently Ji-woon's letter felt like a labyrinth of sorrow, as each sentence was acutely tinged with a remorse and a yearning for life, while a shade of parting was implied in each word like a shadow. To Yun-hee, the transparent emotion of Ji-woon, which could not find its place in this barren world, and the ideal of Yi Sung-ju in pursuit of something great, seemed as precarious as the conjunction of air and wind. Although they were beings indispensable to each other, their relationship seemed as vain as their longing was real. It seemed that they could not come down to earth from the high tower of their love since the very nature of their relationship was so lofty.

It occurred to Yun-hee that people of the same sentiments could never make a couple in the real world. If Yun-hee were of the same nature as Hee-jo, how could she manage to live with him up to now? Perhaps they would have been burned to ashes together like firewood. But this does not necessarily mean that either Hee-jo or Yi Sung-ju was happy with their life simply because they had chosen the mundane life, nor were Yun-hee or Yi Sung-ju's wife content with everyday life. Life is, as a philosopher put it, a thing that naturally ends in remorse.

With this thought Yun-hee called to mind an interview with Greta Garbo in her old age, which she had read before. Retiring from the world at the age of thirty-six, the actress was said to have cut herself off from the intrusion of the outside world, keeping her inner castle ardently, protecting her mystery. At the interview, however, the actress admitted that there had been something mistaken in the life she had led. Yun-hee, who had loved that actress with her unique allure, was astonished a little by such a confession: though choosing the martyrdom of sacrificing herself to beauty by her own will, Garbo revealed regret in the twilight of her life.

In Buddhism, Yun-hee had learned, life is often compared to a bowl of sorrow, and the way people around her lived seemed pitiful. Ji-woon's life was doomed, as her love was forbidden by the custom of the society; Yi Sung-ju's wife lived in barrenness of heart because of the love she could not hold for herself; Yun-hee, for her part, tried to seek compensation in the work of art for the pain of her life with Hee-jo; while Han Min-wha, who had chosen solitude to get closer to the essence of her being, seemed acutely aware of her own limits. As expressed in the idea of Buddhism, all of these people were pitiful human beings, swept away by the sea of pain. Then the only way to endure the sorrow of life, Yun-hee concluded, is just to stand it as it is. There is no use seeking desperately for someone's understanding, so one must live on like the flowing water and submit to what nature ordains.

Now that the children were not at home, the house was as still as a temple. As Hee-jo went to his studio to prepare himself for his next job, Yun-hee set off to visit Han Min-wha after lunch. On a summer day when everything is silently melting under the blazing sun, the best way to escape from the heat is to lie on a bamboo bed under a tree, reading a book. But Yun-hee's mind had remained restless with various thoughts since Ji-woon had left the previous day.

When Yun-hee got to Eunti village, she would find Han Min-wha involved in her work, stepping on the pedals in her breeches. With the roof of the house made of thin tin, the inside was hot and the wind was blowing through opposing windows only. As was usual in Han Min-wha's house, the door was open, and when Yun-hee entered the room, an orange tapestry hanging on the side wall caught her eye. It was a square one with both ends of a pole protruding from the sides like outstretched arms. Its lower end was trimmed into an oval shape and decorated with hanging threads so that it could be used as a shawl.

Hearing footsteps, Han Min-wha turned around to greet Yun-hee. "Oh, it's you. It must be very hot outside."

"I thought you'd not be working in this weather. I'm afraid I disturbed you."

"Not at all—I'm not busy enough to be disturbed. Since there's nothing to tempt me outside, I can concentrate on my work in the summer."

Then, pointing to the orange tapestry, Yun-hee said, "That work seems to have been recently completed, right?"

"Exactly. It suggests twilight," Han Min-wha replied, nodding. "I made it like a clown's stage clothes to get over a feeling I'd get in the twilight. The moment of twilight is hard to endure, you know, since it always feels like the first time. Perhaps that moment might be a time for drinking."

Yun-hee smiled at the reference to drinking, but Han Min-wha said something unexpected. "Actually I did imagine someone when I heard your footsteps a moment ago. My heart was pounding then."

"Really? Who did you imagine?" inquired Yun-hee.

"My old lover—my first love, actually. While I was sitting at the table to take a rest, he appeared at the front door, and I was so surprised. Of course it was nothing but a fantasy, but it was so vivid I even thought he'd returned to this country. He's married and now lives in the United States."

"Why did you two break up?" asked Yun-hee with curiosity.

"Well, it's hard to explain. I know there's something in me like a wild cat. He was a man with a tender heart, but I didn't think we could be happy together. Then I left him, insisting myself that I pursue a life not restricted by anything. Despite that, I wept so many times, because I was afraid to lose him. Although it happened ten years or so ago, the despair of that time still overshadows me."

"Do you still love him?"

"Yes—I love his memory."

With this remark Han Min-wha leaned against the wall and stared at the empty air. Outside, the rice plants were growing under the sunlight, and the blowing wind caressed its laboring children gently, lingering at the window. Then Yun-hee noticed a long string of prayer beads that Han Min-wha was wearing on her neck. With a red silk cloth the size of a tiny coin hanging on its middle part like a decoration, it was made up of pink, red, and purple silk scraps sewn together. It looked like a bag filled with memories that Han Min-wha still cherished. Remembering a tiny paper ship that Sae-bul once made for her, Yun-hee asked Han Min-wha what it was.

"It's a bag containing a red mineral," she answered. "And they say this mineral ought to be wrapped in a red silk bag. It's used as a dyestuff, an herb, and even in making a talisman. A friend in Hong Kong sent it to me."

Because a monk in the Buddhist temple where her mother used to visit would make a talisman sometimes, Yun-hee had seen it before. A mineral ore of deep red, it looked like a hardened fragment of the sun. In a moment Han Min-wha told Yun-hee that she had begun to wear the talisman because something ominous had been happening to her recently. Then she said something Yun-hee didn't know: in obtaining her present house, Han Min-wha hadn't bought the land, but the owner of the land had transferred the land to a real estate agent some months ago, and consequently the new landlord had kept urging her to sell the house.

"As far as I know, the land is designated as belonging to the green belt area," explained Han Min-wha, "so it's of no use without this house."

"If so, why didn't you buy the land from the beginning?" asked Yun-hee.

"The owner of this lot owned a great deal of land in this village—as much as five thousand p'yong. He asked me to buy all of it, but what would I do with so much land? Besides, I didn't have enough money, either."

After a thought Yun-hee suggested: "Then you've no choice but to stand up to him to the end. Even if he's a landlord, the owner of your lot cannot touch another person's house."

"Since he began threatening me to sell my house, my heart has been pounding wildly these days. In a dream last night I heard a loud noise of a machine, and soon after I saw a large building standing like a monster beside this house. In fact, I'm tortured with terrible dreams like this lately whenever I go to sleep."

"Why don't you go and see a lawyer, then?" urged Yun-hee. "How can you expect to beat such a man with your bare hands?"

"Well, I believe my talisman can help me. Besides, I'm certain that nothing harmful would be done to a person who gets close to the essence of humanity," Han Min-wha responded, holding fast to the red bag containing the mineral, and then continued: "It looks as if all my sin were burning inside this bag. I wish all of my defects were burnt away as this red color suggests."

"How can you expect your defects to be burnt away?"

Yun-hee rebuked Han Min-wha, who, oblivious to the trouble concerning her house, merely stared at the talisman. Then their eyes met. The red bag, which was thought to burn away Han Min-wha's defects, seemed to purify even Yun-hee's soul, so she touched it carefully as if handling a sacred object. "You're a very elusive person, Ms. Han. At one time you're as strong as a witch, and at another you captivate me like an ethereal child."

When Yun-hee returned home after helping Han Min-wha plant radish seeds in her kitchen garden, Yi Sung-ju was, to her surprise, sitting in her living room with Hee-jo. It seemed he arrived just after Yun-hee had left. There were two empty bottles of *makkoli* and the head of a dried pollack on the table.

"Damn! You've got to be either a nationalist or a thorough cosmopolitan to live in this land," muttered Yi Sung-ju, indulging himself.

As Yun-hee stepped into the room, Hee-jo stopped talking, and asked her if there was any wine left in the house. He was unaware that she'd brought plum wine made the previous year from her parents' house on her previous visit. Just as Yun-hee was about to bring it in, Yi Sung-ju rose to leave, stopping her. "Don't go. I don't need it, because I'm supposed to meet someone in Seoul at six o'clock. I've got to go now."

"Why are you leaving so abruptly?" asked Yun-hee. "It's been a long time since you came here. And I've also something to ask you about."

"I dropped by my house just before I came here. The next time I visit, I'll offer you a drink, Big Sister."

Yi Sung-ju, who seemed not to have a watch, looked at the clock on the wall and got up. Unlike Park Young-soo, who would enjoy his time of leisure, he was always in a hurry. While watching Yi Sung-ju leave her house as swiftly as the wind, Yun-hee was suddenly reminded of Ji-woon's letter, which she'd put between the pages of a book. Though she hadn't burned it, there seemed no need to give it to him now. If he had come the previous day, Yun-hee thought, he'd have met Ji-woon, so the two persons, as always, had missed each other narrowly.

❧

It didn't seem like autumn was really coming, given this sultry weather, and time seemed to stand still during the past few days when Yun-hee's children were not home. As such, the silent space felt like where water was gathered, giving a dreamy atmosphere. As if trying to escape from boredom, light and shadow were playing hide-and-seek in the yard. In the corner of the yard the male goose was tramping the back of the female goose, pecking her head with his beak.

When raising geese for the first time, Yun-hee, unaware of their mating habits, had merely thought they were fighting with each other. Since the tramped goose would not fight back, Yun-hee considered it as a sign of the weak one's resignation, but then Hee-jo joked about her naivety. It turned out the mating of geese, whose relationship to each other was not harmonious, was literally like fighting. And the female goose would get annoyed when the male goose kept pecking her head with his beak. Such a case, Yun-hee realized, was no different from the relationship between man and woman. Fed up with their mating then, she had given the geese without hesitation to Hee-jo's friend, who had just bought a farm.

In making love to each other, Yun-hee learned later, the geese would express their ecstasy by making loud noises. So a joke goes that a widow cannot raise geese because of their mating habits, yet to Yun-hee the sound they would make during the mating was anything but obscene. While watching the geese enjoying their love as a part of nature, without a weary sense of self-consciousness, Yun-hee was suddenly led to feel a yearning for primitive love to revive in her heart. It might be another expression of her hidden passion, or a secret desire to break through the routine of her life. Then Yun-hee wondered if a primitive love that could repudiate the solidity of daily life still exists on the earth. Like the nature of the modern world, the human mind had become so complicated that the simple purity of mind could never be fully realized.

What is primitive love, then? Yun-hee wondered. It must be above all a state with no need for reason—just like the full blooming of a flower as seen in slow-motion photography. While the scene of geese making love under the blazing sun provided her with a prototype of love, a white butterfly, looking like a flower hidden in the grass, came flying staggeringly to her feet as if dazzled. And staring forlornly at the dancing flower with the coming of the butterfly, Yun-hee felt sorrow all of a sudden, thinking that these lower beings were much more blessed than herself.

Meanwhile Hee-jo went out early the next morning and returned at dusk with three different newspapers. A news item not mentioned in the morning papers attracted Yun-hee's eyes: it was about the female employees of the YH Trading Company, who had protested against the company's shutdown and subsequently had gone on an overnight strike at the opposition New Democratic Party headquarters.

The YH Trading Company, according to the paper, had managed a wig-making factory and recorded in its heyday an export volume of more than ten million dollars. But its management began to deteriorate, to the point where the company had had to pay nearly eighty million *won* a month in bank interest, ultimately leading to the shutdown of the factory. The president of the company, a man of enormous wealth, was said to own a great deal of real estate even in the U.S., whereas a beginning worker's salary at the factory barely reached thirty-six thousand *won*—a fact that made Yun-hee realize to her bones the harsh exploitation of the capitalists. Since the oil price hike the previous month, many people had been worried about the serious job situation and the low wages. Even so, Yun-hee was astonished that female workers' salaries could not even pay for a bag of rice. Looking at the pictures of the female workers protesting, Hee-jo spoke shortly, "Well, I suspect Yi Sung-ju may have been involved in this affair."

Then, two days later, a picture of the female workers being dragged into a police bus appeared in the papers, making people angry to see it. At two o'clock in the morning, the paper said, nearly a thousand policemen rushed into the New Democratic Party headquarters where the protest had been going on and arrested one hundred seventy female workers, even breaking open the office door of the party president. Swinging night sticks, as detailed in the paper, they had beaten the congressmen inside the office and pulled them out into the street. The spokesman of the opposition party had had blood all over his face, making it hard to recognize him, and the picture in the paper showed the party president forced out of his office with policemen holding both of his arms.

In truth, the police action had been so ruthless that night that some of the female workers even attempted suicide by throwing themselves out of the building. And, in the middle of this confusion, one of the female workers had cut an artery and thrown herself to the ground as a sign of protest against the brutal actions of the police. The violence and brutality of the police had proved astounding, the picture of the female workers crying out in the police bus and grabbing the iron bars at the window seeming genuinely pitiful.

Reading such news in the remote countryside, Yun-hee herself felt frustrated. Her anxiety was made even worse by the fact that three of her geese hadn't come back for the past two days. As a matter of fact, Yun-hee had not neglected to take care of the goose pen at sundown since the clever grandfather goose had died. The geese had poked around the yard the previous day, but it was not until evening that she found the three missing geese. So Yun-hee looked for them all through the village, including the banks of the stream, but they were nowhere to be seen.

In the morning Hee-jo, who couldn't afford to worry about geese because of his impending work, spoke to Yun-hee about his dream related to the articles about the YH Trading Company in the paper. "In my dream last night the missing geese returned followed by someone I couldn't identify. I wonder if someone might visit today."

Hee-jo's dream proved correct. As Yun-hee finished pickling cucumbers and pumping water for the cabbage patch, the geese entered the front gate with their long necks stretched forward. Delighted, Yun-hee stood up, and soon after she heard Tan-bee's voice calling, "Mom!" and then Madame Shin entered the yard following the children. The children looked healthier than ever: Tan-bee's yellowish skin seemed to shine in the bright sunshine, while Sae-bul looked taller, with his hair cut shorter.

"Now here come my children!" exclaimed Yun-hee.

As the children rushed to her, Yun-hee held them in her arms. Madame Shin laid down a wrapped bundle on the bamboo bed, which was a bunch of dried corbina fish. Seeing Yun-hee, she said: "I felt quite dreadful on the way here. I saw some strange-looking men lingering around the peppery-stew restaurant."

"A black sedan was parked there, too," Sae-bul interrupted.

"I guess they must be vacationers. I expect many people in this season," Yun-hee replied, not minding her mother's words.

That night, for the first time in a long while, Madame Shin had dinner with her son-in-law. Though Yun-hee had not gone to the market since her children had been away, she was able to prepare a nice dinner with a soup of sour *kimchi* and fried potatoes that Sae-bul liked, together with the dried corbina fish and other side dishes. After dinner, eating yellow melons Yun-hee had bought in the village, the children talked about how much fun they had had while in Seoul. Yun-hee spoke to her mother about Hee-jo's dream:

"I'd been worried about the geese since they hadn't returned home for two days. I even thought of an excuse to make to Sae-bul in case the geese should not come back at all."

"Why, what would you say to me?" Sae-bul asked.

"I'd have to tell you the truth—they went in pursuit of freedom!" Yun-hee answered jokingly. "That may be what they've been dreaming of."

In preparing her children's beds later, Yun-hee heard the front gate open. Looking out the window, she saw a flashlight coming toward the house in the darkness, so, shuddering, she turned on the yard light instantly. In a moment two strange men climbed abruptly onto the wooden floor and opened the door to the living room.

"Who are you?" shouted Yun-hee, uncomprehending.

But almost before Yun-hee had finished her words, a man with darkish eyebrows stepped onto the wooden floor with his shoes on. "We've come to inspect your house," he said.

Yun-hee was momentarily frightened by the man's menacing eyes, yet she felt impulsively that it had something to do with Yi Sung-ju. As the man was about to rush into the living room like a barbarian, with his shoes still on, Madame Shin shouted at him with a tremendous voice:

"What's the meaning of all this? You must know this is a house—not a pigsty! How dare you enter the room with your shoes on? Don't you have any parents to respect? What rudeness before an old woman your mother's age! Take off your shoes right away!"

Furious, Madame Shin shouted at them, sitting in the room. And startled by her angry voice, the men stepped down from the wooden floor and took off their shoes uncertainly. Then Yun-hee opened in spite of herself, "God! You're breaking into my house." Only then did she come back to herself and demanded an identification card from them. The man willingly showed her a card, but in her confusion Yun-hee couldn't make sense of it. As she gave him back his card, another man standing outside followed and started to rummage through the house.

They flung open every door and randomly took all the books out of the shelves to look through them, then went up to the attic holding a flashlight. Yun-hee became nervous, since on a shelf in the attic was *Im Guck-jung* by Hong Myong-hee, a book forbidden by government authority. The book had been given to her by her father, who had cherished it, and Yun-hee had not taken it out of the attic, keeping it all to herself. After a while a man in the attic asked her what was inside the box, when she saw him point to the army ration box. Inside the box were *punch'ong* dishes—though the book was hidden behind the box—so Yun-hee merely answered that it was a military ration box.

"What? You even keep a military ration box in the house, eh?"

Making an absurd remark, the intruder came down the stairs, then told Hee-jo in a menacing tone to come with them for interrogation. Hee-jo gazed back at him and said bluntly, "What's wrong with me anyway?"

Early the next morning, Yun-hee went to Yi Sung-ju's house, but there was nobody at home. His family must have gone to Seoul to seek help for him, Yun-hee suspected. When she left Yi Sung-ju's house, a man who looked like a police inspector was standing around the house and glanced at her. Yun-hee judged that Hee-jo had been taken to the police station to be questioned about Yi Sung-ju's whereabout.

Yun-hee sat up all night with no other choice but to wait. Her children, frightened the previous night by the intruders with their shoes on in the room, had not got over the shock even by morning, and Yun-hee, too, barely took a spoonful of rice at lunch, drinking only water. Looking at her daughter, Madame Shin breathed a deep sigh. "No wonder you're in no mood for taking a meal. Indeed, that's the reality of husband and wife."

"I hope nothing serious happens. It looks like you came here only to see this wretched thing, Mother. If you hadn't been here last night, we'd have had more trouble."

"Well, it's because you relied on me. Naturally, a woman tends to be strong in the presence of her children."

Yun-hee felt ashamed to recall how scared she had been during the house inspection the previous night, despite having done nothing wrong. Due to the incident, Yun-hee discovered, she was merely a naive person accustomed to the dictatorial regime in spite of herself. After the children had left, Madame Shin spoke to Yun-hee in a composed voice:

"Now I must say I've felt sorry for you all this time. I even thought I should have let you do what you wished when you suggested a divorce to me just after you were married. If so, you'd have met an ordinary man and lived happily. Life may seem long, but it never is. It's just as short as a passing dream."

"Mother, I've no regrets about my life. How much happiness could I enjoy in my life? Anyway I think I'm now enjoying more than my share in life. Looking around myself, I find myself happier than I should be."

"I believed in you, since you were always good-natured. At my age all the painful past feels like a haze in spring, and happiness is transient, too. They say that when Buddha discovered the truth at his death, he illuminated it for all the world. It might be lucky, however, if an ordinary woman like me could die peacefully without a sense of attachment to life."

Yun-hee was touched to learn that her mother still remembered what she had said long before, feeling that her mother had become tender-hearted so as to reveal her inner mind to her daughter.

In the afternoon Yun-hee opened a drawer of the chest, looking for the children's sportswear, but found instead a piece of cotton dyed with Chinese ink. Glancing at the cloth, Madame Shin asked Yun-hee what she was going to use it for. It was something Hee-jo had brought from Monk Hyeo when he had visited Tamyang the previous spring; since Hee-jo had shown his desire for a monk's robe, Hyeo had given him the cloth willingly. So Yun-hee had planned to take it to a tailor shop near the Chokye Temple, which specialized in monks' robes, the next time she went to Seoul.

Hearing it, Madame Shin roughly measured the size of the piece and looked for scissors along with Hee-jo's other clothes. She estimated its length by spreading her arms, cut the cloth skillfully with her glasses on, and then began to sew the cloth with a sewing machine. It was actually the first time that Madame Shin had made clothes for her son-in-law. After finishing the robe for Hee-jo, Madame Shin left for Seoul the next morning, saying she could hardly await his return.

The newspaper that day reported that the incident at the YH Trading Company had been completely crushed. According to the paper, the police arrested three of the female workers who had led the demonstration and brought the rest of them back home after allowing a small payment. Accompanied by such ruthless suppression, the police action had been cruel enough to provoke outrage all over the country. The police were said to be in the process of interrogating five dissidents suspected of having secretly led the demonstration. In addition to this, the relationship between the Mission for the Urban Industrialized Region and some of the dissidents was being thoroughly investigated, the paper continued. Two months before, Yun-hee remembered, Yi Sung-ju had begun an evening school for workers in association with the Mission, even acquiring some *punch'ong* cups from Hee-jo to use in that purpose.

She guessed that if Yi Sung-ju were arrested now, Hee-jo would soon be released.

In spite of the hot weather that afternoon, Yun-hee's children went out to collect herbs, which was one of their vacation chores. While Yun-hee was staying home alone, Park Young-soo visited for the first time in a long while. In fact, he had stopped coming to her house since Hee-jo had made such a commotion in drinking, but this time he made a visit abruptly, followed by Yi Jung-dal. Learning from Yun-hee that Hee-jo had been taken to the police station, Park Young-soo, looking distressed, said he himself had happened to be suspected by the police. As Yun-hee inquired in a grave voice if Hee-jo would go through hardship from the police, Park Young-soo answered that it wouldn't be long before he was released, suggesting she should not worry too much for now. Hearing all this, Yi Jung-dal muttered, frowning: "An artist is like a grasshopper singing in the field. So what's the use of arresting him? What a brutal age we're in!"

Yun-hee was glad to see Yi Jung-dal come back to her house, despite the fact that Hee-jo had urinated on him the previous time, but she was now in no mood to smile. Noticing Yun-hee's emaciated face, Park Young-soo stood up to leave, asking her to notify him as soon as Hee-jo was back. Out of the house, Yi Jung-dal stopped by the brook and poured something from a beer bottle into the water. Glancing at Yun-hee's curious look, Yi Jung-dal explained, grinning, that he had put his urine in the bottle. Realizing that he had come to take joyful revenge on Hee-jo, Yun-hee said, smiling, "I won't forget to tell Mr. Hong you've come here with the bottle. I guess he'll be delighted to hear it."

Hee-jo returned late that night. At first, he staggered a little, smelling of wine, and Yun-hee felt her heart trembling to see his gaunt face. In fact, she'd imagined so many horrible things so far—sitting up all night for two days straight, which seemed like a long, dark tunnel. Standing speechless in the yard, Yun-hee told herself that he had safely returned from the darkness. However, Hee-jo avoided her eyes and disappeared past the kitchen garden to the stream. He wanted to be alone for a while, it seemed. Yun-hee entered the kitchen to pour water into the kettle and, after preparing Hee-jo's dinner, awaited him impatiently with a troubled mind. Now the clock struck eleven. When Yun-hee went outside and walked across the stream toward the stony bank, a night wind brushed her neck gently.

Hee-jo, it turned out, was sitting crouched like a rock by the stream; from behind he looked lonely and dwarfed enough to be buried in darkness. For fear of interrupting his reflections, Yun-hee approached him quietly in her bare feet and sat beside him. Under the stars the stream seemed to be opening its arms wide, embracing one of the mountain peaks in the darkness, which was throwing its shadow on the surface of the stream. Watching the stream, Yun-hee said softly: "The family is getting along all right. Mother left this morning and Mr. Park Young-soo dropped by this afternoon."

As Yun-hee spoke, Hee-jo nodded, not even stirring a finger. So she continued, "It looks like Yi Sung-ju must be arrested, right?"

"Maybe."

"Did they torture you there?"

"No."

"Didn't they beat you up?" she inquired again.

"No."

His shoulders shuddered a little as if what he had gone through was an enormous shame. Realizing that his heart was deeply wounded, Yun-hee asked no more and let Hee-jo hold his tongue stubbornly. A doubt passed swiftly through her mind that he'd surrendered himself to the police, trembling like a rabbit at their threats. In a moment Yun-hee began to express how difficult it had been for the past two days while waiting impatiently for his return:

"I could hardly sleep at all after they took you away," she said, "and a scene from a battlefield kept coming to my mind. Dead bodies were heaped up in piles and the roads were littered with abandoned shoes. I wondered how at such a time women could wait for their husbands—if they were taken away like you. With this thought settled in my mind, I became terrified."

Then Hee-jo crumpled down to Yun-hee, burying his head in her bosom, and they fell to the ground together. "It felt like being drowned . . . I remembered my childhood when I drowned and was close to death . . ."

Mumbling, Hee-jo put his feverish lips on Yun-hee's as if trying to seal her mouth. He pushed his face breathlessly into hers like a scared child, and Yun-hee embraced him heartily with open arms— as if receiving a fallen star into her heart. She felt a sisterly compassion for Hee-jo trembling at his nightmarish experience. Feeling her eyes also grow moist, Yun-hee turned her glance toward the stream. With the light of the stars scattered on the surface, the black stream flowed like coal tar.

8

Every Flower Has Its Own Seeds

Now came the beginning of autumn, a time when even a mosquito is said to feel cold. Only a week before, "Judy," the tenth typhoon in the season, had done considerable damage to the southern part of the country, which had been revisited by a local downpour associated with the eleventh typhoon, claiming one hundred and nine lives and leaving nearly thirty-six thousand people homeless. As a result, every corner of the country was suffering seriously from the typhoon, with damage amounting to almost thirty billion *won*.

Yi Sung-ju, Yun-hee heard later, had been arrested along with other dissidents for supposedly plotting social disorder and scheming to subvert the government. Among his personal offenses were such things as circulating subversive documents in his capacity as an evening school teacher and stirring up the protesters of the YH Company to struggle in a solid union.

After her husband came back, Yun-hee had visited Yi Sung-ju's house twice. The first time she did not have a chance to talk with Yi Sung-ju's wife since there was a visitor, and the second time there was nobody at home. On her way home from the first market day in September, Yun-hee dropped by Yi Sung-ju's house to find his wife and her younger brother packing things. Only then did she learn they were moving away.

"Recently I appealed to the Human Rights Association in Seoul," Yi Sung-ju's wife began, sighing. "Regardless of this, I'm afraid they'll sentence my husband to many years' imprisonment. I don't feel like living here without him anymore."

"Did Mr. Yi consent to your idea?" asked Yun-hee with a worried look.

"He told me to do as I liked. And we decided to let his school junior take charge of this house."

"Sounds like a good idea. I hope living in the busy city will make you forget the hardship you're facing now. At any rate, I suppose waiting in the countryside is harder to bear."

Then Yun-hee continued that she had learned how hard it was to wait for her husband after his arrest, and that she had even thought of people's agony in wartime.

"But waiting in wartime would be easier," replied Yi Sung-ju's wife feebly. "This waiting of mine only gives me a troubled mind."

"I hope this incident may change Mr. Yi. Also, your living apart will cause him to miss you and your children very much. Though he was taken away from you by force, it's likely to help you have a chance to think with a sense of distance."

"A sense of distance is not likely to give me peace, though."

With a pale complexion, Yi Sung-ju's wife looked up at the jujube tree in the front yard. This tree is said to bear fruit three times a year through the three peaks of hot weather in the summer, so Yun-hee thought that Yi Sung-ju's wife's tenacious love, like the image the tree evoked, might bear secret fruit under the heart-searing sun.

As the summer receded, a cool breeze rose both morning and evening, with an early cricket already starting to chirp under the stone steps. Yun-hee, who was sensitive to the cold, asked a villager to bring firewood to heat the *ondol* floor every other day. Removing the summer quilt, she prepared a padded quilt for her children and hung out the winter clothes, which had been kept in a box at the attic, in the sunshine to dry.

While the season was changing, Hee-jo, like a mere spectator, did nothing but look vacantly at the field, drinking. Since returning from the horrible dungeon, he would drink fitfully and seek another drink the next morning to chase away the hangover. Hee-jo seemed deeply shocked by the fact that he himself had suffered from the regime's violence, which he'd often heard of. As Yun-hee observed, the two days' experience Hee-jo had gone through must have left so deep a scar on his mind that he even refused to tell his wife about it. She felt sympathetic to see him struggling to wipe out the nightmarish experience by taking to drinking, only hoping that his suffering would not have a bad effect on him.

The day Yi Sung-ju's wife moved away, she came to see Yun-hee to say she felt sorry to have caused anxiety to her neighbors. As a matter of fact, Yun-hee had instinctively held a grudge against Yi Sung-ju since Hee-jo had been taken to the police station. But now her resentment passed away as she felt unburdened that her husband had at least taken a share in their suffering. In such hard times, when many dissidents continued to be arrested, the peaceful life of the countryside that she had enjoyed made her feel guilty despite her antipathy to the common folk ideology.

A month later Park Young-soo, who had visited right after Hee-jo's release, came again with Yi Jung-dal. Hee-jo, now on speaking terms with Yi Jung-dal, burst into laughter to learn from him about the episode of the beer bottle full of urine, and said half-jokingly that he had escaped from being urinated on just because he had been in custody. As is shown in *The Tale of Shim Ch'ong* and *The Tale of Chun-hyang,* both of which have happy endings, few Koreans expect the reality around them to end either tragically or in hostility.

Once sitting down, Yi Jung-dal opened by saying that he had grown restless with the seasonal change. He talked to Hee-jo as if joking: "You know what? A pottery artist's struggle with himself seems less serious than mine, since he deals above all with clay. The clay is sure to awaken the origin of something, right?"

Not responding directly to this remark, Hee-jo spoke calmly. "So far I've only layered and wedged clay to find such an origin. But I must confess my sense of incompetence prevents me from producing even one piece of pottery."

"Incompetence? Nonsense! A potter like you has nothing but to turn the potter's wheel."

Pretending to be indifferent to Hee-jo's feeling, Park Young-soo started talking about a topic that had been reported in the newspaper for a month: a number of artists had instantly objected to the government's plan to impose income taxes on them starting the next year.

"Even the female workers of the YH Trading Company," Park Young-soo continued, "whose monthly earning barely reaches one hundred thousand *won* were obliged to pay income tax. Given this, there's no justification under any circumstances for professed artists not to pay taxes. As for painters, however, I don't believe they have to pay income tax if their annual income from their work is less than six million *won*. And I'm sure neither of you—Hee-jo nor Jung-dal—will have to pay tax, in the sense that eighty percent of an artist's total income becomes the necessary cost of doing business, while only the remaining twenty percent is subject to taxation. You might as well consider this a certain privilege. But I know some artists insist they should not pay any income tax under the present circumstances, where the evasion of taxes is such a prevalent social practice. Surely this is an insult to the low-income workers who must pay their taxes regularly. To my knowledge, the problem arises from the artists' conviction that a work of art, which they regard as the outcome of a noble act of mind, should not be compared with a general commodity. Naturally it's not restricted to money value alone. I'm not certain if all works of art deserve such treatment, but I think that artists should be defined as professionals only if they make a living through their works."

"True, I live on my pots," spoke Hee-jo instantly to Park Young-soo, "so I'll have to pay the tax. But I've no mind at all to consider my work as a profession as you just mentioned. It's not that my work is lofty but that it needs just as much endless patience as is needed—like breaking a rock with your bare hands."

A look of earnestness showed up on Hee-jo's swarthy face even though he appeared to have forgotten pottery for a long while. Agreeing with Hee-jo, Yi Jung-dal stated, "Sure, your work becomes a vocation if you're willing to suffer such hardship for it."

"Mmm, you call it a vocation . . ."

Hee-jo mumbled to himself and resumed in a moment. "Since moving here I have often seen an old woman working laboriously—practically attached to the soil. She plants every tiny seed, however trivial, whenever she gets one. And I came to understand what a vocation is whenever I saw that old woman plowing a field without any complaint or agitation. Her hands are as rough as the bark of a tree, but her face shines like an angel's, though covered all over with dust. Although I've never met an angel, I can hardly imagine a more beautiful face than hers. And the modesty I learned from her is beyond any comparison. Compared with her, I'm only a beginner in my vocation."

"You could claim you attained a vocation if you did this kind of work before."

With this remark Park Young-soo took out something wrapped in paper, and as he unwrapped the package, a small pot resembling a long-necked jug appeared. Without any touch of ornament or craftsmanship, it lay before them like a natural object. Holding the pot in his hand which showed a timeless strength, Park Young-soo disclosed that he had got it cheaply at an antique shop. "In old times this was used as a pot for pickled shrimp in a fishing village. And I'll leave it here for you to observe as long as you want."

With a smile on his lips, Hee-jo put his hands gently around the pot and fixed his eyes on it. "Good! It seemed to be made for a purely practical purpose, and I can see no superfluous lines or curves. Right now I'm thinking of our country anew—I mean I'm pondering on what I should do in my position, since this pot stirs something in me."

Park Young-soo and Yi Jung-dal went back early the next morning. Because he had drunk heavily, Hee-jo began passing dark bloody excrement all through the night. He had been in and out of the room, rummaging through the drawers of the chest, while Yun-hee slept. And the next morning Yun-hee found a heap of blood-stained underwear by the toilet. He must have been searching in the drawers for clean underwear, spilling blood but still drinking heroically like a trouper.

Unable to stand it anymore, Yun-hee urged him to consult a medical doctor. But Hee-jo replied nonchalantly, from the pain in his belly, that it was nothing but menstruation. Suppressing her anger, Yun-hee went instantly to the peppery-stew restaurant to call up an old Buddhist monk in Sungnam. Since hearing of him from Monk Hyeo that he was well known for compounding herbal medicines from secret recipes, Yun-hee had been his customer. As if proving his reputation, Hee-jo had once been cured of duodenitis by some doses of herbs that this mysterious monk had compounded. And a rumor had spread openly among his patients that one patient, confined to bed for a year because of a severe back pain, had been miraculously cured in a week by acupuncture, and that a woman, who had been sterile for nine years, had got pregnant by taking only two packages of prepared herbs.

With blind belief, Yun-hee, over the phone, impatiently asked the monk for help, telling him of Hee-jo's symptoms. "He won't go to a hospital, so send me anything you can prescribe."

"Pshaw! He has destroyed himself with drink again. Damn his

drinking habit! No doubt his weak veins broke because of his cold entrails. If he doesn't get well after taking my herbs, tell him to go to hell immediately!"

"Please send your medicine right now."

Yun-hee entreated him again, since she was already aware that he was a foul-mouthed monk. The monk promised instantly that he would compound a medicine after the morning ceremony the next day. Despite that, Yun-hee thought it fortunate that he was due to get medicinal ingredients that afternoon.

Hee-jo took the medicine for three days like an obedient child. Looking at dried red peppers on a straw mat, he mumbled painfully that autumn had come. One day he struggled with a sketchbook, and then worked at the potter's wheel for two successive days to get his hands ready to work.

It was not until after Hee-jo visited his children's school that he would resume drinking, though his bleeding had barely stopped. On Saturdays the children would return home before noon, but this time they hadn't got back until four o'clock in the afternoon. Worrying that the children might be hungry now that they took no lunch box with them, Yun-hee suspected something might have happened at school. Remembering an incident just two days before when a junior high school girl was raped in a grove near the village, she decided it would be better for her to go to the school than to stay restlessly at home. At that moment, Hee-jo insisted he go instead and changed from his working clothes, as he seemed about to stop his work in the hot weather at noon.

Hardly an hour had passed after Hee-jo had gone out, when the children returned home. As Yun-hee began to scold them for being late for no reason, Tan-bee explained without hesitation, "Since the President was expected to pass by our school, we had to clean the street and pull weeds."

"What? If he ever comes again, all the children will get sick. By the way, why didn't your father get back with you?"

"Father went to the peppery-stew restaurant to drink. He was roaring angrily at the teachers in their office because they made children work in such sultry weather, ignoring lunchtime."

Tan-bee blinked her eyes behind her glasses. Since the child did not seem to tell easily who was right, Yun-hee explained: "I think your teachers are wrong, because they seemed to forget the fact that any child is as valuable as the President himself. Besides, children are weak and should be taken care of as such."

Hee-jo returned at midnight, beastly drunk. On arriving, he unexpectedly put down a bundle of dried corn and said to the uncomprehending Yun-hee, "Ms. Han gave it to me."

It seemed he had dropped in at Han Min-wha's on his way home. Therefore Yun-hee gave up the idea of getting him to take the prepared medicine, and instead inquired about Han Min-wha. In fact, Yun-hee had called at her house just once since her children began school, and had already told Hee-jo about the troubled situation facing the woman.

"Today," said Hee-jo, "I happened to meet the owner of that piece of land there and gave him a good scolding, of course. Maybe he'll never come back."

"What if he should think you're drunk?" Yun-hee asked pitifully, looking at his bloodshot eyes. To believe that he could, though in a drunken spirit, frighten off the money-grabbing speculator who cruelly decided to pull down the small house of a woman living alone . . .

Disillusioned with her husband, who had taken to drinking again to chase away his hangover, and worried about Han Min-wha, Yun-hee left her house the next morning, going toward Eunti village. With Tan-bee going with her since it was Sunday, Yun-hee felt an early autumn breeze refresh them now. All the rice fields that had endured the ordeal of the typhoons now turned yellow with ripened grain. In the face of the withering season when they would depart, various insects such as locusts, grasshoppers, and dragonflies were enjoying their lives to the full.

When Yun-hee had been a child, the fields were full of locusts at this time of year. Children used to catch and tie them in rows in a foxtail shape so they could fry them at home to eat, but the locusts had gradually dwindled because of the overuse of agricultural chemicals. Nowadays it was a delight to find a mantis on the grass, seeming to threaten people with its boldly raised sawtoothed feet and breast. Yun-hee remembered how she had once been afraid of going blind by touching a mantis since, with its swollen eyes, a mantis's triangular face always looked inauspicious.

The odd-looking female mantis eats her mate away after copulation, she heard, but it turns out that her mate's body is necessary to nourish the female as she lays her eggs. As Yun-hee reflected, such a natural fact reveals the very law of nature. In reading Fabre's *Souvenirs Entomologiques* some time ago, Yun-hee learned that all the lowly insects have their own mysterious instincts: locust or grasshopper, each insect keeps the dark secret of life inside its body.

Walking beside her mother, Tan-bee tried vainly to catch some red dragonflies whirling in the air like tiny helicopters. Yun-hee too felt like catching one out of curiosity about their fragile, transparent wings, which looked so beautiful, but the children wanted to catch feeble insects alive out of their destructive instinct.

The other day Sae-bul had come running to Yun-hee, holding five red dragonflies in his fingers. "What did you catch them for?" Yun-hee asked him, assuming a grave face, thinking he had caught too many. "I'll let them fly into the air like this," the child replied, raising his hand, as if dispelling his mother's fear. In a moment the dragonflies were soaring away together. Yun-hee heard some children in the city were often cruel enough to drop chickens from high up in their apartment buildings. But her children, living in the countryside, took even an ant for a friend and wouldn't step on it.

Walking along a field lined with exuberant cosmos into the edge of the mountains, Yun-hee found a bunch of wild white chrysanthemums blooming at a street corner. The summer flowers she liked had already withered; a clump of wild chrysanthemums blooming lonely in the shadow of the trees aroused the autumn sentiments in her. Beside Yun-hee Tan-bee said to herself, Every flower has its own seeds. It's so miraculous!

As Tan-bee stood still, fascinated by the flowers before her eyes, Yun-hee held her calmly by the hand. To think of the flower seeds while looking at the flowers . . . Maybe all humans keep their own seeds in the depths of their hearts, Yun-hee mused. How can a tiny seed grow to be a tall flower? What kind of flower will this child bloom into in the future?

Reaching Han Min-wha's back yard across a brook, they saw many cosmos as tall as Tan-bee blooming like pillars, so Tan-bee rejoiced buried in the flowers. As they passed into the front yard through a path covered with cosmos trembling slightly as if fainting, a piece of weaving hanging under the eaves came into view. Dangling from a laundry line like a bamboo blind, it had a plain geometric formation of such variant colors as orange, light green, and violet. Its gorgeous, rich colors reminded Yun-hee of an autumn field, but Tan-bee commented it looked like a flag. The child's comparison came vividly to Yun-hee's mind as the work seemed to be uniquely woven with the colorful threads of the weaver's mind.

Hearing an indication that someone was around, Han Min-wha emerged to greet her guests. As Tan-bee bowed to her saying hello, she replied with a surprised look, "Oh, you look like a young lady now. I didn't know you wore glasses."

Greeting her, Yun-hee pointed to the work drooping down from the eaves. "It looks more beautiful hanging there than when it was in the frame. It feels familiar with its smooth texture."

"I dedicated it to the Earth Goddess for my stable life on this land. I think it a rather good work since it's in harmony with nature."

"To me it looks like an autumn field, but Tan-bee compared it to a flag," replied Yun-hee.

"Actually it's the flag of my mind."

As Han Min-wha answered, looking at the texture of the work, Tan-bee said, as if in a trance, "This place looks like a lonely castle in a cartoon. And you're an exiled queen weaving textiles."

"Do you think so? But neither a flower nor a flag is strong enough to protect me," said Han Min-wha, before leading them into the room. There was no thread on the loom in the corner now that she had finished weaving. On the table was an open book; Yun-hee thought it might be a collection of poems and took a look at it.

"It's a collection of Tagore's poems," explained Han Min-wha. "I've been reading his poems to calm my troubled mind."

"But what's the use of reading poems under the circumstances?" Yun-hee protested. "I heard the owner of this land came to you again yesterday. Didn't my husband make matters worse?"

As Han Min-wha, not responding to her words immediately, went out to bring in sweet potatoes, Yun-hee clicked her tongue, thinking she was as naive as her husband.

Returning soon, Han Min-wha spoke. "Never mind. There's nothing to get worse anymore. A few days ago when the man came to threaten me, I poured water on the place where he was standing. And I'd even asked my younger brother to take this matter to a lawyer, but the owner of the land didn't seem to mind at all, since he came to me again yesterday. There's no end to the greediness of the rich, you know, because the more they have the more they want. An excessive attachment to something is ugly as it leads people into a trap."

While speaking, Han Min-wha shrugged her shoulders, indicating she had no mind to think of it anymore. She'd innocently tried to preserve her own world, it seemed, but was now groaning as she was unable to handle the attack of harsh reality. Feeling sorry that she couldn't help the woman, Yun-hee mumbled, "I think you should have a dependable person to help you with your chores."

Sensing that Yun-hee had implied the need for a man in her life, Han Min-wha, who had been lost in thought for a while, replied: "Recently my will has been getting feeble along with my weak body. And I even thought of whom I'd call for help in case I should be ill in bed. I remembered everyone I had loved, but should I be in such a condition I'd end up calling up my first lover, I concluded. In spite of having experienced a more mature, reasonable love as time passed, I realized that reason can never surpass instinctive feelings in love. Our first love, in particular, is a thing influenced by a primordial feeling, even though it's considered immature and chaotic. Now I've come to realize how great that primordial feeling is."

The instant Han Min-wha had finished her words, Yun-hee revealed what had been in her mind for a long while. "From the beginning I've known you and my husband love each other very much. I wouldn't call such a relationship 'reasonable' or 'moral'— instead, I'd like to think that neither of you is courageous, even within yourself. There's a friend of mine who once said stability is only a different name for cowardice. Of course you may tell my husband her words. After all, I believe there exists no longer a primitive love in this world that could inflame all the established lives in its passion. And my husband is no exception in this respect. It may even be the same with me."

269

Han Min-wha kept her eyes down, as if she felt ashamed, but she appeared to agree with Yun-hee. By contrast, Yun-hee wondered whether she was herself cunning or not; at first, she had made friends with Han Min-wha, fascinated by her keen sensibility, but soon she had found herself standing in the way, fearing that Han Min-wha's relationship with Hee-jo would develop against her wishes. As Yun-hee remained lost in thought, startled at her discovery, Tan-bee, who had been playing by herself with many colorful threads in the corner of the kitchen, came to them. Staring at a red scrap of cloth hanging from Han Min-wha's neck, the child asked, "What is it, Auntie?"

"A bag for a memory," Yun-hee answered on behalf of Han Min-wha, thinking that Tan-bee was unable to figure out what a talisman means. As the child fixed her eyes upon it, Yun-hee added, "You see, she made it as a necklace to preserve lovely memories."

"Really? Does it help to keep all the lovely memories?" inquired the child with a curious look.

"Of course. This red bag is believed to absorb all the memories like an immense sponge," Han Min-wha replied to Tan-bee.

"I wish I had such a bag."

As Tan-bee was so earnest in her request, Han Min-wha's face became cloudy. "This is not a thing anyone should hope to possess," she said to the child. "Though it looks pretty, you must instead endure many sorrows to keep it. So I think you'd better turn to a visible thing, however small, rather than to invisible memories. Isn't it happier, after all, to live with your mother than to live with a memory of her?"

At the sight of the grave look on Han Min-wha's face, Tan-bee said no more. Child that she was, she now seemed able to perceive the heavy atmosphere lingering in the room. In truth, Han Min-wha's words were a painful monologue for a woman living with only a memory, Yun-hee realized instantly. After a silence Yun-hee opened in a solemn tone: "I've no memory worth keeping since I never experienced a love demanding tears. Now I feel how dreary my life has been. I'm not entitled to claim I know about life."

When Yun-hee got home after eating lunch at Eunti, her friend Eun-kyong had been waiting for her with her husband. Walking up and down the yard, their daughter Hye-ri ran to Tan-bee as soon as she saw her. As a child, she had liked Tan-bee so much that she would tease her mother to give birth to a sister as pretty as Tan-bee. Now, as a junior high school girl, she looked quite composed.

Hee-jo's face was already reddened with drink when Yun-hee entered the room. Seeing a dish of seafood stew on the table, she suspected Eun-kyong had brought sea food, and there was even a little *ume* wine left in the bottle.

Upon looking at Yun-hee, Eun-kyong asked where she had been, so Yun-hee answered nonchalantly, "My husband's lover is living nearby."

"Does he have a lover?" asked Eun-kyong, assuming a startled face. And Yun-hee replied half-jokingly but without malice, "Because he's an artist."

"You mean an artist can have a lover? I wish I were an artist, then," Chung In-ku responded jokingly.

At her husband's words, Eun-kyong looked charmingly askance at him. Laughing quietly, Yun-hee said, "At last, you've become an ordinary wife, too."

As Yun-hee was about to change the topic so as not to embarrass Hee-jo, Eun-kyong abruptly started telling a story about a younger friend from school who had recently been divorced. Although this friend would not tolerate anything wrong, owing to her straightforward nature, Eun-kyong said that she liked her very much because of her thoughtful, clear-minded disposition.

"Then she got divorced this spring," began Eun-kyong. "They had loved each other earnestly and were said to be a perfectly harmonious couple. In the course of their living, however, her husband became enchanted by another woman. One Saturday morning, drunk, he pronounced that he would leave her because he could not deceive her any longer. You can imagine how shocked she was! But even in such terrible circumstances she instantly composed her thoughts and told him at breakfast the next day that it would be their last meal together. Then she told him she had no courage to care for their beautiful four-year-old daughter, and demanded he take the child with him. That day her husband left with only the child and a trunk. Their humble yet happy marriage of six years came to an end that way."

271

"How unbelievable! How old is she?" asked Yun-hee.

"She is my junior by six years. She's thirty."

"Thirty? It's an age when she begins her journey into life like someone just packing things for a start."

Eun-kyong continued her story, which sounded like a French film. "Then her husband came back two months later. He confessed immediately that he'd made a terrible mistake and asked for a reconciliation, apologizing for his act. What would you do in her position? I believe most Korean women would tolerantly accept it, because, despite their sense of mortification, they would expect to make a compromise in the name of preserving their family to the end. In this case, however, she rejected him, firmly declaring that she could not love a man who had run after women like an animal in rut. Of course she loved her husband, and still loves him regardless of her sense of betrayal. Later she told me she would never forget him but that her self-respect did not allow her to accept his entreaty—although she could fully anticipate her misfortune. At first I blamed her for not taking him back, but now I've come to think highly of her decision. She deserves my respect, since she placed her self-respect before anything else. Anyhow it gives me, as a fellow woman, comfort to find such a woman in our land."

As Eun-kyong came to the unexpected conclusion, Yun-hee looked at her in amazement. But Chung In-ku said, grinning, "Look, you're threatening me with such a melodrama."

"No—I'm not threatening you," responded Eun-kyong. "Instead I'm letting you know I'm prepared for it, too. I've lived up to now quite mechanically, as precise as a ruler. Nevertheless, I haven't led my life by my own will, because there's no choice left for me. Who knows, then, whether or not I'll be run over by a car tomorrow? The moment I heard her story, I made up my mind to be ready for any conceivable thing."

"Why is it you women are always thinking of such extreme situations? I guess that's why all the tragic characters in fiction are female. True, she would take to such queer thoughts since her husband was so incompetent as not to help his genius wife be recognized in the world."

As Chung In-ku lovingly made fun of his wife, Yun-hee spoke, filling Eun-kyong's glass. "Still, you're far better off than me, my proud friend."

❧

In the meantime Hee-jo, while taking the herbal medicine, had drunk for two days straight, and on Monday morning he drank again to chase away his hangover. Getting angry with him, Yun-hee remarked, pouring the prepared herbs into the garbage box, "Don't make me waste my efforts like this anymore," but Hee-jo made no response and continued to drink silently. Later, when Yun-hee entered the children's room to clean, he rose stealthily, pretending not to notice her. She went into the kitchen to find a broom only to see Hee-jo standing quietly with his back to the door. He seemed to have looked into the garbage box, trying to confirm whether she had really poured out the herbal medicine.

The next day Wan-kyu came back with a bag, and they began to work earnestly as before. Yun-hee made a soup as a side dish by steaming some ribs in a kettle for a long time. At this time of year she would make a soup from ox bones, since beef was more nourishing in the autumn. After all, Hee-jo's work and having Wan-kyu again in the family made Yun-hee feel as if she were preparing a banquet. With his exhibition ahead, Hee-jo, strained, had stopped drinking and had even been taking the medicine regularly. For Yun-hee it always felt good to watch him involved in his work, and it was delightful as well to hear him talking about pottery after supper with Wan-kyu. The evening after Wan-kyu had returned, Hee-jo brought up a change in the mode of pottery:

"Although we Koreans are considered to have inherited fine and unique pots," he said, "I think modern pottery artists should repudiate the form of the old. And I myself have made an effort to break away from the old pattern and form. As you see, the present form of iron kettles is the same as it was in the Iron Age. The reason it has been handed down over a long period of time is that it has a common denominator in technique deserving to be accepted time after time. Despite that, I believe we must destroy its form—even though it's regarded as flawless. Of course, pottery artists have their own unique method, but what's important for me in pottery is the idea of freedom and change. Although, thanks to our flexible minds, we humans are capable of making a change continuously, we should be careful not to become tied up with something, nor to be fixed to some form as well. Just as a stone is always changing, so everything in life changes."

The next day, when Yun-hee took some steamed chestnuts to the studio, Hee-jo was showing Wan-kyu a tea cup with a hole in it, fresh off the potter's wheel. "At the beginning of this work," he explained, pointing to the cup, "I thought of making a tea cup with a pointed bottom. But in the process of making it I found myself oblivious to my plan, and so I did the work again, trying not to forget. Eventually I ended up with this cup with a hole in the bottom. With this experience I learned that an artist has to work with a transient mind—not attached to established form. Do you know then what a transient mind means, Wan-kyu?"

"I've no idea," replied Wan-kyu, while Hee-jo washed his hands to rest.

"We would often describe our life as transient, but transience doesn't necessarily mean nothingness. Rather, it suggests all things are subject to change. There's actually nothing under the sun that doesn't change. And so we must accept change as it is because there can be no fixed form in this world."

"It sounds rather difficult to me, though."

"I couldn't understand it at your age, either, which means I've changed, too."

In time Hee-jo engaged himself with his work without minding anything else, and in the process he succeeded in making over twenty big pots. Among them were a jar resembling a halo around the moon, a big bowl, and a few square pots with finger paintings on the surface, whose soft curves aroused an abundant feeling. There were also four long-necked jars of a sort Yun-hee had never seen before. Hee-jo seemed to have gotten the inspiration for the jar from the piece used for pickled shrimps. The stripe-like traces of the potter's wheel on the upper part of the jar, which were intentionally made, and the pattern of a few finger-touched lines on the surface had brought a totally different form. While in Hee-jo's studio watching his works, Yun-hee discovered a sketchbook beside the potter's wheel where some fragmentary thoughts were written along with rough sketches.

A soaring form keeping in it a bleeding scar. Though it shows some power, it's not disturbing, but warm.

Yun-hee felt relieved to observe the sketchbook. Despite the deep wound in his heart, which he couldn't reveal even to his wife, Hee-jo had seemed not to lose human warmth. Remembering his assertion that a pot must not look too sharp, Yun-hee thought that his nightmarish experience in the dungeon must have made him search for a more human feeling in his pottery.

While Hee-jo, after finishing the glaze for the second firing, was waiting for the greenwares to dry, President Choi of the Dawool Gallery paid an unexpected visit. Having decided that Hee-jo's exhibition was to be held in November, he now seemed to be anxious how Hee-jo's work had been proceeding. However, Hee-jo showed him nothing, not even the pots finished before the rainy season, suggesting he had accomplished little. President Choi merely requested that Hee-jo help him prepare a catalogue at least ten days before the exhibition, and then discussed who would write an epilogue in the catalogue. After that they moved to the room and continued to talk about their concern.

With a tea cup in his hand, President Choi talked about the Kumdang Shop incident, which he had mentioned before, because the police, who had not caught the murderer until over three months later, had finally disclosed the whole story in the paper.

"Despite speculation that the kidnap victims might have been killed," related President Choi, "we were all shocked and amazed to hear the police announcement. The murderer, in his attempt to collect business money, happened to see the signboard of the Kumdang Shop and ultimately took it for his prey. I just can't imagine how he killed the chauffeur as well as the Chung couple and then buried them all secretly in the yard of their house. To be sure, humans are the cruelest of all living things."

"How horrible! By the way, I heard the Chung couple had four daughters," said Yun-hee. "And their diaries made me so sad.

Yesterday I turned off the television news in order to keep my children from watching it."

At this moment Hee-jo opened in a quiet voice, filling President Choi's cup: "Mr. Chung is said to have followed the murderer in order to buy rare pieces of Koryo celadon and Choson white porcelain, because he heard that the man possessed them. And his last words did not leave my mind."

President Choi, nodding, continued: "Although I deal primarily with wooden wares, I believe an antique dealer must above all handle old china and porcelain. In particular, the Choson white porcelain is so popular that anyone would readily follow someone who claims to possess it. Naturally, Mr. Chung seemed to have followed the man to his death without even telling anyone else."

"When I was in college," returned Hee-jo, "my senior once showed me a white porcelain piece. I was so fascinated by the cracked porcelain that my heart leaped, and then my thought extended to who could have made such a porcelain piece, and when it might have been made. Obviously, the impression I got at the time destined me to get involved with pottery later."

As their conversation deepened, President Choi related an episode about Korean pottery:

"There're so many people who admire Korean pottery, but I'd like to mention, in particular, Bernard Rich of England and Hamata Syogi of Japan, who were commonly known as the two greatest pottery artists of this century. These two people had specified in their autobiographies how much they were touched by Korean pottery. In this respect, there's no doubt we've inherited a great cultural legacy, which could charm anyone else. During the Japanese occupation of Korea, the Japanese had recklessly dug out a countless number of our treasured pots and taken them to their country. In the middle of such a devastation of our cultural property, the collecting of Koryo celadons by the British lawyer John Gatsby, who was then settled in Japan, made a praiseworthy anecdote. In fact, this becomes a telling lesson of how we have to regard our cultural heritage, I think. At first Gatsby was a patron of paintings of the Japanese nobles, but once he saw the Koryo celadons he was thoroughly enchanted by their beauty. He was known to collect the Koryo celadons primarily in Tokyo and other

276

cities of Japan, and even made it a habit to visit our land to buy rare pieces of porcelain. According to the story about Gatsby's collection, he flew to Seoul on the last day of one year with money to purchase an inlaid bottle of Koryo celadon and an incense burner of Choson white porcelain, both of which were rare antique pieces kept by a Japanese nobleman. Ultimately his tenacity enabled him on the first day of the new year to acquire two pieces of Koryo celadon, worthy of the national treasury. I'm told that these pieces, which had been possessed by a foreign connoisseur, were later turned over to Kansong, a then famed collector and preserver of our cultural assets. When Kansong, who had sold his large inherited plantation to buy the cultural pieces, went to Japan to purchase Koryo celadons at Gatsby's house, he first asked Gatsby why he did not collect Japanese pottery. But this foreigner answered flatly he couldn't find anything more beautiful than the Koryo celadons."

It seemed President Choi's affection for Korean pottery was no less than Hee-jo's. And he continued that whenever he sold antique pieces he felt like a father trusting his daughter with a man, adding that he wouldn't sell them to anyone who was not a true connoisseur. Just as love has the power to draw a secret soul from its object, so to him an antique piece was a living thing with a soul.

Realizing he had digressed, President Choi changed the subject. "At any rate, because of the Kumdang Shop incident, many antique dealers have been experiencing their severest and longest days this summer. Added to this incident, the economic depression left them almost exhausted."

After hearing what President Choi had said without a word, Hee-jo spat out sardonically: "Hmph! It's a sad incident caused by a sick society where money—instead of life—is everything. Nevertheless, political leaders have stressed how to live a better life only in material terms, not how to lead a righteous life."

⌒

Regardless of the outside world, farmers were busy preparing for the harvest. It had been raining for two days in a row, but on the day Hee-jo started to fire the kiln, it cleared up; a good omen. The sky seemed to be getting higher, and now a flock of voracious sparrows flew over the roof of Yun-hee's house to the golden fields. Once the fire in the kiln had started, the burner had made such a loud noise that the deserted yard, covered only by chestnut burrs, became lively again. Now that Hee-jo's exhibition depended on the results of this firing, Yun-hee felt relieved to hear the roaring sound of the machine, which seemed to herald fruition.

Twelve hours after the firing began, a roaring sound was heard in the left burner. But, in order to finish the firing as quickly as possible, Hee-jo, assisted by Wan-kyu, opened the insulating brick a little and then continued his work. Three hours after the bag walls on both sides were almost torn off, the soot on the back wall fell off. They had been worrying about the grating sound in the machine, but fortunately no bearings had slipped out during operation. Relieved, Hee-jo shut off the burner at midnight and asked for a drink.

The next morning, after Hee-jo had left for town, Wan-kyu went out to the stream, carrying a book. They seemed to be enjoying a brief rest until they opened the kiln the next day. Since Wan-kyu hadn't returned by noon, Yun-hee went out and found him by the stream, smoking. It had been a long time since she had been there. Yun-hee picked up a stone at her feet, which she found had no warmth because the sun was not blazing as in the summer. Looking at Wan-kyu, she observed, "My! The stream looks even clearer in autumn."

"They say that in autumn a man becomes sentimental," Wan-kyu returned. "As a matter of fact, I've been in an emotional turmoil with no reason."

Sitting on the stony ground, Yun-hee said, smiling: "Once before, I thought men had neither inner conflict nor doubt—I mean they had no heart. So I laughed whenever I heard men saying that autumn is the season for men or something."

"You're saying you had regarded men as insensitive?"

"True. Although it is the men who heroically act in the construction of the world, sometimes I feel horrified to see them sacrifice the little things just in the name of carrying out something majestic. In this regard, it's the women, I believe, who come closer to the essential. Naturally, poetry or art belongs to the realm of women."

"Might be. The Bible tells us that Eve was made from Adam's rib, but all men, in turn, come from their mothers' wombs. I believe woman is an eternal home for men to return to. As a result, art is one form of such a returning instinct."

Wan-kyu put out his cigarette and abruptly mentioned Yi Sung-ju's name, since he was already aware that Yi Sung-ju had been arrested in connection with the YH Trading Company incident. Then he asked about Ji-woon, "The woman who came here with Mr. Yi Sung-ju won't come again?"

"You mean Ji-woon?"

"Right. Before I came over here a few days ago, I had dreamed of a woman forlornly crossing a field, carrying something on her back. I'm sure she must have been Ji-woon—though I saw her only from behind. And the next morning Mr. Hong phoned me to return here."

"Maybe you got such a dream as a premonition of coming here," Yun-hee replied.

"It looks like there's a close relationship between Ji-woon and Mr. Yi Sung-ju, right?"

"Maybe."

Yun-hee had expected Wan-kyu not to learn of their relationship, but since he had already mentioned it there was no way but to tell the truth. He seemed interested enough in Ji-woon to dream of her. But after a while Wan-kyu spoke bitterly but resolutely: "I'll have to forget her anyhow."

Looking at Wan-kyu, who seemed somewhat discouraged, Yun-hee said as if appeasingly: "You know what? The German poet Rilke is said to have been pricked to death by a rose thorn. And I think there're actually some people who are likely to be killed even by the weak poison of the thorn. It seems that the more sensitive we are, the more subject we are to being hurt."

"But how could you imagine there is someone not likely to be hurt at all in life? At any rate, if Ji-woon has something to lament, just tell her to come over to me for consolation."

Yun-hee looked up at Wan-kyu with a refreshed understanding:

up to now she'd treated him as immature since he was, after all, her husband's apprentice, but now she found him as mature as an autumn chestnut. Feeling it, Yun-hee urged Wan-kyu not to be discouraged. "I'll meet Ji-woon soon to let her know what you've said now. I think it'll certainly give her great comfort."

The wavering reflection of a mountain peak in the stream seemed to tinge the water dark green. The mountains were still green, Yun-hee found, but soon they would change to the red color of late autumn. All of a sudden, Yun-hee told herself that life is a midsummer night's dream, remembering a play in which a fairy put a secret liquid into the eyes of sleeping lovers and consequently made them love others by mistake. She had watched the play as if enjoying a children's game, and marveled at the insight of the great writer. As in the play, Yun-hee loved Hee-jo, who, in turn, loved Han Min-wha; and while Ji-woon loved Yi Sung-ju, Wan-kyu appeared to love her. Someday in the future, when looking back upon such an endless chain of relationships, Yun-hee would probably be able to realize that such pathetic love was but a midsummer night's dream.

Meanwhile the result of the initial firing had been quite satisfying this time. Although the duration of firing had been a little long, the weakened absorbing power of the wares seemed to be made up for by putting glaze on them. Among the large pieces only three were broken, so the total number of failed wares, including living ware, was less than twenty.

Following the initial firing, on the first day of October, Hee-jo offered a humble sacrifice to the spirits and was about to start the second firing after putting glaze on the wares. While he made a bow and sprinkled wine around the kiln, a little swallow came in from nowhere and flew near the ceiling. It seemed to try vainly to find an exit as Yun-hee was restlessly watching this unexpected appearance of the swallow.

Despite that, Hee-jo turned the burner on, and then the studio was filled with a loud sound. The swallow flew down to get out through the brightening exit, but happened to go into the ventilation fan. Since the fan was already in motion, the swallow was whirling round and round, unable to spread its wings fully. It appeared the young swallow had mistaken the ventilation fan for an exit to freedom, since the sky was visible through it. All the people in the studio, therefore, watched the swallow anxiously now that it was beyond their reach. But while they were craning their necks to watch the fan, the swallow suddenly disappeared. No sooner had Yun-hee suspected it must be dead than Wan-kyu gave a sigh of relief beside her, saying it had got out safely.

"Are you really sure it got out safely?"

Half in doubt, Hee-jo tried to believe Wan-kyu's words. And seeing Yun-hee's eyes by chance, he brought a chair to search the ventilation fan and then explained: "The swallow is gone. Perhaps it regarded the studio as a remote southern land due to the warm air inside."

"I guess it must have felt warmth even before we turned on the burner," added Wan-kyu.

"Animals are very sensitive by nature," said Hee-jo. "I heard that even ants come out of their holes before it begins to rain."

While Hee-jo was chatting with Wan-kyu, Yun-hee left the studio. Coming out, she went first under the ventilation fan with some suspicion since she didn't believe a swallow could get out through the labyrinthine ventilation fan. But discovering no dead swallow, even on the grass field, she consoled herself, taking the swallow's escape as a lucky sign, after all.

Nearly two hours seemed to have passed since they had started the second firing. By the time Yun-hee went out to hang the clothes on a laundry line, Wan-kyu was working with clay in front of the studio. Looking inside, she found a heavy flame pouring out of a hole in the burner at Hee-jo's right side. He appeared upset, as the flame did not move in the direction he had desired, and tried to close up the hole with clay to retain the heat in the kiln.

After nearly six hours' firing, the back wall as well as both side walls fell off, and in eleven hours the pyrometric cones on both sides began to bend. Since the kiln had been fitted to be fired by a gray-blue reduction fire, its inside was naturally full of smoke. Hee-jo would use a reduction fire for incomplete combustion because it stopped the air supply, making it easy to add fuel only. But this time he supplied a little air, since the kiln had madly begun to pour out smoke. Inside the kiln, the chimney could be seen emitting an enormous amount of smoke in the darkness, like a crater.

With the firing in progress, the sound of the burner hadn't stopped, even at midnight. When Wan-kyu came to bring water, Yun-hee asked him about the situation. "The large pyrometric cone in the center hasn't bent yet," he answered doubtfully. And, he added, Hee-jo was worried there'd never been such a case, that the large cone in the center hadn't melted even after fifteen hours' firing.

The second firing eventually ended at one o'clock the next morning. Besides the unexpected problem that the glaze melted more slowly than before, they'd been anxious due to the sudden rain shower during the firing. Nevertheless, the test pieces turned out fine; their grayish blue color, appearing like stones in water, made Yun-hee imagine momentarily that the whole kiln was a submerged treasure.

With the end of firing followed a sudden silence, making all the people in the house feel as if they were in a dream. Though Harvest Moon Day was only three days away, Yun-hee couldn't feel its coming in her heart. In addition to shopping for the festive day, since she had to go to the rice mill the next morning, Yun-hee needed to get some pine needles on which to steam a rice cake. Writing down in her pocket notebook the names of the foods that would be used for the family ritual, she enjoyed the serenity as still as a vacuum coming after hard work.

In the meantime Wan-kyu roamed about the village for the entire morning, making a sketch, and returned at noon. After lunch, enjoying a smoke with Hee-jo, he happened to be attracted to the dark brown ashtray on the floor, which looked like the thin lid of a crock for soy sauce. So he asked Hee-jo: "Looks peculiar. Who made it?"

"Park Young-soo did it. His work seems to be going well since he moved to the countryside. Does it look like the yard of a country house?"

"I suppose so. As a matter of fact, one of my friends recently opened a shop of living wares. He might covet it if he saw it." Wan-kyu went on, changing the subject: "Tomorrow is National Foundation Day. Come to think of it, today is the last day of Professor Kim Yil-woo's exhibition. Since I didn't attend the opening day because of the work here, I must at least go there today."

"Did he hold an exhibition, too?" Hee-jo inquired rather scornfully.

Although Kim Yil-woo was a professor in the pottery department in Wan-kyu's college, Hee-jo had had little respect for him, since he would boast of his pots, looking at best like a wrapping cloth, claiming that it retained the modern style of pottery.

Even so, Wan-kyu took a glimpse at his watch and, putting out his cigarette, said to Hee-jo: "Anyway I must go to his exhibition and will come back soon. In any event he's my professor."

"Go if you want," replied Hee-jo bluntly.

"If I'm unable to return tonight, I'll at least be back by tomorrow afternoon because we're going to open the kiln the day after tomorrow."

As soon as Wan-kyu had stepped down to the front yard, Hee-jo spat out himself, "Hmph! Here is another young man without enough patience to be in one place for very long."

The next day, while resting on the bamboo bed after coming back from the mill, Yun-hee was startled to see Wan-kyu, who turned up wearing a cast on one of his arms. Standing up at once, she inquired of him, "What's the matter? When did you sprain your arm?"

"I sprained my arm slipping in an underpass. I'm afraid Mr. Hong will be angry at me."

"Don't worry about Mr. Hong. You should have been careful not to slip like a child. Why, then, did you come back with a sprained arm, instead of taking a rest at home?"

"I was aware we'll open the kiln tomorrow. It's fortunate I sprained my left arm only," Wan-kyu consoled himself absurdly. And at this moment Hee-jo emerged from the studio, furrowing his brow to find Wan-kyu. As Yun-hee was about to explain, Wan-kyu spoke first. "Sorry. I found the exhibition had already closed when I got there yesterday. I slipped, as I was worn out. It's all because of the ashtray that I went to Seoul in vain and sprained my arm."

"Because of the ashtray?" returned Hee-jo angrily. "Did it order you to go? Don't ever make such an absurd excuse! What kind of excuse will you make if you fail later in firing the kiln?"

As Hee-jo looked at the plastered arm deploringly, Wan-kyu

again admitted his mistake remorsefully. Then Hee-jo mitigated his anger, finding it admirable that Wan-kyu had decided to help with the work to the end. "Everything is a mirror of ourselves," said Hee-jo as if to soothe him. "True, I've always made an excuse for anything I did. As a child, I even ascribed my mistakes to God. Then I came to learn it was my lack of self-restraint that had made my life so hard to bear."

As it was a holiday, Yun-hee and her children gathered pine needles at the village grove, and in the evening they made rice cakes. Imitating Tan-bee, Sae-bul struggled clumsily to make some of his own, so Yun-hee gave them the boiled chestnuts necessary for making rice cakes. On his first attempt, Sae-bul ended up letting the contents of the cake show through the dough, although it was fairly easy to make. But he made much progress on his third attempt, shaping his cake like a Chinese bun with creases. For her part, Tan-bee made her cakes look pretty by pressing their rims with her fingers, and then showed them to Sae-bul, asking him to follow her method.

"But if I make mine look like yours, Sister, who can tell which is mine?" Sal-bul retorted.

Looking at Tan-bee, who was a bit embarrassed by this remark, Yun-hee smiled quietly as it reminded her of her past. In fact, the cakes Yun-hee had made in her own way as a child were all clumsy-looking, with the sesame scattered around their surface, but nonetheless they were more delicious to her than any other cake. Perhaps such satisfaction, combined with naive self-respect, must have come from the simple fact that she herself had taken a role in the family event. But, she learned later, such a feeling turned out laughable, as it was getting broken off little by little by her contact with harsh reality.

Early the next day, when Yun-hee was about to go to the market for Harvest Moon Day, Hee-jo stopped her, saying, "My brother's family may come here today. I think it would be better for you to prepare the meal for the rite alone, though. I wish they'd come tomorrow."

"I think so, too, because we're going to open the kiln today," replied Yun-hee.

Since Hee-jo's parents had passed away, his older sister had moved to Cheju Island, leaving his younger brother, living near Seoul, as the only sibling. This brother being different from Hee-jo in nature, however, they would rarely meet except on days such as big holidays when they got together to affirm brotherhood— though in name only. Accordingly, the wife of Hee-jo's brother would come to Yun-hee's house a day before a holiday to help with the meal as an act of courtesy.

Regardless of the family event, Yun-hee suspected, it would be a great delight if the result of the firing were successful before Harvest Moon Day. But who could possibly predict the result before the opening of the kiln? Hence, the day they took the pottery out of the kiln, they felt as if they had been waiting for a verdict that couldn't be appealed any further—with hope and resignation crossing each other in their minds.

While Hee-jo and Wan-kyu were taking pots out of the kiln, Yun-hee went to the market, as it was the day before Harvest Moon Day. Naturally the market place was quite crowded with various kinds of colorful refreshments displayed on the street. In the rice cake shop, Yun-hee found all kinds of cakes—*songpyen,* glutinous rice cakes, rice cakes with bean jam, and those with a flower pattern. Of course all of these cakes were for housewives who were too busy to make them at home. Also, Yun-hee found red-ripe persimmons, which appear in early autumn, and mudfish stirring loudly in pails of water. While walking leisurely around the market, she bought three kinds of greens, some taros for soup, meat to fry, and a sacrificial hen. Not knowing they would be offered in the Harvest rite, the live hens were craning their necks, crowing in their cage. An animated sight with the festive day just ahead, the market was so lively that even a tiny steel spoon looked gorgeous.

Along with a bottle of refined rice wine and new fruit, Yun-hee bought pepper seeds ground at the market. Her shopping bags were so heavy her shoulders felt stiff already. Though people were saying the rememberance rites for ancestors had been simplified in recent years, Yun-hee could not feel any difference in preparing for such a family event. Besides, she was not to neglect such preparation, since Hee-jo was so filial a son.

When she had been young, Yun-hee's family had kept the rite so faithfully as to offer it even during wartime. For her part,

Yun-hee had taken it as a matter of fact. But when, as a senior in college, she had seen the ritual at the ancestral temple of the royal family, which looked all solemn, she had felt repelled for the first time; the complex process, requiring innumerable dishes, had made her feel doubtful about the great effort of preparing it. Seeing the ritual at the time, Yun-hee had been reminded of an earlier time when people had given more respect to the family line than to the individual. Though respect for one's ancestors was a custom worth preserving in itself, she believed, the clan society of the Yi Dynasty had been torn apart by too much emphasis on such formalities. Contrary to her belief, however, common people might think the spirits of their ancestors, like living souls, would be pleased to eat the rite offering. If she died, Yun-hee felt, her spirit would not be likely to come back happily to taste such an offering. Despite this, the offering rite might be regarded as a simple means of self-confirmation for a clan society in an intense struggle for existence. Considered in the light of primitive humanity, even a tiny offering of wine on the morning of a festival ritual would be an expression of such an earnest mind.

When Yun-hee got back from the market, the greenwares had already been taken out of the kiln, the front yard filled with living wares. The pots showed only a tint of yellow smoke—even though their color was to be bluish. At this moment Yun-hee felt drained to see Wan-kyu, who, with his plastered arm, was sitting vacantly on the grass in the yard. As she began to find the big pieces in the yard, Wan-kyu, who had been silent till now, opened: "Because the firing went on too long, the wares got tinted with the yellow smoke. Only twenty or so pieces were left intact. In fact, we've broken all the big pieces except one vase."

As Wan-kyu pointed to the wall, Yun-hee moved toward it to find a heap of broken pieces in the grass. To her that scene seemed like a cruelly unrealized dream. Looking down at the pieces under her feet, lying like wounded souls, Yun-hee felt as if she herself had been thrown away. "All has come to nothing," she murmured in spite of herself, staggering out into the dazzling autumn sunshine.

9

A Morning Road

It was reported that the temperature had dropped abruptly around Harvest Moon Day, with the stream in the valley of Daekwan Height freezing up. In fact, the cold water in the basin felt chillingly fresh when Yun-hee put her hands in it to wash in the morning. The field was already suffused with gold, the rice plants harvested, and the trees were changing colors to prepare for the coming winter.

Three days had passed since Hee-jo had left home. He hadn't taken his children to visit his ancestors' graves on Harvest Moon Day, taking instead only his brother's two children. A trip might do him good, Yun-hee judged, if it returned his mind to his work, so that he could start out fresh after coming back. The day after Hee-jo had left, Yun-hee had asked Mr. Yang, a brother of the owner of the peppery-stew restaurant, to make balls of clay. Though he was an idle man who disliked farming, she thought it was fortunate to have a person like him around in a busy season.

The reason for the kiln's failure was that Hee-jo had covered the hole of the burner with mud, which in turn had resulted in a lack of oxygen. By covering the hole, Hee-jo had supposed he would prevent the fire from shooting out and so reduce the heat loss. However, since there had been no exit for the smoke in the kiln, it had stained the pots while the glaze was melting out.

After analyzing the cause of his failure, Hee-jo accepted the result without emotion. In Yun-hee's eyes, he controlled himself in a manner worthy of a teacher—as when he had told Wan-kyu, who had returned with his arm in a cast, that he should not make excuses for his mistakes. Obviously, while away from home, Hee-jo had seemed to be able to suppress his anger, but Yun-hee thought he should return soon to resume his work. Now that the exhibition was only about three weeks away, he still had time for one more firing in the kiln.

The day after Harvest Moon Day was Saturday, and so Tan-bee

kept begging Yun-hee to call on her grandmother. Because the children had talked about their grandmother until they fell asleep, Yun-hee finally promised that they would go there. On Sunday morning Mr. Yang came a little after eight, earlier than the day before and, stopping doing dishes, Yun-hee treated him to pears. He was saying that although the crop was said to be abundant this year it would be a bad year for the farmers due to the low government purchase price. "A good government makes farmers rich," he asserted.

Yun-hee agreed with him. And as she was about to leave the studio, she heard the sound of a motorcycle. It was the postman's motorcycle. "A telegram for you!" he shouted.

A telegram for me? Wondering what it was about, Yun-hee walked toward him. But his hard expression made her heart pound. A telegram so early in the morning . . . Has something happened to Hee-jo? she continued to wonder. The postman handed her a yellow paper without a word, then turned around. Yun-hee opened it anxiously. It read: "Mother Dead. Come Immediately. From Sung-ho."

At that moment Yun-hee felt numb and looked at the paper once again to see if she was mistaken. All she was able to see, however, was the word, "Mother." Feeling dizzy, she was on the verge of collapse, unable to believe it. How on earth could it happen? Murmuring, Yun-hee dragged her trembling legs into the house and summoned her children. As she changed her clothes with great difficulty and was about to leave with only a bag, Sae-bul asked, pointing to her shoes, "You're wearing those shoes?" Only then did Yun-hee realize they were worn-out sports shoes that she used to wear at home.

After changing her shoes, Yun-hee came back to her senses and left home, telling Mr. Yang of the news of her mother's death. Not looking back to see whether her children were following her or not, she hurried to the peppery-stew restaurant to telephone to Seoul. Asking first where she was, Sung-ho told her that Mother had died early in the morning after coming out of the bathroom, leaning back against the wall as if dozing off.

"We're all gathered here, Sister. Come right away."

"Lying! You're lying!" Yun-hee hung up sobbing, unable to

control her copious tears. Then the restaurant's owner offered to call a taxi for her, but she declined and hurried out of the place.

"Is Grandmother dead?"

The instant Tan-bee heard what had happened, her face became contorted as if she was about to burst into tears. And Yun-hee grasped the child's hand firmly. She could not believe her mother was gone, still vividly picturing her raging at the police investigators when they had raided the house at midnight with their shoes on. Also, an image of her mother driving geese into the pen flashed through Yun-hee's mind. "No, it's only a dream—merely a dream," she murmured over and over to herself.

When Yun-hee saw the gate of her parents' house lighted by a lantern for the dead and approached a yard full of floral wreaths, tears blinded her eyes, making her feel as if she were falling into an abyss. Struggling in the depths of the abyss, she stepped into the house like a ghost, when her father and the rest of her maiden family members hovered around as if their souls had left them. Without stopping to greet her father, Yun-hee broke into tears the moment she saw her mother's picture in the open door, framed by a black cloth.

"Oh, Mother! All my life I've been dependent upon you," Yun-hee said to herself, sobbing. "Your tender shoulders have been a shelter for all of us. Your hair always neatly combed, you've been like the Good Earth embracing all your seeds! To whom will I confide my joys and sorrows now that you've passed away?"

In fact, Madame Shin had been like a guardian angel, who provided a wonderful remedy to fight back whenever Yun-hee felt overshadowed in the face of the potential enemies. Her remedy was like the red, yellow, and blue bags in a fairy tale: if the blue bag labeled "patience" was thrown into the middle of danger, the thorn bushes before her would burn down and an open field would appear. Now Yun-hee felt like a terrified child, with her magic bags gone, standing before a deep, blue river she would have to cross alone. Sobbing, she felt her body drawn into endless darkness.

Just as darkness exists along with light, so was held a feast for the living in the place of the dead. Her tears hardly dried, Yun-hee had to help out since there was too much work to be done for the funeral. Indeed, her mother's death hit the whole family like a shipwreck; yet they were united in sharing their grief—like animals that lick each other's wounds. The lantern, the floral wreaths in the open air, and the condolences from guests—all of these seemed to bring consolation to the grieving hearts of the bereaved. Autumn moths hovered all night in the yard resplendent with flowers and lights; a red cockscomb quivered under the fence as if it were the spirit of the dead. Death is not separated from life, Yun-hee realized, but they are the continuation of each other. Indeed, the feast held at the mourners' home seemed to be prepared for the living, who looked indifferent to the essential components of living such as grief, happiness, and eternity.

Working beside the exhausted Yun-hee, who was barely able to help out in the kitchen, her aunt was envying Madame Shin's blessed life even at her death. Looking at the house full of guests, she remarked that Madame Shin had been given special treatment in her death, as her husband was still in power. Recalling her own husband's funeral ten years before, when abundant floral wreaths had been sent even by some prominent politicians of the day, Yun-hee's aunt sighed deeply. Perhaps she might have predicted her own desolate funeral someday. At the funeral of some high official, Yun-hee heard, as many as seven hundred floral wreaths were reported, which shocked the common people keenly aware of the Simplified Family Ritual Standards set out by the government authority. It seemed that even in the ritual for the dead, the living seemed to identify themselves by, and comfort themselves with, the amount of donations received.

In any event Yun-hee's grief and her aunt's envy had nothing to do with the death itself. When her mother's dead body was being laid in the coffin, Yun-hee wailed and writhed. However, upon seeing the face of her dead mother, she stopped crying in spite of herself; her stiff hands and purple fingernails indicating death, the dead woman was lying on her back as if determined not to get up again. Now her soulless face was incomparably peaceful—a peace returned to its root—as it revealed the completion of life. So Yun-hee wondered if her mother had been already aware of the beauty of her last journey. Dressed in the silk shroud that she herself had prepared, Madame Shin was lying in the coffin as her family wailed showing vividly the contrast between the eternity of the other world and the suffering of this world.

Hee-jo arrived at night on the day the corpse was placed in the coffin. Finding Yun-hee dressed in mourning clothes, he lowered his eyes, then went straight to the room where the coffin was. After burning incense, he bowed to the deceased as if repenting. He was wearing the grey cotton suit that Madame Shin had made with her own hands; perhaps predicting her own death, she seemed to have made those clothes as a token of reconciliation with her son-in-law. Nevertheless, because of the distance that had existed between them, Hee-jo, arriving late, was not able to witness the body of the deceased. Having managed to come to her senses, Yun-hee remembered she had called Hee-jo's uncle in Puyeo in the afternoon the previous day. But since it was long after Hee-jo had left, his uncle had come to Seoul that day with Yun-hee's brother-in-law and his wife to offer their condolences beforehand.

The mourning family seemed much eased after the body had been laid in the coffin. That night people, including Hee-jo, joined the family gathering in the room and were absorbed in memories of the dead. At this time Yun-hee told them of the serene look of the deceased, thinking of her father, who seemed to have aged with his wife's death.

"Probably my grief can't be compared with yours, Father," she said. "But I won't grieve anymore, since Mother has completed her life. Our grief is not for Mother's death itself, I think, but for our own sorrow. And we're all confused because things have changed suddenly with the absence of Mother. It must be especially hard on you, Father, as you've been sharing joys and sorrows with her for over forty years."

"Well, I think it's fortunate that your mother died without pain," returned Father. "She passed away as neatly as she'd lived all her life. Now I feel empty, as if part of my body has been cut off, but I'm relieved to think I'll meet her again when I die. Because she has taken care of me all her life, I thank God I could be of service to her on her last journey."

Father controlled his emotion in a manner worthy of the head of a family.

Then Sung-ho spoke to Yun-hee. "I had the same feeling as you, Sister, when I saw Mother's dead body. Recently, while reading a book by Chang-tzu, I found a passage that goes like this: 'Although people merely fear death, who can tell after they're dead whether they regret having struggled and clung to life with all their might?' In this regard, I think Mother's death is not something entirely sorrowful."

"Look, Sung-ho faces the meaning of death directly like a grown-up," marveled Yun-hee's older sister, who belonged to the old generation. And Yun-hee, too, felt proud of Sung-ho as he now accepted his mother's death bravely in order to comfort other family members. In fact, she had treated him as her own son, since he was the youngest in the family.

Turning his glance toward Hee-jo, who had agreed with Sung-ho, Father asked him how he had been doing. "So, did you cut the weeds and tend your mother's grave? If Tan-bee's mother had gone with you, she would not have heard of her mother's death."

"If I went to the grave with him," interrupted Yun-hee, "I'd have dropped by on the way and seen Mother one last time."

It occurred to Yun-hee, then, that Hee-jo's uncle had dropped by, so she told him about it. And when the conversation turned to his uncle, Hee-jo brought up an interesting story.

"During an idle talk we had," said Hee-jo, "he noticed my shabby features and then urged me to seek out a fortune-teller in the village who had a fairly good reputation. This fortune-teller, he told me, was marvelous enough to predict the exact date his cousin would get a promotion. Also, predicting the death of another person, the fortune-teller told the family that had come to see him to prepare a shroud in advance. If I'd gone there, I'd have been the first to learn of my mother-in-law's death."

"Why, then, didn't you go and ask him when you'll have a great success?" asked Yun-hee jokingly.

"Life wouldn't be that interesting if we knew what would happen next," replied Hee-jo, "so I made an excuse about being busy and ran away."

Upon hearing this, the husband of Yun-hee's sister burst into laughter, which, in turn, made the rest of the family laugh. Then he spoke:

"That's well said. Even though I myself keep talking about money—not knowing whether I might die tomorrow or not, I've no mind to predict my own future. If my destiny is already fixed, why is it that I've got to go through all these troubles to earn a living? Now I work and have hope for my children just because I don't know my own future."

Hee-jo was right, Yun-hee told herself. If we knew our own future, there would be no necessity to work, and we would end up becoming nothing but robots. We could dream of the unknown and overcome hardships, just because we don't know what tomorrow will be bringing to us.

The next day they buried the coffin in the family grave in Songchu and put a memorial tablet in the Yunheung Temple near Pyukje. Because Mother had often sought that temple, they asked the monk there to do the Forty-Nine Rememberances Rite for her. In addition, a sacrificial ceremony calling the departed soul home was held that day.

After seeking the mourning family's understanding for his early departure, Hee-jo went directly home from the burial place to resume his work. Yun-hee, too, returned to Choha-ri as soon as the three-day mourning period was over. When she got home, Hee-jo handed her a thick envelope. Looking at the handwriting, which seemed familiar to her, Yun-hee, to her surprise, found that it was from Ji-woon. Because she had talked to Wan-kyu about her a few days before, Yun-hee was delighted to hear from Ji-woon. So, sitting on the sunny front step, Yun-hee opened the letter:

Although I went to bed much exhausted after arriving at a Buddhist hermitage late tonight, my mind was still as hard and clear as a crystal. And I was all shaken up to discover this unfamiliar site. It was the second day of my trip, but I couldn't sleep at all perhaps because I felt I had flown ever so high from the gloomy days.

I had set out yesterday and stayed at Anmyun Island for the night. Today I passed through Haemi and unpacked my suitcase at this hermitage on Mt. Kyeryong. Despite a heavy itinerary, I didn't have any regrets since I was able to spend a day at the mountains and a day by the sea. The best part of my trip, however, was when I stopped near Haemi. It was a historic site where a stone castle built five hundred years ago had remained unbelievably untouched. Its sacredness captivated me the instant I stepped off the bus. Though the nearby surroundings had no peculiar features, the mountains protecting Haemi Fortress, now ruined, seemed too spirited to pass by without noticing as they opened up like a father's bosom.

It was not until I got off the bus, as if enchanted, and wandered around the fortress that I came to learn where the sacred spirit was emerging from. It turned out that this was a place of great ordeal where thousands of Catholics, fighting for their religious beliefs, were buried alive in a hole. Many followers were said even to have jumped down themselves for fear that they might change their mind while waiting for their turn to die. And so, the blood of those martyrs had made this place that sacred.

While strolling around the holy place where martyrs sacrificed themselves, I suddenly found myself consoled, feeling that my sorrow-stricken soul was getting purified. And when I found out that the root of being sacred lay in the total sacrifice of one's own self—like a lotus blossom arising from a slough of suffering, I felt I could perceive a faint gleam of light, and realized that my suffering in the past was far from being in vain.

Up to now I've lived a life in death, but now I am ready for a day when I will stand up bravely. Whenever recalling the hot day I went to Choha-ri to see you, I would feel pain as if jabbed by a darning needle. I attended the morning mass every day to purify myself of my sins and wrote something in the form of a meditation, which became a poem at one time and a prayer at another. In fact, I'd been writing like this for the past five years. And a few days ago I looked through these writings and discovered in them a stream of consciousness like a flow of water.

How splendid it would be if meetings between individuals were like a stream. To part with someone, I believe, might be better dealt with if we considered it the way we saw the stream. If meeting and parting with someone flowed like a stream, it would not hurt us as much as it does. Now I am trying to learn what the *flow* is—I would not push myself to possess something, nor grab something to satisfy myself, so that I could love my empty serenity as if enjoying a game.

It had been a long time since I had seen myself experiencing the miracle of encountering something new by emptying myself like this. Therefore, things that could not touch my mind when it was full of something, began to penetrate my empty heart like the sound of wind or water, or like a ray of sunshine. As in a miracle, after I started to attend morning mass, a little boy would appear in my dreams like soft sunlight. And while I was repenting my sins with a tear, he observed me with his eyes as deep as a well and shook his head silently. When I wrote a poetic prayer after clearing my head, he handed me a long pencil with a shining face.

This glorious boy, hovering around me like the air, with eyes that seemed to understand every human condition, must have been a shadow of love sent by God himself to console my heart. I suspected instinctively that when very young, he was an altar boy helping the priest say mass. And although in my vision I never saw him wear the robes of an altar boy, I came to know him little by little. One day in my dream I was stroking his head like a sister, staring at his eyes, which were like rays of sunshine and would never hurt a soul. At first, he was at a loss in a mixture of delight and embarrassment. But I said calmly, shaking my head, "Don't worry. I won't hold you that long. All I want to learn from you is how to love, and you can teach me, since everyone has his own path in life."

Afterwards I came to perceive that this boy had already belonged to the order of God. But, because of his presence on my behalf, I resolved not to reveal the secret encounter with him to anybody. Perhaps the desolate, empty space where the sunshine and wind could rest might be a consolation to some other lonely souls who might seek spiritual communion.

A while ago, I strolled in the back garden of this hermitage. With autumn maturing, the moonlit valley of the opposite mountains caught my eyes. In a flash I saw a vision of a woman who I thought must be my former self, walking along toward the dark valley. Then I thought that even in my former existence I must have been wandering in an unfamiliar darkness. With this vision I felt relieved that I had climbed all the way up here today and seen my former self. That distant valley might be a distant place in my heart, and until I am distinctly aware of it, I'll be wandering around the maze-like valley of life.

October 6, 1979

Ji-woon

Reading the letter, Yun-hee felt that Ji-woon was now composed and mature, having suffered a tremendous agony lately. In contrast to this, the letter she had sent to Yi Sung-ju two months before had been as precarious as the edge of a knife, and sorrowful, but now she seemed to accept all her suffering with a certain distance, in an effort to heal her wounds. As Wan-kyu once put it, nobody is without a wound; if one could transform a wound into a precious experience as valuable as a pearl, then it would become far better than blind happiness. Perhaps Ji-woon felt obliged to write to Yun-hee, who had seen her in her worst times, but her letter gave Yun-hee an opportunity to reflect on her own life as well.

How true it is, Yun-hee mused, that suffering rather than happiness gives humans consolation. Wealth alienates those who have not, but the blind confirm the happiness of those who can see, just as suicide gives consolation to those who seek death. As a result happiness, which is sufficient in itself, has nothing to bestow, and distribution is possible only when there is deficiency. Perhaps Yun-hee could be as close to Han Min-wha as she was because she had gained relative comfort from her loneliness.

The day after she had returned from her mother's funeral, Yun-hee paid a visit to Han Min-wha's house. Before starting for Seoul for the funeral, she stopped by Eunti to ask Han Min-wha to look after her house, and so Han Min-wha had stayed in Choha-ri until Hee-jo came back after the burial. Because she just couldn't stay at home with the emptiness in her heart, Yun-hee set out to thank Han Min-wha for her help.

The rice plants had been cut during the interval, with the sheaves of rice piled up in the fields. Only the sound of a threshing machine heard in the barren fields, not even a flock of birds could be seen. It seemed only yesterday that farmers had planted rice, but it was all cut and gone now. "Where did we come from and where should we go?" Yun-hee mumbled to herself. A certain inescapable fate had brought us to this world, only to cast off our shell when it came time to leave. Oh, Mother, Yun-hee uttered to herself, if you're still attached to this world, brush it away like dust and break your agonizing connection with this life. May you never return to this world of suffering with a heavy burden, and may you fly to eternity ever so lightly, like a butterfly.

The mountains were ablaze with autumnal tints like a red cloud. While watching the dust from the threshing machine scatter around and spread over the field like the ashes of a cremation, Yun-hee wiped the tears from her eyes. Nothing lives forever, except the earth and the mountains. A death song by an Indian, who fell in a rain of bullets, suddenly occurred to her. And it gave Yun-hee, still overwhelmed by her mother's death, a momentary relief, and washed away her fear for life.

With the wave of waning heat sweeping Eunti village, cosmos surrounding Han Min-wha's house had already withered. The grass in the front yard was on the wane, and the piece of weaving, which had been draped under the eaves like an autumn field, was now barely hanging by one corner, as if tossed by a typhoon. Yun-hee attempted to straighten it out but gave up since it was out of reach. The colorful tapestry, which drooped to the earth, was like an old banner hung in a ruined temple. The door was wide open, but it was so quiet that it seemed almost ghostly. As she was about to close the door, suspecting that no one was inside, Yun-hee was startled to find Han Min-wha leaning like a ghost against the wall of a room, smoking.

"Oh, you're at home now," said Yun-hee, glad to see Han Min-wha.

But Yun-hee stood in amazement with her mouth open to find

the room totally in disorder. In front of Han Min-wha the loom was falling down. Also, the spoon case cast aside, spoons were scattered all over the place like scrap metal, and sweet potatoes rolled here and there under Yun-hee's feet. Judging from the scene, someone must have dumped out a sack of sweet potatoes. Under the table was a purple bowl broken into three pieces—it was the porcelain that Han Min-wha had once referred to as being the color of happiness.

Only then did Han Min-wha, who had been sitting as motionless as if watching a performance on a stage, put out her cigarette and get up, saying: "Ah, when did you come back? Did the funeral go well? You must still be dazed by your mother's death."

"Such feeling will go away gradually, I think. Everyone has to depart someday, and I've experienced it a little earlier than others."

After exchanging brief words with Han Min-wha, Yun-hee asked her what had happened, pointing to the floor.

"I'd gone to the grove to gather chestnuts," answered Han Min-wha, "and when I got back I found this mess."

"Who did it anyway?"

"Who else could it be? It must have been that crazy speculator," Han Min-wha said with a sigh.

"My God! Why don't you bring charges against him for breaking into your house?"

"But there's no one I can rely on now. Even my lawyer is urging me to sell this house. Apparently he must have been bribed by the real estate broker."

Upset to see the mess, Yun-hee began to pick up the scattered sweet potatoes and put them back into the sack. Han Min-wha tried to hold her back but gave up. And while Yun-hee cleaned the place, Han Min-wha was barely able to set up the loom in the corner. Picking up the broken pieces of the purple bowl and then putting them on the table, Yun-hee told Han Min-wha that since the broken pieces were large, she would go home to find out if they could be put back together. But Han Min-wha replied, shaking her head, "After all, happiness is apt to break like this bowl."

No sooner had they straightened up the room than Han Min-wha shuddered in terror as if remembering the landlord's violence again. As Yun-hee persuaded her to find ways to cope with the problem, Han Min-wha muttered, "Horrible! There's no way to beat such greed. Since this house is like prey to this beast, he won't let it slip away."

"But it's your right to protect what belongs to you," asserted Yun-hee.

"It's mine—legally. But law alone is not sufficient to protect my life."

After a pause Han Min-wha told Yun-hee about a dream she'd had, adding that recently she'd had the same dream again and again: "I entered an exotic temple, as if enchanted, and found a path as narrow and dark as a tunnel. In spite of my fear, however, I walked through the tunnel for a while, and when I finally got out of it, there appeared a big, empty road with three branches. I kept looking for a way out in my dream, which was like the situation I am in now."

"Don't be so hard on yourself. You chose your way of life yourself, anyway," Yun-hee consoled her.

"It looks that way because I keep wandering."

"You're too ambitious, Ms. Han. Most people are content with a little happiness and settle down. But you're ceaselessly seeking something more."

"Well, there's only one thing I want—that is the progress of my soul. It may sound selfish, but I can't leave myself to the common destiny. Till now, I've been weaving with an immature passion, groping for the meaning of life. I asked myself if I've been living to exhibit my own peculiarity or to gain a worldly reputation. And I also tried to analyze myself and cast off my shell. Whenever I encounter people who possess much but still remain in spiritual darkness, I strive to get out of my state of darkness quickly. What we see coming out of our mother's womb is only the light of this world, but I yearn to see the eternal light. At times I've a faint idea of what it'll be like in that moment."

"What will it be like?" asked Yun-hee earnestly.

"Like a morning yard swept clean by a bamboo broom. I wish I could see a person with such a vision."

Han Min-wha's expression was so vivid that Yun-hee could picture the traces of the broom in her mind. Hearing her words, she was able to imagine a sacred monk or a wise poet in that morning yard deep in the mountains, walking around in communion with the leaves of grass.

After a moment Han Min-wha spoke in a low voice, fingering the red bag containing her talisman. "In my former existence I might have been a fallen monk driven out of the temple in the middle of penance."

"If you go on like this, you might become an enlightened person in the life hereafter."

"Do you want to be reincarnated? If so, what do you want to be?" Han Min-wha asked Yun-hee with curiosity.

"A person like my husband or you might desire to become God—a being who rules himself or herself. But an enlightened person who serves as the salt of the earth is sufficient with only two of you, I think. I want to be a flirt in the life hereafter because a perfect woman or mother does not appeal to me. If I died, only my tough shell would be left."

Raising her eyebrows, Han Min-wha responded to Yun-hee's words. "My! You still want to be born as a woman again? I don't ever want to be reborn as a woman."

"It's not so with me. Women often dream of being men or want to father a son to inherit their vested interests. But to me it's nothing more than an escape from reality, since they must claim first of all their own freedom. In fact, the world of women is narrowly confined because they've been trained to live that way for thousands of years."

"If so, be born as a liberated woman in the life hereafter," Han Min-wha said. "That's the way to live life to the fullest. You seem to love life, but I want to get out of it."

As the exhibition drew near, Hee-jo locked himself in his studio, making it difficult for Yun-hee to see him. Although in the past he did not usually work at night, Hee-jo, now sitting at the potter's wheel, worked far into the night for nearly three days in a row. Devoting himself to large pieces only because he had no time to make living wares, Hee-jo proceeded as scheduled, since the ideas for his work were already mapped out.

After molding a dozen long-necked jars on which he'd made patterns just like the traces of wounds, Hee-jo explained to Wan-kyu that they were far from an ordinary form.

"It's unconventional," he said, "though it's not against the traditional form. A long form is liable to look fragile, you know. This time I'll try a neutral, pale yellow fire in the kiln in order to give warmth to the simple *punch'ong* wares. And I'm going to reveal the inherent force of the common folk—not an ideological but a spontaneous aspect. I believe ideology must not come first under any circumstance. After all, it's the innocent hands of the potters who created the simple beauty of the *punch'ong* wares as well as the kindness and purity of the Choson white porcelains."

In a few days the greenwares were put into the kiln chamber. And when they had dried, Hee-jo finished grinding their foot rims and then began to apply the slip. Pressing hard on the straw-brush that Yun-hee had bought at the market, he applied the slip with swift strokes across the surface of the wares. Soon the slender, pale brown pots, full of warmth and vitality, seemed to have sprung from the earth. Although Yun-hee could picture how they would turn into a concrete form in the kiln, she kept such a vision in her heart: Ever since the silent kiln had been installed in her house, she had learned to keep both agony and hope within her heart, taking them out only to use, as a child would do her toys.

The weather had been clear for several days; the day after Hee-jo finished slipping the wares, Yun-hee sliced sweet potatoes, squash, and eggplants, then spread them out in the yard to dry. In the old days when autumn drew near, barely having time to enjoy the season, women busied themselves preparing for the coming winter. Before Yun-hee had married, her mother would dry these vegetables and give each of her daughters a handful of them when winter came. Since moving to the countryside, Yun-hee had sent dried vegetables to her mother instead, but now it had become a sad memory for her.

Unlike Yun-hee, her children were not much touched by their grandmother's death. So Tan-bee, not grieving, believed that her grandmother was somewhere in heaven; Sae-bul, indulging in a childlike fantasy, wondered whether the grave was too cramped for his grandmother.

Today, Yun-hee found Sae-bul playing in the yard singing an odd song. While listening to it, she was able to recognize it as a song praising Genghis Khan of Mongolia, the first emperor of the Yuan Dynasty. Unaware of the historical fact that Mongolia had invaded Koryo about seven times and ravaged the whole country, Sae-bul sang the song over and over again: "Genghis Khan, a hero in my heart . . ."

"Where did you learn that song?"

Yun-hee asked abruptly as she could not bear to listen any longer. But Sae-bul replied, undisturbed. "Why, it's very popular these days, you know. All the students in my class knew it . . ."

"True, Genghis Khan was a hero, since he had founded a great empire that extended over Europe and Asia. But you must also know that he invaded Koryo seven times and caused our ancestors innumerable sufferings and sacrifices."

With this explanation, Yun-hee told the child a brief history of the Koryo Dynasty and Genghis Khan. Sae-bul opened his eyes wide, startled, to learn how King Won-jong of Koryo had gone all the way to Mongolia to surrender, and of the subsequent struggle of the civil army, Sambyulcho, against the royal force.

"He was an invader, after all. So you must not sing that kind of song again," Yun-hee admonished him.

"Then, why did they write it?" inquired Sae-bul innocently.

At this time Hee-jo seemed to hear the conversation between mother and son. He looked dumbfounded when Yun-hee entered the room, unable to find an appropriate answer for the child.

"Praising charisma justifies tyranny, you know," he explained shortly. "And they're brainwashing people now through popular songs. To be sure, it's one of the last symptoms of a regime before it falls."

Meanwhile, the newspapers showed, the political situation had been in greater disarray recently than any other time. The very evening of the day when the October Revitalizing Reform had been proclaimed seven years before, the government had declared Emergency Martial Law in Pusan where a massive demonstration had broken out.

Hee-jo had reported this news when returning from Seoul around curfew. Three thousand university students in Pusan had marched in the streets, shouting for the abolition of the October Revitalizing Reform as well as for the overthrow of the dictatorship, while many civilians had joined the students in a protest that had continued until the next morning. The fierce demonstrations had continued for two days, the paper said. People had attacked provincial and central government offices; twenty-one police branches had been destroyed, with even the picture of the President being burned, and six police vehicles had been set on fire. Many people had reportedly been injured in the ruthless suppression by airborne troops swinging oak batons.

Despite the unstable political situation, however, the autumn sky had been so clear that the slipped greenwares were completely dried. While Hee-jo was planning to put the wares into the kiln the next day, Monk Hyeo stopped by unexpectedly. It had been four months since his last visit, yet his shaven head was still pale blue and his patched monk's robe was the same. Already informed of Madame Shin's death by Hee-jo's letter, Hyeo first gave Yun-hee words of consolation. "I imagine you've gone through a tremendous hardship recently. No wonder you look gaunt, since death brings hardship to the living first."

"Mother used to say that to live is to live up to one's fate. I believe it, too." Yun-hee replied.

"No one could find a fragrance or a red flower in a seed. By the law of cause and effect, an appropriate soil, with bright sunlight and timely rain, will make a flower blossom, enabling it to emit fragrance. But when the autumn comes, that flower vanishes as its life ends. Our life is certainly like the sound of clapping hands because there is no coming and going—let alone dying and being born. Just as the sun and the moon appear each day and night, the birth and death of our body is only a symptom of change."

As Hyeo finished his words, Hee-jo spoke. "Once I saw the phrase 'Unseparable Gate' at a Buddhist temple. When we're saying that the world involves opposing forces, its end can be condensed into a matter of life and death, I think. If so, what is the end of life and death? And what is the ultimate end? With this notion in mind, I am now able to gain a faint vision of *Unseparable*."

With Hee-jo joining him, Hyeo brought up the worship ceremony of Buddhism, telling about a foreigner who once came to his temple to ask whether the ritual of bowing to the statue of Buddha was idolatry or not.

"Our posture in bowing to Buddha," Hyeo explained, "is that of a fetus crouching in his mother's womb. Naturally the Buddhist posture is conceived as the best we can find. It's actually what the ascetics discovered after several decades of penance—so it's clear why we humans bow to Buddha. It's even scientific to bow repeatedly to Buddha in that posture, since we've yet to get beyond that stage. And we bow until our heart is lit by the divine light. The East and the West have different notions of the divine, but I think it's the Easterners who have a complete understanding of the universe."

"Did the foreigner understand what you said?" asked Yun-hee.

"Certainly not. First of all, I can't speak English, ha, ha!"

Turning his smiling face toward Hee-jo, Hyeo suggested, "How can you make good pottery? Do it the same way you bow to Buddha."

"Now I've found the answer after searching for it all this time," Hee-jo replied delightedly, then asked Hyeo if he had something to do. Shaking his head, Hyeo said he'd left his temple because of a bad dream.

"Do you, Monk, have bad dreams, too?" inquired Hee-jo.

"Of course. The human body is a microcosm in which all things interact with one another. To put it simply, the human body has an instinct. Children play well on good soil, for instance, but if the spirit of the soil is not good, they tend to leave without even being aware of the reason. Naturally a monk like me is more intuitive than ordinary people distracted by worldly affairs."

Hyeo then started to talk about the current political situation, which he had rarely mentioned before. "They say that on receiving the report of the Pusan-Masan affairs, the President ordered that the people involved in the protest be crushed by armored tanks. It may be a groundless rumor, but last night I dreamed of blood pouring like a flood."

"It's the politicians themselves," Yun-hee interrupted, "who should learn how to be thoughtful, because their slightest word or gesture has a great impact on the happiness or misery of common people. Look at the people's hostile expression in the street these days and you'll realize everybody is devoid of love. Since the government has no regard for the lives of people, each part of the great wheel of the country is deteriorating as well."

Having stayed overnight, Hyeo left early the next morning. Then Hee-jo resumed his work at the kiln after nearly twenty days; since, fortunately, he'd already made some works before the rainy season, he felt less pressure to finish the rest of the work by the exhibition. However, with only large pieces going into the kiln this time, there would be some tension because it would be easier to fire them along with living wares. Thus, Yun-hee did not approach his studio when she heard the burner starting to pulse again.

With the temperature dropping two days earlier, it had suddenly become as chilly as in early winter. A clump of reeds were swaying desolately in the wind at the corner of the field, and the mountains were changing their color to brown. In Yun-hee's yard the paulownia leaves, which were bigger than her palm, had withered to yellow, blotting out the sky. Looking at the withering leaves, Yun-hee recalled that little Sae-bul had once asked her if the trees were sick. But Sae-bul, she thought, wouldn't have felt compassion for the trees had he known the fact that they were only returning to the soil after spending their lives passionately under the blazing sun, and that the leaves heaped in layers in the November grove were welcoming the feet of a wanderer, willing to cover and fertilize the soil with their bodies.

After eleven hours, with the bag wall on the right side of the kiln falling down, the initial firing was finished. There had been no specific difficulties in the firing this time, yet Hee-jo, going to bed, considered postponing the exhibition until a little later.

A week before, when President Choi of the Dawool Gallery had come to see him, Hee-jo had taken out some of the pots he had made in the summer so that pictures could be taken for the catalogue. He had promised President Choi that he would do his best, although it was hard to predict the results until he opened the kiln. President Choi, optimistic, was satisfied to see the large pieces that had just been slipped, and returned to Seoul.

"I'm a little bit worried about the turbulent political situation," said Yun-hee, "but just go on with your schedule. I think they must have started printing the catalogues by now."

But Hee-jo replied as if indifferent. "Don't mind it. We could still hold an exhibition even if a war broke out."

Concerned about making a living, Yun-hee was, above all, thinking of selling the pots, but Hee-jo, as an artist, didn't seem to worry about that at all. Taking a break while waiting for the kiln to cool off, he began to prepare in detail for the exhibition by selecting the names of people to be invited. Meanwhile, the sound of the threshing machine was heard on and off from the field, and in front of Yun-hee's house people were busy harvesting cabbages from the patches.

That day they welcomed guests who hadn't paid a visit to their house for a long while. Even though they would enjoy entertaining visitors, Master Chu Myong-whan was the one whom Yun-hee respected more than anyone else. It had been a year and a half since she had last seen him, so she was as delighted as if seeing her own father. As Hee-jo's mentor, who saw the works sent back by Hee-jo while he was studying in Japan, Master Chu had urged him to return immediately for fear that the student's work might become Japanized. Now sixty, he was a traditional pottery artist who had succeeded in reviving the Choson white porcelains.

Yun-hee discovered that a slim woman followed Master Chu. Unlike most women of her age, she was tall and wore gold-rimmed glasses; Yun-hee was instantly able to recognize her as Master Chu's gentle and graceful wife. After they had exchanged greetings in the room, Hee-jo spoke to Master Chu, smiling. "I thought of you while making a list of people to send invitations to for my exhibition, and expected to meet you soon. It's not easy to see you, although we're both living in the countryside."

"Ha, ha! It's better to engage ourselves with work, forgetting time. We can meet like this abruptly whenever we wish."

"I didn't expect your wife to come such a long way here," said Hee-jo.

"My wife is my goddess, you know, so it's my duty to take my goddess wherever I go," returned Master Chu with a laugh.

"Oh, don't tease me. Actually he's the one who controls me all the time." Master Chu's wife said, smiling shyly.

Yun-hee had first met her two years before at Master Chu's exhibition, and at first glance she discovered an elegant beauty in her, who, despite her age, evoked an image of a daffodil. Once a reporter who had come to interview Master Chu asked Mrs. Chu her name, but she modestly had declined to disclose it, merely saying she was no more than an ordinary woman. Even when a magazine reporter had asked to take her picture with her husband, she had refused stubbornly. Her modesty, Yun-hee realized, was not the intentional refinement commonly seen in the intellectual; rather, it was an innate thing, as if bestowed by Heaven, that would make anyone feel touched.

That day at the exhibition Yun-hee realized that the most beautiful thing in the world was modesty itself. It was not mere exaggeration, therefore, that Master Chu would praise his wife as a goddess. A feminist who could genuinely distinguish a woman's beauty, Master Chu deserved to live with a woman as precious as a gem. As such, they looked like an ideal couple to Yun-hee.

Finding red wine that Eun-kyong had brought earlier, Yun-hee set a table, roasting ginkgo nuts and peeling chestnuts, along with *kimchi* she'd pickled without using hot pepper four days before. And Hee-jo took out white porcelain cups made by Master Chu, suggesting they might go well with wine. Then Master Chu set a long square box before him, and Hee-jo opened the box and found a white porcelain bottle inside. It had been fired recently and had a little crack on the surface, Master Chu explained, but he had brought it anyway, since the color was worth observing. In truth, blue coloring added to the blue-white porcelain did not evoke a cold feeling, bringing in fact a look as clear as his wife sitting beside Yun-hee.

With a cup in his hand, Master Chu told Hee-jo: "You'll find everything around us consists of straight lines or angles. For instance, a house has a line and a room or a table has an angle. I can't stand this because I want everything to resemble the natural state, but our society prevents this from happening as it prefers standardization. This can be resolved by color, I think, since everything is supposed to have its own color. Of course, you may have a different idea about it, Hee-jo, as you've specialized in *punch'ong* wares. To me, however, color is the most important element in the art of pottery—more than its form and line. So I feel a need to create an untainted color, like the color of a blue-white porcelain that shows white piercing out of blue. I've been using white clay to make my pots, and the well made pots emerge from the glaze white while the badly made ones turn blue. The crude porcelain of bluish white never satisfies me, since its tainted color makes us feel less pure. In this respect, I believe, the superiority of Koryo celadons and Choson white porcelains lies above all in their color. I assume you must have heard the words 'the mystical Koryo color.'"

"Since I was captivated by your revived work of porcelains," Hee-jo responded, "I've never been satisfied with modern styles of works—just as it's difficult to go down once we see the top."

Following Hee-jo's praise, Master Chu continued: "For the things I can't handle by myself, I ask God to help me in my heart. But it always brings me a great deal of agony when the results of my experiments are far from satisfactory. Usually it doesn't take much time to make a sample work, as it can be done by my own skill, but reviving the old work is to be literally dependent on the data. Up to now I've attempted to mix various colors almost a hundred thousand times, and made more than a thousand experimental works. At my first exhibition four years ago, I was ninety percent successful in reviving the original color. This time I'm close to a hundred percent, so I don't need to try the Choson white porcelains anymore. However, in the matter of restoring the original color of the Koryo celadons, I've yet to reach the last stage."

Then Master Chu added he had been destined to the life of a pottery artist from the moment he had majored in mining at a technical high school during the Japanese rule. He was, in fact, so obsessed with clay as to fill his pockets with pretty-colored clay whenever he discovered it. Having been living like a disciplined monk in a deserted mine at Yeoju, where he had discovered white clay about ten years before, he had spent his days entirely in experiments, with mixing various colors in the laboratory with the help of his assistant. Three years before, he had undergone an operation to remove the cataracts resulting from measuring the flame in a conventional kiln without using a thermometer.

"At the time," his wife explained, "he would weep behind his glasses, which were heavy enough to tear his ears off. Since he had no time to return home in Seoul, I took my children to where he was. But the children were even unable to recognize their father with his hair tied back with a rubber band and wearing a beard."

"Although I've devoted myself to traditional pottery for nearly thirty years," resumed Master Chu, "my mind is still drawn to our Korean pottery. I've always believed that Chinese pottery can be imitated, but that our Korean pottery can't be. So it brings me great comfort whenever I think of my mission to transmit our pottery to the next generation. Nevertheless, I can't be called an artist, since I do not create pottery in the genuine sense. To me, pottery is science as well as scholarship. In other words, my work is no more than scientific archaeology."

Master Chu went on to talk about the hard life of a craftsman. Confessing that just like any other craftsman he became sharp and nervous while involved in his work, he told a story of something he'd gone through several years ago.

A big corporation had invited a well-known calligrapher to produce inscriptions for Master Chu's white porcelains. The calligrapher, with whom Hee-jo was also acquainted, was displeased by having to visit the remote countryside to write in person. Therefore, he kept complaining about the site he visited even after finishing his writing and, flaunting his reputation, asked arrogantly whether Master Chu had heard of who he was. This had caused Master Chu to explode in anger: "So I shouted at him, 'How can I know you when you don't even know me?' But, come to think of it, I should have ignored him from the beginning. This incident aside, I would get especially angry when I was not satisfied with the results of my work. Unlike the peaceful mind I'd have while working at the potter's wheel, violent passion often swept me. Perhaps it's because I learned the negative side of the artist, I believe. The positive aspect of art improves our mind, while the negative aspect does not."

Master Chu's face, while talking, showed wrinkles as deep, simple, and mature as Choson white porcelain. All this time, Hee-jo had been drinking without a word, as if ashamed. Looking out at the darkening field through the window, Master Chu uttered softly: "The sunset is more beautiful than the sunrise because the sun blazes for the last time before setting. And it's the same with pottery. The moment the glaze begins to melt down, unable to bear high temperature, it reveals the most magnificent color."

"It looks painful to me at that moment, though—like a labor pain just before giving birth to a baby," added Hee-jo.

"Absolutely so. It's the pain of pottery as well as the pain of a potter. There is an anecdote about a potter who took a pillar from his house and used it as firewood. In the ultimate stage, artists lose their sense. That's the road to art."

Master Chu then pointed to the blue-white porcelain bottle, while Yun-hee listened to him as if enchanted. "When I see this blue-white porcelain, I'm reminded of my mother in my hometown as it has the color of *chogori* I used to wear. My mother had dyed it jade-green, which I think is a really natural color, and that's the essence of the Choson white porcelain. I believe that when we die we return to the world of white porcelain."

As Yun-hee poured wine into the gradually emptying decanter, Master Chu poured wine into her cup, too. Feeling a sense of plentitude, Yun-hee merely observed the white porcelain cup without drinking. When we die, we return to the world of white porcelain. . . . Thinking it marvelous, she repeated this expression to herself. It was in order to approach the world of self-completion, and to show the way to the ultimate end, that Master Chu had devoted virtually all his life to creating the transparent, jade-green color, Yun-hee reflected.

After a while Hee-jo opened all at once, as if awakened from the intoxicated state. "Indeed, the industrial art you've engaged yourself with suggests a great awakening to me."

"Well, it's rather for the enjoyment of the general public. If I were born again, I would become a showgirl and entertain people with the French cancan."

Master Chu replied jokingly, then praised Hee-jo's works with a comment that he felt like embracing them. He started home at sunset without taking his usual amount of drink. Though wearing long *turumaki,* he strided as energetically as a teenager. And when they reached the darkening field, the elderly couple stopped suddenly to face each other. Then Master Chu exclaimed to his wife, "How dull! We haven't had a date for a long time."

With this remark Master Chu's wife shyly locked her arm in her husband's and smiled, looking back over her shoulders. So Yun-hee waved good-by to them, saying they looked well matched. While she was watching Master Chu, who, fluttering his long hair, disappeared into the darkness with his wife, a smile spread over her lips. Walking home side by side with Hee-jo, Yun-hee spoke with a modest heart: "After all, he made me realize we live in order to die well. Now I can imagine what life is about."

❧

The result of the initial firing had been good. There were no serious faults this time except that the two vases at the top of the pile were broken, and the soot was not completely wiped off the wares at the bottom. Hee-jo began putting glaze on the wares immediately after he finished grinding the foot rims. He had done most of the work by himself, needing Wan-kyu's help only in putting on the glaze. And he could finish his work on time, since there were no living wares to fire, which would demand extra time.

Yun-hee went shopping the day when Hee-jo, having cleared the soot off the hole of the burner, put the wares into the kiln. When she returned, Hee-jo told her that Han Min-wha had dropped by two hours before. So Yun-hee asked if something had happened to her.

"She said she's going to leave next week," answered Hee-jo, knitting his brows. "Obviously the owner of the land lot must have pestered her. And, it seems, she's going to leave her home vacant for a while, and asked us to go to Eunti for a change and look after her house."

"Oh, my! She won't be able to resist any longer if she leaves her home now. If she had a man to rely upon, this kind of thing wouldn't happen," Yun-hee replied worriedly.

"She could live well without a man, I think."

Glancing at Hee-jo for his seemingly indifferent attitude, Yun-hee asserted, "She needs love—if not a man. I think her heart became bleak while trying to overcome the conflict of love."

The second firing began at eleven o'clock the next morning. While they were checking the oil tank, which they did not have time to fill the previous day, the postman came by a little earlier than usual and, stopping his bicycle, shouted, "Registered mail here!"

So Yun-hee went out and received a book addressed to Hee-jo. The postman handed her a newspaper and asked, glancing at the front gate, "Why didn't you hang a mourning flag?"

"A mourning flag?" Yun-hee countered him, not knowing why.

"You don't know yet? President Park Jung-hee died."

"What?" Yun-hee responded uncomprehendingly.

"While attending a dinner party at a secret place near his official residence, he was shot to death by the director of the Central Intelligence Agency, Kim Jae-kyu. Five people were also killed—including the director of the Presidential Protective Forces. All this was reported in the news this morning."

"My God! Are you sure?"

Astonished, Yun-hee couldn't believe what she had heard. But, shaking his head, the postman added: "The news was so stunning that everyone lost their senses. I'm also in no mood to deliver letters today. What will become of this country?" Too stunned to think of anything, she read the newspaper, standing. A headline, "A SERIOUS INCIDENT CONCERNING PRESIDENT PARK," was printed in big, white characters on a black background, followed by the statements, "Prime Minister Choi appointed as Acting President—Emergency Martial Law declared all over the nation as of 4 a.m. today." Then words that seemed to compete for attention came into her eyes: "The President was dead," "An official government announcement expected at 9:30 A.M.," "Closing of all universities and colleges," "All gatherings banned," "An extension of the curfew," and "Tanks entered the central parts of the city."

Along with these words, there was in the paper a picture of fully armored soldiers stationed in front of many public buildings. But Yun-hee's family couldn't have had the slightest idea of what had been going on because they didn't usually listen to the radio and because, in particular, their house was far from the village. Trembling, Yun-hee was about to go out when Hee-jo came in. As she told him the news of the President's assassination, Hee-jo refused to believe it at first. But after listening to the special broadcast on the radio, he muttered with a bitter expression: "Late spring is the effect of early spring and the cause of early summer as well. So no one could escape from the law of cause and effect. . . ."

Meanwhile, Tan-bee returned home from school crying at the news of the President's death and hung a flag at half mast. Although they stood at a turning point of history, Hee-jo started the kiln on schedule. Instantly, the burner sounded clamorously as if to open a new era. From the radio in the studio, a special message by Acting President Choi Kyu-ha was repeated over and over, with a statement that he was now appealing with indescribable grief for the people's patriotism and unity, asking them to trust the government and the army, and to do their daily duty without disruption.

With the exhibition season approaching, many artists and galleries had been in great confusion since the unthinkable Emergency Martial Law had been in force. Despite this external event, Hee-jo watched the kiln with serenity. In the meantime he had had to repair the burner on the left side, as he had found it out of order after the back walls on both sides had been removed. This time, the cones on the left side were beginning to bend in ten hours of firing. And around three o'clock the next morning, Yun-hee, who had fallen asleep after seeing the glaze starting to melt, was awakened from a light sleep and found Hee-jo peeping through a fire hole of the kiln.

As Yun-hee approached, Hee-jo stepped aside for her to look inside. And, it turned out, the four cones of the bag walls on both sides had been entirely bent down. The flame, which had been whirling around the wares like a lost soul, calmed down also, revealing its most transparent moment. The transparent flame, with a color like a ripe persimmon, was burning silently, and the brilliant tranquility was actually so pure that even dust did not seem to intrude on it. If we call such a state one of peace, Yun-hee told herself, then the flame has demonstrated what genuine peace is—just as a lotus blossom blooming in the mud shows genuine nobility.

After extinguishing the kiln two hours later, Hee-jo walked out into the bluish morning air. Although his face was smeared with soot, he was like a spirit emerging from the abyss, removing the shell of his body. Chaos and the dregs of a frenzied passion now cleared from his face, he looked as clean as a morning yard swept by a bamboo broom. While drawn to Hee-jo, Yun-hee was suddenly reminded of Han Min-wha and felt a yearning to show her this purity in Hee-jo.

In a moment Yun-hee left home like a sleepwalker, wheeling a bicycle laid in the yard. She had to pedal with bent legs because the bicycle was so small, yet the cold morning air seemed to purify her lungs. In the bluish daybreak the empty field unfolded like scenery in the sky while the town was still buried in tranquility. Here and there were lying sheaves of rice like weary souls, and an out-of-season scarecrow was lying on its back, pointing to the empty space with its exposed bosom. As she pedaled serenely along a dark brown road curving like a snake past a village grave, magpies startled by the sound of the bicycle flew away in a flock, shaking the empty cornstalks.

Glossary

bandaji   a clothes chest with a hinged front flap

changgi   an Oriental chess game, with round wooden pieces and a board. Each piece has its own name with a Chinese character printed on it.

chima   a pleated skirt, extending to the feet and worn by women

chogori   a shirt, crescent-sleeved with a tie attached on each front gore and worn by men and women

Choson   the name of Korea from 1392 to 1910 when the Yi Dynasty reigned

Chung Jung-boo   a military officer in the Koryo period

Chung Yak-yong   a pragmatic scholar in the late Choson period

Chusa   a pen name for Kim Ch'ong-hee, a calligrapher in the late Choson period

devil post   a wooden post carved in the shape of devil which serves to mark distances

dolmen   a group of upright stones supporting a large flat piece of stone

The Dream Journey to the Peach Blossom Spring   a painting by Ahn Kyon of the Koryo period

gut   an exorcism

hanji   the traditional Korean paper with fine texture and muted color

Hideyoshi   a Japanese general who led a military campaign to Korea in 1592

Im Guck-jung   a chivalrous robber in the Choson period whose act was widely admired by peasants

kimchi   pickled cabbages or radish, seasoned with spices such as garlic and ground hot pepper

Koryo   the name of Korea from 918 to 1392

Kyumje   a pen name for Chong Son, a painter in the Choson period

makkoli   rice wine

Meiji   emperor of Japan (1867–1912) who opened his country to Western civilization

menhir   a single upright crude monolith usually of prehistoric origin

moodang   a female shaman

ondol   a heating system of traditional Korean homes. The level of a room is raised so the fire in the fuel hole can heat the large stone block under the floor.

Paekche   one of the three divided kingdoms in Korea that continued from 18 B.C. to 663 A.D.

Prajna-paramita-sutra   one of the Buddhist scriptures that teaches the way to Nirvana

punch'ong   the standard pottery of Korea. It was produced in a large number of kilns in the country and was commonly given a light coating of slip before being painted.

p'yong   a unit of land. One *p'yong* is equivalent to 3.3 square meters.

Sambyulcho   Started as Three Elite Patrols, this special army was famous for its struggle against the Mongols who invaded Korea in the late Koryo period.

sarangbang   a room used exclusively by the master of the house during the Choson period as a study and guest room

The Secret Garden   the royal garden inside the Changduck Palace in Seoul

sijo   a traditional Korean ode, usually with three stanzas

soju   wine of grain

songpyen   a half-moon-shaped rice cake stuffed with beans

The Tale of Chun-hyang   a folklore that appeared in the late Choson period. It deals with a girl, Chun-hyang, who devotes herself to a man through all kind of hardship.

The Tale of Shim Ch'ong   a folklore that appeared in the late Choson period. It deals with a filial girl, Shim Ch'ong, who serves her blind father.

Three Kingdoms   the period of Korea when three divided kingdoms—Silla (57 B.C.–668 A.D.), Paekche (18 B.C.–663 A.D.), and Koguryo (37 B.C.–668 A.D.)—reigned.

turumaki   a robe-like overcoat

ume   a Japanese apricot

won   a monetary unit in Korea

yangban   Referred originally to two classes (civil and military) of nobility that ruled throughout the Choson period. It now means any of their descendants.

Yu Kwan-sun   a girl who was active in the March 1st Independence Movement from Japan in 1919

Yuan Dynasty   the dynasty established in 1279 in China by the Mongol tribes. It stretched throughout most of Asia and eastern Europe.